For Lawrence

Praise for the Novels
of Dawn Halliday

"Watch out for your fingers . . . *Highland Obsession* is on fire—a scorching page-turner from cover to cover! [With] sexy Highlanders and wickedly erotic romance, Dawn Halliday is the hottest new voice in Scottish romance."   —National bestselling author Monica McCarty

"Dawn Halliday blasts onto the erotic romance scene with a well-written, passionate debut certain to keep readers up all night."
          —Jess Michaels, author of *Taboo*

"I found myself eagerly reading through the pages waiting to find out what would happen next . . . a wonderful summertime read."
          —Romance Junkies

"Joyfully recommended! There was nothing about this novel that I didn't like. Well, other than the fact that it made me sweat. Ms. Halliday gets two thumbs up . . . impressively awesome."
          —Joyfully Reviewed

"Passionate . . . a wonderful read."   —Just Erotic Romance Reviews

"If you like your romance hot and sexy, this book is the one for you."
          —The Romance Studio

"[An] erotic treat . . . plenty of sensual thrills. Great job and I look forward to reading more from this author in the future."
          —Fallen Angel Reviews

"Absolutely sizzles . . . [a] well-crafted plot and steaming-hot sex. Definitely recommended!"   —TwoLips Reviews

ALSO BY DAWN HALLIDAY

Highland Obsession

HIGHLAND SURRENDER

DAWN HALLIDAY

A SIGNET ECLIPSE BOOK

SIGNET ECLIPSE
Published by New American Library, a division of
Penguin Group (USA) Inc., 375 Hudson Street,
New York, New York 10014, USA
Penguin Group (Canada), 90 Eglinton Avenue East, Suite 700, Toronto,
Ontario M4P 2Y3, Canada (a division of Pearson Penguin Canada Inc.)
Penguin Books Ltd., 80 Strand, London WC2R 0RL, England
Penguin Ireland, 25 St. Stephen's Green, Dublin 2,
Ireland (a division of Penguin Books Ltd.)
Penguin Group (Australia), 250 Camberwell Road, Camberwell, Victoria 3124,
Australia (a division of Pearson Australia Group Pty. Ltd.)
Penguin Books India Pvt. Ltd., 11 Community Centre, Panchsheel Park,
New Delhi - 110 017, India
Penguin Group (NZ), 67 Apollo Drive, Rosedale, North Shore 0632,
New Zealand (a division of Pearson New Zealand Ltd.)
Penguin Books (South Africa) (Pty.) Ltd., 24 Sturdee Avenue,
Rosebank, Johannesburg 2196, South Africa

Penguin Books Ltd., Registered Offices:
80 Strand, London WC2R 0RL, England

First published by Signet Eclipse, an imprint of New American Library,
a division of Penguin Group (USA) Inc.

First Printing, April 2010
10 9 8 7 6 5 4 3 2 1

Copyright © Jennifer Haymore, 2010
All rights reserved

LIBRARY OF CONGRESS CATALOGING-IN-PUBLICATION DATA
Halliday, Dawn.
Highland surrender / Dawn Halliday.
   p. cm.
ISBN 978-0-451-22924-3
1. Highlands (Scotland)—Fiction. I. Title.
PS3608.A54835H57 2010
813'.6—dc22   2009040778

Set in Goudy Old Style
Designed by Alissa Amell

Printed in the United States of America

PUBLISHER'S NOTE
This is a work of fiction. Names, characters, places, and incidents either are the product of the author's
imagination or are used fictitiously, and any resemblance to actual persons, living or dead, business es-
tablishments, events, or locales is entirely coincidental.
   The publisher does not have any control over and does not assume any responsibility for author or
third-party Web sites or their content.

ACKNOWLEDGMENTS

Huge thanks to the two people without whom I wouldn't have had the opportunity to write this book: Barbara Poelle, my fantastic agent, and Becky Vinter, my amazing editor.

To all the writers who helped me so much in crafting this book: Evie Byrne, Tessa Dare, Kate McKinley, and Maya Banks—I appreciate your honesty, your talent, and your friendship. Thank you so much! And to Jody Allen, who helped me to research this novel and whose knowledge of all things Scottish is amazing.

Finally, huge thanks to my husband and children, who are so generous with their support. I couldn't do it without your never-ending encouragement.

HIGHLAND SURRENDER

CHAPTER ONE

Scottish Highlands
April 1717

The Earl of Camdonn urged his horse to a canter. Ears pricked, the animal willingly obliged, sensing its rider's eagerness. From the gentle hills of Hampshire to the craggy Highland mountains, Cam had followed behind the two black-lacquered carriages rumbling toward Camdonn Castle. Today, however, on the final leg of the journey, he'd stopped to speak with one of his tenants, and the carriages had drawn ahead.

He leaned low and became one with his mare as they sped along the ragged path leading to Camdonn Castle. Since they had left England, he'd clung to the image of leading his bride-to-be and her uncle through the castle gates. A rider had gone ahead to bear the news that they would arrive this afternoon, and Cam had indulged in a vision of his people lined up along the road leading through the castle gates, smiling and cheering as they welcomed him home.

He wanted to make it clear that he was back to stay this time. He intended to become the leader his Highlanders needed.

Only a few miles to go—they now rode through the pass in the forested mountains bordering the southern side of Loch Shiel. Cam had doubted the duke's coaches would survive the journey, since the rutted paths in this part of the world didn't come near to qualifying as roads. They'd engaged the services of a wheelwright and had made use of him often along the way, and somehow they had succeeded.

Cam could now breathe easy, and the sweet, fresh smells of pine and heather—of *home*—washed through him. Cam hoped Elizabeth would grow to love the Highlands as quickly as he had.

He thought she might. Just shy of twenty, Lady Elizabeth was young, titled, and rich. A proper innocent English lass and the perfect wife for him, politically speaking. The Duke of Argyll himself had suggested the match, and the king had endorsed it.

Even better, though she was beautiful and alluring and would be no hardship to bed, her demure nature didn't rouse him to all-consuming desire, a state Cam was determined to avoid at all costs.

He hardly knew her, but that didn't matter. Cam had gone to England in search of someone precisely like Elizabeth. He was pleased his quest hadn't taken too long. He'd been in England for five months, and already he ached for home.

His horse rounded a bend in the wide path, and a faint commotion ahead drew Cam from his thoughts. Cam frowned and leaned forward in the saddle, straining his ears. Men shouting? Suddenly the crack of a gunshot resonated through the air, and his horse surged into a gallop.

What the hell? Cam gave the animal its head as another shot sent a flock of birds bursting from the branches of a nearby pine.

The road opened into a clearing where men on horseback swarmed around the larger, gold leaf–trimmed carriage—the one bearing Elizabeth, her uncle, her lady's maid, and two of the duke's trusted servants. The attackers all wore black, and scarves covered the lower halves of their faces. The second vehicle carrying the duke's remaining men and the wheelwright was nowhere to be seen.

Cam bared his teeth. *Highwaymen.*

As he thundered closer, he saw the sole man on foot drag Lady Elizabeth from the carriage. She didn't make a sound, nor did she fight back. The poor chit was petrified with fear.

Protective rage swelled in Cam's chest, and he yanked his pistol from his belt. "Let her go, damn you!" he bellowed, heedless of the fact that she'd hear his foul language.

All four attackers swiveled in his direction. Just as well. If he diverted their attention away from his helpless family-to-be, perhaps he could keep them safe. He focused on the villain, whose filthy, calloused hands wrapped around Elizabeth's tiny waist.

"Release her!" He leveled the pistol at the man's chest, though the bastard probably knew Cam wouldn't dare risk shooting and injuring Elizabeth.

Astonishingly, the man obeyed. He shoved her aside. She stumbled backward, tripping over her voluminous silk skirts and tumbling into a gorse bush. The villain leered at Cam as the three others on horseback turned toward him. Someone tossed the man on foot the reins of a riderless horse, and he mounted quickly.

Looked as if they all intended to come after him. Good. He'd draw them away from Elizabeth and the duke.

Garbled shouting came from inside the carriage, and Cam's attention snapped to the rig. The coachman, gazing wide-eyed over his shoulder, raised the reins.

"Ho! On with you, then!" He whipped the animals into a frenzied gallop. The carriage lurched forward, leaving Elizabeth stranded in the bush.

None of the highwaymen pursued the carriage or paid attention to the bright yellow flurry of Elizabeth's skirts—all four focused solely on Cam.

It was him they wanted, he thought grimly. *So much the better.*

But they were closing in.

He aimed his pistol at one of the bandits and fired. The horse reared, and the man toppled off the animal, but the rest lunged closer, weapons drawn. Three guns aimed directly at him.

Turning away from them, Cam bent low over the mare's elongated neck and dug in his heels. A bullet whizzed past his shoulder.

Air streamed through his hair as the mare leaped smoothly over a fallen tree. *Brilliant*, he thought with pride. Another excellent acquisition from his trip to England. As with Lady Elizabeth, he hadn't spent a fortune on this animal for her beauty alone.

A man shouted behind him, and the villains' horses drew nearer. Cam unsheathed his sword with a whoosh of steel against leather.

He had been on the move for the greater part of the day—it was the only reason their horses could outrun his. As one approached his rear flank, Cam held out his sword as if he were jousting. He yanked on the reins, turning in a tight circle only a well-trained and well-bred horse could manage. The abrupt motion sent the animal just behind him catapulting past. The weapon pierced the man's side, jerking him off his horse. Cam yanked his sword away, and his attacker fell to the ground, blood staining the tear in his tattered black coat.

The second bandit was gaining on his other side. Spinning in his saddle, Cam arced his sword through the air and cut him in the shoulder. The horse shied, and the man hunched over in the saddle, clutching his wound.

The final man chasing him had time to slow his mount, and Cam caught a glimpse of the barrel of a musket. Again he made a tight turn and spurred his horse, leaning low. The animal leaped ahead, passing through a thick screen of greenery. Leaves whipped at Cam's face.

Just as he decided he was safe, the loud report of a gunshot shook the trees, and fire exploded through Cam's body. He jerked, yanking on the reins, and the mare reared. He toppled from her sleek back. Bracken and moss softened his fall, but he felt nothing but the all-consuming pain.

God help him. Finally, just as he was about to turn his life to rights, he'd been killed. And worst of all, he'd left the sheltered, innocent Lady Elizabeth alone in the wild Highlands of Scotland.

The hair prickled on the back of Ceana MacNab's neck. Someone was in her cottage. Watching her.

She tightened her grip on the pestle she was using to grind herbs. With her lips twisted into a snarl, she spun round.

"Rob!" Lowering the pestle, she took a step backward. "You scared me."

Robert MacLean leaned against the doorframe and crossed his arms over his chest. The barest hint of a smile touched his lips before it faded. Smiles never held on Rob's face. They passed over it like specters, and if a woman blinked, she'd miss them.

She wished she could draw out the source of his melancholy, but so far she'd failed. Yet she couldn't fault him for his reticence. After all, she kept secrets from him as well.

"Good morning," he said, his voice low and smooth.

She set the pestle on the long, low table where she mixed her medicines. "You could announce your presence, couldn't you? I heard gunshots a few moments ago, and—"

"I heard them too."

She released a low noise of disgust. "Poachers again."

"Aye, must be. You ought to speak with the laird about them."

"I already have. As long as they don't infringe on the needs of his people, Alan turns a blind eye." She hid a shudder—the crack of muskets made her skin crawl. "He's too lenient, that one. If it were me, I'd have skinned them alive by now, just for disturbing my afternoon repose."

Rob pushed himself off the doorframe and took a step toward her. His blue tartan plaid shifted over his knees as he walked, and his whisky-colored eyes scanned the dim interior of her cottage. "You haven't any patients?"

"None so far today." Warmth traveled across her chest, and she looked down lest he see her blush.

Ceana lived an isolated existence, made bearable only by her work and the superficial associations she maintained. She'd arrived at the Glen two months ago and had lived in lonely seclusion until she'd been summoned to Camdonn Castle to care for a man with an ague. She'd met Rob, the stable master, there, and the attraction between them had flared, instantaneous and powerful. When she'd left Camdonn Castle, it had been near dark and he'd offered to ride home with her on one of the horses. They'd talked along the way, and his quietly confident demeanor had appealed to her. When they'd arrived at her cottage, she'd asked him to come inside for some ale.

By the time he'd left it was nearly dawn, and they were lovers.

He wasn't her first lover. As with the others, whenever she was with Rob, she diligently followed the rules for carnal relations she'd established for herself after she'd left Aberdeen. *Never share your past. Never let him into your heart. Always keep him at a distance.*

Most men she'd known were more than happy to abide by the rules she set forth, for they allowed them to have a willing bed partner without any expectations of a long-term attachment. The arrangement worked perfectly well for Ceana, too. Without someone to occasionally warm her bed, she'd have gone mad from the loneliness.

Rob, however, was different from the others. More complicated, more guarded, more difficult for her to understand. He possessed many appealing qualities, from his hardened demeanor to his sheer, raw strength. Ceana didn't intimidate Rob as she did most men. He was a man of few words, a man who lived inside himself. For the most part, he communicated with his eyes, with subtle gestures and variations in stance.

Ceana had grown to care for this mysterious man. A great deal. More, perhaps, than she should.

He took another step toward her. A calloused finger pressed her chin upward, forcing her to look at him. "Take off your clothes."

Her eyes widened. "What did you say?"

"Do it." His voice was quiet, commanding, and it sent a shudder down her spine. It had always struck her as a supreme injustice that he was a stable master. He should be a lord of something, of someone, not only of horses.

"I don't—"

He gazed down at her through those compelling eyes, now glittering with heat. "I haven't much time. Lord Camdonn will return sometime after midday."

She blinked. His intent was clear. He wanted her. He wanted to take her fast and hard before returning to his duties at the castle.

Ceana wasn't one to blindly follow men's orders, and God knew the women in her family weren't known for their complacency. But something about Rob inspired obedience.

With his hot stare focused on her, she unclasped her brooch and belt and allowed the sleeves of her *arisaid*, her tartan overdress, to slip down her shoulders.

She glanced at him from the corner of her eye. He stood tall and still, watching her every move. His gaze raked down her body, leaving trails of gooseflesh in its wake.

She quickly divested herself of her petticoat and stays, and laid them over one of her tall-backed wicker chairs. Finally naked, she turned to face him, raising her chin in challenge.

Their eyes locked for a long, agonizing moment. Ceana gritted her teeth against the tremors rippling through her, trying not to make it obvious. She was naked, he was fully clothed, and the air around them crackled.

As usual, Rob had sought to put himself in the position of power, and it drove her to distraction. Half the time she didn't know whether to slap his face or sink to her knees in supplication. Nevertheless, right now, his domineering behavior was a relief, for it took her mind far away from her unsettling worries about their future.

Leaving her standing in the center of the tiny room, he turned away to pull his dirk free from the top of his stocking and set it on her table. His sword and pistol followed. He unclasped the circular pin securing his plaid at his shoulder. Unbuckling his belt, he allowed the plaid to fall to the floor. He grasped the bottom of his shirt, pulled it over his head, and tossed it away.

She caught only the briefest glimpse of his backside before he turned and stepped to her. In that instant, his pale, muscular thighs flexed, and his taut buttocks hollowed. Oh, but he was a gorgeous specimen of a man. Her fingers twitched, and she could hardly contain her need to touch him.

What took her two strides took him only one, and in an instant, he'd snagged her body and pressed her against him, his shaft heavy against the lower part of her belly.

"Mmm." She smiled, squirming against the pressure. His skin was hot and hard. His cock solid yet silken. Exquisite.

His hand slid between their bodies. "Are you ready?"

She didn't bother to respond—the slickness he found as he stroked between her thighs was answer enough. Just looking at him, watching him, and interpreting his dark intent had been enough to prepare her body for him.

"Good," he murmured. "Come."

They stumbled toward her bed. His lips pressed against hers, firm and delicious, as he lowered her onto the heather-stuffed mattress. She wrapped her arms around him and sank back, opening for him as he took complete ownership of the kiss.

"Turn over." His voice was gruff against her mouth. He propped himself on his hands to give her room to turn. She flipped over before she could give it a second thought, and then she almost chuckled. What an obedient little servant she could be for young Rob MacLean.

Out of nowhere, his hand came down hard on the cheek of her arse. *Smack!* Her body lurched in reaction, and she yelped in surprise.

"You oughtn't resist me, Ceana."

"What do you mean?"

His fingers feathered over her arse cheek, now tingling pleasantly with the aftereffects of his spank. The sensation trickled to her core, and she released a measured breath, gritting her teeth against the urge to ask him to do it again.

This she hadn't expected. Ten minutes ago, if someone had told her Robert MacLean was going to march into her cottage, demand she strip, and then strike her buttocks, she would have snickered and said, "I hope to see him try." Then she'd have dreamed up a hundred different ways to avenge her arse, all of them involving bodily harm and misery to the man who'd wronged it.

"You obey readily enough, but I still see the resistance. In your muscles. In your eyes. In your voice."

"Rob, I cannot—"

"Hush," he ordered.

She allowed her eyelids to sink shut. God knew she didn't want to argue with him. Not now.

One hard arm wrapped beneath her stomach and hefted her onto her knees. He spread a soothing hand over the place he'd smacked, and then, before she had a chance to take another breath, he thrust inside her.

A strangled gasp erupted from her throat, and she curled her fists into the bedsheet. His fingers tightened around her waist, holding her immobile, locked against him.

Lodged deep inside her, he froze.

Her arse cheeks, one of them still tingling erotically, pushed against the warmth of his pelvis. Her slick channel pulsed around the steely length of his cock.

"Rob," she murmured. It felt so good. "Move."

He didn't. He didn't move, and he didn't speak. She tried to wriggle, to grind against him, but his grip on her waist was too firm. When this was over, the marks of his fingers would be imprinted on her skin.

"Move!" she demanded.

More pulsing, deep within her body. She didn't know which one of them it was, but she groaned with pleasure as sparks ignited beneath her skin.

Still he didn't move. The tiny fires in her veins faded, leaving her trembling in their wake.

"Rob," she groaned.

His fingers tightened, but otherwise he didn't budge. If he didn't move soon, she would jump straight out of her skin. Closing her eyes, she clamped her jaw and twisted the linen in her hands.

"Please," she begged, flinching at the desperation in her voice.

One of his hands released her waist, and he slid it beneath her body and up her torso until his rough fingertips brushed the underside of her breast. Ceana shuddered.

"Better," he murmured. Two of his fingers found her nipple, scraping over the hardened tip, then tightening around it and giving a tug that made her exhale in a gasp.

His palm closed around her breast. He pulled out of her until the hot, blunt head of his cock rimmed her entry, and then he plunged deep.

"Oh," she groaned. *More*. But she didn't dare voice the command for fear he'd stop again.

With his hands on her breast and on her hip, he yanked her against him as he thrust forward in each long, deep invasion of her body. Every one of Ceana's muscles engaged, until she undulated beneath the sheer power of his possession.

She'd long forgotten the chill in the air. Sweat beaded over her back and ran down her temple as his breaths grew ragged behind her. Her channel clenched spasmodically around his shaft, and he grew even larger inside her, until she was sure she couldn't endure any more.

Sensation centered between her legs in a whirlwind, rising to the power of a gale. Dimly, she heard whimpering and abstractedly knew she was making those sounds of pleasure as Rob rammed into her, hard and relentless.

The whirlwind tightened and compressed, tighter and more intense, until it exploded, and she came apart, crying out. Rob groaned behind her, but he didn't stop; he kept her going, squeezing her breast until her muscles softened like butter, and she sank to her elbows, gasping.

With a final harsh exhalation, he yanked out of her, and the warmth of his release spattered over her lower back.

She sank onto her stomach, eyes closed. A cloth stroked her just above the crack of her arse as Rob cleaned his seed from her skin. Then he brushed her hair aside and kissed the back of her neck.

She turned her head and opened her eyes. "Must you go? So soon?"

"Aye." His voice had gentled. Pulling his shirt over his head, he sat on the edge of the bed, and for a long moment he simply gazed at her. She looked into his beautiful golden brown eyes, feeling no desire to speak, basking in the moment.

Then he shattered it.

"We should marry."

She stiffened.

"I care for you, Ceana. Marry me."

They'd come together in mutual understanding—or so she'd thought. Their needs had aligned, and they supplied each other with a basic, fleshy need. Rob had never implied that he was looking for a wife or a commitment from anyone.

Never share your past. Never let him into your heart. Always keep him at a distance.

Once, she'd laughed away those vital rules passed down from her mother and her grandmother before her. She'd mocked them, dismissed them as superstitious fancy. She was enlightened, she'd thought. She'd trained herself in the ways of the modern masters of medicine and knew better than to acknowledge superstitions handed down for generations by ignorant, unlearned women.

How stupid she'd been. Because she'd been so stubborn, because she'd refused to listen, she'd suffered and others had suffered. Others had died.

There was truth in science, but there was also wisdom in the old ways. Now she knew to respect both. She'd never second-guess her mother's and grandmother's warnings again.

Never.

She released a deep breath. She admired Rob. She cared for him. She wished to know more about him, about what made him into the man he was. But—praise God—she didn't love him.

Despite the words he'd just spoken, she was certain he didn't love her, either. If he did love her, he'd reveal more of himself. He'd truly talk to her, share himself and his past. He'd wish to stay with her longer after he'd bedded her.

He stared at her, searching her face. "You don't want me," he stated after a moment of silence.

She hated this. Hated that she must do this to Rob, whom she liked so very much.

She shrugged lightly, carefully schooling her expression to indifference.

He looked away, shaking his head. "I don't have much to offer you, but—"

She hissed out a breath, interrupting him midsentence. When she spoke, her voice was tight. "That has naught to do with it."

There was so much more. Yet she wouldn't speak of it to him. The curse was her own burden, not to be shared with Rob, or anyone.

She'd made a critical error and had allowed their liaison to go on too long. It pained her to admit it, but it was true.

She took a deep, strengthening breath, and managed to infuse a measure of haughty arrogance into her voice. "MacNab women never marry."

"Aye," Rob said grimly. "So I've heard. I've also heard you're man-hating shrews and I shouldn't go within shooting distance of any of you."

She raised a brow. "For fear of being gunned down?"

"Aye."

Yet the people of the Glen came to her daily pleading for medical help. She curled her lip. "Perhaps they are right to warn you off."

He shook his head firmly.

She drew in a silent breath but kept her face immobile, frozen into a mask of disdain. *The moment people cease to fear ye*, her grandmother had warned, *is the moment ye'll be in true danger.*

Sliding his hand under the plaid covering her, he turned to her, his eyes dark. His hand came to a stop when it rested on her belly. "What if I were to get you with child? I try to come outside your body, but—"

"No."

She'd already made certain that event would never come to pass. She'd never again risk bringing a child into this world only to be subjected to the stigma of bastardy. One would think that after five generations, MacNab women would learn. But no, each repeated the mistakes of her mother. Ceana had sworn four years ago that it would all end with her.

She pushed Rob's hand from her skin. "You speak nonsense. You don't love me."

His lips tightened. "I do. As much as . . . as much as I'm capable."

No, she wanted to say, *you're capable of so much more.* As reserved as Rob was, she sensed a great passion in him. But she kept her lips sealed shut and her expression flat. He was younger than her, with less experience of the ways of love. Someday he'd learn. Hopefully with far less pain than she had suffered.

"I care for you," he said. "I admire and respect you." His voice lowered, and his gaze dipped to peruse her form. "I take pleasure from your body."

"Aye, and I take pleasure from yours. However, carnal attraction doesn't promise a good marriage, now, does it?" Propping herself up on her elbow, she leaned toward him. "Listen to me, Rob. For a marriage to work, the bond must be deeper."

"I must go." Rising abruptly, he turned away to don his plaid and weapons in silence.

As he strapped on his belt, she asked, "Will you come back?"

"Next week." He strode to the door, where he paused, his back to her. "Think on it."

He stepped out and pushed the door closed behind him.

Ceana closed her eyes and lay for some time listening to the spring breeze rustle the thatch. Her body was still languid from their lovemaking, but her heart pounded and her mind whirled.

She'd tarried too long with Rob, but the truth was, she feared letting him go. The boundless loneliness ate at her, and she'd suffer without Rob here to soothe it.

Nevertheless, she'd taken their liaison too far. She thought she'd been careful, but she'd already led him to think she might offer him more than she could.

Let him go.

It frightened her, but she wouldn't lie to him. She couldn't continue to hurt him.

Sighing, she thrust the plaids aside and gathered her petticoat and stays from where they lay discarded on the floor. She had work to do.

She pulled her underclothes on with jerky movements, and then

wrapped her *arisaid* about her body and pinned it on with her grandmother's silver brooch.

Alan MacDonald, the laird of the MacDonalds of the Glen, had
promised to come to the cottage before dusk to bring her some herbs
from his wife Sorcha's garden. He planned to head Ceana's direction
on his way to Camdonn Castle to welcome Lord Camdonn home, and
said he'd spare her the walk to their manor. Alan appeared to consider
the earl a close friend, though they'd once dueled over Sorcha, a
story that always made Ceana chuckle. Men and their honor were
two things she'd never fully understand.

Alan didn't go today solely to welcome his friend home, however.
He went to warn the earl, for since the official surrender of the Jacobites after last year's uprising, the mood of the earl's tenants had
soured, and many were unhappy about his return from England. Rumors abounded that he brought a new wife home with him—an English lady—and that had served only to heighten the ripples of
discontent. This area was rife with true-blooded Jacobites, and the
idea that their loyalist lord was on his way home to lay down the law
made their blood boil. Alan had worked tirelessly to calm the sentiment, but it was as contagious as an infectious disease, and he hadn't
been able to suppress it.

Ceana wanted to be here when Alan arrived, to discuss the problem of the poachers with him again. First, however, she needed to find
some foxglove for a tonic for one of her patients who'd recovered from
a case of scarlet fever but now suffered with the dropsy.

She drew her jacket from the peg by her table, grabbed the basket
containing her tools, and ventured into the cool afternoon, closing
her woven wicker door securely behind her.

Slinging the basket over her forearm, Ceana headed toward the forest on the slope of mountains behind the clearing surrounding her cottage. She vaguely remembered where Moira Stewart, her grandmother's
old apprentice and now the midwife's apprentice, had shown her foxglove. It grew in a sheltered, rocky area somewhere near the pass through
the mountains that led to the Lowlands, about a mile away.

When Ceana had last visited the spot at the end of autumn, a thick frost had clung to the branches of the barren trees and the pine needles. Now the forest had come alive, growing thick and green in the crisp, moist springtime air.

Ceana lifted her skirts and strode uphill, remembering the poachers had been out this way earlier this afternoon. She hoped they were long gone—she'd prefer not to be mistaken for game. Still, she kept alert for signs of human movement as she picked her way through budding rowan trees and stone brambles. Scanning for foxglove, she avoided muddy spots and clumps of weeds, and took a wide circle around a thick copse of alders.

A low, inhuman noise stopped her in her tracks. It came from a nearby cluster of bushes, and she swung her head around but could see nothing beyond the thick screen of green. When the sound faded, silence settled through the forest, but she remained frozen in place, listening intently. And then there it was again. A low groan. A sound of pain.

An animal must be injured in the brush. Those cursed poachers had probably shot the poor creature, and it had run away, only to eventually collapse in the bushes. Ceana yanked her dirk from her basket. If she was wrong, or if the thing mistook her for a predator and attacked, at least she could defend herself.

Slowly, she approached the source of the noise, peering through the thick greenery. Leaves rustled as the creature moved, and another soft moan permeated the air.

A black mass came into view through the branches and leaves, and then Ceana froze, the breath whooshing from her lungs.

It wasn't an animal at all. It was a man.

CHAPTER TWO

Elizabeth crawled from the awful thorny bush, praising God her uncle couldn't see the ungainly way in which she performed the awkward action. In fact, she thought as she yanked her sleeve from a bramble and grimaced at the screeching sound of fabric tearing, she'd like to see him attempt to accomplish the feat with more grace. First she'd strap him into her stays and her stiff stomacher, and then she'd watch in satisfaction as he floundered helplessly in the thorns.

Finally straightening on the dirt path, she shook out her skirts and gazed regretfully down at her dress. Moments ago it had been a beautiful yellow silk sack gown, pleated at the shoulders and trimmed with lush embroidery and the finest lace, but now the nasty leaves and branches had snagged the expensive material, tearing her skirts and leaving lace bits to dangle haphazardly from her bodice and bell-shaped sleeves.

Pursing her lips, Elizabeth glanced up and down the path. No one was about. Thank heavens Cam had driven those awful men away. Heaven forbid he see her in such a state.

She sighed. Her thoughts just went to show how jaded and dissolute she truly was. If she were truly innocent, if she were truly a lady, she'd be terrified. She'd be a shaking lump, utterly petrified by fear.

Instead, she worried about Uncle Walter and Cam seeing her in disarray.

A masked stranger had pulled her from a carriage and might have killed her, or worse, but she couldn't bring herself to feel the requisite terror. How pitiful. She tilted her head to search her emotions, but they were a blank slate. She didn't feel a bit of fear—or much of anything else, for that matter.

She was no fool. If another soul stood nearby, she'd make a show of fright, just so they wouldn't grow concerned for her sanity. But since she was alone, there was no need to school her actions. She could be herself.

She could thank Uncle Walter for her strange, improper reaction, she supposed. Had this been his goal? To eradicate her ability to respond in an appropriate way? To eliminate the instinctual response to fear for her life?

And then she did feel a little something. A tiny flicker of terror. Not of the highwaymen, though, nor for her life. Of Uncle Walter himself.

Elizabeth stared down the path in the direction Cam and those awful men had gone. What if they had injured him? She squeezed her eyes shut and pictured Cam with a hole torn open in his chest. Taking gasping, wheezing breaths as his lifeblood drained from him . . .

Uncle Walter would take her back to England.

No. She shook off the thought. Cam was capable of defending himself. Those men were rough and dirty and unskilled compared to her betrothed. She had faith in his ability to overcome them, even outnumbered as he was.

But why hadn't he come back?

A bird cackled nearby, and she cast an acerbic glance in the creature's direction, then scoured the edge of the path until she found a sharp stick to use as a weapon. Who knew what kinds of ferocious beasts could be roaming this wild place?

Perhaps this was where she belonged, after all. It was wild, just like her. She smiled a little and gripped the stick tighter.

She'd go after Cam. If something had happened, if he was hurt,
she'd help him.

Suddenly, the clomp of a horse's hooves sounded from around a
bend in the path. Wielding her stick like a sword, she braced her feet
in the center of the narrow strip of dirt, not knowing whether she'd
face the earl or one of the criminals come back to ravish her. Or hold
her for ransom. Or both.

It was neither. A dark-haired man approached on horseback. He
wore one of those Highland plaids that gave the men in this region
such an untamed, scandalous appearance. Young Scotsmen in their
plaids always made her chest tighten in pleasant appreciation. Even
this one, who wore a tartan of a most appealing shade of blue but was
particularly wild-looking, made her stomach flutter, when instead she
ought to be scared to death—or at the very least on her guard.

He couldn't have been involved with the attack. The difference
between him and the highwaymen was obvious in his bearing, his
dress, and in the horse he rode—a much finer animal than the short,
skinny Scottish creatures the highwaymen had ridden.

As he drew near, she straightened her spine, lowered the stick, and
adopted her "Lady Elizabeth" facade. Her uncle approved of this particular air she affected—said it made her look as haughty as a queen.
Over the years, she'd refined and polished it until it shone like one of
the golden Roman statues adorning the Duke of Irvington's foyer.
Until it solidified into stone, as hard as one of the Greek alabaster
busts in the library.

The horse's back legs sprayed mud as it halted before her. For a long
moment, the man's dark amber eyes perused her. Assessed her. Then
one corner of his mouth twitched upward. "Who might you be?"

His rumbling accent sent a chill of awareness down her spine, but
she hid it, knowing full well her visceral reaction to him was utterly
ridiculous.

How had he known to speak English to her? Was her foreignness
so very obvious?

She lifted her chin and narrowed her eyes, doing her best to look down her nose at him, though his position on the horse put him several feet above her. Anyone who knew anything about manners would have dismounted before speaking to a lady of her status.

"I am Lady Elizabeth Grant, a guest of the Earl of Camdonn. Our carriages were attacked by bandits. Surely you heard the gunshots."

"Aye." He scanned the area. "So where are they now?"

"The earl chased them away," she said primly.

The man seemed to do a rapid mental calculation; then he dismounted smoothly. A master horseman, she deduced. Not a peasant, certainly. She imagined a majority of the population of this poor country had no idea whatsoever how to handle a horse.

He bowed his head. His hair was dark—the color of coffee with just the barest touch of cream—but not as dark as Cam's. "I am Robert MacLean."

She nodded coolly. Keeping her stiff composure, inwardly she indulged in a brazen smile. Here she stood in the wilds of Scotland with a scandalously torn dress, alone on an abandoned path and at the whim of a young and handsome stranger, and they were exchanging introductions. Days ago, she could never have imagined such an absurd scenario.

Robert angled his head at the horse. "Come."

She was surely mad. Any of the girls back home would be terrified, but Elizabeth . . . No. Again she wasn't frightened in the least.

"Indeed I will not 'come,'" she huffed. "I shall walk. I do not know you, sir. However, you must—" Before she had the opportunity to command that he go back and search for Cam, his hands encircled her waist, lifted her, and deposited her upon the horse. Then he mounted and settled behind her in the saddle. Shockingly close. *Deliciously* close. The rough wool of his plaid scraped the delicate silk of her dress, and when she inhaled she smelled him. Clean hay and leather.

He adjusted the reins and wrapped one hard arm around her waist, presumably to keep her from toppling off the animal.

She looked over her shoulder, directly into Robert MacLean's eyes. Not quite brown, not quite gold, they reminded her of autumn. No, of sweet burnt sugar. She found them as absorbing as a whirlpool. He didn't meet her gaze; instead he stared steadily ahead. Nevertheless, she read something in the dark gold depths. Dislike, perhaps.

She turned and stared ahead at the rutted path as Robert coaxed the horse into a walk. It didn't matter. As delicious as he appeared—coffee hair and burnt-sugar eyes, indeed!—it was certainly for the best if he didn't like her. In any event, she wasn't a very likable person. Nobody liked her. Which was perfectly fine, really.

Cam, however, was infinitely polite, infinitely solicitous in her presence. Did he like her? As a person, as a human being, as a woman, a lifelong companion?

Probably not. Maybe someday he would. That would be ideal, of course, but ultimately she didn't care. As long as Cam didn't hate her, nothing else mattered.

All she desired was freedom from Uncle Walter. And if Cam was hurt . . .

She turned to Robert MacLean. "Stop immediately. You must go back to search for Lord Camdonn. I'll continue on foot to the castle and inform them that the earl is missing. But if he's in dire need, you might find him first and save him. If we delay any longer, we could be too late."

Robert MacLean didn't respond. He didn't even deign to look at her—instead his eyes focused unerringly on the uneven surface of the path.

"Stop at once. I insist." She pushed at the arm clasped round her waist, but it wouldn't budge.

"Nay."

"Where are you taking me?"

"To Camdonn Castle."

She sat in rising frustration as the horse plodded forward. When they arrived at Camdonn Castle, Uncle Walter would take control, and she would be impotent. Desperation surged through her. She didn't trust her uncle to help Cam. If Cam was hurt, the Highlander sitting behind her was her only hope.

When she spoke, it was in her quietest, most lethal voice. The voice that made her servants at home blanch in fear. "You must obey me."

"Why?" He seemed mildly amused.

"Because I am the niece of the Duke of Irvington, of course."

"Aye, and the betrothed of the Earl of Camdonn. You'll find high-and-mighty English titles mean a wee bit less to Highlanders."

Highlanders. The word rolled off his tongue carnally, and her stomach fluttered even as she clenched her fists in her skirts. How dare he dismiss her order so lightly? She ground her teeth, hating him, hating even more how her body responded to him. Still, her desperation to help Cam overwhelmed it all.

"I could have you horsewhipped."

Her threat sounded as though it came from the mouth of a petulant child—no, worse. She sounded as horrible as her uncle, and a flash flood of shame thundered through her.

If Robert MacLean hadn't hated her before, her words certainly sealed the impression. He didn't make any move to obey her; instead, his arm stiffened about her waist, and steam seemed to billow from his body. He was so warm, she struggled not to sink into him like the softest of down quilts. Even though he was hard as stone.

It suddenly seemed far more likely he'd have *her* horsewhipped.

The fight drained out of her, dripped right out of her toes. She'd lost, and it was her own fault.

She closed her eyes in self-loathing. She was such a horrid brat. Lord knew she would never inflict a terrible punishment like a horsewhipping on such a delicious man. Whether he deserved it or not. She'd never consciously inflict such a punishment on *anyone*, no matter what they looked like, no matter how evil their disposition. He believed he was doing the honorable thing by taking her to Cam's home. He couldn't be faulted for that.

She should apologize for making such a vile threat. Certainly she should. She *must*.

But she couldn't. The harder she tried to push *I'm sorry* from her throat, the tighter it closed, simply refusing to release the words.

Uncle Walter surely had Cam's best interests in mind. She had to trust in that, if nothing else. Her uncle had no reason to wish for Cam's demise. If her uncle had a desire to see Cam dead, he'd already be long gone.

The horse shifted abruptly, and Elizabeth opened her eyes. Here the road began a steep descent down the back of the mountain. At the bottom, probably a bit less than a mile away, water stretched in a placid blue line, calm and pristine. A lake—no, a *loch* was what they called it here. Green cliffs speckled with great white boulders rose from the opposite bank, ascending steeply toward the puffy clouds. A handful of boats floated on the loch's surface, mere dots from this distance, and she couldn't tell if they were moving.

Her gaze followed the far shoreline until the loch came to a rounded tip. Smoke curled lazily from a cluster of structures tucked into the valley leading off from the bank. She couldn't remember the name of the village—Glen . . . Glen-something-or-other. She studied how the bank curved back around, her gaze skimming over the few brown cottage roofs among the prevailing green on this side of the loch. A bucolic scene, like something from an Italian painting, but even more vivid, more lovely.

Her gaze careened to a stop when it landed on the castle.

"Camdonn Castle," she murmured.

Robert MacLean, still angry with her, still sitting like a statue behind her, didn't respond.

Sighing, she gazed down at the structures directly below them. Situated on a spit of land jutting into the loch, Camdonn Castle wasn't just one building but many, all built from gray stone. With the loch serving as its moat and a solid rock wall barring entrance to the spit, it appeared more an ancient fortress than the glittering silver fairy-tale palaces she'd seen on the trip north from Hampshire. Camdonn Castle looked stony and cold, and altogether *harsh*.

This cold, gray, awful place, this place that looked more like a medieval prison than a house . . . this was to be her home forevermore.

A tremble resonated through her body. Was it her imagination, or did Robert MacLean's arm tighten around her?

They continued down the mountain in rigid silence. All along, the raw strength of Robert MacLean simmered behind her, and regret for her rash, childish outburst continued to bite through her like scampering mice.

It was too late to take back what she'd said. She'd missed her opportunity to apologize, and she'd probably never see him again.

As they descended to the entryway to the castle, Robert urged the horse into a trot. The animal obliged readily enough, probably anticipating the promise of oats and the release of the heavy weight from its back.

A big, black, heavy iron gate rose from the sheer rock walls. A group of guards stood before it, eyeing them warily as they approached. When they recognized the man riding behind her, they called to Robert in Gaelic, regarding Elizabeth with an unfriendly glimmer in their eyes that curdled her stomach.

Robert dismounted. Leading the horse by the reins, he walked the rest of the way. Elizabeth sat stiffly in the saddle, clutching the horse's mane so hard her knuckles turned white, but remaining outwardly calm as she eyed the men with disdain.

Robert cocked his head in her direction. He spoke in English, likely for her benefit. "This is Lady Elizabeth Grant, his lordship's intended. I found her on the road."

The men glanced at her, then looked away, none of them offering a reasonable semblance of an obeisance. Elizabeth kept her expression even. A huge man with a pockmarked face and a red nose rattled off something in Gaelic.

Elizabeth arched a regal brow at Robert. "Translate, please, Mr. MacLean."

"He says His Grace, your uncle, is here, but there's been no sign of his lordship. They're sending a party to search for him."

Elizabeth released a silent breath, and a shudder of alarm rippled through her body. She clenched every muscle to combat it, to remain outwardly serene. It was what she did best, after all.

The gate swung open with a loud squeal.

Without sparing another glance at her, Robert strode forward, leading the horse across the narrow length of the spit and then up a winding path to the castle grounds.

People crowded the graveled courtyard in a disorganized mass. Men shouted orders, but nobody seemed to be listening, and Robert made a disapproving noise in his throat.

As they approached, a group separated from the rest and rushed at them. Elizabeth immediately recognized her uncle's fashionable white wig among the darker heads of the Scots.

"Elizabeth," he blustered, breaking from the crowd. The gold of the round buttons down the front of his coat came into view, and Elizabeth noted that he'd placed his wig carefully askew to give himself an anxious demeanor. As always, he played the concerned, doting uncle to a T. Now all the residents of Camdonn Castle would spread the rumor of what a fine, caring man he was, and if she ever disputed it, well, they viewed evidence to the contrary right this very instant.

"Oh, my dear." He reached up to pull her from the horse. Her feet hit the ground with a jolt, and he loomed over her, his face a mask of concern. "Oh, Lizzy. How I have worried. Thank God you are unhurt."

She managed to smile up at him. "I am fine, truly." She risked a glance at Robert, who watched the scene dispassionately.

"Come, child, let us go inside. It is warm there, and your maid awaits with fresh garments and a warm posset for you."

"But what about Lord Camdonn, Uncle? He's lost. I fear he's been shot or fallen from his horse—"

"Never fear, dear girl. Lord Camdonn's men will find him. They will scour every inch of the countryside, and I have no doubt he'll be home by dusk." He gave her arm a fatherly pat.

From the corner of her eye, she saw Robert take up the reins and lead the horse away. She knew better than to stare, and she tore her gaze away from the Scot as Uncle Walter ushered her toward a long rectangular building with a tall square tower rising from one end. Long ago, this building must have served as the keep.

She'd felt utterly safe with Robert's strong arm locked around her body. With his powerful legs encasing her behind. As he moved farther away from her, so did that warm, sweet sensation of security.

She looked up at her uncle, saw the silvery glint in his eyes as he slanted his gaze at her disheveled gown, and steeled herself against the panic threatening to consume her whole.

Ceana pushed through the brush and dropped to her knees beside the man. Eyes half lidded, he didn't seem to register her presence as she assessed his condition. Blue tinged his pale skin, a stark contrast to his red lips and dark lashes and brows. High, slashing cheekbones, a sloped straight nose, and black brows arching over long-lashed, wide-set eyes all worked together to create an artistic masterpiece.

She tore her gaze from his face, which required no further analysis, certainly, for it was uninjured. Only the paleness of his skin offered information; he'd lost too much blood.

Once she escaped the snare of his far-too-handsome face, it was simple enough to diagnose his malaise. Sticky blood covered his shoulder and most of his arm, darkening the black wool coat covering his torso. He'd been dealt a crushing blow to his arm—or maybe he'd been shot. She shuddered, remembering the poachers. Perhaps they weren't poachers after all.

His rich clothing left no doubt that he was a fine gentleman. Not that it mattered to her—she wasn't the obsequious, sniveling sort, fawning over the higher orders like they shat gold. People were equal to her, no matter their station in life, and while the difference between her class and his might be clear as day, she'd care for him as she'd care for anyone else. He deserved no more and no less than the lowliest whore or the poorest beggar.

People could either accept her as she was or leave her be. She didn't care one way or the other, and ultimately, when it came to a choice between living and dying, neither did anyone else. Of any class. No one cared about her appearance or her social standing if she was saving their life.

"Can you hear me?" she asked in Scots. She tried again in English. When he didn't answer, she spoke more sharply, smacking his smoothly shaven cheek lightly with her palm. His skin was clammy, cold to the touch, his breathing rapid.

His eyelids fluttered, revealing the dark orbs beneath. "Mary MacNab," he murmured, his lips twitching into a skeletal grimace. "Will you save me this time?"

She stared at him. He'd responded in crusty Gaelic, and he'd mistaken her for her dead grandmother. She didn't know whether she ought to feel offended or honored. Blinking away her surprise, she pressed her fingers to his neck and found his pulse weak and rapid.

"It's Ceana MacNab, not Mary," she snapped. "Mary is dead." Her words sounded awfully similar to the way her grandmother might have spoken them.

She turned his head to the side in the event he vomited and unbuttoned her jacket to remove her *arisaid*. Her mind rapidly calculated his status: It was essential to keep him warm, to stop the bleeding, to encourage the flow of blood to his heart . . .

She shivered in her petticoat as she shook open her *arisaid* and spread it over him, then tucked her jacket on top. She could survive the cold, but he wouldn't. Gathering an armful of bracken, she used it to raise his legs.

Reaching under the wool covering, she found the buttons of his coat. She unbuttoned it, then carefully peeled the heavy material back over his arm as he groaned in complaint. Blood stuck his linen shirt to his skin, but she'd take care of that later. The wound was clearly visible through the torn cloth, and she studied it, emitting a small sound of satisfaction. A musket ball had gone clean through him. It hadn't shattered a bone, and the blood ran clean. He'd be good as new in no time at all. If she could rouse him and get him out of the forest before darkness came and he froze to death, that was. How on earth could she move him?

Gritting her teeth, she ripped the skirts of her petticoat. Using her dirk as a tool, it took her a few moments to fashion a bandage-cum-sling, which she wrapped around the wound and tied tightly at his neck.

"Can you walk?"

He'd drifted into oblivion, and she rapped on his good shoulder. "Can you walk?"

He kept his eyes shut. "Not a chance, Mary."

"It's Ceana," she gritted out. "You must rise and walk."

He released a shaky breath. "Stop, I pray you. Can't you see I'm dying? Allow me to do it in peace, if you please."

"Surely a man who's capable of such a fine speech is capable of taking a few steps."

She wasn't going to share that he'd have to walk nearly a mile before they reached the nearest shelter—her cottage. If he knew that, she didn't have a hope of his even trying.

He didn't respond, and she wasn't surprised. He'd lost too much blood and the flow of liquid remaining in his veins was too sluggish for him to see reason. Ceana rocked back on her heels, gazing at her surroundings. The brush grew thick in this area. She presumed he'd fallen from a horse, and if she was right, the animal might be nearby. She didn't know the first thing about horses, but she might be able to lead it back and coax him onto it somehow.

Of course, whoever had shot him might be lurking about too.

Leaning forward over him, she vigorously rubbed his uninjured arm and his legs to encourage the flow of blood. Then she pressed her fingers to his neck again and found his pulse had slowed. *Good.*

"Very well, then." She lowered her voice in the event his attacker was close. "I shall have to fetch someone to help."

His good hand shot out, clutching her arm with far more strength than she'd expected him to have. "No! Don't leave me."

"Don't be an idiot. We cannot stay here."

"Why not?" he murmured. "Comfortable. Warm. Hurts to move."

"Because," she said with exaggerated patience, "it will be dark soon, and you'll get cold, and we'll *both* freeze to death."

The fool still hadn't opened his eyes, but his lips turned down. "I don't want you to freeze. Too pretty."

She cast her gaze heavenward. "Exactly. Now, I insist you save *my* precious life by leading me to shelter."

His lips twisted. "You're tricking me, Mary."

"I'm not Mary."

"Sure you are," he mumbled. "Mary. Mary turned young and beautiful and haloed like an angel . . . Pretty Mary with creamy white breasts . . ."

Grinding her teeth, Ceana glanced down at her bosom, which was indeed brimming over the top of her petticoat, and yanked the material as high as she could as she looked over her shoulder.

Through the branches, the sun dipped low in the sky, sending streams of light all around them. No doubt it did have a halo effect on her appearance. But honestly! Could the man truly think he'd died and met a young version of her grandmother in heaven? She laughed out loud. Delirious fool. "Get up, you oaf."

That made him open his eyes. "I've been called many things, but never an oaf." His pupils contracted, and a crease appeared between his brows as he frowned at her. "Who are you?"

A flush of relief rushed through her at seeing him awake—*truly* awake this time, she thought.

"Ceana." She cupped his face in her palm. His skin was warmer now—not so clammy. He'd come out of the worst of it. "Remember? I told you before."

He gave a small shake of his head. "I was shot," he murmured. "My shoulder . . ."

"I know. I've already bandaged it."

He tore his gaze from her to glance at his arm, confirming it was, indeed, bandaged; then he looked back to her. "I thought . . . I thought you were—" Glancing at her chest, he broke off, and red crept into his cheeks. A good sign, for certain. "Forgive me. I think . . . I wasn't a gentleman."

"Nothing to forgive," she said brusquely. "Can you walk?"

"I'll"—he swallowed, and his face seemed to whiten even more—"try."

She smiled. "Here, I'll help you up. Then we'll find a walking stick for you and get you home."

"Home . . ." he repeated wistfully. Then his eyes widened and he lurched upward. The movement undoubtedly sent pain streaking through him, and he groaned. "Elizabeth!"

"Elizabeth?"

"Lady Elizabeth, my wife. Uh, my betrothed," he amended. "We were attacked by highwaymen . . . They left her on the side of the path—"

"The highwaymen left her?"

"Yes. No." He dropped his face into his uninjured hand. "I don't know."

Blood already seeped through the cloth wrapped around his arm. At this rate, she'd never get him home.

Alan would be at her house within half an hour. "Listen to me . . ." She took in a breath. "Who, exactly, are you?"

"Cam," he said quietly, almost as if the truth of it embarrassed him.

The Earl of Camdonn. She should have known.

She stared at him for a long moment, too shaken to speak, as an unfamiliar, awed feeling settled within her. The earl didn't meet her eyes, just stared off into the brush. So *this* was the infamous earl. The man who'd debauched Sorcha MacDonald, whom the locals never spoke of without sneering, who'd dueled with Alan. From the way the people talked about him, she'd expected a lecherous monster. What could provoke such viciousness? The Earl of Camdonn was the most beautiful man she'd ever laid eyes on.

Ceana shook off the strange, fluttery feeling in her stomach, mentally slapping herself across the face. She was behaving like a simpleton maiden on the verge of swooning. Ridiculous. She didn't know this man at all. Perhaps inside that beautiful shell he *was* a lecherous monster. After all, look at how he'd just spoken of her breasts.

She cleared her throat. "Listen to me. Alan MacDonald is due at my home in less than an hour. I'm sure he will do whatever is necessary to find the lass. You cannot do it. You're near to fainting for lack of blood, and you must use all your remaining energy to walk to my cottage."

His attention had seemed to wander at the beginning of her speech, but now his gaze sharpened on her. "Why are you naked?"

"I am not naked. You required my *arisaid* for warmth."

He glanced down at the tartan fabric covering him; then his gaze snapped back to her. "Is Alan MacDonald visiting you? Will he be alone?"

She choked out a laugh. "Is this an attempt to protect my virtue or his?"

His lips pressed into a firm, straight line. "Just tell me."

They didn't have the time for this nonsense. She released a harsh breath. "I don't see how it is any of your concern, but he's bringing me some herbs from his wife's garden. Are you satisfied?"

"Will your husband be at home?"

It took her a moment to realize her jaw had dropped, and she snapped it shut. What kind of man asked a woman such questions moments after having met her?

"There is no husband at home. It is just me. If it interests you, I arrived at my grandmother's house at the end of autumn, and the laird and his wife have been generous in welcoming me to the Glen." She narrowed her eyes at him. "Now, does that satisfy your rampant curiosity? Might we walk now?"

He gave her a soft smile. "I heard Mary MacNab had passed. She was your grandmother? I'm sorry."

"Aye. Well, thank you." A surprising, and unwelcome, surge of emotion crowded her throat, and she looked away.

Reaching out with his good hand, he pressed his fingers against her cheek, turning her face back toward him. "We'll return to your cottage to meet with Alan. He'll have a horse. He'll help me find Elizabeth. Much more expedient than me on foot and injured."

She blew out a breath. Wasn't all that what she'd been trying to tell him this entire time?

The earl frowned. "There's no time to waste. We must hurry."

CHAPTER THREE

When they finally descended the slope leading to Ceana's cottage, the gloaming had arrived, sending streams of dusky light through the clouds to settle across the land. The earl took harsh, rasping breaths and was so white-faced she knew he remained upright only through sheer force of will.

A big black horse was tied to the tree nearest her cottage, and she saw movement near the corner of the building. "Ah, look. Alan has arrived."

The earl remained quiet as they plodded steadily closer. He leaned heavily on her now, and sweat stuck her shift to her back, though the air grew cooler by the minute. When they were a few hundred yards from the cottage, he murmured, "I might not be able to hold on."

"Oh, come! Not this nonsense about dying. I already told you your wound wasn't serious—do you think I'd lie to you? Dragging you halfway through the forest is hard work. If you were going to die, I'd rather've left you where you were."

"No," he pushed out. "I just . . . I don't think I'll be able to maintain consciousness for much longer. It's . . . it's dragging me under. It's like a game of tug-of-war I'm starting to"—he drew in a shaky breath—"lose."

She softened, knowing he spoke the truth. If she'd ever seen anyone on the verge of fainting, it was him.

"It's all right for you to sleep," she soothed.

"Elizabeth . . ."

"Alan will find your Elizabeth for you. Come; it's only a few more yards. My bed is soft and comfortable. We'll lay you down . . ."

She continued to murmur encouragement as they stumbled within shouting range of her cottage.

"Alan!" she called. "Are you there? Help us!"

The earl stumbled. "Oh, hell."

"Oh, hell!" she gasped in agreement. His knees buckled and her back bowed—she couldn't support his weight.

"Cam!"

On hearing Alan's gruff voice, Ceana breathed a sigh of relief so acute, tears pricked at her eyes. Her legs collapsed under the earl, but she couldn't let him go down too hard, jar his arm, hit his head on a rock. Lord, she couldn't fall on top of him. She gritted her teeth, groaning with the strain of holding him up. She couldn't. She wasn't strong enough.

Just as they crumpled, Alan lunged at them, catching the earl. Muscles bunched beneath his shirt as he disentangled Lord Camdonn from Ceana and gently eased him to the ground. Ceana collapsed onto her knees beside the earl, breathing heavily. His eyes had closed. His face again took on that quality of an angel in repose.

The laird thrust his plaid higher onto his shoulder. "What the hell happened?" he ground out, his blue eyes narrow as he stared down at his friend.

Ceana looked at him in surprise. She'd never heard Alan curse before. "He was shot. He said they were attacked by highwaymen."

"Where is everyone else?"

Ceana shrugged. "I don't know. He only mentioned Elizabeth."

"Lady Elizabeth? What did he say?"

"He said they left her."

A muscle twitched in Alan's jaw. He removed his bonnet and rubbed a hand over his curly blond hair, his lips turning down. "She's a young English lady. She won't have the faintest idea what to do alone in the wilderness. I must go find her."

"That's what he said." Her voice was soft. Gentle. It didn't sound like her. Compassion for the earl flooded through her, and even for Alan she couldn't muster her usual matter-of-fact tone. The earl had put enormous effort into walking here. She was no fool—as much as she'd prodded and cajoled him, it had taken every ounce of strength he could muster to come all this way after having lost so much blood. She'd been a healer all her life, and she had seen many people in various states of weakness. It took a powerful will to accomplish what he had—and all so he could get to her cottage in time to intercept Alan—to ask Alan to help him find his betrothed. His obvious love and concern for his Elizabeth made Ceana's chest tighten.

Why? Was it admiration of him, or envy of his lady?

She brushed a knuckle over his cold cheek and stared down at him. She was all twisted up inside with some emotion she couldn't comprehend. She pursed her lips, battling back the strange feeling. She saved lives all the time. This one was no different.

"Can you manage if I leave you with him?"

She glanced up at Alan. She'd been so lost in the unconscious earl, she'd forgotten all about the laird. "Of course. But you must help me bring him inside."

Alan nodded tersely.

Together, she and Alan managed to carry Lord Camdonn into her cottage and settle him on the bed. Seeing its disarray, Ceana remembered Rob's earlier visit. How Rob had smacked her behind. How she'd liked it . . .

The earl had turned clammy again. Pushing aside the memories of that afternoon, Ceana covered him with layers of plaids.

Alan clapped his bonnet on his head and buttoned his jacket. He took the torch she offered him and paused at the door. "I might not be back for some time, Ceana." He glanced at the earl. "Will he be all right?"

She considered the man lying limply in her bed, his features ashen and drawn. "I'll do my best."

That seemed good enough for Alan. "Are you certain you don't need anything?"

She gestured at the shelves of medicines above her worktable. "I've everything I need for him here."

"You've done well, as always." He paused, and then said in a low voice, "You have my thanks."

"I've done no more than my profession requires of me."

"I'll return as soon as I can."

The next time she tore her eyes away from the earl to glance at the door, Alan was gone.

Cam dreamed about the angel. "I'm not Mary MacNab," she'd said in that cutting voice, sharp as a blade. "I'm Ceana."

Pretty Ceana with her blond-streaked brown curls and clear gray-blue eyes. The eyes, the shape of the face. The voice. They'd all reminded him of the old woman. In his dream, Ceana spoke to him.

"I think you're the angel, not I." She stroked a soft finger down his nose. Over the bones of his cheeks. Across his jaw. Around the edges of his hair.

Only someone in his dreams would call him an angel. In real life, he was a pariah.

She peeled off his shirt, poked and prodded him, and gasped at the scar at his side.

"Alan's work," he whispered. "He saved me."

She harrumphed. "Near killed you, more like."

"Too complicated . . ."

He opened his eyes, clutching her wrist in sudden fear. "Elizabeth!"

"Shh. They're looking for her. They'll find her."

Ceana. She must be the old healer's heir. He wondered if she was as talented at healing as her grandmother.

He drifted back into darkness.

When Cam opened his eyes again, time had passed, for she no longer stood at his side. Instead she stood at the foot of the bed, her heart-shaped face framed by wildly curly golden-streaked hair.

She was changing her clothes. She stripped off her torn petticoat and shimmied out of her shift. Her body glowed in the moonlight as she bent over to splash water over her face and chest. Large, high breasts, narrow waist, flared hips. She reminded him of a ripe fruit, of a plump, juicy pear. Surely she'd be just as sweet. His mouth watered, and long-denied lust surged through him.

And she called *him* the angel? The absurdity of it nearly made him laugh out loud.

She pulled a clean shift over her head and wrapped a cloak around that luscious, rounded figure. Cam's heavy eyelids drooped as she returned to his side, reached under the blankets, and laced her fingers with his. Why did she hold his hand? How could she know how much the simple touch soothed him?

"Don't let go," he murmured. "It feels . . . safe."

"Delirious fool," she muttered, but she squeezed his fingers tighter.

She sounded like Mary. He chuckled and then allowed sweet oblivion to claim him again.

He awoke to sharp pain in his shoulder. His eyes snapped open to utter blackness, but he heard her. Ceana MacNab's breaths came in long, deep draws. Hair tickled his lips, and with effort, Cam turned his heavy head. She sat on a tattered wicker chair beside the bed. She'd crossed her arms on the bed and rested her head on them. Her untamed mop of hair tumbled across the blankets. With a pang in his chest, Cam realized she lived in a one-room cottage, and he'd taken her only bed.

With his good arm, he reached up to touch her hand, brushing away a soft strand of hair. Her fingers were icy. Gritting his teeth against the pain moving wrought on his shoulder, he managed to push two of the warm plaids off his body and tug them over her without waking her.

She turned her face into the single stream of moonlight coming in from the cloudy window, and he stared at her glowing silver-streaked skin for a long while. Such lush lips—he'd never seen anything like them. Plump and gently rounded, the top one curved into a perfect bow. Ever so gently, he swept a finger over them. Her lips parted, and a warm breath whispered over his fingertip.

Satisfied, he drifted off again. This time he dreamed of those lips moving over his body, down his chest, over the tip of his straining cock, and swallowing him deep into her mouth. Her fingers wrapped around him along with her lips, squeezing tight, and together they created a rhythm that shot sparks of pleasure through his body.

God, he was close. He drew away, staring down at her—his angel—as she gazed up at him from her kneeling position, her lips shiny from sucking him.

Her pink tongue flicked out, licking around her lips as if he were the most delicious thing she'd ever tasted.

"Why did you pull away?" she asked.

"I don't want it to end. Not now." He wanted it to go on and on, this feeling of pleasure, of contentment, of wholeness. He didn't want to rush his release, because if he did so, it would mean he must release *her*.

He would hang on to her, to it, until he had no choice but to let go.

Maybe not, though. Maybe if he showed her how he felt she'd understand. Maybe she wouldn't leave him. More than anything in his life, right now he needed an angel at his side. Someone to help him, to guide him when he began to go astray.

She still looked up at him, those gray-blue eyes questioning him, searching for a reason for his withdrawal and for his hesitation.

"I want you," he said simply.

She rose to her feet, her garments vanishing from her body as she did so, leaving her bare.

"Beautiful," he whispered.

She opened her arms, welcoming. "I want you, too."

He knew then, without a doubt, that he was dreaming. No one he'd wanted so much had ever wanted him in return.

Dream or not, he'd take it.

He stepped into her arms, pressed his body against her soft flesh, gently lifted her, and slid into her warm, willing body.

*   *   *

Rob stepped into the fresh air and turned his face toward the sky.

He should be angry after all that had happened today. He should be grief-stricken that his lover had rejected his proposal of marriage, and he should be annoyed at the behavior of the haughty English lass he'd met on the road. He should be with the other men in the barracks, drowning his woes in ale.

Yet he was none of those things. Instead, he was oddly reflective.

He stared up at the moon, an arcing slice of silver surrounded by a thick wash of stars.

Ceana was right: They had shared little beyond their flesh. He'd never felt compelled to tell her anything about his true feelings or about his past, and she seemingly felt the same.

Marriages had been built on less, he knew. Yet there was more to it than that, something she didn't seem to recognize. He held himself back with her. In bed, he showed her a slice of his nature, but he kept the rest of himself hidden. Like the moon, part of him glowed and part lay buried in shadow. He'd never met a woman he could reveal himself to, and long ago he'd resigned himself to living half hidden from the world.

He still hoped Ceana could be that woman. He hoped he could somehow prove himself to her, show her that they could work together, build a life together. Though he once might have sneered at what had become of his life, he was content with his position as stable master at Camdonn Castle. It was a quiet existence, on the land that was part of his spirit and soul. He'd rather live in a more secluded, private place, but his flat in the stables would do for now.

It was a lonely life, though. His apartments were too big, too quiet. Someday he would like to share them with someone. Have a family, infuse the idea in his children that they belonged and they were loved—all the elements lacking in his own childhood.

Someday.

From the beginning, it had discomfited him to think that he was using Ceana like a whore, and today he had proposed to her on impulse, half out of genuine affection and half in an attempt to create something honorable from their affair.

Now, though, as he stared up at the crescent moon, it dawned on him that she might be using him too.

To his surprise, that revelation didn't anger him. Instead he felt relieved, like the weight of an enormous responsibility had been lifted from his shoulders.

Smoke billowing from one of the tower chimneys blotted the bottom tip of the moon, and he lowered his gaze to the tower. The highest room was brightly lit, and through the arrow slits, he could see a figure pacing inside.

He knew the room. He knew who occupied it. Once, long ago, the last countess had occupied that tower chamber. Cam's mother. Of course Cam would choose to put his betrothed there.

Rob gazed up at the tower and watched the shadow move back and forth past the arrow slit. He had never met anyone like Lady Elizabeth. Such a haughty, sneering woman. And yet he sensed a deep-seated vulnerability in her. He'd felt it resonate beneath her skin during that long silence as the horse had plodded down the mountain. He'd seen it in the mottled red flush that crept up her neck. He'd heard it in the choppy sound of her uneven breathing. And her seemingly "perfect" responses to her uncle conflicted with every one of her behaviors until that moment.

Who was she, really? Why did she hide? Why did she fascinate him so?

Was she like him?

She passed the arrow slit again, her white shift flowing in her wake, and, unbidden, a vision came to him. Her beautiful body undulating beneath his. Her perfect pale flesh crisscrossed with the red marks of his lash. Her lips parted in ecstasy as she knelt at his feet and begged him for more.

He tried to push away the fantasy. It was dangerous. Reckless. *Impossible.*

His cock hardened and pressed against the wool of his plaid as she passed the window once more.

In his debauched fantasy, he drew out his dirk and sliced her shift open, from the top of her neckline straight down to the bottom of the skirt, revealing more of her creamy skin with each inch of fabric he cut. The tip of the dagger pricked at her flesh, making her gasp, but he did not draw blood.

"More," she whispered. "More."

She didn't fight him. She wanted more. She asked him to expose himself. She begged him to emerge from behind the shadows, to give her what she knew he was capable of giving.

Rob blinked hard. His dissolute mind conjured this fantasy, but from what? From the minutes she'd spent pressed against him on the saddle of a horse? He knew nothing about her. She was a spoiled Englishwoman, and it was likely she'd never spare him another glance.

And she was betrothed to the Earl of Camdonn. She was untouchable.

Elizabeth paced the tiny castle bedchamber, her stockings sliding over the slick, worn wood planks of the floor. The afternoon and evening had passed in a flurry. Fortunately, Cam's housekeeper, Janet Mac-Adam, had remained with her and her lady's maid, Bitsy, for most of the night, and Elizabeth hadn't had a moment alone with Uncle Walter. Thank the Lord, for she'd caught his narrow, pale blue gaze assessing her more than once.

Mrs. MacAdam had given her a tiny room high up in the tower. Elizabeth might have scoffed at it, but its other qualities more than made up for its small size. First off, arrow slits lined each of its four walls, a most excellent way to discreetly view the happenings on the castle grounds. Secondly, Mrs. MacAdam, with a conspiratorial smile on her wrinkled face, had moved aside an ugly, faded tapestry depicting some awful battle, and had revealed a door.

"A secret staircase to the ground floor," she'd confided with a twinkle in her round eyes. "Once, this was the countess's bedchamber, and legend says her lover took this passage to her bed every night."

Elizabeth had shuddered and pasted an appropriately appalled expression on her face. "How despicable," she'd murmured, but inside she squealed with joy. She'd known every means of entrance and exit to her uncle's Hampshire estate, Purefoy Abbey, but none was as mysterious or exciting as this one. When her maid finally left her, Elizabeth's first order of business had been to grab a candle, slip behind the tapestry, and venture down the dusty, spiraling stone stairs. She encountered nothing, living or dead, along the way, and at the bottom, she'd pressed her ear to the rotting slats of a wooden door. It must lead to a room where people gathered, because she heard a low-toned conversation between several people. Unfortunately, it was in Gaelic and she couldn't understand a word.

She returned to her chamber, and for the remainder of the night she kept watch on the activities in the courtyard below, growing more and more frustrated. Nobody bothered to keep her apprised of anything. Would they search for and arrest those awful highwaymen? She didn't know whether they'd found Cam, whether he was alive . . . How in heaven's name could they expect her to sleep?

Her shoulders tight with frustration, she drifted to one of the windows to look out over the night. This arrow slit faced the building she'd learned was the stable that housed Cam's fine collection of horseflesh.

A figure stood beneath the eaves. A striking Highlander wearing a blue tartan plaid, his face tilted up. Strong jaw, straight nose, lips parted to reveal clenched white teeth, he stared at the tower. She spun away from the arrow slit and leaned weakly against the cool stone wall, her heart pounding.

For the briefest of seconds, Robert MacLean's hungry gaze had locked onto hers, held her prisoner.

Blood rushed through her veins, and her quim tingled in reaction.

Perhaps he didn't hate her as much as she'd thought.

Or perhaps he did hate her.

But one thing was abundantly clear: He wanted her.

Ceana opened her eyes to dim light permeating her cottage through the tiny pane of her window. She raised her head from her arms to see the earl's fingers entwined with her own. His hand was long-fingered, paler than hers, smoother. Aristocratic. If nothing else, that ought to serve as a reminder: He was from a different world than she.

She straightened, feeling a weight on her shoulders. He'd covered her with blankets, and she was still holding his hand.

Ceana's spine stiffened, and her breaths became shallow. She freed herself shakily, more roughly than she'd intended. It was foolish to hold his hand.

MacNab women were strong. Renowned for their force of character, for the unbreakable shell that kept them aloof from the rest of the world.

She glanced at his face. He was awake, watching her, his dark eyes intent.

Damn it. Tucking strands of tangled hair behind her ears, she smiled down at him. "Good morning."

He returned her smile. Color had seeped into his cheeks, and he looked much better. "Thank you."

She took a shaky breath. "For what?"

"Saving my life."

"Ah. Well, how do you feel?"

"Weak. But better."

"And your shoulder?"

"Sore. Tolerable, though." He flinched as she reached to adjust his bandage, and then gritted his teeth as she peeled it back to check the wound. She turned to her medicine shelves to find the Saint-John's-wort salve.

"Why aren't you married, Ceana?"

Her back to him, she froze. Closing her eyes, she remembered Rob's proposal. Then she gathered her wits. "That, my Lord Camdonn, is none of your business."

"I'm merely curious. Someone as beautiful as you ought to be married. It is odd to me that you aren't."

"MacNab women never marry," she said, her voice flat.

He remained silent as she made a show of taking up a long-handled spoon, dipping it into the small clay pot containing the salve, and mixing—though it didn't need to be mixed.

Finally, he said, "Alan hasn't returned."

She turned back to him, carrying a bit of the medicine on the edge of the spoon. "He did, in fact. He came in the middle of the night, and you were sound asleep. I told him to let you rest. They're coming to take you home to Camdonn Castle later this morning."

Worry clouded the earl's dark eyes. "Did they find Elizabeth?" he asked through gritted teeth as she gently rubbed the salve over his wound.

Still she couldn't look at him. "The lady is well. Robert MacLean found her on the road and brought her to the castle late yesterday."

"Robert MacLean?"

"Your stable master. He was returning to Camdonn Castle . . ."

Her breath caught. Lord, how to finish that sentence? *After tupping me hard, slapping my arse, and listening to me cruelly reject his offer of marriage . . . ?*

"Ah. Yes, of course." His eyes squeezed shut. "Thank God she is unhurt."

Ceana's jaw tightened a little even as she smiled at him. She set the spoon back on the table, took the swath of linen she planned to fashion into a sling, and busied herself by folding it. "It sounds like you love her very much."

"She's a lovely girl. Perfect, really."

"I see."

For God's sake, she did *not* want to talk about the perfect, rich, and undoubtedly beautiful Englishwoman this man was going to marry. With her stomach clenched tight, Ceana turned away from him.

As soon as Alan arrived, Cam would have to leave her.

He didn't want to. He didn't like the thought of her alone in this tiny cottage in the forest. Especially with murdering highwaymen roaming the nearby lands.

Cam watched as she busied herself with her work. She ground herbs, chopped leaves, boiled something sweet-smelling over the fire.

God help him, his dreams had been carnal, and she'd featured in all of them. He'd woken with a painful erection, unimpeded by the stabbing ache in his shoulder. Her name had been on his lips, but he'd managed to swallow it down before he said it aloud.

He remembered one of the dreams. They'd both knelt on the bed, facing each other. She'd raised her arms over her head, lifting those heavy, pale breasts for his perusal. He'd taken one sweet pink nipple into his mouth as he'd brushed his fingers over the other. He'd pinched gently, scraped his teeth over the taut peak, and she'd moaned . . .

Hell, it was happening again. Deliberately, he focused on the ordinary. The peat fire circle on the floor at the foot of the bed, fingers of smoke spreading under the rafters as if searching for the hole in the roof. The thatch of the ceiling overhead . . .

He had no intention of betraying Elizabeth. Nevertheless, he wasn't married to her, not yet. He'd made no promises of fidelity.

Hating that damned devil inside him clamoring to be set free, he pushed the thought away.

Lady Elizabeth was going to be his wife. Months ago, he'd locked up that dissolute creature within him and tossed away the key. Never again would he allow a woman to control him. Never again would he surrender to the power a woman could wield over him.

He was stronger now. A year ago, he'd been impulsive and arrogant, driven by lust. In the past few months, he'd reined himself in. Now he displayed a self-possessed, serious, calm facade, and henceforth he pledged to do what his duty and position required. He'd already gone to England and found a suitable lady to become his wife. Within a month, they'd marry, and within a year, she'd give birth to his heir. Meanwhile, he'd focus on his tenants and his lands, and try to help his people break free from the crushing poverty that swelled like an endless plague through the Highlands.

He hadn't spent a great deal of time with Elizabeth, but he sensed a core strength of independence in her he found appealing, and he thought she might eventually assist him in the monumental task ahead, unlike most fragile Englishwomen, who'd certainly hinder his efforts. She was intelligent and curious, and when they had taken walks together, though their conversation had felt stilted and stiffly polite, she had shown an interest in matters that were important to him. All of these traits boded well for her future as a Highland wife.

He also sensed her unhappiness with her life in Hampshire. Her smiles rarely reached her eyes, and at times when she thought no one was looking, Cam saw her gazing longingly at the horizon. He attributed her melancholy to the loss of her parents at a tender age, and he understood wholeheartedly, having lost his own mother young and never having achieved closeness with his father.

She was beautiful too. Though he knew the task of bedding her wouldn't be unpleasant, he didn't lust after her like he had Sorcha. He didn't know why, for she was a lovely woman—it was simply that he didn't feel that visceral, inescapable desire in her presence. That was precisely what he was looking for in a bride. He couldn't become so physically wound up over a woman again.

He glanced at Ceana and caught her gazing at him. She looked quickly away.

Damn it. If only she were more like her grandmother. In truth, she was very much like her grandmother, but different in all the ways that mattered . . . in the ways that affected him most.

Strangely, he felt safe with Ceana. Comfortable. As if he'd known her his whole life. For some reason, he wanted to explain himself to her.

"I hardly know her, you see," he admitted in a quiet voice.

Her gray-blue eyes locked on his once more. "Who?"

"Elizabeth."

"Ah."

"The Duke of Argyll suggested the match. He introduced me to her uncle in London two months ago."

A week later, they'd traveled to Hampshire to see Elizabeth at her uncle's seat, Purefoy Abbey. The young woman had quickly shown him that she possessed all the traits required to make him a proper wife. After three weeks in Hampshire, he'd done what everyone expected and offered for her. Everything about the match was perfect. *She* was perfect.

"Can I tell you something?" he asked Ceana.

Why was he talking to a stranger about this? Something—God knew what—compelled him to give Ceana the truth. Hell, maybe he just needed to tell someone. He'd kept everything bottled inside for so long. Alan and Sorcha had remained his best friends, had seen him through his worst moments, but after all that had passed between them, there were so many things he couldn't share with them.

He watched the struggle play out on Ceana's face. Shadows seemed to pass over her expression as she debated. Her eyes shifted away from him.

He understood her dilemma. She feared getting too close to him. He knew why—he was dangerous. Poison.

"Of course you can," slipped from her lips, and she closed her eyes in a long blink, as if she regretted her acquiescence. She sank onto the chair beside the bed.

"I've loved only one woman in my life."

"Sorcha MacDonald."

That took him aback. He was silent for a long moment, but then he gave her a rueful smile. "I'd forgotten you told me you knew Sorcha."

He'd never love another woman like he'd loved Sorcha. He was solely responsible for the disaster he'd made of his obsession with her, and he'd never forgive himself. Partially in penance for his past deeds and partially in pure self-preservation, he couldn't allow that to happen again.

"Do you still love her?" she murmured.

"Yes," he admitted. "I'll always love her. But—" He broke off, staring up at the rafters. In the past year Sorcha had stopped appearing in his dreams, stopped occupying his every thought. His thoughts of her usually occurred in conjunction with thoughts of Alan, and were no longer carnal. Sorcha and Alan were like a brother and sister to him. Closer than that, perhaps—he couldn't know. He'd never had a brother or a sister to compare.

"I no longer desire her," he finished belatedly.

"Well, good," Ceana said on an exhalation. "I'd prefer not to witness Alan eviscerating you."

"Indeed." He released a low laugh that resonated in his wound. Though it didn't hurt as much as it should—he felt almost too well for having been shot less than a day ago. Must be the MacNab family secret. The MacNab witchcraft, some would call it.

He returned his gaze to her and closed his hand over her palm. "I haven't even been home yet, and you've already saved my life. I suppose, given my luck, you'll have the opportunity often in the future. So I think we should be friends."

Friends? He nearly laughed aloud at his own words. He was a damn fool, and Ceana saw right through him.

She raised a cynical brow. "Friends?"

He kept his gaze fastened on her. Hell, those lips. Such a deep red. Now slightly parted, they showed the hint of white teeth behind them. He wanted a taste.

"At another time, in other circumstances, I'd ask for more than friendship."

"Would you?"

"Yes." He'd demand more. Insist on more. He wouldn't give her a choice.

Or maybe he would. It would be gratifying to know she'd choose him. And right now, with the spots of color high on her cheeks, her dilated pupils, the pulse pounding rapidly in her neck, he knew she would.

As much as he'd tried, the beast inside him was impervious to all his efforts to destroy it. He'd never succeed in exterminating it. His reserved behavior in England was a sham, and now that he was home, his true nature emerged. He was debauched to his soul.

"What . . . would you ask?"

Her question sucked the air from his lungs. If he were free from his promises to himself and to the Duke of Irvington, what would he ask of this woman? A kiss? A one-time tumble? Or would he ask her to be his lover? His mistress?

His throat closed, and he couldn't answer her. She seemed to understand, for she turned her palm up beneath his hand and curled her fingers around his.

He'd ask for a kiss, surely. A kiss would be the first in line of many other things he'd ask of her.

She leaned closer. Their lips brushed . . . so softly that he barely felt it. But the connection hummed through his veins, all the way to his toes, softening the sharp pain in his shoulder.

"Ceana."

He said her name against her lips, and he felt a violent shudder roll through her.

Reaching up, he wrapped his fingers around the back of her neck and yanked her closer. Her hand dove into his hair, sifting through the strands. Her fingertips rubbed his scalp. He deepened the kiss, tracing the softness of her lips with his tongue until she groaned, opening to him.

She fisted her hand in his hair, and he tightened his grip on her neck. They resonated together as if they'd been struck by the same bolt of lightning and its electricity vibrated through them.

A knock sounded at the door, and it creaked as someone swung it open.

"Cam?" Sorcha's voice.

Ceana stumbled backward so fast, her chair toppled. Her chest heaved. Her curls framed her head like a halo, her cheeks turned fire red, and her eyes widened to blue pools. God, she was beautiful.

Finally, Cam tore his gaze from her. Alan and Sorcha MacDonald, the latter heavy with child, stood frozen in shock in the doorway, their mouths agape.

CHAPTER FOUR

Ceana's cheeks burned with mortification, the effect heightened by her knowledge of the tumultuous past between the three people now crowding her cottage. Did Alan think the Earl of Camdonn had seduced her like he had Sorcha? The truth was the opposite, she feared—she'd been the one to do the seducing. How could she have prevented the kiss, though, when every inch of her body craved the caress of this man's lips?

I am a MacNab. Men don't affect me.

Her mantra succeeded to an extent, and she diligently kept her eyes off the earl, for the sight of his pale, handsome face would crumble her resolve.

She gazed at Alan's rugged countenance instead, trying to ignore the surprise written all over it—the raised brows, widened blue eyes, parted lips.

"Good morning." She glanced at Sorcha, then away, for the shocked expression on the other woman's face made her own burn even hotter.

Sorcha seemed too dumbstruck to speak, so Alan took the reins. "Good morning, Ceana. Cam."

The earl made a noncommittal noise, and Alan glanced at her. "How is he? Ah"—he cleared his throat—"his wound, I mean."

"He's better." Ceana spoke curtly, brushing her hands as if they'd just been immersed in sand. "Ready to return to his grand castle, I daresay." She turned to her worktable and began to sift through her medicines. "There are a few things you must take to give to his physician. They will aid in the healing process." She raised a small jar of salve so they all could see it. "This is to be rubbed on the wound twice daily."

The rustle of skirts heralded Sorcha's appearance at the bedside. Sorcha seemed to have come to her senses, for now she appeared more like herself. She smiled down at Cam. "From the way Alan described your injury, I was certain you were at death's door. I wanted to come to you last night, but Alan forbade me to—"

"Your condition, Sorcha," Alan cut in from the doorway. "You seem determined to forget about it."

"—and so I came as soon as I could, only to find you debauching wenches." She glanced up to give Ceana a saucy wink. "Now, why did my husband cause me to fret when it is clear you are as right as my leg?"

"I'm sorry to have caused you worry. It is good to see you, my dear."

Sorcha knelt to kiss Cam on the lips. "I forgive you. I'm happy to see that you're not quite at death's door."

Cam's gaze rested on her rounded stomach. "You've . . . grown."

Sorcha laughed. "Aye, so I have. He's huge, isn't he? I think he intends to grow until he bursts right out of me."

"You think it's a boy, then?"

"A lass wouldn't have the impudence to stretch me thus."

Ceana watched their easy camaraderie in bemusement. Cam and Sorcha had been lovers, and with Alan in the same room, Ceana would have expected some tension. But while Alan was silent at the threshold, his stance was relaxed and she detected no animosity from him. How extraordinarily odd.

As Ceana handed Alan the medicine, Sorcha turned to her. "Ceana, do you know the surgeon at Camdonn Castle?"

"No, I haven't had that pleasure," Ceana stated dryly. With a few exceptions, Ceana was wary of those formally trained in the ways of medicine. When she encountered them, her claws invariably extended. Besides being pompous and generally ineffective, these men could be dangerous to her kind. In the middle of the last century, Ceana's great-grandmother had been burned as a witch on the evidence of such "learned" men.

"Well, he's a fool," Sorcha said. "Rest assured, if you place Cam's well-being in that man's hands, he'll encourage ill humors rather than stave them off."

Ceana sighed. "If you supply specific instructions—"

"—he'll know they come from you and he'll intentionally countermand your orders," Alan finished. "I think you should accompany the earl back to the castle and stay with him until he's healed."

"That's not necessary," Cam said. "I'm already halfway healed, and Ceana has—"

Sorcha raised her hand, halting his words. "Do you trust your surgeon, Cam?"

"Well . . ." He hesitated and then said in a sheepish tone, "No."

"Neither do I." Again she turned to Ceana. "He needs proper care, doesn't he? What will happen if he does not receive it?"

Ceana shrugged. "The wound will fester and he will die."

"Then you must stay with him."

Cam must have seen the hesitance in Ceana's eyes. "She has other patients, Sorcha. I daresay I can manage my wound and the medications well enough on my own."

Certainly there was someone at Camdonn Castle he could trust to care for him. Ceana blew out an exasperated breath. "If your surgeon is such an idiot, why do you continue to employ him?"

"He worked for my father, who promised him the position for life. Further, he is well liked. I haven't the heart to cast him away."

Ceana frowned at him. She'd been told the Earl of Camdonn didn't have the heart for anyone. Certainly someone so ruthless wouldn't keep a member of his staff out of sentimentality. Every min-

ute she spent with the man drove home deeper the fact that the people of the Glen had misjudged him.

"Please, Ceana," Sorcha said quietly. "When Cam was last injured
like this, the wound festered and he nearly died. Your grandmother's
healing skills were what saved him in the end." She shuddered and
placed a protective hand over the swell of her belly. "We were so close
to losing him. I don't wish for that to happen again. I beg you to stay
with him, at least until the wound is out of danger of festering."

Ceana sighed. "Very well, then. For a few days."

She felt Cam's dark, soulful eyes boring into her, and she had a
premonition that she'd live to regret that decision.

A few hours later, Ceana stood beside Cam's grizzled manservant,
Duncan MacDougall, in the earl's cavernous bedchamber. Duncan
was a round, small man with a haggard face and beady blue eyes, a
circle of white hair his crowning glory.

Tapestries draped the stone walls of Cam's bedchamber. Midday
light filtered in through a single window, conveniently placed in a location to make full use of the sun's trajectory. On the rightmost wall,
two doors flanked a massive stone fireplace.

"Och," Duncan murmured gruffly, "here they are, then."

Ceana turned to the entrance of the room as four men appeared
bearing the earl on a stretcher. He leaned up on his good elbow, scowling. When the men jerked to a halt just inside, he caught sight of
Ceana, and his scowl deepened. "I can walk."

She shrugged. "I'm here to ensure your welfare."

Beside her, Duncan snickered silently. At least he was on her
side.

Oh, but she'd see to Cam's welfare. She'd see to it so well and so
thoroughly, he wouldn't be able to endure it. And in a day or two he'd
throw her out of his castle, and she would be free to go home. She
didn't like the message she sent by staying at Camdonn Castle: that
the earl's well-being was more important than anyone else's in the
Glen.

But beyond that, for some reason, this place discomfited her greatly. Here, she was ultimately at the earl's mercy. She didn't like being under anyone else's power. She preferred to be queen of her own tiny domain rather than a servant in someone else's massive one.

"My welfare isn't dependent upon my being treated like a god-damn invalid."

Good. Her plan was already working. She gave him a serene smile and gestured to the bed. "Take him over there," she instructed the men. She knew one of them—Bram MacGregor—a tenant of the earl whom she'd nursed through the ague when she'd first arrived in the Glen. She smiled at Bram, but he didn't meet her eyes. Instead, he gazed at Cam with open dislike as the four men laid the stretcher at the edge of the bed.

"Should we move him over onto 'is bed, Ceana?" one of the men asked.

Ceana opened her mouth to answer, but before she could, Cam interrupted in a growl, "I shall move myself, thank you. Now leave us, all of you."

Duly dismissed, the four men and Duncan strode out, Duncan grinning and two of the other men raising sympathetic brows at Ceana as they passed her. She marched to the bedside, hands on hips. "You are a surly patient."

"Do you know Alan pinned me down on that damned stretcher so they could carry me up here?" he grumbled.

"Only because I asked it of him."

"You didn't treat me like a piece of glass yesterday."

"I'd no choice yesterday. I had to make you walk through the forest to save your sorry life. Today, however, I have everything I require to heal you quickly at my disposal." She cracked her knuckles. "And I intend to make use of all of it."

His lips twisted. "Sounds to me like you're preparing to inflict torture."

"Ah, well. Sometimes healing can be a kind of torture. Especially for men of action, such as you." She allowed herself a drifting gaze down the length of his body. "Well, I assume you are, in any case. You might be one of those noblemen who sits about all day drinking brandy and gazing at your beautiful visage in a gilded mirror."

He raised a single black brow. "You think I've a beautiful visage?"

"I didn't say that," she snapped.

A shadow cast a pall over his face, and his gaze skittered away from her until it came to rest on the opposite wall. "I shouldn't taunt you."

Needing to occupy her hands, Ceana turned to her medicine trunk. She'd brought more than Cam would require, for she suspected Cam wouldn't be the only one to request her healing skills at Cam-donn Castle.

"That kiss . . . at your cottage . . ." Cam's halting voice came from behind her, and, squatting before her trunk, she paused.

Without looking back at him, she said, "It was a mistake."

"Yes." He sounded almost relieved.

"You are betrothed." She tried—and failed—to infuse a scoff into her voice. "I am a MacNab." That statement held quite a lot of mean-ing in the Glen. Most of the residents here had feared her grand-mother.

"Yes," he said quietly. "Yes on both counts."

As much as she wished it didn't, his agreement pricked her in the chest. It hurt.

Nevertheless, she reminded herself that this was for the best. She didn't want this man pursuing her. She had no desire to be the mis-tress of the Earl of Camdonn, and she had even less desire to become a rival of the future countess.

She should be thankful for his dismissal, because God knew she didn't have the willpower to resist him. One touch and she'd be lost.

Yet she would be forced to touch him. Over and over again, until his wound had healed enough for her to leave.

Ceana closed her fist around a tiny pot of medicine and rose to her feet, looking wildly about for a means to change the subject. She ges-tured at the wall where the hearth was flanked by the two doors. "What lies beyond those doors?"

"Why don't you go see for yourself."

She strode to the rightmost door first. Opening it, she found an enormous dressing room with a wardrobe, a clothespress, and shelves brimming with clothing and accessories. Enough to clothe the men of Glenfinnan for a year, she gathered. After a few moments, she backed out the way she had come.

She walked to the other door and opened it to reveal a receiving room elaborately decorated with silk-covered furniture dyed in dark, masculine browns and rusty reds. At the far end of the room stood an exquisitely carved rosewood desk that matched Cam's bed. Crystal bottles filled with clear and amber liquids covered the similarly styled sidebar that ran nearly the entire length of the wall backing the dressing room. Several plush chairs and a long sofa scattered the vast area between Ceana and the desk. The room was almost the size of Cam's bedchamber, and equally elegant. Combined, the rooms were ten times as large as her cottage.

Most women of her status would swoon with ecstasy to walk into such a room. Ceana, however, was a MacNab. It took more than this to impress her. She retreated and returned to Cam's side.

"Did you see the wine bottles beneath the sidebar?"

"No."

"I could use a bottle right now."

"Absolutely not," she declared. "Spirits make wretched aids to healing."

"Perhaps I ought to have called in my surgeon after all. He'd have allowed me to drink as much as I pleased."

She chose to ignore that statement.

He frowned. "Even your grandmother allowed me a bit of whisky when I needed it for the pain."

"My grandmother wasn't nearly so erudite as I am."

He laughed. "Is that so?"

"Aye. Her expertise was in the old ways. I have found many of those methods to be effective, but I've studied newer forms of healing, and I possess far more knowledge of the science of it."

"What do you mean, 'newer forms of healing'?"

"Techniques of the East, for example." She tore her gaze from him, an unsettled feeling fluttering in her chest. She often used the techniques she'd studied, but people rarely questioned her, and she'd never shared her knowledge of them before. She'd accomplished most of her learning through secret reading and sly observance. At first it was a matter of self-preservation that she didn't discuss her knowledge, for no one would allow any woman, never mind a woman of her lowly and questionable status, to study as she had. Eventually her secrecy had become a matter of habit. Nevertheless, it was disconcerting to talk about it to anyone, even after all these years.

"Techniques of the East?"

He seemed intrigued, and Ceana's cheeks heated. She never blushed, but with this man, it had developed into a distressing, embarrassing habit. She pressed the backs of her hands to her face and kept her gaze resolutely on the stone hearth. "Aye, well, yes. I lived in Aberdeen for a time, where I had access to certain resources."

"How?"

"I was employed as a maid at King's College. Everything I required was available to me there." She remembered those quiet nights, fervently reading "borrowed" works of Galen, Aristotle, Hippocrates, and many others by the light of tallow candles. Those days hovering in the background and pretending not to listen to the professors reading their lectures.

"What did you find?"

"Learned men who'd traveled to Arabia and India and beyond. I read books by esteemed scholars that taught me, among other important facts, that spirits aren't wise for the sick to ingest."

"Ah, well, I'm not sick," he said in triumph.

"You must remain strong, my lord. Spirits weaken the body, render it unable to fend off the ill humors."

Cam's lips twisted. "Well, then, what would be wise for me to ingest?"

"Heavy cream. Boiled cow's blood. Sowans—whisky free, of course."

He made a disgusted face, and she laughed. "Don't fret—I'll not force you to drink anything you find offensive. The force of the vomiting would be more costly than the benefits supplied."

"Good."

She gazed down at him. "We must get you onto the bed. Now, why didn't you allow the men to help you move?"

"Because I can do it myself."

She placed fisted hands over her hips and cocked her head at him. "Is that so? Show me, then."

With tight lips, he awkwardly shimmied onto the other side of the bed. Resisting the urge to help, she stood still and watched him as he painfully made his way off the stretcher. He finally sank onto the pillows.

"There."

"You're sweating."

"Am I?"

"Aye. Was it difficult?"

"Not at all."

She grinned. "Good. Because this will be." She held up the small pot she'd kept hidden in her hand.

"What's that?"

"A healing medicine for open wounds. But unlike the Saint-John's-wort salve I used this morning, this one contains spirits and stings like the very devil."

He closed his eyes. "So you *do* intend to inflict torture on me. I knew it was so the moment you cracked your knuckles."

"Aye. Until you are healed."

"Ah, well." He released a sigh. "Better you than the surgeon."

"Well, I'd prefer to cure you of a wee hole in your shoulder rather than a deadly fever."

"I agree." With his eyes still closed, he gave her a ghost of a smile and slumped against the cushions, apparently exhausted. "Do your worst."

She walked around the monstrous bed and sat on its edge, pushing away the green-and-black-striped bed curtain. It fell back down on her shoulder and she frowned up at it.

"Tie it back," Cam said. "There." He gestured with his chin at the elaborately carved post at the corner. Halfway up the post and dangling from a hook was a golden rope.

Ceana shook her head. "Decadence."

Cam chuckled.

She slid her gaze to him as she wrapped the silky rope around the heavy curtain. "What's so funny?"

"Only you have the ballocks to say such a thing about my bed. No one else would dare."

She smirked. "I haven't any ballocks."

"I've yet to see the proof of that."

"Aye, well. It'd be best if you never did see proof of it." Finished tying the cord, she perched on the edge of the bed and pulled the stopper on the medicine jar.

"Would it?" he asked quietly.

She glanced at him. His eyes were closed. Two spots of color flared high on his cheekbones. His muscles tensed, and he lay very still, as if he waged some inner battle.

"Aye," she said after a pause. "It'd be better if you didn't see me at all."

It was true. They both knew it. An inexplicable, impossible pull had developed between them in the hours they'd spent together since she'd found him in the forest. The harder she tried to sever it, the stronger it seemed to grow. The best solution would be to keep far away from him.

She must cure him and return to her cottage—her safe haven—as quickly as possible.

He opened his eyes. Their gazes clashed and held for a long, suspended moment. Ceana didn't move, didn't breathe. The air surrounding them seemed to pause in suspense. His finger touched her bunched fist, a single, hot point of physical contact between them.

A knock sounded behind her. Ceana sucked a breath into her air-starved body, and Cam jerked his gaze to the door. "Come in."

Rob pushed open the door.

"Yes?" Cam asked.

Rob's gaze skimmed over her and then he looked at Cam. "You wished to see me, milord."

"Ah, Robert MacLean," Cam said. "Of course. Please come in."

Warily, Rob stepped into the room. He stopped a few feet away from Ceana, and awareness streamed through her. The presence of these two men crackled in the air. They were similar in subtle ways. Perhaps it was in their facial expressiveness, or maybe it was just their eyes. Rob's eyes were lighter, but when he wanted her, the carnal gleam in them was similar to Cam's.

Cam truly wanted her, she realized. He was trying to fight it, trying to hide it, but it was there, apparent in his eyes.

"I wished to thank you for bringing Lady Elizabeth safely home."

Rob's lips flattened. "I'd have done the same for anyone."

"I'm glad to hear it. But Lady Elizabeth . . ." Cam blew out a breath. His gaze flickered to Ceana and then away. "I am thankful you kept her safe."

Rob remained impassive, his back straight. "'Twas nothing, milord."

"I'm told I shall be well enough to sit at the table, at least for a short amount of time, by tomorrow. I'd hoped you would dine with us."

Silence.

"There will be just a few of us." Cam glanced at Ceana. "Are Alan and Sorcha still here?"

She shook her head. "No, they've gone home. Said they'd return to check on you in a few days."

"Just me and Lady Elizabeth and the Duke of Irvington, then. And Ceana MacNab." He looked from Rob to Ceana. "Do you know each other?"

"Aye," Rob and Ceana said in unison.

An awkward silence followed before Ceana added, "We met the first time I came out to Camdonn Castle to see one of your men who was sick."

"If I might be excused, milord. They'll be requiring me in the stables. And as for dinner . . ." A muscle jerked in Rob's jaw. "Aye, I'll be there. Thank you."

Ceana cast Rob a faltering smile. She'd never encountered him in a group setting, but it wouldn't surprise her to discover that he dreaded them.

He didn't return her smile. Instead he simply glanced at her with narrowed eyes. There it was—that gleam she recognized well.

"Of course you may be excused," Cam said. "Thank you again. I'll see you later."

Tearing his gaze from her, Rob turned and strode away.

"Thank you, Bitsy."

After an hour of painstaking attention to Elizabeth's coiffure, Bitsy shoved one last pin into Elizabeth's hair and dropped her hands to her sides. Possessing a sallow complexion and narrow features, the lady's maid looked like a woman who'd lived a long, hard life, though she wasn't much older than her mistress.

Bitsy *had* lived a hard, long life. Elizabeth was reminded of that fact—and the fact that it was her fault—every time she laid eyes on the woman.

"Only trying to make you look respectable, milady."

"Thank you, but I doubt Lord Camdonn will pay any mind to my appearance today." The man was probably in too much pain. Finally, late this morning, Mrs. MacAdam had told Elizabeth that one of the gunshots she'd heard in the wood had sent a bullet through Cam's shoulder. Elizabeth leaned away as her maid held up a cosmetics brush. "I shall go to the earl now."

Dropping her hands, Bitsy backed away. "Very well, milady."

Elizabeth rose and strode to the heavy wooden door, closing it behind her with a thud. She paused for a moment in the hall to catch her breath. Bitsy's presence, as always, made her uneasy. Elizabeth had never worked out how best to manage her. Whether she should treat her as she would any other servant, be apologetic and remorseful, try to make friends with her, or give her extra attention and recompense for what she suffered on Elizabeth's behalf.

Elizabeth had tried all of those tactics and nothing was effective. No matter what she did, Bitsy was sullen and dour. She performed her duties without complaint but never met Elizabeth's eyes or engaged in conversation with her beyond the necessities. Elizabeth understood that withdrawal was the only way the woman could survive, but she still wished she could find a way to help.

Elizabeth walked down the stairs and into the long, dark passageway that led to Cam's bedchamber.

She reeled to a halt when a figure emerged from the shadows. She recognized him immediately from his stance alone. *Robert MacLean.*

Elizabeth's heart beat frantically, and she clenched her fists in her skirts to prevent herself from slapping her hand over her chest. He didn't hesitate as she did; instead he came inexorably closer.

Straightening her spine, she resumed walking, holding her chin high. When a few feet separated them, they stopped. Elizabeth dropped her skirts, smoothed them, and inclined her head. "Mr. MacLean."

"Milady." He kept his facial expression perfectly schooled, revealing nothing of how he felt upon seeing her.

"Have you come from seeing Lord Camdonn?"

"Aye."

She clenched her teeth. His infernal one-word answers were bound to drive her straight to madness.

"How is he?"

"Well."

This time she couldn't contain her frustration. She stamped her foot. "Stop that!"

He raised one dark brow. "Stop what?"

Did he mock her? Something glimmered in those amber eyes.

"Why must you always answer with one word? It is annoying."

"I apologize." He didn't appear in the least contrite.

She glared at him. He exhilarated her. He frustrated her. Drove her mad.

He made her *feel*.

The sudden awareness gave her an unsettled, fluttery sensation, as though a family of blind butterflies had just found themselves imprisoned in her belly.

"Good day, milady." He made to walk around her, but before she could give it a single thought, her hand snaked out and caught his arm.

"Wait."

He stopped, looking from her hand clutching his arm to her face in curiosity. Elizabeth stole a glance up and down the corridor. It appeared empty.

"I'm sorry," she said in a rush. "I'm the one who must apologize. What I said to you yesterday—it was unforgivable. And I wish to thank you for delivering me safely to Camdonn Castle."

Before she could pause to think with shocked incredulity on the fact that she was apologizing—to a *servant*—she swallowed and confessed something she'd never confessed to anyone. She lowered her voice to a whisper. "Sometimes it is difficult for me, you see. Sometimes . . . pride doesn't allow me to admit when I'm wrong."

He stared at her. But the cold stillness she'd sensed in him when she'd threatened and insulted him seemed to melt a little.

"I wish . . ." . . . *to kiss you?* No, that wasn't right. She blinked away the thought and tried again. "I wish for us to be . . . friends. Perhaps you might show me the stables sometime. I possess a more than trifling interest in horses, and his lordship has offered me the pick of his fillies."

He glanced pointedly at where she still gripped his arm, and she dropped her hand. "Sorry."

His lips quirked upward, and he tilted his head in the tiniest gesture of respect. "Good-bye, milady."

With that, he strode off. Elizabeth watched him until he turned toward the stairs and disappeared, leaving her alone in the corridor scrambling to reassemble her fractured wits.

After Rob left them, the balls of tension in Ceana's shoulders had loosened, and she had lowered herself back onto the edge of the bed beside Cam. "Let's clean that wound, then."

She pulled down the side of his shirt, which she'd cut to allow access to his arm, and unwrapped the linen bandage.

"Looks to be healing well," she murmured.

"Good." His voice was tight, but he held still for her as she applied the stinging medicine, neither flinching away nor complaining, as most patients were wont to do with a wound of this magnitude—more proof of the strength of his will.

Even so, as evidenced by his paleness and the tightness of his features, it was plain that he was hurting. In an attempt to divert his attention from the pain, she asked, "Are you happy to be home?"

There was a long pause before he spoke. "Yes. Though I wish I could have arrived in grander fashion."

"Why?"

"How does it look for a leader to return home flat on his back after having been shot?"

"Brave, perhaps?"

He scoffed. "Or weak. I wanted there to be fanfare. A celebration. I wanted to show the people that Elizabeth and I were home. That we were here to stay, that we were ready to lead."

"You speak as though you were already married."

"I could have been," he said, "but I thought it would be better to marry here. If she marries me at Camdonn Castle, it will give her a greater sense of belonging, and the people a stronger sense that she belonged."

Ceana tilted her head, gently rubbing the inflamed area around the edges of the wound. "That is a wise justification. I think you are right."

"I am not well loved," Cam said quietly.

Ceana almost choked. *Not well loved* was an understatement of grand proportions. "Why do you think that is?"

"I have been home seldom, and when I have been here, I have been distracted by personal dilemmas unrelated to my leadership." He firmed his lips. "But that will change now."

"Will it?"

"Yes. There is nothing more important to me than the earldom. Than my tenants. I spent years stupidly ignoring both, but no longer. My intention is to spend the remainder of my days on Scottish soil, working to improve the lives of the people who occupy my lands. I wish to return this estate to its former glory."

Ceana paused in her ministrations to stare at him. She'd known a number of Scottish nobles in her time, and the vast majority of them were more concerned about their relations with the powerful English rather than the welfare of their own people. "Truly?"

"Yes."

Ceana believed in his sincerity and she admired his aim, but she also pitied him. The tide had long ago turned against him, and to coax it to shift again would be nearly as difficult as reining the moon and forcing it to change direction.

A tentative knock interrupted her thoughts, and she met Cam's eyes. He took a fortifying breath and turned his head toward the door. "Come in."

The door opened to reveal the most elegant young woman Ceana had ever seen, a slightly built, delicate creature with cascading blond curls, dressed in skirts of rose pink festooned by yards upon yards of exquisite lace. She reeked of foreignness.

It could be none other than Cam's English bride. Lady Elizabeth.

CHAPTER FIVE

Lady Elizabeth glided to the opposite side of the bed from Ceana, concern lending a pink tint to her creamy complexion. Cam smiled up at her and spoke in English. "I am so glad you escaped unscathed, Elizabeth."

He slid his eyes toward Ceana, as if wondering whether she understood. Of course she did. Her return smile communicated that fact. She tried to keep the bitterness from it, but she feared her expression resembled a snarl. His assumption that she was ignorant of the English language was insulting, especially after their conversation about her studies.

Furthermore, this English girl, a youthful lady with such a sweet voice, delicate figure, and rich, beautiful garments, made her feel dirty and coarse in comparison. Ceana thought she'd long ago overcome such ridiculous notions, but there they were, rearing their ugly heads.

Lady Elizabeth was—outwardly, in any case—far superior to herself. Why had Cam wasted his time kissing Ceana when he had such perfection at his fingertips?

She was jealous. How utterly pitiful. She couldn't remember experiencing that despicable emotion since . . .

No. Hastily, she pushed the memory away.

"Oh, my lord," Elizabeth murmured in a lilting voice. She clasped her hands in front of her. "I was so very, *very* frightened for you."

She fluttered her fingers in a dismissive wave at Ceana, and Ceana stared at her in challenge, rooting herself in her position on the edge of the bed. She was no servant, and she refused to be sent away like one.

Elizabeth's eyebrows drew into a frown above cornflower blue eyes as her cool stare landed on Ceana. "You may go," she said. "I shall ring if his lordship requires anything else."

Ceana crossed her arms over her chest and proved her fluency in the lady's language with her response. "Oh, I'll not be leaving. Not yet." She cut a glance at Cam. "Not till I've finished with 'his lordship.'"

"Elizabeth, this is Ceana MacNab," Cam said. "She's the woman who found me. She is a healer from a renowned family—her grandmother has kept about every person in the Glen alive at one time or another. Now she is gone, and Ceana has come to take her place. Ceana, meet my betrothed, Lady Elizabeth Grant."

Elizabeth pressed slender fingers to her bosom. "Oh! I am so sorry, Mrs. MacNab. I thought you were a—"

"Maid?" Ceana shrugged. "Aye, well, that's understandable, I suppose. And that'd be 'Miss' MacNab. I've no husband, nor do I ever intend to have one."

Elizabeth's blond eyebrows arched. "Oh? Why is that?"

"MacNab women never marry," Cam supplied, his lips twisting as he met Ceana's eyes.

Ceana tore her gaze from the earl. "Aye, it's true. We never do. My mother never married, nor did my grandmother before her, nor my great-grandmother, who was—"

Elizabeth released a little gasp. "You are illegitimate?"

Ceana smirked. "Aye, it's true. Bastard daughters, all of us."

"Oh, my." Wide-eyed with interest, Elizabeth studied Ceana, and Ceana smiled. The green-eyed monster slithered away, and Ceana locked it deep inside her as she gazed at the younger woman. Something told her there was more to this lady than met the eye.

Cam's cleared throat drew the women's attention back to him.

Elizabeth sighed and reached toward him. "Does it hurt very much, my lord?"

"Not so much," he soothed, covering her hand with his. "Thanks to Ceana."

Elizabeth cut her a glance. "How fortuitous you were the one to find him."

"Indeed," Ceana said. "If I didn't, I warrant he'd be stone-cold dead by now."

Elizabeth's slender throat moved as she swallowed. "Oh."

Cam frowned at Ceana. "You're frightening her."

Ceana fought the compulsion to laugh as yet another knock sounded at the door, this one louder.

"Come in," Cam called.

An older, heavyset man entered the room. If Elizabeth's foreignness was apparent, Ceana could smell the English on this one. He possessed a red complexion and a round face with a bulbous nose. He wore a stylish wig and a patch above his lip. His cheeks were rouged— quite unnecessarily, given his skin's natural flush—and his lips painted into a perfect moue.

"Ah!" he bellowed. He came to a halt beside Elizabeth, towering over her petite frame. "Good gracious, Camdonn. It is so very fine to see you in the flesh after the drama of yesterday's events. Elizabeth and I were so worried when you did not return last night. Thank goodness that . . . Oh, dear, I forgot his name"—he waved a big, blunt-fingered hand effeminately—"that burly Scottish man . . ."

"Alan MacDonald," Elizabeth reminded him gently.

"Ah, yes, thank you, Lizzy, dear. Thank goodness the MacDonald chap came to tell us you had been found and would return forthwith!"

"Thank you for your concern, Your Grace, but I have fared very well indeed," Cam said, all gentlemanly politeness. "I am relieved neither you nor Lady Elizabeth was hurt by those villains. I only regret they caused you such distress so near to my home."

"Do you have any idea who they were?" asked the Englishman.

Cam shook his head somberly. "None at all. But I'll get to the bottom of it."

"I am certain you will."

Ceana sighed. Cam's shoulder was oozing. It required her attention, and she'd delayed long enough. It was time to take advantage of her healer's prerogative.

Clapping her hands, she rose from her perch at the edge of the bed. "Well, then, enough blathering. Out with you both."

Elizabeth nodded, but the Englishman scowled at her. "What did you say?"

"I said you must leave. I must continue to clean the earl's wound and apply medicinals, and you've wasted enough of my time."

The man's mouth dropped open and his astonished gaze moved to Cam, who raised his good hand in a placating gesture. "I fear my doctor has a tendency to be officious."

The man's brows shot halfway up his tall forehead. "Doctor?"

"Your Grace, this is Ceana MacNab." Cam continued on with his description of her healing prowess and pedigree, as he had with Elizabeth, but Ceana just stared haughtily at the man, drumming her foot on the floor planks and reveling in the tapping sound it made.

The man looked down his nose at her. "Come, Elizabeth." He glanced at Cam. "We will see you soon, Camdonn. Again, we are so thankful to see you well. If you need anything . . . anything at all . . . please feel free to call on me or one of my men."

"Of course. Thank you."

The man pressed his hand on the small of Elizabeth's back and nudged her out.

"The likes of him must be stopped if we want King James to prevail."

Rob set his currycomb on a bench and turned to face Bram MacGregor. Bram was a brawny man with shoulder-length thick black curls and a bushy beard. He had come from Edinburgh to work the earl's land ten years ago. He hadn't lived in the Glen for generations, like Rob's family and most of the other residents, and that made him an outsider. It also meant his views were worldlier and more insurgent than the majority of the earl's tenants. Nevertheless, due in part to his warriorlike demeanor and in part to his engaging manner, the people of the Glen listened to him.

He and Rob had formed an alliance of sorts. Though his family hailed from these parts, Rob had spent most of his life in the busy port town of Glasgow. Life on the docks had given Rob a wider worldview, and he and Bram MacGregor understood each other in a way no one else in the Glen could.

"You should guard your tongue," Rob said quietly. "Do not speak out so openly against the earl. Remember you are his tenant, and the reprisals will be severe should he hear you're rabble-rousing."

Bram's lip curled. "Nay, Rob. I needn't rouse any rabble. They all hate him. Ye're one of the few who hasn't openly slandered him. Even his personal guard, Angus MacLean, has turned against him, when last year he trailed after him like a puppy."

Angus MacLean—no near relation to Rob, thank God—possessed the intelligence of a gnat. Calling him a puppy was far too generous. Rob took a measured breath. "I haven't enough evidence of the man's character to make a judgment. And neither have you."

"Och." Bram spat on the dirt. "Come. He's a Whig and a Presbyterian. He bows to the Hanoverian bastard. Hell, he supports a government that forbids us to bear arms."

"He has a right to his politics. He's well aware that there be Jacobites on his lands, and he doesn't deny us our right to remain." Nor had he upheld the newly passed Disarming Act.

"Aye, because he's afraid to face us."

"You cannot believe that."

"I'm certain of it. We could overcome him with no effort at all, and he knows it, so he pretends to be at peace."

Rob wasn't so sure. The earl had never been popular among the people of the Glen. He'd been absent for the past half a year, but he'd been in residence the year before that. Granted he'd been distracted by Alan MacDonald's wife during the majority of that time, but Rob had observed the man more closely than most. And though the earl might never completely agree with the Jacobite cause, Rob sensed he preferred peace and tolerance over strife and war.

He could be wrong. Yet one very influential and respected man remained the earl's steadfast friend: Alan MacDonald. Without Alan, Cam would be long dead by now. Rob wondered if the earl knew it. Rob doubted even Alan was aware of the extent of his influence.

"And now he's brought that damnable Sassenach wench . . . Hell, he's a damned fool if he thinks we'll simper to that bitch."

Remembering Elizabeth's rushed apology, Rob stiffened. He wasn't going to discuss Lady Elizabeth with Bram, or anyone.

He couldn't think of her. Not now. Not tonight. God knew he'd thought of her enough last night. Thought of her as he'd stroked himself to a groaning orgasm, imagining his cock sliding through her sweet, hot English flesh. Imagined her pink lips parted in ecstasy; his own lips possessing them.

Christ, it was bloody torture thinking of her. He had to stop.

Bram was talking—about Elizabeth's silk and lace, and how her dresses alone could feed the poor on the earl's land through the winter months. God knew the man was right, but all Rob could imagine was sliding that silk off her body.

Thrusting away the carnal images, he forced his attention back to Bram. "Don't judge until you are certain. They've only just arrived. Before you say or do anything, be sure it is the wisest course."

Bram made a scoffing noise, and Rob had the sinking feeling his warnings might come too late.

Dinner the following evening was a decidedly awkward affair. No one felt at ease, besides, perhaps, the grouse and salmon set on the table. Rob sat straight in his chair, his torso stiff, and ate uncomfortably from his silver spoon.

The earl, pale faced from the ordeal of descending the stairs, sat at the head of the grand table, and the remainder of the party sat at the end nearest him, for if anyone were seated at the opposite end, he'd have to shout down the length of the table in order to be heard.

Elizabeth, dressed in a cream satin that Rob's fingers itched to touch, sat at the earl's left and the Duke of Irvington at his right. Ceana sat beside Elizabeth, and Rob sat beside the duke, facing both women.

Each time Rob looked up, he met either the solid gray-blue stare of Ceana or the crystalline blue of Elizabeth's skittering gaze. It was as if the English lady didn't want to be caught looking at him, yet felt compelled to do so. As he did her. His gaze was drawn to her again and again, and he discreetly absorbed her every feature and her every move. Her narrow waist emphasized by the taper of her bodice, the straight lines of her back and shoulders, the creamy flesh over her collarbones, the curling wisps of blond hair drifting over her shoulders.

Ceana remained mostly silent, but her shrewd gaze took in everything. Including Rob's constant assessment of Lady Elizabeth; of that Rob had no doubt. He ought to feel guilty, perhaps, but his pride still smarted from her rejection. Still, he had no wish to taunt her. Not to mention the foolhardiness of continuing to allow carnal thoughts of Lady Elizabeth to wander into his mind.

"MacLean."

Rob's attention snapped to the earl. Ceana had wrapped the man's shoulder in a bulky bandage. A regal velvet dinner coat was draped over his shoulders, and the long fingers of his good hand tapped his wineglass as he regarded Rob with a steady gaze.

"What do you make of the attack on our party?"

"Disturbing," Rob answered truthfully.

"Have such random attacks become common since my departure from the Glen last year?"

Rob and Ceana exchanged a glance. Ceana spoke first. "No, they haven't. I haven't heard of any similar crime since I arrived at the Glen."

Elizabeth patted her silk napkin to her lips and demurely gazed at her lap, hands folded. What an innocent she tried to appear in mixed company. Rob had seen a very different side of her on the ride down to the castle. There was a scorching-hot fire inside her, sparkling and blue, like her eyes.

She was a study in contrasts, in fire and ice, in delicacy and strength, in refinement and impropriety. He craved to know her, to understand what instigated these odd disparities in her behavior.

"How unfortunate to arrive at one's home at the same time villains choose to infiltrate the area," the duke said on a shudder. He dragged his napkin over the greasy remnants of grouse on his chin, then deposited a forkful of meat into his mouth.

Cam's gaze never left Rob. "The populace of the Glen was aware I was returning home that day, correct?"

"Aye," Rob said.

"Do you believe it was a random attack, or was it planned?"

Rob hesitated, then said, "What do *you* think, milord?"

Cam lifted the glass to his lips and drank. Lowering the crystal, he gazed at Rob over the rim. "They weren't after the riches from our luggage. If that were the case, they'd have focused the attack on the carriages."

Again, the man beside Rob shuddered. "Lord above. I'd heard about the wilds of the Highlands, but little did I know I'd risked my very life by visiting here!"

"I wouldn't have allowed any harm to come to you," Cam said, his voice hard. "Nor Elizabeth. Please trust I would have kept you safe."

That earned Cam a gracious smile from Elizabeth, a smile that made Rob desperate to be awarded one of his own. Hell, haughty and spoiled as she was, she was the most alluring, engaging, confusing woman he'd ever laid eyes on.

He glanced at Ceana, who studied him with her observant gaze, her face devoid of expression. She was beautiful too, but in an opposite way. Where Elizabeth was refined and contained, Ceana was wild and free.

He still wanted Ceana, despite her less-than-gentle set-down of the other day.

Was it possible to want two women at once? He glanced from one to the other. Apparently so, he thought uncomfortably. Nevertheless, Ceana had refused him, and Elizabeth was as unattainable as the Virgin Mary.

"Of course you would have kept us safe, Lord Camdonn." The duke nodded vigorously. "Of course."

"But those men—they weren't after our riches. They were after me."

A stillness settled over the room. The people at the table took on the quality of the footmen standing silently in the shadows. They all sat staring at Cam.

After a long moment of silence, Rob cleared his throat. "Are you certain?"

"Yes. Yes, I believe I am."

"Well," Ceana said in her no-nonsense way. Earlier tonight, it had come as no small surprise when she'd opened her mouth and Rob heard her speak English for the first time. She was quite fluent, too. It struck him that Ceana had experienced a more varied past than she'd led anyone to believe. "Seems they're unhappier with you than you suspected."

"What's this?" asked the duke, his pale eyes narrowed.

"The people of the Glen are heavily in favor of King James," Ceana explained.

The duke scoffed. "The Jacobites surrendered to the government months ago, and the Pretender is languishing in France."

"Aye, but that does not mean the desire to have him on the throne no longer exists." Ceana gestured toward Cam. "So, you see, to many, our earl represents the enemy."

"Their defeat was final." The duke grunted. "Seems to me that the poor and illiterate masses are unable to comprehend the meaning of surrender."

Rob remained silent. The man possessed no understanding of the Highlands, yet Rob had no desire to enlighten him. It wouldn't be worth the effort.

Elizabeth sat quietly, a prim expression on her face, but she watched everyone with interest, and Rob could almost see the wheels churning in her head. She might be an impulsive Sassenach, but she was no fool. A fact that would benefit her if she truly planned to make a life here.

Ceana—Ceana the intrepid, Rob thought—did respond to the duke's statement, her tone mild. "Ah, but there you're mistaken, Your Grace. Surrender is an understandable concept, but many have refused to concede defeat. The uprising might be delayed for a time, but it isn't over. Not yet."

The duke snorted dismissively. "The Jacobites are too weak to rise again."

"Perhaps not soon, but Highlanders don't forget easily."

The duke raised his brows at Cam as if to express astonishment at the woman's gall in engaging in a political discussion with a duke of England. Cam missed the implication, however—he remained focused on Ceana. "Why do they persist in viewing me as the enemy?"

"To many of them, you are naught but a Presbyterian English Whig," Ceana said.

"As he well should be," the duke muttered.

Cam looked thoughtful, and despite Rob's silence, the earl addressed him again. "Do you have any idea who might've been behind the attack, MacLean?"

"No." Rob sincerely hoped Bram MacGregor hadn't been behind it—that it hadn't been instigated by one of the earl's own people.

"I'd like you to keep your eyes and ears open, then," Cam said. "If you learn anything, report it to me immediately."

"Aye, sir," Rob said mildly. Though he had no desire to come between the earl and the Jacobites, should it come to that. Ultimately, he reminded himself, he didn't know the earl or his motives. Cam had been more absent than present, and perhaps it was solely in hopeful optimism that Rob had already judged him innocent.

"In the meantime," Cam continued, "Elizabeth and I shall do our best to ingratiate ourselves to our tenants."

"You must continue to take advantage of your friendship with the MacDonald laird," Ceana said.

Cam slid his finger around the top rim of his wineglass and shook his head. "No. I must do this alone." He glanced at Elizabeth. "With the help of my betrothed. What say you, Elizabeth?"

"As you wish, my lord," she murmured.

After midnight, the door clicked shut as Bitsy left her for the night, and finally, *finally*, Elizabeth was free. She leaped out of bed and threw her cloak over her shoulders. Pulling the edges tight, she grabbed her candle, slid behind the tapestry, opened the door, and descended the spiraling stone staircase.

When her feet touched the dirt under the bottom step, she tiptoed forward and listened at the door. No sound emerged from the room beyond, for most of the castle occupants were abed by now.

She shoved hard at the bolt preventing the door from opening from the other side, and the corroded metal finally gave way. Taking a deep breath, she grabbed the equally rusty handle and turned it. The handle squealed and the hinges groaned in complaint as she forced the door open and peeked out as the smells of onions, ashes, and salted meat rushed into the stale air of the stairway.

The vast ground-floor room contained a massive cooking stove, rows of pots and pans hanging from the ceiling, a hearth big enough for a man to sleep in, and several tables piled with kitchen implements and foods in varying states of freshness. She tiptoed past the cold ovens and the brimming shelves and into the next room, the servants' dining room.

She passed the long, rough-hewn table and opened the door on the opposite end of the room. A brush of cool outside air raised chill bumps across her flesh and blew out her candle. The lack of candlelight didn't matter—there was enough moonlight for her to find her way. She set the candle down near the door and stepped outside, pulling her cloak close around her body.

It was quiet tonight. Watchful eyes continually roamed the castle grounds, but the courtyard between the stables and the main building was shrouded in shadows, and unless someone stood within a few feet of her, Elizabeth wouldn't be seen.

On impulse, she lifted her skirts and sprinted across the graveled clearing, her slippers soundless as she flew over the rocks.

When she reached the closed door of the stables she slowed and walked around to the side door, which was propped open to allow the fresh spring air to circulate through the building.

She slipped inside. Animals rustled in their stalls, but otherwise all was silent. Immediately to her left were the stone stairs that led to the upper story of the complex—the stable master's apartment. Staring at the steps, Elizabeth chewed on her lip for a long moment.

She knew what was up there. Or rather, *who* was up there.

Before she could take too much time to think about the ramifications of what she did, she gathered her skirts and tiptoed up the stairs.

Halfway up, she heard a gasp. Tilting her head, she paused to listen.

"Rob . . ."

Elizabeth blinked hard. If she wasn't mistaken, that was Ceana MacNab's voice.

Rob gave a one-word answer—a Gaelic word Elizabeth didn't understand. Rob's voice had that edge of roughness she'd heard in it when Elizabeth had first met him—that edge that made her spine tingle as if a hundred feathers stroked it.

Slowly, she took another step up, and then another. Neither Rob nor Ceana spoke again. Now all Elizabeth could hear was their breathing, heavier than usual. Her mouth went dry. She dropped her skirts and continued up the stairs until her head was level with the passageway on the second level of the stables. She raised her gaze to the landing.

The corridor traveled the width of the stable building, with bales of hay piled high against the wall on one side. Rob and Ceana were both turned away from her, facing the small, square window at the opposite wall. Rob held Ceana captured in his muscular arms, and she threw her head back as Rob's lips ravaged her neck and jaw.

Raising her hand, Elizabeth gripped the edge of the floor to steady herself.

Rob moved Ceana ahead until he pressed her face forward against the wall between the window and a bale of hay. Leaning over, he bunched his hands in her wine-colored skirts, pulling them upward until he grasped the back of her knee at the top of her garter. Ceana flattened her hands and pressed her cheek against the wall, making no attempt to stop him.

He lifted her leg and propped her foot on the bale of hay, then ran his fingers downward over the wool stocking covering her calf. She shuddered against the stone wall. Rob tugged her dress higher, flipping it over her back, and then, wasting no time, he slid his fingers between the pale globes of her buttocks. Ceana jerked and whimpered as he stroked the flesh between her legs in harsh, rough passes. He kissed her cheek, her jaw. He yanked her dress down past her shoulder and kissed the skin he exposed to the damp midnight air.

Elizabeth's tongue circled her lips as she stared at them.

"Rob," Ceana groaned. "Rob."

With one hand, Rob grasped her just above her hip bone. With the other, he pulled his plaid aside and grasped his cock. Elizabeth caught a glimpse of the flushed tip as he guided it between Ceana's legs. Notching himself in her entrance, he gripped Ceana's waist in both hands and jerked her toward him. Ceana cried out. Rob was utterly silent.

Elizabeth's heart pounded in her ears, loud as a drum. Surely they could hear it. Perhaps not, not with their joined harsh exhalations each time Rob thrust into Ceana. Rob's fingers bit into her white flesh, and his head dipped down.

Ceana reached back, and her fingertips grasped the fabric of his blue plaid and yanked him closer.

His teeth closed on her shoulder.

Ceana groaned. Her body arched and undulated beneath him. Rob held her flush against him, his profile an agonized mask of restraint. She went limp, and Rob began again, this time at a quicker pace, thrusting into her fast and hard, his eyes closed, his lips in a tight white line. Ceana pressed her forehead against the wall and took his battering.

A cold, cruel sense of unjustness and the hot flush of excitement tangled together within Elizabeth, coalescing into a perverse agony. Just as Elizabeth was certain she must move, must cry out, must run away or do anything rather than endure watching them for one second longer, Rob pulled out and, with a low groan, released his seed over Ceana's lower back. Elizabeth watched in fascination as ropes of white covered the dimple at the top of Ceana's buttocks.

Rob slumped over her, supporting himself with one hand on the wall beside her smaller one.

Elizabeth stood as still as a statue, watching. Tears stung her eyes. Lord help her, she wished it had been her.

Finally, Rob straightened and murmured something to Ceana in a low voice. He turned, but not before Elizabeth's wits returned. She flew down the stairs, out the door, across the darkened corridor, through the dining room, kitchen, and storage room, and back up the secret stairs to the frigid loneliness of her room.

CHAPTER SIX

Ceana leaned against the wall, her strength sapped, as Rob stroked the soft cloth over her skin. When he finished, he gently lowered her skirts, and she let her foot slip off the bale of hay and onto the planked wood floor.

Slowly, she turned to face him. Heat crept into her cheeks. Perhaps it was a mistake to have allowed him to touch her tonight. In truth, she'd needed it as urgently as he had, but that didn't make either of their motivations acceptable.

"We can't do this anymore," she said.

His lips tightened. He held out his hand. "Sit with me."

She grasped his hand and followed him through the arched doorway into his quarters. The stable boys lived in the barracks with the earl's men, so Rob possessed the entire upper level of the stables as his quarters. The large chamber was split down the middle by a partition separating the living and dining space from the sleeping area. The area possessed the added benefit of a stone fireplace at each end. Altogether royal accommodation, but the Earls of Camdonn, she'd learned, had always taken their horseflesh seriously.

Castoffs from the keep furnished the room, creating a comfortable, if mismatched, ensemble. She chose a frayed velvety plum-colored sofa and sank into it as Rob knelt at the grate to start a fire.

At dinner, she'd observed the furtive glances Elizabeth had directed at Rob, and in return his heated stares at her. All night long, a fierce spark had buzzed between the stable master and the future countess.

Ceana doubted anyone else had witnessed it, but she was intuitive in these matters. At first she was surprised that Rob would be attracted to a woman like Elizabeth, but as she observed them, it began to make more sense. Elizabeth's intelligence and poise shielded a core of soft vulnerability that had shimmered beneath her skin and deep in her eyes all night long.

Rob would like a woman like that. Ceana was neither soft nor vulnerable, and Rob, though he'd never said it outright, wished she were. He wanted a woman he could protect and shelter. Ceana was too independent for that. Perhaps Elizabeth, despite her cool demeanor, wasn't.

Ceana felt neither resentment nor jealousy toward either of them—a further sign that it was over between her and Rob. Instead, her heart panged with sympathy for them both. Anything between them was impossible. She sighed. It seemed matters of love extended their cruelty to people beyond herself.

"How long will you be here?" Rob asked, his back to her.

"Until the earl is completely healed, I suppose. I want to be certain the wound heals well."

"Why?" Rob asked.

"I . . ." Her voice faltered. "I would do the same for anyone."

But would she?

"You could make it easier for many."

"What do you mean?"

"If you encouraged the wound to fester. Allowed him to die." Rob crouched beside the fireplace and looked back at her with eyes that glittered with gold flecks in the light of the fire.

She spoke through clenched teeth. "It is against my nature as a healer to allow that to happen to anyone, friend or foe. And Cam isn't . . . Well, he isn't a foe." She paused. "And who would be his successor? A remote English cousin who cares naught for this land?"

"Some say the earl himself doesn't care."

"He does," she said flatly.

Rob turned back to the hearth.

"Did you hope I'd agree to such a thing?" she asked in a low voice. The idea that he might wish Cam dead made her feel like a boulder had settled in the pit of her stomach.

After a long silence, Rob said, "No."

She released a long breath of relief.

He rose and came to sit beside her. "But there are others who would."

"I know."

They sat in the quiet for a long time, the only sound the whisper of the fire. Rob's hand rested comfortably on her thigh. She didn't try to remove it.

"What are we doing, Rob?"

He just gazed at her, eyes hooded. She had no idea what he was thinking. She wished she could read him better.

"I'm not the one you wanted tonight," she said. *And you're not the one I wanted . . .*

They'd come together in mutual frustration. Ceana couldn't deny that she'd sought him out because she craved release from the tension of being near the earl. And after witnessing the feral need in Rob, she suspected the same held true for him, with Elizabeth.

"You are drawn to the English lass."

He straightened. "That would be daft."

"Nevertheless, it is true."

He sighed. His eyes flickered away. "I am drawn to you too, Ceana."

"I'm not enough for you," she said gently. "You need something more. A wife. A family."

"I need . . ." He paused, staring at the fire. "I don't know what I need."

"Don't risk it," she murmured. "Stay away from Lady Elizabeth. She also is incapable of providing you with what you need."

"How can you know that?" He clamped his lips shut, as if the words had emerged before he could stop them, and looked away.

"You cannot marry her. You cannot *be* with her. To pursue her would be folly."

He said nothing, just thrust a hand through his dark hair.

"I say this only as someone who cares about you. I would not begrudge you her, but the earl—and the duke—surely would."

"I know," he ground out. He looked like he'd rather not be a part of this discussion. Ceana sighed and covered his hand with her own.

"I won't be returning," she said quietly. "I'm sorry."

"You needn't be."

"I still care for you."

His bronze gaze rested on her for a long moment, and then he nodded, his fingers tightening on her thigh. "Aye."

She gave him a faltering smile, affection for him overwhelming her. If only there were no curse. If only they were right for each other. She closed her eyes, remembering the powerful rush of sensation she'd experienced that very first night when he'd taken her in her cottage.

But it was never meant to be. It was a carnal relationship, nothing more. And if they continued it now, it would only damage them both in the end.

Gently, she pushed his hand off her thigh. "Good-bye, Rob."

Ceana stared at the sleeping earl. Dinner last night had sapped his strength. His color wasn't nearly as good as yesterday morning. He must keep to his bed until he was stronger. If he pushed himself too hard, he'd succumb to a fever, just as he had when Alan wounded him in the duel.

Reaching forward, she brushed a strand of black hair from his cheek. His eyelids fluttered, then opened. The dark orbs settled on her, and his lips twitched into a lazy smile.

"Ceana." His voice was rough with sleep.

She smiled at him. "I didn't mean to wake you."

He reached up. His hand curled behind her neck, and he pulled her down. Before she could think, his lips moved against hers in a silken glide and her hands were sifting through the satin strands of his hair.

His fingers were hard on her neck, but his lips were soft and warm. His tongue flicked against the side of her mouth, and he took the kiss deeper.

Heat bloomed between Ceana's legs and spread through her body, softening her muscles and making her blood rush through her veins. Her breast pressed against the side of his chest, the nipple hardening as it brushed over the blanket covering him.

She wanted him, but . . .

She couldn't do this. There were a thousand reasons not to.

She jerked away.

"Cam . . ." There was a pleading tone in her voice she didn't try to hide. Cam had burrowed past her brittle facade. He must know how much she wanted him, what a battle she raged against herself to do what was right. "I can't . . ."

How blissful it would be if she could strip off her clothes and lie beside him now. Press her body against his from head to toe. Make sweet love with him all day long.

His dark eyes locked on her as she pushed a stray curl out of her eye.

"I can't help it," he murmured in a gruff voice. "I will go mad if I don't touch you."

"You must not touch me."

He closed his eyes wearily. "There are certain things that I cannot control. I wish I could . . . but I can't."

"Of course you can."

He opened his eyes, and there was a deep sadness in the brown depths. "No."

"Why?"

"I don't know. I believe I know how I'd like to be—how I should be—but I cannot." He ground his teeth in frustration.

"Are you referring to what happened between you and Sorcha

MacDonald? What did you do to make Alan duel with you?" Ceana
tried to picture the earl pursuing the very pregnant and very happily
married Sorcha, but the image was not forthcoming.

"I kidnapped her."

She raised her brows.

"I knocked down their door, snatched her naked from her marriage bed, and brought her here. To my bedchamber."

Ceana fought to keep her jaw from dropping. Keeping her breaths
steady, she gently pulled the bandage from behind his shoulder. In
truth, the wound shouldn't need cleaning today. It was an excuse to
stay with him longer. To have him to herself.

"What happened?"

"She denied me. For the first time."

At that, she did look at him. "You'd been lovers."

"Yes."

"But she wouldn't have you after she married Alan."

"No . . . not for . . . Well, no. Not really," he said uncomfortably.
"She escaped from me. Alan nearly killed me before he went to Sherrifmuir. And now we have all come round full circle." He stared at the
wooden beams in the ceiling, his gaze turning wistful. "I'm glad they
found happiness together."

"And now it is your turn." Rocking back, Ceana studied his lips,
resisted the urge to trace them with her fingertip.

"Is it?"

"Of course."

"I must be a good leader. I must marry Elizabeth. But"—his eyes,
dark and full of longing, locked onto hers—"Ceana, I can't stop thinking about you."

Ceana drew in a measured breath. "You mustn't think anything of
me. I'm only a simple country healer. That is all I can be to you."

"I know that."

Again, she felt that dart in her chest, and a part of her acknowl-
edged that she'd wanted him to argue with her. Somewhere deep inside, she wanted him to fight for her.

She yearned for his regard. She cared for him.

No. Impossible. She'd warned Rob against a similar folly last night, and in her case, the folly would be even greater.

"Why can't it be simple? Why can't Elizabeth occupy my every thought?"

"I don't know." Ceana spoke the words she knew she must, but they emerged without intonation. "Your betrothed *should* occupy your every thought."

"She doesn't. Why is that?"

"I don't know."

"She's a lovely girl."

"Aye, and perfect for someone of your rank too." Again, Ceana took a deep breath. She hated this, but it was absolutely necessary. "She is a true lady."

Cam shook his head, and grooves formed in his brow. "I thought the people would admire her as I do, but instead they hold themselves aloof."

"She's English. People are distrustful of the English. As they well should be."

"But Elizabeth? She's all innocence and sweetness. Surely they can see that?"

"Outwardly, she is perfection, but she also holds herself aloof. She doesn't give away her true nature to anyone."

His frown deepened. "What do you mean?"

"Like most people, she is more complex than she appears."

"Do you think so?"

"Aye. I know it."

"She is the niece of an English duke." Cam frowned. "I wonder at times why she agreed to marry a bucolic little Scottish earl, why her uncle agreed to the betrothal."

Ceana snorted. "I'd hardly call you bucolic. And little . . . ?"

Before she could stop herself, her gaze wandered down his long body, pausing at the bulge between his legs. Unable to quell the ridiculous heat creeping across her cheeks—for heaven's sake, she was behaving like a virginal maid—she wrenched her gaze to his shoulder. "Your wound looks well. I'll rewrap it. Tell me if it begins to pain you."

He remained silent as she folded the linen over his arm, but she could feel the heat emanating from him. She didn't dare risk glancing over his form, covered only by a thin blanket that revealed every contour and every bulge.

She took a deep breath. "I must leave to gather some herbs. I'll return by early afternoon."

She needed to escape. Energy shimmered around his body, and she knew he was restraining himself from touching her. She could scarcely keep herself from touching him. Only the wound in his shoulder held him anchored to the bed. If not for that, they'd surely be lost.

"Remember your betrothed," she said in a low voice. "She is the most beautiful English girl I've laid eyes on. Think of her. And I'll think of . . ."

No one.

She tied off his bandage and stood. "There, now."

He reached out, skimming the top of her hand with his fingertip before she turned away and nearly tripped over her skirts in her haste to flee from his bedchamber.

Downstairs, she let herself out, leaned against the smooth rock face of the outside wall, and gulped in deep breaths of cool, fresh air. She stared at her hand. Why could she still feel his touch? Why did she care?

Why, why, why?

The man was driving her mad.

He was an earl. An *earl*. And even if he weren't a man of consequence, she shouldn't be having these thoughts—these obsessive, protective, needy thoughts—about any man.

She stared off toward the loch. An overgrown lawn stretched between the path circling the main castle and the edge of the cliff that descended to the water. She'd always loved coming to Camdonn Castle, because as far as she was concerned, this part of Loch Shiel was one of the most beautiful places in all of Scotland.

The sky was hazy today, with a thin cloud layer obscuring the sun and sending a shimmering gray cast over the water. There was no wind, and the loch glowed like an expansive mirror. From here she faced the inlet that led to Glenfinnan, the nearest village and where the bulk of Alan's clan lived.

"Good morning."

Ceana's head whipped toward the lilting voice. Lady Elizabeth stood on the path, wearing a shimmering garment of some fashionable and expensive fabric Ceana didn't care to name.

"Lady Elizabeth."

The younger woman offered her a tentative smile. "What are you doing out here?"

Ceana pushed herself off the wall. Maybe spending more time with the lady would ease her resentment. Perhaps not. In either case, Ceana couldn't deny her curiosity about Cam's betrothed. Further, she had observed that no one had made an effort to befriend the future countess, and the lass had very few duties with which to occupy herself. Though she tried to hide it, there was a restlessness in Elizabeth that might be cured by meaningful activity and friendly conversation.

"I'm off to gather some herbs for some medicinal preparations." When Elizabeth didn't answer, she added, "Would you like to come?"

"Why, yes, I would."

Ceana allowed herself an assessing gaze. "We shall have to walk a ways. At least a mile."

"I am able to walk."

"Very well, then."

Elizabeth followed her as she slipped into the kitchens to fetch an extra basket from one of the maids before returning outside. They crossed the courtyard and passed through the castle gate, Ceana exchanging polite words with the guards. When they were out of earshot, Elizabeth asked, "What did those men at the gate say to you?"

Ceana chuckled. "Well, one was complaining of his gout. I told him to imbibe a wee bit less of Cam's whisky if he wished to ease it. The other was just wishing us a good day."

Elizabeth sighed. "Your English is very good, for someone of your . . ."

Her voice dwindled, and Ceana smiled. "Aye, it's very good, isn't it?"

"You do have quite a heavy accent, but—"

"But you understand me well enough, don't you?"

"Yes." Elizabeth paused. "I wish I knew Gaelic."

"You should learn," Ceana said. "It would be wise."

"Why do you say that?"

"People will be more willing to offer you their trust if you spoke their language. At least if you tried to learn it."

"Will you teach me?"

Ceana shrugged. "I don't live at Camdonn Castle. I will leave soon, and then you shouldn't see me unless someone is ill and asks for me to come. But until then . . . aye, I'll teach you what I can."

Both women were silent as they turned down the road, headed in the direction of the village of Glenfinnan.

"What are you searching for?" Elizabeth asked finally. "Perhaps I can help you to find it."

"Foxglove and groundsel," Ceana said. "Foxglove is poisonous, but in small amounts it is helpful for patients with the dropsy. I use groundsel for festering wounds. If we happen to find some in bloom, I'll take the flowers to mix with vinegar for another kind of salve."

Elizabeth ground to a stop, staring up at her with blue eyes wide with dismay. "Is the earl's wound festering?"

The younger woman's oval face had gone completely ashen. It ought to satisfy Ceana that Cam had chosen someone who wasn't entirely indifferent to him, but instead the green monster within her clawed for release. She closed her eyes, valiantly battling it until it once again slunk away.

"No," she said tightly. "It hasn't festered. It would be a precautionary measure in his case."

Elizabeth released a relieved breath and began walking again.

Ceana fell into step beside her. "Do you care for the earl so much, then?"

"Of course I do. He is to be my husband. It would be improper for me not to care."

"It's all that matters to you, isn't it?" Ceana kept her gaze fastened to the edges of the path, looking for signs of the herbs.

"What do you mean?"

"What's proper and what's not," Ceana said. "Frankly, I couldn't care less about all that nonsense. I'm interested in what you really feel."

"All right," Elizabeth said after a moment, her voice steady but quiet. "I really do care that Cam heals from his wound. Perhaps not for the reasons someone such as you might suspect, but I want him well, and I want to marry him." She paused, then asked quietly, "Does that satisfy you?"

Ceana shrugged. "Almost. We'll see how long your candor lasts."

Elizabeth huffed.

"Don't worry, my lady. I won't reveal your secret to the world. It seems everyone is oblivious to the inner workings of your mind."

"And you think you are not?"

"Not completely, in any case. I know there's something more to you. Something you'd prefer not to reveal. It's always there, under your skin, hidden in your eyes. Its origins will remain a mystery until you choose to reveal them."

"What if I never choose to reveal them?"

"Then they will be a mystery to me forever, I suppose. Ah! There!" Ceana veered off the path and knelt before the patch of groundsel.

Elizabeth crouched beside her. "That wasn't difficult to find."

"Aye. Groundsel can be a nasty weed. It is a most helpful plant for a healer, however. Here." She thrust the basket into the other woman's arms and withdrew her dirk from her skirt.

"Tell me what that is in Gaelic," Elizabeth commanded.

"Groundsel?"

"No, that." Elizabeth pointed at the dirk.

"Ah." Ceana turned it in her hand. Its blade glimmered in the silver-gray light. "This is a *sgian achlais*. It was my grandmother's."

"*Sgian achlais*," Elizabeth repeated dutifully.

In silence, aware of Elizabeth studying her every move, Ceana sawed off the branches and leaves that would be most beneficial for her salve.

"Do you like Robert MacLean very much?"

Ceana paused, then plucked off a healthy leaf and placed it in the basket. "Aye, I do like him."

"You are lovers." It was a statement, not a question. A very direct statement for a lady of Elizabeth's status. Too direct.

Ceana took a shaky breath. How on earth could Elizabeth know anything about her and Rob? Had Rob told her something? "Aye, we were. Not anymore."

Something flared in Elizabeth's eyes. "Why not anymore?"

"Your questions are of a personal nature." She dropped the *sgian achlais* at her side and gazed steadily at Elizabeth. "My lady."

Elizabeth shrugged. "I am merely curious."

"You are attracted to Rob."

The lady flinched, and then her mouth set in a mulish line. Her eyes flashed a challenge at Ceana.

"There is no need to deny it," Ceana said on a sigh. "It was obvious from the glances you kept stealing at him over dinner."

"I did no such thing!" The denial was too rapid to be anything but a lie.

"Rest easy, lass. No one else noticed."

Making a sound of distress, Elizabeth surged to her feet.

"I think that ought to be enough." Ceana brushed her hands off, then collected the basket and rose.

Elizabeth suddenly stood directly in front of her. "You mustn't tell anyone. If you do—"

"Don't be a fool," Ceana interrupted. "Why ever would I have reason to cause trouble for Rob?"

"Because your affair is over." Elizabeth's pretty pink lips twisted. "Or so you say."

"Aye, we have parted ways, but it was amicable. I shouldn't wish Cam's wrath to rain down upon him. Or the duke's."

"Not the duke's," Elizabeth repeated, shaking her head somberly. "You don't want to witness the duke's wrath, I promise you."

Ceana stared at her for a long moment. "Tell me something. If you're attracted to Rob MacLean, why should you care whether Cam lives or dies?"

"I care deeply," Elizabeth whispered. "I care because Cam is my savior."

Later, Elizabeth climbed the stairs toward her bedchamber, deep in thought.

Ceana MacNab possessed no fear. While an Englishwoman of Ceana's status would scarcely dare to glance at Elizabeth, Ceana looked her in the eye and told her exactly what she thought. She didn't mince words, nor did she pretend to be something she was not.

After what she'd seen happen between Rob and Ceana in the stables, Elizabeth was perplexed by her reaction to the healer. She'd expected to be disgusted by her, or at the very least jealous. But she found Ceana oddly fascinating.

Elizabeth had never known anyone quite like her. She admired her. More than that—she truly *liked* her. Elizabeth grasped onto this strange feeling, this genuine respect for another, and smiled. Perhaps, as unlikely as a friendship would seem between the two of them, she could work to forge one.

She pushed open the door to her room and stepped inside, only to jump backward when she saw who stood at one of the arrow slit windows.

Uncle Walter.

He turned to face her. "Close the door, Lizzy, dear."

Trying to stifle the fear leaping into her throat, Elizabeth reached for the handle. Once the door was closed, there would be no more *Lizzy, dears* from the duke. Her doting uncle would be gone.

Elizabeth had spent the better part of her life trying to avoid being alone with her uncle. Since her parents and brother had died, she'd been his tool—the object he'd used to show the world what a good, kindhearted, heroic man he was. But when she was alone with him, that pretense disappeared. She was one of the very few people who knew exactly what he was—she'd known his true colors since she was six years old.

Lord, he frightened her. Elizabeth understood what he was capable of. He was a monster. A murderer. And she spent a great majority of her time in abject terror that if she pushed him too hard, he'd repeat the horror of what she'd witnessed when she was a little girl.

He'd come close many times. Poor Bitsy had been the object of his wrath. Through the years, Elizabeth had watched him hurt her innocent lady's maid, slowly stripping the woman of her humanity.

Elizabeth's own impetuous, reckless actions were responsible for Bitsy's suffering. Elizabeth was naughty. She was impulsive. She couldn't stop herself from acting out, even when she knew the consequences.

Elizabeth was a wily child and a cunning young woman, and her impetuous nature, her need to escape from her stifling confinement at Purefoy Abbey, and her desire for a bit of normalcy and happiness had often prompted her to sneak out of the house. She'd usually gotten away with playing with the village children and exploring the nearby forests, but Uncle Walter occasionally caught her. Six times total, in thirteen years.

She made a heroic effort not to shrink against the door. "Good afternoon, Uncle."

His lips twisted, causing his patch to nearly disappear into the crevice of a deep wrinkle. "Enjoy your walk?"

"Yes."

"You were with the healer woman Camdonn has employed."

"Yes, Uncle."

"You are not to associate with that woman. She is a heathen."

"But Lord Camdonn said—"

"Lord Camdonn's injury has affected his mind in a most unhealthy manner." Uncle Walter's scowl deepened. "If I weren't certain he'd recover, we'd have already returned to England." He shuddered to drive home his point. "From their language to their filthy ways, these people disturb me."

"Yes, Uncle." Elizabeth was glad her uncle was nearly as eager to be rid of her as she was to be rid of him. He was too deeply involved in his scheme and wouldn't take her home now—not when he was so close to her being out of his life and far away from him forever.

Now that she was an adult, Elizabeth's usefulness had come to an end. He could no longer exploit her to show himself to the world as the doting, caring uncle, as the hero and savior of his poor orphaned niece. She was too old, and if he kept his young, marriageable kinswoman sequestered in Hampshire, people might question his motives for doing so. Yet if he married her to a nearby lord or someone with a strong connection to London, she might someday reveal the truth about him. His plan to marry her to a Scottish earl who lived in a remote corner of the earth and had no plans to return to England was, in his mind, the best way to safely—and admirably—get rid of her with the least risk to himself.

"You must not fall into the trap of becoming like them," Uncle Walter said. "You are young yet, Lizzy, and vulnerable. However, you are also English, and I have spent many years training you to rise above those who are below you. You and I possess far superior bloodlines to any single person within scores of miles of this place. We must never forget that fact."

"No, of course not, Uncle."

"It would be unseemly for you to befriend any of them. You must stand apart. Revel in your distinction. If you desire companionship, there is Lord Camdonn himself, but beyond that, there is no one acceptable. If you desire a confidante, you must look to your friends in England."

Elizabeth nodded. "Yes, Uncle."

Uncle Walter assumed that there existed ties between her and her

"English friends," but there weren't any. There never had been. She'd write to none of those witless girls whose company had been foisted on her through the years. The feeling was entirely mutual—she wouldn't be hearing from them, either.

"Good." He paused and tilted his head. "You will make me proud, Lizzy. I will not have you denigrating yourself and embarrassing our esteemed family. I have trained you sufficiently, I hope, but if it becomes clear that I have not done my duty well enough, I will not hesitate to punish you most harshly."

His words stabbed directly into her lungs, leaving her struggling for air. "But . . . but we are in Scotland. I am to be married soon . . ."

"Until the day of your marriage, you are mine to manage—and to punish—as I see fit. I will continue to endeavor to mold you into the fine young woman your lineage demands until I place your hand in the Earl of Camdonn's. And then I can only pray that he will take as firm a stance with you as I have."

"I'm sorry," Elizabeth breathed finally. "You are right, Uncle. I shall be conscious of my superior status hereafter."

But a part of her, that rebellious part that she tried so hard to squelch, rose up and screamed in denial. She liked these people; she liked this place; she wanted to talk more, know more, learn more. But she forced these desires down. Uncle Walter would not be here forever, and Cam was nothing like him. There would be time for all that once her uncle had gone back to Hampshire.

"Above all, you must stay away from that witch Ceana MacNab. There is something about the woman that is pure evil."

Ceana wasn't evil; that much Elizabeth knew to the depths of her heart. She knew evil intimately already, and Ceana MacNab didn't qualify.

CHAPTER SEVEN

She didn't venture to the stables again. Elizabeth couldn't fathom what had drawn her there to begin with.

Well, that wasn't being completely honest. She could fathom it. Rob MacLean had lured her there.

She'd never felt this pull with anyone. Not even Tom, a footman at Purefoy Abbey, the only man she'd ever touched. Tom was handsome and young, but there had been nothing to her feelings for him beyond interest and curiosity . . . and the irresistible compulsion to be bad.

Nonetheless, Elizabeth wasn't stupid enough to expect that she and Rob would have a torrid affair beneath the Earl of Camdonn's nose. She might have wicked thoughts, but even she couldn't go that far. To hurt Uncle Walter, maybe. To risk her marriage to Cam . . . no. She wouldn't do it. No matter how strongly Rob drew her, she must stay away from him.

So when she slipped out tonight to enjoy her small taste of freedom, she ventured in the opposite direction from the stables. She drifted to the edge of the cliff facing the loch and wedged her body between two bushes blooming abundantly with white flowers.

She felt safe out here. Safer than in the castle proper, in such close proximity to her uncle. Being inside stifled her. Outside in the clear, star-studded Highland night, she could pretend she was free.

Even though she wasn't.

Almost, Elizabeth. Almost.

She didn't care about the dewy ground soaking through her wrap and robe. She sat in the grass, her legs drawn up into the circle of her arms, and gazed out over the smooth black surface of the loch.

It was so beautiful here. How could she ever have thought this was a wild land? It was a peaceful land. So varied, full of life, altogether marvelous. Mrs. MacAdam told her that in the winter, snow would blanket the surrounding mountains in white. In the summer, everything that so hesitantly came to life right now would flare into full, prodigious bloom.

Elizabeth could love it here. She'd known since the day she'd been stranded alone up in the mountain. Something about this place called to her in a far deeper and more primitive way than anything in Hampshire.

Rob stood in the shadows of the keep, watching her as she tucked her slender frame between the two small blooming hawthorns.

The hawthorn bush was known by Highlanders as the entrance to the fairy world. Some unsuspecting onlooker might see her flitting over the castle grounds with her blond curls and her white robe flowing behind her, and think she was one of the fae when she disappeared into the hawthorn.

She hadn't escaped into another world, though. Her white garments flashed among the similarly colored blooms as she shifted her position.

What was it about her?

Ceana was right: Even so much as talking to Elizabeth was dangerous. Touching her could mean his doom. And yet the compulsion to do both was too strong to resist.

He must learn more about her. Understand what it was that drew him to her. He wanted to touch her. To care for her. To make her shudder in his arms.

His shoes silent on the grass, he ducked into the hawthorn behind her and clamped a hand over her mouth so she wouldn't scream. "Shh." His lips brushed over the satin of her hair. "It's Rob MacLean."

Instantly, she relaxed, and he forced himself to let her go, as strong as the urge was to keep her pinned in the safe circle of his arms.

"Sorry to startle you." When his arms fell away, she looked at him over her shoulder. "I gather you didn't wish to be discovered," he murmured.

"You gather correctly."

"Well." He looked to the right and left of the bush. "It seems I am the only one who has spotted you. Anyone who looks this way will think I'm only pissing in the bushes."

She grinned, an expression that was as surprising as it was beautiful. "Who'd dare to say such a thing to me besides Robert MacLean?"

He shrugged.

"I'd invite you to sit, but there isn't any room."

As it was, branches scratched at them both, threatening to tear her robe. "I know a better place." He held out his hand. "Come."

She stared at his hand for a long moment, then reached forward tentatively. *This*—this clear vulnerability in her actions—contradicted her haughty demeanor and tugged at something deep within him.

He pulled her to her feet, then led her around the bush to pause at the cliff's edge, where the hawthorn's height still blocked them from the view of the guardhouse.

"I'll go first, and you follow." Releasing her, Rob crouched down and then dropped over the edge, finding his footing on one of the rock outcroppings.

She knelt at the edge of the cliff, peering down at him. "Where are you going?"

"I'll show you."

Tentatively, she adjusted herself to a sitting position, allowing her legs to dangle into black nothingness. Her skirt bunched up over her thighs, revealing the fact that she had removed her stockings and wore her slippers over bare feet.

"Very good," he murmured, trying not to let the sight of her legs affect him. "Hop off and I'll catch you."

She stared down at him, haloed by the moonlight, biting her lip as if she were considering whether to obey.

"I trust you," she murmured finally. Closing her eyes, she pushed herself off. He caught her around the waist and gently lowered her until her slippered feet rested on solid stone.

She gazed into Rob's face, her expression darkened by shadows. They touched from head to toe. Shudders rolled through her.

Gathering himself, he pulled away and glanced down. "The stones here create natural steps, but you must be careful. Follow me."

They progressed slowly down the cliff wall. It wasn't far to the bottom, but the trail was steep and the narrow stone steps only a gray glimmer in the starry night, and he made certain she placed every foot firmly so she wouldn't slip.

Soon they descended onto a small, muddy beach. Here, lilies grew at the water's edge, and a small boat bobbed just offshore. A rope led from the boat to a stone mooring on the beach. A few steps from the water's edge, the cliff collapsed inward as if the hand of a giant had punched a hole in it to form the beginnings of a cave. Just inside the shallow impression lay two flat stones that looked like low chairs and had probably been placed there for that purpose. Rob sat on one of the stones and gestured to the other. Elizabeth adjusted the skirts of her shift and robe and settled onto the rock.

"No chance of anyone finding you here," he said.

She nodded, her expression sober. "It is a much better hiding place."

"What do you hide from?" he asked softly.

She paused, then licked her lips. "Everything."

A long silence followed her admission. Rob watched the small, dark ripples lap against the shore.

He understood. Not so long ago, he'd wanted to hide from everything too. He glanced at her. She stared at the water, her hands clasped tightly in her lap. He didn't think she would have admitted that to just anyone.

"When I was a lad, I'd escape from Glasgow and disappear into the countryside," he said. "Sometimes for days on end. I'd seek out stables, horses, other animals. I felt safer with them."

"Safe from what?" she breathed.

"From my da." She stared at him, and his lips twisted. "He was a drunkard . . . and he wasn't overly fond of me."

He'd never told anyone about his father, but in Elizabeth's presence he felt comfortable. He wanted to tell her. It was more than a compulsion to share his past with her; it was a desire to draw her out as well. To explore and put a name to that feeling that they shared something, some deeper bond. She was so familiar to him—too familiar, given their outward differences—and he wanted to understand why.

"I'm sorry." She blinked, revealing a deep sadness in the depths of her blue eyes. "My father . . . He wasn't like that."

"When did he die?"

"I was . . . six years old. He died of smallpox on the same night as my mother. And my younger brother—he died soon after."

Rob nodded. "Did you contract the pox?"

She turned to stare out over the water again. "Yes. I brought it home to my family. I survived, with only one small scar to prove I had it. They did not."

Her words emerged tight and emotionless, and Rob's chest tightened as she pulled her hair back and gestured at a spot high on her forehead. "There it is. The reminder of what I did."

He couldn't see the scar, but he nodded, and she dropped her hair. "I miss my mother. I miss both of them."

"I never knew my mother," Rob said. "She died at my birth. It's part of why my da punished me for the remainder of his life."

"Only part?" Elizabeth asked.

"Aye."

"Why else did he punish you?"

Rob paused. When he finally spoke, his voice was low. "My mother . . . She had strayed. I was my da's son only in name."

"Not in blood?"

Staring out over the loch, Rob said, "No. Not in blood."

Soon she would have to leave him. Sighing, Ceana lowered her hands into the basin and scooped clean water over her face. She'd remained at Camdonn Castle a full week. A healthy scab covered Cam's wound, and he had resumed most of his regular duties.

There had been no further hint of his attraction to her. This brought forth in her a confounding mixture of regret and relief. She should only be relieved, but much to her disgust, she yearned for the earl's attentions.

To make matters worse, she'd spent time with his betrothed and she liked her. Ceana wasn't the kind of woman to steal away another woman's man, and yet some demon within her commanded she grab Cam and cling to him for all she was worth. *To hell with the Sassenach*, it said. *To hell with the damnable curse*.

She was a fool. She splashed another handful of water over her face and thanked God for Elizabeth. Because if the English lady didn't exist, Ceana would have tumbled Cam the very first day she knew him, and if that had happened, she'd be far worse off than she was now.

A knock at her door had her looking up in surprise. She grabbed a towel and swiped it over her face. She was wearing only her petticoat, so she quickly threw a plaid over her shoulders. "Come in."

The door opened to reveal Cam, dressed in buckskin breeches, tall black boots, and a white shirt with a ruffled collar that made him look like a pirate.

She stepped back out of sheer self-preservation.

He smiled at her. "Ceana."

"I'm leaving tomorrow," she blurted.

She hadn't planned to go quite so soon, but his sinful appearance and her body's reaction to it drove home the truth that sooner was better than later.

His eyes widened. "Why?"

"Because you are healed."

"Not entirely healed."

She kept her gaze steady. "You wish me to stay for reasons that have naught to do with your injury."

"Do you think so?"

"Aye."

He broke their eye contact first. His smile had faded, and his gaze moved over her shoulder toward the pair of long, rectangular windows on the opposite wall. "I dislike the thought of you leaving."

"Why?"

"I don't like the thought of you away from me." Cam stepped fully inside the room and closed the door. He must have seen the panic flare in her eyes, because he ground out, "I have no intention of touching you."

She released a breath. If he had intended to touch her, she could not be held responsible for her actions. Even now, her fingers twitched and a fire burned low in her belly.

"Don't leave, Ceana."

"I must."

He shook his head, pushed his good hand through his hair. "I need you close."

"You don't need me."

"There is so much I must do. So many amends I must make. So much time to make up for. You could help me."

"I will not stay here on anyone's whim, earl or not."

"You're a MacNab woman," he recited, his tone dull. "You don't heel to any man's orders."

"Precisely."

She remembered Rob's orders in bed, how quickly she'd submitted. But in life, in real life, such as this was, she had never submitted. Not even when it had mattered most. And still she had lost everything.

He took a step closer, his heat reaching out in long fingers to stroke her, sensuous and seductive. "Do you heel to your body's orders?"

"I tread a perilous line," she whispered. "It is best for all of us that I go."

"What do you mean?"

"Do you think it is easy for me? To see you with that . . . *duke* and Elizabeth?"

He made a low sound of frustration.

"What would you ask of me were I to stay? Your words and your actions make no sense at all. You ask me not to leave when you've already chosen the woman who will stand by your side. *She* must be the one to help you make amends to your people."

"Elizabeth is different. She isn't you. She doesn't understand—"

"Are you looking to gain both a mistress and a wife? Do you think she'd honor and obey you if she were to discover your infidelities? Elizabeth is no simpleton, and neither am I."

"No!" He spun away from her and paced the room in agitation. "No. I must never betray my wife."

Holding her ground at the foot of the bed, she laughed bitterly. "Then what? I am to stand by your side as . . . as your *adviser*? As your *friend*? When we have this . . ." She jerked her hand back and forth between the two of them. "When we have this pull between us? How long do you think it would last before one of us succumbed to it? A week? A month? Then what would happen to your vows of fidelity to your English lady?"

Again Cam made a noise of frustration. "I don't know! All I know is that I cannot stand the thought of you leaving."

"As I said. It is for the best."

He covered his face with his hands, then pushed them both through his hair, making it stick up in clumps. Ceana clenched her fists, resisting the urge to go to him and smooth his hair. To soothe the anguished look on his face with a kiss. She knew she held the power to do so.

But her kisses would leave behind another kind of anguish. One far worse than what they endured now.

"I must go," she said quietly. "I must."

He stared at her, his expression a heavy mix of desperation and need that nearly made her knees buckle. Then he gave a crisp nod.

"Duncan is more than capable of caring for your wound. And if you need someone to help you in any other way, go to Rob MacLean," she said. "He is an honorable man."

He nodded again.

"If you are ill, you may come to me."

"Only if I am ill?"

"Aye. Only then."

He stared at her in silence for a long moment. Then his lips thinned into a flat line. "As you wish, Ceana MacNab."

He swiveled on his heel and left her alone, slamming the door behind him.

Ceana stood in the center of her room for long minutes as her heartbeat returned to normal. Her chest was so tight, she thought she might weep. It was an odd, unfamiliar sensation—she hadn't wept in a very long time.

As she stood there, reeling in her emotions, her grandmother's voice sounded in her mind. *Remember Brian, child. Remember what happened when ye fell in love with Brian . . .*

Ceana spun to the shelf where she stowed her medicinals. She'd discovered a fine collection of containers and stoppers in one of the castle's storage rooms, and the housekeeper had encouraged her to take whatever she needed. She turned her focus to remixing and filling the tiny, clean bottles with her medicines and then carefully packing the containers into her trunk.

An hour later, another knock sounded at her door. The sound of it—a rapid-fire rapping—was different from Cam's knock, and Ceana rose. "Come in."

A harried-looking manservant entered, followed by a stout, sandy-haired woman Ceana recognized as one of the whores from the mountain. Ceana stepped forward, frowning. "What is it?"

"It's Gràinne," the woman cried. "She's been hurt. Terribly hurt."

Gràinne was a member of the tight-knit community of the mountain whores. Ceana turned to fetch her satchel. Kneeling at her trunk, she searched for the most useful medicines and tools.

"How was she hurt?"

"Beaten."

Ceana couldn't repress the angry growl that emerged from her throat.

"It happened at noon. She was well enough to come tell us, but oh, she needs seeing to, Ceana."

Groundsel and vinegar potion for the wounds. Periwinkle ointment for bruising. Foxglove salve for swelling.

Slipping the medicines she would need into her satchel, she turned back to the woman. "Let's go."

Ceana nearly collided with Lady Elizabeth on her way downstairs. The lady had been avoiding Ceana for the past few days, though when her uncle wasn't looking she'd cast a few smiles in her direction. Ceana wasn't surprised. The puffed-up man had probably told Elizabeth that Ceana was unworthy of their attention.

The lady studied the party, taking in the harried expression on their faces. "What has happened?"

"A woman has been hurt, and I must tend to her," Ceana said.

Elizabeth glanced up and down the passageway, then lowered her voice. "Lord Camdonn and the duke have just left to go fishing on the loch. May I go with you?"

Ceana raised her eyebrows in surprise, but could think of no reason to deny her. Perhaps the lass could learn something by going to the mountain—and Ceana knew no one else would have the ballocks to take her there. She gave a brusque nod.

Elizabeth drew up alongside Ceana as they strode out of the living quarters and through the courtyard. Sometime later, they reached the row of scattered cottages near the top of the mountain. The whores of the Glen clustered into a small community here on MacDonald land. Men from the clan and from Camdonn Castle visited the mountain to make use of the services offered by the women, and the whores raised their children and lived in communal peace, for the most part. Ceana had traveled up here occasionally to address some mild women's complaints, and once to deliver a baby when Moira Stewart and the midwife had been unable to attend the birth. Never for this reason, for the MacDonalds weren't the sort to use their females ill, whether they be whores or wives.

Elizabeth studied the row of thatched cottages. "What is this place?"

There were about ten cottages, all told. Primitive one-roomed structures, each occupied by a whore and, if she had any, her children.

Ceana glanced at Elizabeth. "We call it the mountain. It's where the whores live."

Elizabeth's eyes widened, but she didn't comment further. In fact, a small, twisted smile appeared on her face as they strode toward the closest structure—the cottage belonging to Gràinne.

Ceana knocked brusquely and pushed open the door before anyone could answer. This cottage was appointed far more richly than the others. Though the floor was simple hard-packed dirt, there was a glass pane in the window. A rough-hewn table and two spindly wicker-backed chairs occupied the center of the room, but pushed against the wall stood an opulently carved bed, and next to it a fancy chair, with a cushion of red velvet and legs carved to resemble a lion's paws.

It looked like furniture one might find at Camdonn Castle.

Several women crowded the cottage, concern creasing their faces as they looked up at the sound of the door opening. Gràinne lay on her side with her back facing the door. Red hair cascaded around her, and though she burrowed beneath the coverlet, a spray of dark spots covered the red silk. *Blood.*

Ceana squeezed between the women standing at the bedside. "Gràinne."

The whore smiled up at her, but her face was puffy and her brown eyes dim with pain. "Ceana MacNab," she said by way of greeting.

"Where are you injured?"

"Aye, well, my hand is the worst of it."

"Will you show me?" Ceana asked through tight lips. She didn't know this woman well, but that didn't matter. She wanted to kill the bastard who had done this. Any man who treated a woman with such cruelty deserved to be shot.

"Aye."

Ceana pulled down the cover and studied the woman's hand and arm, which were swollen from fingertips to elbow. Gently, she prodded the bones in the fingers, stopping when she came to the wrist. Broken.

Ceana glanced at the women surrounding them, their eyes rounded with curiosity. "Begone, all of you," she commanded. She nodded at Elizabeth, who'd pushed through to stand beside her. "Even you, my lady."

Elizabeth nodded, but Gràinne reached out her uninjured arm. "Nay. You must stay, lass." Her voice was thready, full of pain.

Elizabeth glanced to the right and left, unsure whether the woman had addressed her. "Me?"

"Aye." Gràinne spoke in heavily accented English. "You be the lass our earl brought home from England, is that not so?"

"Yes."

"You must stay. Ceana will require your help, and I wish to know you better. Might be my only chance."

"Certainly I will stay, if you wish it." Elizabeth lowered herself to the edge of the bed and stroked a clump of fiery red hair off Gràinne's cheek. "I will do what I can to help."

Everyone else, meanwhile, had gone, leaving Elizabeth and Ceana alone with Gràinne. Gràinne was one of the most mature of the women on the mountain but, at forty-one years of age, still beautiful and, to her clients, desirable. She kept a brisk business, and while competition sometimes was a destructive force on the mountain, the other women seemed to admire Gràinne.

Ceana continued to assess her injuries and found a broken collarbone, two probable broken ribs, and scrapes and bruises in a dozen other places. Elizabeth was silent throughout the examination, and finally Ceana glanced at her. Whatever feelings Elizabeth had about the beaten woman lying on the bed, she kept them well hidden. Her tight, pale lips were her only evidence of emotion as she gently tugged away strands of Gràinne's red hair from blood dried on her skin.

Well, who would have thought the wee Englishwoman would have such a pleasant bedside demeanor? If she were a villager, Ceana might have considered apprenticing her.

Ceana turned her attention to an open wound on Gràinne's arm. It looked like someone had sliced at it with a dirk. She prodded the angry, swollen flesh around it. "Have you any water?"

"Aye," the woman breathed. "On the fire. Should be well warmed by now."

Ceana glanced at Elizabeth, who turned to fetch it. Ceana withdrew a clean cloth from her satchel. "First we're going to clean the wounds; then I'll set and bind your wrist. The cut isn't deep enough to require stitches."

"Aye."

Ceana met Elizabeth's gaze across the bed. "Will you help me clean off the blood?"

Elizabeth nodded, her expression grave yet free of fear or revulsion.

Ceana took a small bottle from her pouch and poured the contents into the pot of water Elizabeth had placed on the floor beside her. "This will disinfect the water," Ceana murmured. "It possesses a charm to remove the evil spirits."

She spoke in terms Gràinne would understand, not mentioning the antiputrefaction qualities of the herbal ingredients, which she knew to be as effective as any charm.

In silence, they cleaned Gràinne's wounds. The woman's forehead glistened with sweat, and she clenched the wool blanket in her hand but kept her lips pressed together as if she were determined not to cry.

Elizabeth was the one to break the extended quiet. "Who did this to you?"

Gràinne opened her lips, and a gasp leaked through before she responded. "'Twas a man I knew long ago in Inverness. I haven't any idea why he came."

"Alan will punish him," Ceana promised. Alan MacDonald possessed a gentle nature and an abiding respect for women. He wouldn't tolerate this.

Gràinne closed her eyes. "I think he's gone. Or hiding. He . . . he was an acquaintance of my husband's. Long ago, when I was married."

Elizabeth's slender throat moved as she swallowed. "Tell us what happened. How did he do this to you?"

"He came up here in innocence, I suppose. He always had violent tendencies . . ." Grainne shuddered. "But I think he desired a fast tup before moving on. I didn't recognize him at first, and I served him a bit of claret in exchange for his silver." A tear seeped from the corner of her eye. "I recognized him then. I demanded he leave. I shouldn't have done that. When he remembered who I was, he . . . tried to tie me to the bedposts. I . . . fought him. Perhaps not the wisest idea for a woman in my position, but I wanted nothing of that man."

Ceana ground her teeth. Her cheeks were hot with anger. "Did he rape you?"

Gràinne blinked. "Aye."

"Is there pain? Did he hurt you?"

"Nay," Gràinne said quietly. "That part of me, at least, is well enough. He had the forethought to ease the way with goose grease."

Blowing out a breath through her pursed lips, Ceana dumped the soiled cloth into the hot water. She pushed up her sleeves. "I'm going to manipulate your wrist now, Gràinne. I'll do it as gently as I can, but it's going to hurt. Do you want me to call in some of the others to hold you down?"

"Nay." Gràinne's eyes shifted to Elizabeth. "Tell me what you think of our earl, lass. It'll help take my mind from the pain."

Ceana concentrated on Gràinne's wrist, searching for the location of the break. Gràinne gasped.

"I . . . Well, he's very kind," Elizabeth said quickly.

This elicited a tight smile from Gràinne as Ceana began to press harder on the bone. "Aye? I believe so too, but many others would disagree. He's . . ." She paused, wincing. "He has the reputation of a self-serving kind of man."

Elizabeth shrugged. "Be that as it may—of course, there's some consideration one must pay to one's status in life—I daresay he's kind in his heart."

"Do you—" Again, Gràinne gasped. "Do you love him deeply?"

"Oh, yes."

Elizabeth's response was automatic, and Ceana read the disingenuousness immediately. As did Gràinne, who chuckled humorlessly.

Ceana pushed the bone back in place, and all was silent in the cottage save Gràinne's rasping breaths as she valiantly attempted to prevent herself from screaming. Water leaked from the corners of her clenched eyes. With her good hand, she clasped Elizabeth's fingers in a death grip. Elizabeth kept her lips tight and squeezed Gràinne's hand, her face awash with sympathy.

Finally, long minutes after Ceana had finished manipulating her wrist, Gràinne opened her eyes. "You needn't spout falsehoods, milady. Most of us understand that love often comes far into a marriage and oftentimes not at all."

"I love him," Elizabeth said mulishly. "It is no lie."

"Well, then." Gràinne's eyelids slipped closed again as Ceana began to bind her wrist.

"Why do you ask me these questions?" Elizabeth murmured. "Do you know my betrothed?"

"Oh, aye. I do."

"You know him well, I think," Elizabeth accused. "Better than most. Most of the people of the Glen do not understand him, but you do."

Ceana's heartbeat ratcheted upward. Elizabeth had observed more about Cam's nature than she'd let on.

Ceana glanced from Gràinne's wrist to her pale face to the carved bedpost. Had the whore been Cam's lover? The thought did not elicit tender feelings within her.

Taking a deep breath, she gently released her tightening grip on Gràinne's arm and finished tying off the bandage. She'd need to fashion a sling, for she didn't want Gràinne to be using her wrist at all for some time.

"I do know him well," Gràinne said in a low voice. "He is a friend to me, and he has been for many a year."

"Do you share his bed?" Elizabeth asked bluntly.

Ceana snapped her head up in surprise. She didn't speak, for Elizabeth's words had yanked all air from her body. Like all the MacNab women, Ceana was known for her directness. But it seemed this young Englishwoman had her beaten.

Gràinne chuckled again. "No simpleton, are you, lass?"

"No," Elizabeth said tightly. "At times I choose to feign it, but I am not." Her embroidered bodice rose as she took a deep breath. "The earl's past liaisons shall not affect me. It would really be rather silly of me to react at all."

Ceana's surprise dwindled, leaving a lingering respect. Elizabeth was not going to be a sniveling, jealous wife prone to crying jags and fits of vapors. She was as strong as any Highland woman.

"Our earl has chosen well," Gràinne murmured.

Elizabeth suddenly leaned forward, her eyes bright. "Tell me everything about him, Gràinne. I haven't the faintest idea how to please him, and I do hope you will teach me."

Ceana took a measured breath, certain the gods had placed her with these women solely to torture her. What had she done to deserve this torment?

She ground her teeth and locked her jaw. She was not one to shelter her thoughts, but it was imperative she do so in the company of Cam's mistress and his future wife.

It would be a miracle if she survived the afternoon.

CHAPTER EIGHT

Elizabeth was tending to the fire when the door to Gràinne's cottage flew open. She glanced up to see Cam stride in, followed by Rob MacLean, who paused at the door. His amber gaze perused the room until it landed on her.

She'd hardly seen him since the night they'd met at the cave. But she'd dreamed about him, and a flush prickled over her body as she remembered his lips, soft and supple, gliding over her skin in her dream as she'd stroked the dips and curves of his muscular arms and shoulders.

She'd already had an odd afternoon, filled as it had been with honesty and lined with compassion for the woman who'd been so wretchedly mistreated. But when she locked eyes with Robert MacLean, a whole host of new emotions burst through and then exploded in a shower of bright sparks. When his gaze collided with hers, a million tiny burning lights settled over her heart. She sighed with the beauty of it. She felt trust . . . comfort, relief, excitement, and fascination with the man who'd followed her betrothed into the cottage.

As impossible as it was, how freeing, how wonderful it felt, when she'd thought she'd never experience any of those emotions again.

Rob's warm gaze lingered on her; then he stepped outside and closed the door behind him.

"What happened?" Cam demanded, his focus entirely on the sole occupant of the bed. "Speak to me, Gràinne."

"I'm quite all right. Ceana has taken good care of me."

Cam closed his eyes, then opened them. In this light, his eyes appeared black and hard, reminding Elizabeth of a shiny obsidian rock she'd seen once in London.

"Where is the bastard? I'll kill him."

So this woman wasn't only Cam's occasional bedmate. He cared for her. The truth should have made Elizabeth mad with jealousy, but oddly, it warmed her to him.

"Och," Gràinne said to the earl. "Don't fret over him. He's long gone, and he'll not be back."

Elizabeth glanced at Ceana, who stood quietly beside Cam, her eyes downcast. She didn't understand the woman. One moment she was the strongest person Elizabeth had ever seen: direct and forthright, intimidating and unstoppable. The next she was quiet, almost shy.

Cam still hadn't seen Elizabeth. She didn't know him well enough to guess how he'd react to discovering her in a loose woman's abode, and she didn't dare contemplate what might happen if Uncle Walter found out. Better she remained hunched beside the fireplace than draw attention to herself.

Cam loomed over Gràinne, fists clenching and unclenching at his sides. His gaze slid to Ceana. "How bad is it?"

"She'll recover. I've tended to her wounds. She should remain in bed for a day or two."

"I'll send someone up to look after her."

"Nay," Gràinne said. "My friends will care for me well enough. Better my peers than someone down the mountain who will look upon me in disgust and resent the help you force them to offer me. Unlike your young bride over there, who's been generous in contrast."

Cam's gaze snapped to the hearth, and his eyes widened to black pools. "Elizabeth?" His jaw worked as he searched for something to say. "What . . . what the devil are you doing here?"

Ceana straightened. "She came with me."

As Elizabeth rose from her crouched position, a deep red spread across Cam's cheekbones. He looked back and forth from Ceana to Elizabeth. "You shouldn't be here."

"I am all right, my lord."

Cam's lips tightened. "No, you are not all right. It is inappropriate and unseemly for you to be anywhere near the mountain. I shall take you home. Immediately." He straightened and backed away from the bed, but Ceana caught his arm.

"Don't be absurd," she snapped. Elizabeth was relieved to see that Ceana's more natural demeanor had returned.

Cam glowered at Ceana. "What?"

"You mustn't shelter the lass, Cam. Don't think you can keep her locked away in Camdonn Castle for the remainder of her days."

Cam's brows arched. "Why not?"

"She's to be your countess, not your prisoner."

Cam flicked a glance at her, then returned his attention to Ceana. "You don't understand. You do not know how delicate she is. How sensitive. She's a duke's niece. She's unused to Highland ways. She's *English*, for God's sake. Not a Highlander."

All three women met these remarks with silence. Ceana's expression turned hard as stone. Gràinne looked in Elizabeth's direction, her lips curving wickedly, as if daring her to contradict the earl. Elizabeth lowered her gaze. She was trained—perhaps too well—not to interfere when others spoke of her. Her opinion didn't matter. She'd been reminded of that fact time and again through the years. And if Cam were to tell her uncle she'd opposed him . . . she didn't dare imagine the consequences.

In any case, if she did speak, what would she say? Did Cam truly expect her to live like an English lady here? The differences between this place and her home were too vast. Even if she remained sequestered within the castle, her life had already changed irrevocably.

Ceana glanced at her, and when Elizabeth didn't come to her own defense, she narrowed her eyes at Cam. "That's a foolish thing to say. Take a hard look at the lass. Not at her past, but at her. See who she is."

Elizabeth felt Cam's gaze burning into her bowed head. "I see a frightened girl who wishes to go home. I cannot believe you brought her here, Ceana. I thought you wiser than that."

"And I took you for something other than a fool!" Ceana spat.

"Come, Elizabeth. I'll take you home." He took her arm and led her toward the door. "Will you wait outside for me? I must speak to . . . to Gràinne for a moment."

"Of course," she murmured.

"MacLean will look out for you."

He left her on the front stoop and turned, shutting the door behind him, leaving Elizabeth to meet Rob's steady gaze.

"Good afternoon."

He inclined his head. He didn't say a word, but his eyes spoke volumes. He wondered why she'd come here, what she'd learned, what she was thinking.

It was a warm afternoon, and Elizabeth adjusted her bonnet so that the sun wouldn't shine directly on her face and cause her skin to freckle. She glanced down the dirt path strung between the cottages. A group of women stood clustered a short distance away, casting curious glances toward them. Elizabeth pulled her gloves from where she'd tucked them into her belt and tugged them on.

The door opened and Cam emerged. "Forgive me."

She took his proffered arm. "Nothing at all to forgive."

Cam blew out a frustrated breath. Rob glanced at him, then away. Elizabeth nearly smiled. Everyone knew exactly what had happened here, understood the association between Cam and Gràinne, but the men were too cowardly to discuss it in her presence. Cam was deeply concerned for the whore, and he likely expected Elizabeth to be either angry or appalled. He couldn't possibly understand that she was only curious and interested. She wanted to see Gràinne soon to make certain she was all right. Perhaps Ceana would bring her to the mountain again.

But Uncle Walter . . .

He and Cam had said they'd return from their fishing expedition tomorrow. The weather was fine, and there was no reason for them to have returned earlier. Unless someone had gone after Cam to inform him about Gràinne, she realized. Lord, what a fool she'd been. She was so stupid, so terribly stupid. She'd been a fool to think she'd be safe today. Her selfishness was responsible for this. Her impetuous, thoughtless nature. Her craving to explore, to be outside, to spend time with Ceana . . .

Elizabeth shuddered. Uncle Walter would be angry, and there was nothing she could do to prevent the repercussions. Bitsy's tortured face imprinted itself on her mind. *Please God*, she prayed. *Make him lenient.*

Cam cursed under his breath. "I'm sorry, Elizabeth. You should not have seen that. I cannot fathom what Ceana was thinking."

"Truly, it is all right," she murmured. "Please don't blame Miss MacNab. I . . . I wanted to come. I asked her to bring me along."

There. She'd said it. The truth. She held her breath.

He frowned down at her. "Why?"

"I like Ceana. She is . . . my friend."

He frowned harder. But he looked away without comment, leaving an unsettled feeling fluttering in her stomach. She'd half expected him to forbid her to associate with Ceana, as her uncle had.

"I . . ." Cam's voice faltered. He took a deep breath and tried again. "Gràinne . . . She is an old acquaintance of mine."

Looking up at him from beneath her eyelashes, she nodded.

"I just wanted to let you know." His voice sounded strangled as he spoke. "You must know that she is no threat to you, Elizabeth."

"Oh," Elizabeth murmured. "I didn't—"

"Of course you did not," Cam interrupted. His stance was so taut, she thought if she pushed him, he might break into a thousand pieces. "I merely didn't want you to succumb to any notion that she could threaten you or your status. In any way."

As always, their communications were formal, even awkward.

Would it always be this way? She took a breath. "Yes, my lord. Of course. I understand. As the earl, you are concerned about *all* of your neighbors."

Cam glanced heavenward as if in thankfulness; then he relaxed a little and smiled at her. "Yes, that's right. That's exactly it."

Rob and Cam flanked her as they walked toward two horses. Elizabeth's breath caught. "Ceana said you weren't to ride, my lord."

"I didn't have a choice," Cam said grimly. "I had to make . . ." He glanced at her, looked away, then continued. "I had to be certain Gràinne was all right."

"How is your shoulder?" she asked quietly.

"Ceana bound it tightly this morning, and the scab held."

Elizabeth released a breath of relief. "She'll throttle you if she hears you rode."

"Yes." He glanced at Rob. "We'll keep this between the three of us, I think."

Focused on the horses, Rob nodded but didn't speak.

Cam mounted and then reached down with his good hand to pull her up. Elizabeth paused. She didn't hesitate because she'd rather ride with Rob. Truly, she didn't. She hesitated out of concern for her betrothed's injured shoulder.

"My lord." She twisted her hands. "Please. I don't wish to risk your wound."

Rob, already mounted, turned his horse until it stood behind her. "She ought to ride with me, milord. So as not to cause you further injury."

Cam ground his teeth and muttered under his breath, but he relinquished her to Rob. Just the thought of riding with Robert MacLean— a joy she'd thought to never experience again—sent shivers of delight coursing through her.

Under Cam's watchful eye, Rob dismounted and, in a fluid motion, lifted her onto the saddle and then remounted behind her.

Cam motioned them ahead, for the path was too narrow for two horses side by side. They began the slow climb down the mountain in utter quiet.

As they descended, Elizabeth studied the details of her surroundings. Baby leaves had begun to sprout on the trees, speckling the dull brown branches with vivid green. She'd always loved spring best of all the seasons, and surely there had to be some significance to her leaving Purefoy Abbey to be married at this time of year.

Heather grew everywhere, covering the ground in long, stretching clumps. They rode past tall pines, clumps of thin-trunked trees, and bushes budding with violet flowers. She wondered what they'd look like when they opened. Whether they'd smell sweet or bitter, or have no smell at all.

Rob's knee pressed against her thigh and his arm was clamped around her waist so she wouldn't fall if the horse sidestepped or fumbled. Yet he held himself as stiff as a pike, no doubt aware of the earl's eyes boring into them from behind.

"You were easier with me that night at the loch," she murmured.

"Aye."

She glanced over her shoulder at him. "And you responded to me. With more than one word."

His lips twitched. "Aye, so I did."

"But you don't now."

"It wouldn't be wise."

She sighed. "Well, that's likely true." She let her fingertip trail over the top of the hand clamped over her middle. Quietly, she traced every long finger up to the edge of his sleeve cuff. He had beautiful hands.

"Elizabeth," he said on a soft groan. "You shouldn't touch me."

She dropped her hand, fighting a smile. "You called me Elizabeth."

"You'd prefer 'milady'?"

"No," she said instantly. "Not from you." She liked the sound of her name rolling off his tongue in his brogue.

She looked back over her shoulder to see him smiling at her. It was beautiful, natural, and she realized she'd never seen him smile before. It stole her breath away.

"Tell me . . ." She paused. She wanted to know more about him. About his childhood, about his life, about his dreams and desires. "Do you have brothers and sisters?"

"Nay."

"What about your mother? Do you know anything about her?"

"Very little."

"Do you know why she . . . ?"

His hand tightened around her waist. "She was seduced," he murmured after a long pause. "By power. By silver. That is what my da told me." He sighed. "I believe him."

"Did she love the man she . . . strayed with? Your real father?"

"I don't know."

She was silent for a long moment. She touched his hand again, pressing her palm against it. Every inch of her body burned for him. Yet she could never have him. He would remain an unfulfilled dream, because even when Uncle Walter was long gone, she could not risk her marriage to Cam.

She wished it were different. She willed it to be different. But the truth remained. Rob MacLean with his burnt-sugar eyes and his thick coffee hair was an untouchable dream. A fantasy.

Life consisted of sacrifices; she knew that well. She wanted Rob MacLean, but she wouldn't die for lack of having him. In her lifetime, she'd suffered far worse. She would enjoy their stolen moments—she would enjoy the present—and try not to crave more.

Stiffening her resolve, Elizabeth returned her attention to their surroundings. Ahead, through the scrubby trees and brush, the sun cast a metallic gleam over the rippling waters of the loch. The tower of the main keep at Camdonn Castle peeked above the rocky terrain and foliage.

Soon they traversed the winding path across the narrowest part of the spit leading to the castle gates, and with each step closer, Elizabeth's chest grew tighter. She couldn't call back to Cam now. The realization that she should have ridden with him, somehow convinced him not to tell Uncle Walter of this afternoon's excursion, came too late.

She closed her eyes against the welling panic. Rob's hand tightened over her belly. "Are you well?"

Of course Rob sensed her distress. He understood her like no one else. She nodded numbly. Nothing Rob could do would stop Uncle Walter if Cam told him where he'd found her.

As soon as they opened the gates and rode into the courtyard, she saw the familiar white-wigged head bobbing toward them.

"What's wrong, Elizabeth?"

She scarcely heard Rob's concerned voice. All she could see was her uncle coming into view. All she could hear was the blood roaring in her ears.

The horse came to a halt, and Rob dismounted and lifted her down. Cam stopped just behind them.

Her uncle, concern creasing his face, hurried up to them. Ignoring the men, he asked, "Where have you been, Lizzy?"

"She was up the mountain with Ceana MacNab," Cam supplied before Elizabeth could say a word.

Elizabeth held herself rigid as her uncle's cold gaze skimmed over her.

"Is that so?"

"I thought it would be best if I brought her home."

"Of course." Rage—rage she knew well—flared in her uncle's pale blue eyes, but it disappeared before anyone else could identify it.

It was all she could do to stay upright. She considered falling at Cam's and Rob's feet, sobbing, revealing everything, and begging for them to protect her . . . to protect Bitsy.

But Uncle Walter had a way about him that made him appear sane in the face of everyone else's insanity. She would lose the battle. She always did.

She blinked hard. She felt Rob's eyes on her, but she didn't dare glance in his direction.

"Well," her uncle said pleasantly. "We've half an hour before dinner, Lizzy. You should go ready yourself."

She made a small curtsy. "Yes, Uncle."

Woodenly, she strode toward the keep, feeling the weight of all three men's stares as she disappeared inside.

CHAPTER NINE

The duke shook his head as they watched Elizabeth disappear into the living quarters. "My poor niece looks exhausted. She is truly a delicate creature. A precious gem. I shall have her maid make her a posset."

"That sounds like a very good idea." Cam had studied Elizabeth's relationship with her uncle for the past several weeks. Irvington was protective of his niece to a fault, and it was clear that she deeply respected him in turn. "I am sorry we were forced to call our outing short, Irvington."

The duke waved his hand. "No matter. It is likely for the best that we came back early." He pressed his fingers to his chest. "Sometimes Elizabeth can be impetuous, and she forgets her place. I do worry for her safety in these circumstances. Cavorting with a commoner—"

"Everyone in the Glen knows Ceana MacNab. A friend of hers is a friend to all. She is safe with Ceana."

The duke took a deep breath. "And yet the woman is a pagan healer of dubious reputation. Should a duke's niece be seen with such a woman?"

Cam remained very still, battling the rage that swelled in him at the man's disparaging remarks toward Ceana. Finally, he said tightly, "The Highlands are different from England."

The duke nodded gravely. "Yes, of course. In this, as in all things, I trust your judgment, Camdonn."

Adjusting his wig, the duke hurried after his niece, and Cam turned to the stables. He'd needed to do right by Elizabeth and make sure she arrived home safely, but now he must return to the mountain and see to Gràinne. He needed to speak with her, glean more information about her attacker and where the man had gone. The bastard would be caught.

Cam chose a fresh mount and began to saddle it himself. Sensing movement, he glanced up to see the figure of Robert MacLean blocking the stall door.

"I can do that for you, milord."

"It's not necessary."

"You're returning to the mountain?"

"Yes."

MacLean nodded. As Cam cinched the buckle around the horse's girth, he glanced up at the other man. "Any news on the highwaymen?"

"Nay. I believe people have information, but they've seen me with you. Might be they no longer feel I am to be trusted."

Cam nodded. He trusted MacLean as much as he could trust any man, save Alan, whom Cam had scarcely seen since his return to the Glen. He knew it was for the best. Alan had become his crutch, but he no longer required a crutch. This was a problem he must manage by himself. Hell, if he couldn't get to the bottom of the attack without Alan's help, he deserved whatever fate befell him.

As he rode up the mountain, Cam thought of Gràinne and the man who'd abused her. Could there be some connection between the attack on her and the one on himself?

His shoulder throbbed with every step of the horse, and his thoughts turned to Ceana MacNab. When he'd grown angry with her for bringing poor Elizabeth to the mountain—hell, what had the woman been thinking?—she'd stood up for her choices, despite the folly of them.

Cam knew Englishwomen. He'd lived among that particular breed of woman most of his life. He knew exactly what was required to keep an English female content. It was simple: Protect her from harm, coddle her, keep her clothed in the highest fashion, loosen the purse strings, and shower her with compliments and attention when she was near. They were simple creatures—easy to please, easy to keep. Elizabeth had never hinted that she was any different.

He hoped Ceana hadn't upset her too greatly by bringing her up to the mountain. What thoughts had run through her mind when she'd seen the abuse inflicted on poor Gràinne? He shuddered at the thought. Hopefully the girl would soon be able to push the experience from her memory.

Meanwhile, he rode back toward Gràinne, the woman who'd served as his on-and-off lover for years, and Ceana, the woman he'd never touched carnally but whose body he craved every second of the day.

This morning when Ceana had said she was leaving Camdonn Castle, the beast within him had reared its head and roared for her, bringing to life thoughts similar to those he'd had in the month before he'd abducted Sorcha from her marriage bed. Need. Desire. *Obsession.*

The urge to force her to stay at Camdonn Castle had surged through him. Before he could stop the thoughts, he'd considered locking her in his room, tying her to the bed, holding her down and kissing her, touching her body, taking her until she was insensible to anything other than his body, his need.

He banished those debauched thoughts. Nevertheless, they shimmered on the edge of his consciousness, thrilling him, tempting him.

Ceana had best go. Before temptation overruled reason. He'd quell the beast until his marriage a few weeks hence, and then his future would be set in stone.

There was more at stake now than there had been with Sorcha. He was about to be married, with the endorsement of the king and the Duke of Argyll, to the lovely niece of an English duke. He couldn't botch this, for this time the repercussions would extend far beyond the borders of his own lands. He'd embarrass the man who'd suggested the match—the Duke of Argyll. He'd disappoint the king. He'd lose the respect of the powerful lords of England and Scotland that he'd struggled so hard to attain.

The way Ceana made him feel made no sense. His feelings for her conflicted with all his carefully laid-out plans.

After all that had happened, he hadn't learned, hadn't changed. He was no better than he'd been more than a year ago, when he'd taken Sorcha from her marriage bed. He was debauched to his soul. He was a man incapable of learning from his mistakes, unworthy of leadership. He was not an honorable man.

He'd tried so hard to change his goals, to follow the right and proper path. He'd chosen the perfect woman to take to wife. He'd re-aligned his goals for the betterment of the people who surrounded him.

But it was not honorable to feel this burning, raging need for Ceana when he had pledged himself to someone else. It was not honorable to allow himself to be diverted from his aim.

Once again, he was dreaming about something that could never be. He'd thought he could be a true gentleman and make wise choices that befitted his rank, but when he began to feel desire, the line between what he should do and what he must do faded away, leaving him with nothing to grasp onto but his own base needs.

This time, he could not let the obsession overwhelm him. This time, he risked so much more. He must not allow the fire to consume him.

As much as it tried to slither away from him, he must . . . he *must* keep a firm hold on his honor.

Reaching Gràinne's cottage, he tied his horse to the post beside the door and let himself in. Ceana rose from the bedside and hurried toward him, raising her hand to stop him from speaking. "She's asleep," she whispered. "I gave her a calming draft."

Cam jerked his head to the door and Ceana nodded, then followed him outside. He closed the door behind them and walked to the side of the cottage, where they would be hidden from the curious eyes of the other women.

"Did she give you any more details?" he asked.

"No." Tiredly, Ceana tucked a stray curl behind her ear. "Just that he was an acquaintance from Inverness."

Clenching his fists, Cam stared at the spindly pine trees that lined the path leading down the mountain.

"You care for her," Ceana murmured.

"Yes."

"You and she—"

"Yes." Cam swallowed. "She was my first."

Ceana's eyes widened with interest. "Is that so? I thought you spent your childhood in England."

"I did, but I returned home on occasion. On one of those visits, I came with the goal to be relieved of my virginity."

"So you went to the mountain."

Cam nodded. The tip of Ceana's tongue swiped over her lips, and Cam's cock jumped to life. He glanced away. "I hate that she's hurt."

"So do I." After a pause, Ceana looked up at him. "Is she still your lover?"

"No."

She pursed her lips. "Good."

He reached out and slid his fingers over hers. They stood for several minutes in silence, their hands clasped as they looked down the heather-covered slope of the mountain.

Elizabeth didn't eat a bite of her dinner, for she was certain that if she did force something down, it would travel straight back up. She managed a taste of claret, but even that made her stomach rumble and complain. Her uncle watched her throughout the meal with eyes narrowed into slits, but he didn't comment beyond the banal dinner conversation they had spent endless nights perfecting.

The fact that Cam and Ceana hadn't appeared made it even more unbearable. A sickening fear stormed incessantly through her, leaving her adrift on a violent ocean, unable to combat the seasickness.

Afterward, she and Uncle Walter retired to the drawing room, where Cam eventually joined them. She and Cam continued the game of chess they'd been playing, but it couldn't hold her attention.

"You look fatigued this evening, Elizabeth," Cam said stiffly. "I hope you are sufficiently recovered from this afternoon's adventure."

She flicked a glance at Uncle Walter, who sat in one of the silk-covered armchairs reading a religious treatise. "Everything is very well, thank you, my lord. Perhaps I am a little tired."

The gentlemen excused her, and shortly afterward, Elizabeth lay rigid in bed, eyes closed. She tried not to shake, tried not to imagine the forthcoming punishment.

Please let Uncle Walter come in alone. Please let him give me one more chance. If he comes alone, I shall never speak to Ceana MacNab for the rest of my life. I swear it.

As she did each time she'd earned a punishment, her mind filtered through her options. Could she go to someone? Cam? Explain everything to him? What then? He'd approach her uncle, who would convince Cam of his innocence. Uncle Walter was a duke, above reproach.

The last time she'd trusted someone enough to ask for help—her governess—the woman had believed her uncle when he said she'd been altered by the deaths of her parents. They'd threatened her with Bedlam. For so long, people had looked at her with pity in their eyes. It had taken years to undo the rumors that she'd gone mad.

Perhaps she could run away. She'd escaped from Purefoy Abbey on one occasion, when her uncle had gone to fetch Bitsy for a punishment. Uncle Walter had forgotten all about Bitsy until his men had found Elizabeth shivering in a nearby abandoned barn the following afternoon. She'd learned two important lessons as a result of that ordeal. The first was that if she wasn't present, her uncle had no reason to abuse Bitsy, and her maid would be safe. The second was that when Elizabeth returned, the repercussions would be severe.

She couldn't run away. Where would she go, and what would she do? She didn't know the Highlands well enough, and if she was found, she didn't doubt that the reprisal to Bitsy would be more than either of them could bear.

Hopeless options still tumbled about in her mind until the clock struck one and Uncle Walter opened the door. "Are you awake, Lizzy?"

She couldn't summon the voice to answer.

He entered her room, and relief coursed through Elizabeth, for he was alone and empty-handed. But the relief turned into ice-cold panic when wavering candlelight came into view behind him.

"No," she whispered.

"You leave me no choice." He sounded tired. "You will never learn."

Bitsy appeared at the door, holding the flickering candle, her face sallow behind the yellow light. "You should beat me, Uncle," Elizabeth said breathlessly. "Please. Beat *me* instead. Perhaps then I will learn."

He sighed. "I wish I could, but you know the many reasons why I cannot. You're to be married in less than a month. We can't have you unable to sit at your own wedding feast, now, can we?"

Bitsy set the candle on the table beside the door and stood just inside with her arms clasped behind her back, staring at the floor.

This couldn't be happening. Panic surged through Elizabeth as she looked desperately from the windows to the door. "Please . . ."

She couldn't scream, couldn't fight. She'd tried both before, and to punish her for being difficult, he'd made it worse for Bitsy.

All she could do was watch. She slid her gaze to her maid, who stood still, her thin body vibrating like a plucked violin string.

"Go to the bed," Uncle Walter ordered, not deigning to look at the frightened woman.

Mechanically, keeping her gaze averted from Elizabeth, Bitsy walked to the bed. She lay on her stomach beside Elizabeth, hitching up her skirts until she revealed her pale, bare buttocks.

A small whimper leaked from Elizabeth's throat, and she looked away.

"Pay attention," he snapped.

Her eyes watered. Streams of liquid rolled down her cheeks. "Please," she whispered.

"Quiet!" He strode to the side of the bed and shoved Bitsy's skirt higher up her back. "Your mistress has been disobedient again, girl, so you must take another punishment for her."

Elizabeth choked back a sob. "No!"

"You defied me, Elizabeth. After I warned you, very clearly, against doing so."

Uncle Walter's reptilian eyes flicked to Elizabeth, ensuring she watched. She was well trained by now. Knew that she must observe every moment, every detail. She must follow the rules he'd laid out at the beginning, or he would make it worse.

"How many strokes? Ten?" He shook his head gravely. "No, twenty. I think twenty will do it."

Elizabeth released a low sound of disagreement and shook her head vehemently. The last punishment she'd received was at Purefoy Abbey a year ago. He'd caught her sneaking into the village to deliver a satchel of stolen books from his library to a boy who wanted to learn how to read. Twenty strokes. It was the harshest beating to date. Bitsy wouldn't sit for days.

He pulled his paddle from an inside pocket of his coat. It was a long, narrow strip of wood that, when hit against flesh, made a *thwack*—a sound Elizabeth had grown to equate with suffering.

Bitsy made a low murmur, anticipating the pain.

"Be still, or I'll make it thirty," Uncle Walter commanded.

When the first strike came down over her buttocks, the maid flinched and released a low, gravelly cry. Uncle Walter closed his hand over the top part of her skinny thigh and pinned her to the bed as he released another hard blow low on her back. Elizabeth watched, stoic, frozen, but a deep, dark emotion twisted inside her, scraping against all the shields she'd built to keep it contained.

Blows rained down on her maid's back, thighs, and buttocks. At five strokes, the pale flesh pinkened, and at ten, welts erupted over her skin. At fifteen strokes, blood streaked her buttocks, and she began to make sobbing noises that tore at Elizabeth's chest.

Elizabeth watched it all, her body quivering, the coverlet held to her throat.

Since she'd arrived in the Highlands, she'd been lured by the promise of friendship, by the idea that she someday might belong, and that had begun to soften her. But she would never find that elusive happiness, acceptance, desire. She wrought only pain and suffering on others. She was a naive fool to have forgotten it.

Her uncle finally stopped. Mottled red spots covered his face, and sweat beaded on his forehead. His close-cropped graying hair stood up in sparse, damp spikes over his head.

He leaned down over Bitsy and gave her his standard warning. "You speak of this to anyone, and the pain you feel now will be merely a soft caress. Do you understand?"

The steely hardness of his tone made it clear that he did not exaggerate. Elizabeth wondered why he bothered with his warning. Bitsy believed every word Uncle Walter told her, and she had never dared to speak to anyone of the beatings. Elizabeth knew that some of the servants at Purefoy Abbey had suspected what was happening, and she'd noted their special kindness to the withdrawn maidservant, but still Bitsy never talked.

He shoved the paddle back into his coat. Elizabeth didn't watch him leave. Instead she scrambled off the bed, only a dim part of her brain registering the door clicking shut behind her uncle.

She reached down and touched Bitsy's cheek. "Stay there. Don't move."

Long ago, she'd bribed one of the older housemaids at Purefoy Abbey to give her a gallon of the soothing unguent the woman had once made for her brother when he'd fallen and scraped his knee. As a child, Elizabeth had seen the sweet-smelling concoction as a miracle cure, because his tears had turned to smiles and he'd jumped out of her lap and continued running about the countryside, with Elizabeth and their nurse trailing behind him.

I'm sorry, Bitsy. And William, and Mama and Papa. I'm so, so sorry . . .

Now all that was left of the unguent fit into a small jar. Elizabeth stumbled to her dressing table, finding the bottle where she kept it among her lotions and perfumes. Removing the stopper, she returned to Bitsy, who still lay on her stomach on the bed, unmoving but for her chattering teeth.

Elizabeth swallowed. "I'm sorry, Bitsy."

Bitsy stared at her with blank eyes. There was no pain, no anger. Just a dark, fathomless blankness.

Biting her lip hard enough to draw blood, Elizabeth smoothed the medicine over the hot, flame-red marks on her servant's backside.

Her fingernail scraped the bottom of the little unguent bottle. Irrational panic bubbled up within Elizabeth. What would she do the next time this happened? She'd have nothing with which to help Bitsy.

Impulsively, she jumped off the bed and returned to her dressing table to open the single drawer. She removed the smallest of the jewelry boxes, the one containing her mother's diamonds.

She returned to the bed, carrying the box. "Bitsy, look at me," she commanded. "Look here."

Slowly, Bitsy's eyes came to focus on her.

Elizabeth opened the lid and tilted the box so that Bitsy could see the contents. "I want you to take these. I want you to run away."

Some life flared into Bitsy's eyes. "No." Her voice was a harsh croak. "No, milady."

"He hurts you . . ."

"If I weren't here, he'd hurt you. Or someone else."

Elizabeth's eyes stung. "I don't care." For goodness' sake, she *wanted* Uncle Walter to hurt her. It would be far less painful than being responsible for someone else's suffering.

"I won't go."

"Please, Bitsy. Please. I cannot bear to watch him do this to you again."

Bitsy closed her eyes. "There is nowhere for me to go."

Elizabeth remembered Gràinne, the mountain, how all the women there had rallied around her. If Bitsy told them her story, they'd protect her as well. She knew they would. "I know where you can go."

"He will be gone soon." ·

But that didn't satisfy Elizabeth. She knew herself. She knew her uncle. He'd executed tonight's punishment with more glee—and more might—than usual. For some reason, his desire to punish her had increased with their imminent separation. He was searching for a reason to punish her. And she couldn't promise she could prevent him from finding another reason. She didn't trust Uncle Walter. Worse, she didn't trust herself.

"Very well." She sighed and replaced the lid. "The offer shall remain open. If this happens again . . ." She took a gulping breath. "I fear for your safety, do you understand?"

"I will be all right," Bitsy said tonelessly.

"You take the diamonds if you like. Anytime. You know where I keep them."

"I shan't be needing them."

Elizabeth shook her head, and as she gently tugged down her maid's skirts, she recited precise directions to the mountain.

A loud, hollow noise resonated downstairs. Rob leaped to his feet, dirk in hand, before he registered that someone was banging at the door to the stables, which he'd bolted before going to bed.

Gripping the dirk, he took the stairs three at a time and threw open the door, convinced someone had come to tell him disgruntled Jacobites had finally killed the Earl of Camdonn.

Instead, with her golden hair falling over shoulders covered only by the material of a thin shift, the future wife of the earl stood before him. Elizabeth's blue eyes were wide, and her shoulders shuddered beneath the thin linen.

Rob glanced beyond her into the empty courtyard, then at the darkened windows of the keep. He took her hand to pull her out of the way of curious eyes and shut the door behind them before relocking it.

He clasped her upper arms. "Why are you here? What happened?"

"I . . . I . . ."

She buried her face in her hands and burst into tears.

Rob gathered her close and lifted her in his arms. She grasped his shirt and turned her face, weeping into his shoulder as he carried her. Once upstairs, he gently set her down on the sofa.

Her sobs subsided as he added peat to the fire, and he felt her eyes coming to focus on him. Already abed when she'd knocked, he wore only a linen shirt that covered him to midthigh.

He glanced at her over his shoulder, then rose and went to sit beside her. Her tears had turned silent, but they still coursed down her cheeks in two clear streaks.

He wished he could kiss them away. Kiss that haughty look back onto her face.

Pulling her against him, he reached up to stroke her hair. "What happened?"

"I . . . cannot tell you."

"You can tell me anything."

Still, she didn't speak.

"What was it? Was it the earl?" *Goddamn*. He stiffened all over but tried not to let her see it. Despite everything, despite his increasing trust and confidence in the earl, he'd kill Cam if he had anything to do with these tears.

"No." She gulped. "Not Cam."

Her fingers curled over his arms and gripped the backs of his shoulders, and she burrowed into his chest. Rob shifted, pulling her more fully onto his lap. She seemed to take comfort from his touch, so he wrapped one arm tightly around her while continuing to stroke her hair with his other hand. After just a few seconds, his cock was so tight and hot, he thought he might explode beneath her.

Hell—this wasn't the time or place for that. He shifted to adjust himself, then ground his teeth and tried to ignore it.

"Who, then, Elizabeth?" he gritted out. "Who has made you cry?"

Her fingers tightened over his shoulders, and she looked up at him with glassy blue eyes that widened when she saw the rage in his own. "You mustn't say or do anything, Rob," she said in a hushed, urgent voice. "Please. Swear it. I don't want you in the middle of this. He's too . . . too powerful."

Those final words melted his confusion.

"Your uncle," Rob said flatly.

Pressing her lips together, she turned her face to the fire.

Rob continued grazing her hair with his fingertips, but inside him a battle raged. What had the man done to her?

God, how could he promise to separate himself from this when she'd chosen him as the man to reveal her sorrow to? Not Cam. It should have been Cam. Yet the thought of thrusting her off his lap and taking her to her betrothed made nausea swirl in his gut. He held her more tightly.

"I'll take care of it," he said quietly.

She whipped her face around so fast, a strand of blond hair stung his cheek. "No!"

"What did he do to you?"

"You are just a stable master. If you face him, you will not win. He'll crush you."

"I am no weakling."

"You're just a servant."

"I'm more than that."

She laughed bitterly. "I might know that. I see the strength in you. But to the Duke of Irvington, you're no more important than a gnat."

"I'm the Earl of Camdonn's brother!"

He blinked in surprise at his outburst, and his eyes stung. He quickly looked away from her in an attempt to regain his composure.

"You're . . . you're Cam's brother?"

He clenched his teeth. What in hell had possessed him to blurt out the truth?

It was *her*. She weakened him. Her vulnerability brought out his own.

"What? How? Does he know?" she said softly.

"No."

It took her several moments to absorb this. "How can he not know?" She gazed up at him, her teary eyes thoughtful. "That is why your father resented you. The earl and your mother . . ."

Rob nodded briskly. "Aye. He never forgave her. Or me."

"I should have known," she murmured. "You are so like him."

He stiffened further. "What do you mean?"

"You remind me of Cam in many ways. You . . . you have the same mannerisms. The same hands."

Rob was silent. Too many unfamiliar feelings tumbled within him. He'd never before revealed his true parentage to anyone.

"Why haven't you told Cam?"

He shrugged. "He hasn't been here to tell. He's spent most of his time in England."

Rob had come to Camdonn Castle seven years ago in hopes of learning more about his father and only brother. He'd remained in the shadows, never approaching the old earl, just watching and learning. The truth of it was, when Rob was younger, his da had said the Earl of Camdonn would never accept him as his own. He'd said Rob belonged to no one.

Upon meeting the earl, he quickly realized it was true. The late Earl of Camdonn was a dour man, a hard man who'd brought only misery to those around him. He'd never have accepted Rob as his son. As the years went by, Rob's disenchantment had grown, and by the time Cam returned home after his father's death, Rob had little desire to reveal their bond.

Despite his resentment and despite his status as a bastard—and an unknown one at that—Rob had remained quietly steadfast first to the old earl and then to Cam. They were his family, even if they didn't know it.

A tear slipped down Elizabeth's cheek, and he brushed it away with his thumb.

"It's all so unfair," she whispered.

"What is?"

"Your life. My life. Bitsy . . ."

"Bitsy?"

"My lady's maid. Uncle Walter . . . He . . . he beats her when I displease him."

He pulled back from her in disbelief. "Why?"

"He is determined that I shall remain untouched. She has always borne my punishments for me. And each time it happens, something in me dies a little more."

Rob sat stunned. "Elizabeth . . ."

"No." Desperation brimmed in her blue eyes before she looked away from him to burrow into his chest again. "Please. Please, Rob, just hold me. You make me feel so safe. When you touch me everything is pure and white, and I am safe from my own horrid self. Everyone is safe. Everything will be all right."

He closed his eyes. Bending his head, he pressed a gentle kiss to the top of her head.

"Very well," he murmured. "I will hold you."

CHAPTER TEN

Cam stared into the face of one of his tenants. Bram MacGregor was angry; that much was clear. The man was itching for a fight.

Cam leaned back on his chair and stared up at the burly man prowling his study, plaid swishing over his hairy legs with every long stride. Robert MacLean stood by the door, his eyes wary and alert as he watched the proceedings, and Cam's young factor, Charles Stewart, stood near Cam's desk. Before he'd left Scotland last year, Cam had taken on Charles, who was Sorcha's brother, as his new factor. Though young, the boy was quick-witted, and since his father had served in the capacity before him, he'd adapted to the duties easily.

Cam had agreed to this audience only because Rob had intervened. Now he was beginning to regret it. Since Ceana had left, his shoulder had not stopped aching, and exhaustion crept through his bones whenever he considered the daunting task that lay before him. How to turn men like Bram MacGregor to his side? Hell if he knew.

"How can I help you, MacGregor?"

"I've come on behalf of Hamish Roberts."

"Ah." The man he'd had removed from his lands as soon as he'd arrived home. Two years ago, Roberts had been leading mobs of MacLeans into Argyll's land to steal and slaughter his cattle. Cam had put a stop to that as soon as he'd heard. Since then, the man—a surly bastard he was, too—hadn't paid his rents. The whole ordeal put a sour taste in Cam's mouth.

"The Robertses have been tenants of the Earls of Camdonn for a hundred years."

"I know that," Cam said.

"And ye've tossed them out. Not only Hamish, but his mother, his wife, and his six bairns."

"He didn't pay his rents. Hasn't paid for quite a while, if my factor's reports are correct."

"Aye, my lord," Charles said from beside him. "It's been over a year since Roberts last paid."

MacGregor drew to a halt in the center of the room, turning furious eyes on Cam. Cam stared back at him, undaunted. First off, though Cam hadn't enforced the Disarming Act on his lands, he didn't allow his tenants to bear arms on castle grounds, so MacGregor carried no weapons. Second, Cam didn't fear anyone. Certainly not this man. The worst he could do to Cam was kill him with his bare hands, but that wouldn't be wise.

Perhaps Bram and the others who treated him with such distrust didn't comprehend exactly how stupid it would be to kill him. If Cam died, the earldom would go to his cousin, a man who'd never stepped foot in the Highlands and possessed no tolerance for anything non-English and non-Whig. At the first sign of seditious intent, he would trample these people into the dust.

Did Bram know this? Cam sighed. Lack of foresight was a problem with many of his Highlanders.

MacGregor threw a sneer across the room. "And how'd ye expect 'em to pay rents? There be no way do so anymore. What with the restrictions ye've placed on the acquisition of cattle, 'tis impossible for them to survive."

"The *acquisition* of cattle?" Cam raised a brow. "You refer to my desire to prevent Argyll's men from slaughtering my own."

"'Tis the way of things." Bram clenched his fists. "Cattle filching is a time-honored tradition. How Highlanders have endured since the dawn of time. 'Tis the only way they know how to survive."

"I won't argue tradition with you, MacGregor. But I won't advance my wealth through thievery, and neither will anyone who lives on my lands."

"Then they'll be starving."

"There is no need for that—not on my lands. There is an abundance of work to do." And plenty of capital with which to do it.

MacGregor's hand flew up. "Where?"

Cam took a deep breath. "I've several projects in mind. I wish to build a road from here to Glenfinnan. Fortify the cliffs and build a larger wharf. Redo the inside walls of the castle outbuildings. Build a new mill. Institute a loan program for the farmers and cattlemen. I need men. The MacDonald laird and I are investing in more stock, so management of the herds will require more manpower. If you know of a man whose family is going hungry due to his idleness, have him come to my factor or myself, and if he proves himself worthy, he will have work."

MacGregor narrowed his eyes. Still he didn't trust him. Cam hadn't expected it to be easy, but he couldn't let this man believe he held the power. Cam was still the master here. "You are dismissed."

A muscle jerked in the man's jaw; then he swiveled around and marched out. Casting Cam a grim look, Rob followed after him.

As if relieved that the men had gone away, Charles's stomach growled. The boy ate with the usual abandon of a still-growing youth.

"Go on, Charles. I know you're hungry."

Charles nodded somberly. "I'll be back in under an hour. Do you wish to work out the details of your loan program this afternoon, sir?"

"Yes, that's a good idea, lad."

After the door closed behind his factor, Cam took a deep breath, pressed his fingers to his temples, and lowered his head to stare down at the surface of his desk.

Ceana had left more than a week ago. Since the morning of her departure from Camdonn Castle, he'd split his time between work and entertaining the Duke of Irvington, taking him hunting and fishing, and showing him his lands, but all the while a flicker of panic had burned in his gut. As much as he'd tried to quash it, as the days passed, the flicker grew into a steadily burning flame. Standing at his drawing room window a few nights ago, he'd watched a Beltane fire burn in the courtyard below, and that fire had fueled the flames of his own.

He'd come to the conclusion that his feelings for Ceana were different from the way he'd felt about Sorcha. His need for Sorcha had been a selfish thing—wrought by arrogance and lust. Something told him that Ceana, however, had the power to change him, to change his world. His life.

Yet, as much as the ache for Ceana plagued him, he couldn't forget his reasons for coming home. He understood his goals, what he needed to change, and what he needed to accomplish. He must ensure the well-being of his people. He must win their confidence and their loyalty. In doing so, however, he must count on the backing and support of the most powerful men of England and Scotland: Argyll, Parliament, the king. Cam's plan wasn't a simple one, but three weeks ago, he'd been prepared to implement it without any knowledge of Ceana MacNab's existence.

That was the problem. Now he knew she existed. And an existence without her seemed very bleak indeed. He sighed, and confusion swirled around the fire within him. He had no choice—he must make good his promise to Elizabeth. He could no longer allow Ceana to occupy his thoughts when his pretty bride should be the one doing so.

Diligently, he turned his focus to his betrothed. Except for her foray up the mountain, he had been occupied with her uncle and had little knowledge of how Elizabeth had busied herself during the days. Perhaps he should pay more attention. How did she feel about her new home? About Scotland and the Highlands? Was she adapting to the people's ways? Was she worried about her acceptance here? Terrified of their upcoming nuptials and of the life that had been chosen for her?

If so, it was his duty to allay her fears. He had avoided that particular responsibility for too long. Thrusting Ceana's sharp gray-blue eyes and snapping voice from his mind, he left the study in search of his wife-to-be.

It was almost half an hour later when he found her curled up comfortably in the corner of the leather sofa in the small library. He smiled in surprise upon seeing her. He'd never taken her for a book lover.

She dropped the book onto the sofa and scrambled to her feet. "Oh! My lord! You startled me."

He gave a small bow. "I apologize. I didn't mean to disturb you. What are you reading?"

Pink crept over her cheeks and she glanced back at the book. "Oh . . . It is a religious text, my lord, but though I was staring at the words, my mind was wandering elsewhere. I'm sorry."

She dropped her gaze to the floor, and Cam ground his teeth. Guilt swirled through him. He'd been thoughtless, as usual.

"I am the one who is sorry."

Her blue eyes were wide when she looked back up at him. "Why, my lord?"

"I have not given you the attention you deserve. This place must be so unfamiliar and frightening to you."

She shook her head. "Oh, I don't require any attention. I understand you have been preoccupied with more important business since you arrived home."

He gazed at her, clasping his hands behind his back and struggling to think of something to say. Conversation flowed so easily with Ceana, but he always struggled with Elizabeth.

"Do you like the Highlands? Tell me what you think of Camdonn Castle. How do you feel about your new home?"

Her chest rose and fell, showing the creamy tops of her bosom, and she smoothed her hands over her pale pink bodice. She was lovely. A portrait of feminine beauty.

Why, then, didn't she move him like Ceana did? Visions of Ceana's wild curls, her rounded breasts, her bowed lips, her gray-blue eyes, crossed through his mind in rapid succession. He pushed each one away ruthlessly and systematically.

"The Highlands are very beautiful. There is so much variety here that I never saw at home," she said. "I am looking forward to learning all about this new world. And Camdonn Castle is lovely. It's such an ancient seat—it truly does give one the impression of power. I will be proud to call it my home."

Her answer did not bring him the contentment it should have. Why not? Something about it didn't seem right. It wasn't that it was disingenuous, but . . . He couldn't place his finger on it. It felt almost rehearsed. Like she'd formed every word into exactly what he wished to hear.

"I am glad."

A faint smile crossed her face.

"In two weeks we will be married, Elizabeth."

"I know." Her voice was breathless.

Maybe . . . maybe if he tasted her as he'd tasted Ceana. She would be sweet, he knew. Sweet and supple—she was so young—not yet twenty. Maybe she would obliterate the taste of Ceana from his mouth, from his heart and mind.

He stared at her little pink mouth. He had to kiss her. He wanted to, damn it. He'd always known she'd be easy to bed. That hadn't changed.

Another step. She tilted her head to look up at him. Her blue eyes focused on his as he reached his hand to her face.

Gently, he traced her hairline. "You're so beautiful."

"Thank you." She swallowed. "My lord."

"I don't want to frighten you."

She gave a minute shake of her head, a gesture of disagreement.

"I'm going to kiss you," he murmured. He watched her carefully, searching for any sign of terror. Finding none, he bent forward, simultaneously curling his palm around the back of her head and tugging her toward him.

He bussed his lips over hers. They were tight and warm, like her small body standing before him, arms straight at her sides. He brushed tiny kisses over her mouth, then gently touched his tongue to her upper lip. A spasm jerked through her, and he jumped back.

He stared down at her. "Elizabeth?"

Slowly, her eyes opened and gazed up at him, blue and guileless. It was as if the kiss had never happened. Nothing had changed. She was still his perfect English rose.

And he was completely unaffected as well. His body hadn't responded to the kiss at all. Unlike the kiss with Ceana that had incited an inferno blazing through him—an inferno doused only temporarily by the appearance of Sorcha and Alan.

"Yes, my lord?"

"Never mind." He fought to form a smile. "I'm sorry to interrupt your reading." Belatedly, he remembered she hadn't been reading at all.

"It is quite all right."

"Well. I've business to attend. I'll see you at dinner."

She curtsied. "Yes, my lord."

He turned and left her.

He kept his hands clasped behind his back as he strode down the passageway. Perhaps there would never be true passion between him and Elizabeth. And was that so bad? He could focus on his other goals. In his search for a bride, passion hadn't been one of his requirements. In fact, it was a detriment, in his opinion, after what had happened with Sorcha.

Still, it ate at him. How could he spend a lifetime with a woman he felt no passion for when there was a woman he burned for within his reach?

No, that was wrong. Ceana wasn't within his reach. He was an earl, and she was a pagan Scottish healer. Not only that, she was a MacNab. *MacNab women never marry.*

He walked to the stables, where he and Rob exchanged brief words about Bram MacGregor and his aggressive attitude during their meeting earlier. Rob believed that Cam's reception of MacGregor, while it hadn't changed the man's overall attitude, had been a start.

Then Cam mounted his mare and rode up the mountain, taking a group of men with him to relieve the men stationed at Gràinne's cottage. Gràinne was up and about, scrubbing her table when he entered without knocking. He pursed his lips, set his hands on his hips, and stared at her menacingly.

"What, love?" She brushed a strand of red hair out of her face and tossed her soiled cloth into a bucket on the floor. A solid ring of blue had formed around one of her eyes, and Cam's fingers itched to punch someone—preferably the worthless bastard who'd done that to her. "Did you expect I'd sit in bed for a week?"

"Yes."

She hissed in annoyance, but her wide lips remained spread in a smile as she cocked her head at him. "What brings you, Cam?"

"I wanted to check on you." Dropping his hands, he walked inside and closed the door against the cool breeze behind him.

"I am well, as you see. Near whole again. Ceana MacNab is a miracle worker."

She eyed him, assessing his reaction to her words. Gràinne was far too observant when it came to him. He would not discuss Ceana with her—that would be a grave mistake. So he smoothly diverted the conversation.

"How is your wrist?"

She glanced down at the sling Ceana had fashioned that held her arm bound tightly against her body. "Better. It can be a wee bit of a challenge to perform certain tasks. But I have friends to help me." She gestured at a chair. "Sit. I'll pour you some whisky."

"No, I'll fetch my own. You sit."

She did as she was told, watching him as he strode to the shelf by the hearth and poured whisky into the two clay cups beside the small cask. He brought them back to the table and lowered himself onto the chair across from her.

He curled his fingers around the cup and gazed up at Gràinne. The act of looking on her beautiful face marred by violence did strange things to his insides. It made him want to cause pain to the person who'd done this to her, but it also roused his gentle and protective instincts. He could hardly prevent himself from gathering her in his arms, taking her to the bed, tucking her beneath the blankets, and soothing her until she fell asleep.

"I am well, Cam," she said quietly, reading his mind.

He gestured with his chin toward the door. "My guards?"

"I don't require them."

He didn't bother to answer. They would stay until Cam was certain the menace was gone. He had no intention of negotiating that.

Gràinne sighed. "They have been surprisingly good to me, though none has seen any sign of my attacker. Nor will they." Her lips curled as she studied him over the rim of her cup. "It was an honor to meet your betrothed."

"Ah." Cam took a reassuring swallow of whisky. "What did you think of Lady Elizabeth?"

"I liked her."

That surprised Cam. He raised a brow. "You're not madly jealous?"

Her smile widened. "You know I am not. Of course, I'll miss you." Her gaze flicked to the bed and then back to him. "But you know I won't tumble you when you're married. Even when you're betrothed to another. However"—she raised her hand as if to interrupt him from whatever he might be thinking—"trust that is not due to any honorable feelings on my part. It is in due consideration for you."

"Me?"

"Aye. 'Tis *your* honor I consider. You couldn't bear to destroy a woman by being unfaithful to her. This is the reason I won't seduce you now."

His lips twisted. Sometimes it seemed Gràinne understood him better than he understood himself. She'd always been a good friend to him. He'd always love her for that. He'd always take care of her—though he'd done a damn poor job of it of late.

"What did Elizabeth say to you?" he asked, curious.

Gràinne grinned. "She wanted me to teach her how to please you."

Cam sputtered on his whisky. "No!"

"Aye. She did. She was very open about her desire to give you carnal satisfaction."

The air depleted from his lungs, Cam stared at Gràinne dumbly.

Gràinne pushed a finger around the rim of her cup. "That surprises you."

"Hell, yes, it surprises me! I didn't even know . . ." His voice dwindled and heat crept through his cheeks. "Well, hell."

"What didn't you know?"

"It never occurred to me that Elizabeth knew anything about sexual congress."

Gràinne broke out into a peal of laughter that lasted several moments. When she finally calmed enough to speak, she wiped the back of her hand over her glistening eyes. "Oh, that's rich, love. You think she's the epitome of perfection—and, of course, she is—but to you the natural progression of that is that she's utterly virginal, untouched in heart, mind, and body. Poor Cam."

"Are you implying she isn't?"

Gràinne snorted. "Of course she is not."

Again Cam was too stunned to speak.

"She's far more experienced than she'd let on. Even to me." Gràinne relaxed back in her chair, a smug look on her face. "There are certain things even an expert at deception like Lady Elizabeth cannot hide from me."

"But she hides it from me." Cam frowned. "Why?"

"Because she must, of course. Wouldn't she be 'ruined' or 'disgraced' if she behaved in any other way?"

Cam murmured something noncommittal.

"Would you have chosen her if you knew she was interested in ways to please a man? If you knew that perhaps she'd pleased a man before?"

That required some thought. Cam cocked his head, thinking of how he'd approached the task of finding a wife. To Cam, the perfect wife first and foremost must be different from Sorcha MacDonald—he couldn't choose someone who reminded him of the woman he'd been so obsessed with. But certain other elements were critical as well: title, riches, youth, beauty, intelligence, political and social ties, easy personality, strength of constitution. Elizabeth had qualified in every way.

Innocence wasn't on his list of requirements, but perhaps that was because it was an implied condition. If she'd been disgraced as a wanton, the other qualities would have been affected negatively, and he wouldn't have considered her.

"No," he said finally. "I wouldn't have agreed to marry her if I knew she wasn't innocent."

Gràinne studied him. "Does it anger you to learn that she isn't exactly what she seems?"

He drummed his fingers on the table. "No."

But his answer disturbed him. Nothing about Elizabeth affected him—not their kiss, and not learning that she was more sexually experienced than she'd let on.

If he'd just discovered Ceana wasn't what she seemed, that she'd pretended to be someone other than who she'd shown to him, he'd be throwing furniture through the window. But when it came to Elizabeth, he felt nothing. Gràinne could have told him something as ordinary as the fact that she'd eaten porridge for breakfast and he'd have the same response.

"Why aren't you angry?" Gràinne studied him, her brown eyes narrowed in assessment.

He shrugged. "She's not a fool. She knows she cannot reveal such secrets to the world."

"Aye, well, that's true."

"If she told me right away . . . Well, I don't know what experience she's had, but, for example, if she told me she'd sucked a man's cock, I would have called off our engagement immediately, and she knew that. She's not simpleminded."

"Aye, well, I gathered that much."

He drank the remainder of his whisky in silence, thinking about the way Ceana's curls bobbed at her shoulders. The way her eyes sparked at him when she made one of her ridiculous commands. When he set the cup back on the table, Gràinne asked, "And what of Ceana MacNab?"

His head snapped up. "What?"

"What do you think of our new healer?"

Desperately, he tried to form a coherent sentence. "She's a MacNab," he finally muttered.

"Aye." Gràinne grinned. "Through and through. And yet . . ." Her voice dwindled, and the smile slipped from her face. "She was not very MacNab-like when the English lady and I were speaking of the finer points of bedding you."

"Oh?" He tried to sound unaffected. Instead he sounded like a noose were being drawn tight about his neck.

"No, she was quite . . . withdrawn," Gràinne said thoughtfully. "She didn't look at either of us. She wasn't focused on my wounds, either, though she tried to pretend she was."

"Hm."

Gràinne's dark eyes sharpened on him. "Cam?"

"Mm?" Abruptly, Cam rose, his chair scraping over the dirt as he pushed it back. He turned to fetch more whisky. God knew he needed it.

"Ceana MacNab went red as a beetroot as I discussed your cock with your lovely wife-to-be."

"You shouldn't have been discussing my cock at all," he choked out. The thought of the three women in here, talking about how to please him . . . It made him want to squirm out of his skin. At the same damn time, he was harder than a rock.

Gràinne chuckled. "It is what women do."

"They shouldn't," he grumbled, pouring the whisky.

"You spent a night in Ceana's cottage. Something happened between you, didn't it?"

"I was shot." He waved his hand at his shoulder, as if his injury could explain everything.

"Aye. So?"

"I'd lost half the blood in my body. I could hardly move."

"And yet . . . something happened. I smell it. On both of you."

"You don't smell anything, Gràinne."

"Oh, but I do. I have a nose for such things."

Wicked woman. "Nothing. Happened."

She snorted.

"I'm betrothed to the niece of an English duke." Warily, he lowered himself back onto the chair across from her. At least now he had a fresh cup of whisky with which to fortify himself.

"Ah! That's it." She smacked her good hand down on the table. "What would have happened, then? If you weren't betrothed to the niece of a duke?"

"Don't ask that."

"It's important, love."

"How's that? How can this be important to anyone? It's irrelevant. I have brought my betrothed and her family hundreds of miles. I'm to be married in two weeks' time. Anything between myself and Ceana MacNab is over, and it must be forgotten."

"But what if it cannot be? What if you and Ceana are unable to forget?"

"We must," he said stubbornly.

"You want her."

He groaned softly.

"You want her badly. Your body craves her beneath it. Your cock aches to sink into her."

"Stop it."

"You want to fuck her, Cam," Gràinne crooned. "You are mad for her. Obsessed. You can't stop thinking about her."

"That's not true," he pushed out.

"It is. Is this how you felt about Sorcha MacDonald?"

"That was different."

"How?" she demanded.

"I was a stupid fool about Sorcha."

"You tried to force yourself to stop thinking about her. You couldn't, though, could you? Your longing for her increased day by day until you couldn't control it any longer. And then you did a foolish thing."

He pushed back from the table and rose to his feet.

"You are putting yourself at risk, love. It could happen again, and this time, you could destroy yourself—and Elizabeth and Ceana. Don't be blind."

"Stop!" he said harshly. "This has naught to do with Sorcha MacDonald."

"Doesn't it?"

He leaned forward, placing his hands flat on the table's surface. Rage trembled inside him, softened only by the obvious abuse to Gràinne's face. He would not shout at her. "I intend to make good on everything I promised Elizabeth and her uncle." His voice was lethally quiet. "I intend to make a life for us here. My plans will not change. Not for anything. Not this time."

"How, Cam? How is it different?"

"I learned from my mistake."

"And what are you doing to prevent a similar disaster from occurring again?"

"I'm simply not going to allow it."

"And wasn't that the same approach you took last time?"

"No. Not at all," he said, lying through his teeth. He let out a harsh breath. "I must go. Return home to Elizabeth before she wonders what I'm doing up on the mountain with you."

Gràinne leaned back. "Aye, love. You should hurry home. You don't want poor Elizabeth thinking you've been unfaithful. In deed"—she cast him a wistful smile—"or in thought."

He ground his teeth. Both of them knew he'd been unfaithful to Elizabeth in thought, damn it.

Hell. He was doomed. He didn't have an answer, but Gràinne was right: The more he tried not to think of Ceana, the more he thought about her. In the end, his obsessions could ruin them all.

"Take care of yourself, Gràinne," he pushed out, eyeing the bruises on her face. "My men will report all your actions to me. I know you are too stubborn to remain in bed, but if you leave this cottage . . . or if you take a client into your bed . . ." He allowed the threat to remain unspoken.

She nodded and batted her long russet lashes at him. "Oh, aye. I'll not allow another man to step foot inside my house until you give me your permission, love."

"Good."

Rising, she held the door open for him as he strode out. He felt her smile burning into his back until he turned his horse onto the path and disappeared from her view.

It was after midnight when, lying in his bed in the dark, he realized to his disgust that he'd forgotten to question Gràinne about her attacker.

CHAPTER ELEVEN

eana had neglected her herb garden during her stay at Cam-donn Castle, but the weather had been fine, with just the right amount of rain to help it flourish. Weeds had begun to sprout in the fertile soil, however, and today she knelt in the dirt, determined to pluck them all away.

She missed Cam. She missed everything from the planes of his face and his aristocratic nose, to his belligerence about his wound, to his determination to do right by his tenants, to the mixture of anger and compassion in his expression when he'd set eyes upon Gràinne.

Everything reminded her of him. The blankets on her bed smelled like him. The medicines she'd mixed for him still stood on her shelf. The bowl and spoon she'd used to feed him lay beside her dishpan. Even her garden reminded her of him, for he'd collapsed on its fringes when she had tried to drag him to her cottage.

Ceana sighed. It was utterly ridiculous, but she envied Gràinne. The whore had been the one to introduce the young earl-to-be to the pleasures of the flesh. She'd always been there for him, as a friend and a lover.

Ceana wished she'd known him that long. Wished she could have known him when he was a green, faltering youth. Wished she could have seen how he had become the man he was today.

"Good afternoon!"

Shading her eyes, she glanced up in surprise. "Sorcha!" She rose to her feet, brushing the dirt from her hands, and saw the servant standing beside the laird's wife. "Good afternoon, Margaret. What are you two doing here?"

Sorcha shrugged. "Alan is being . . . oh, I don't know. Too *motherly*. I needed to escape from him awhile." She glanced gratefully at the servant woman. "Margaret agreed to come with me. I fear my foolish husband will be furious when he hears I've been traipsing about the countryside, but I simply cannot stay trapped at home one second longer."

Ceana grinned at her. "Men tend to be a wee bit protective of the women who carry their offspring."

She invited the women into her cottage and they sat in the chairs Ceana had placed near the hearth. She poured them each a glass of cold fennel tea, and after drinking hers down Margaret asked if she might take a closer look at Ceana's garden. Ceana gave her approval, then watched in suspicion as the older woman closed the door behind her. Margaret had never expressed an interest in herbs before.

Sorcha tilted her head, turning her cup around in her hands, and a far-off, wistful look clouding her green eyes. "I've been meaning to ask you . . ."

Ceana stiffened. Sentences begun in that manner generally led to things she'd prefer not to discuss.

". . . about Cam," Sorcha finished.

Though the tactic likely wouldn't work—Sorcha had seen them kissing, after all—Ceana opted for playing innocent. "What about him?"

Sorcha chuckled. "You were near to crawling right inside him when Alan and I walked in here after he was wounded."

Ceana took Sorcha's cup and then rose to place it in her dishpan. "'Twas a lapse of judgment," she said. "It didn't happen again."

Sorcha's dark brows rose. "Why ever not?"

Wearily, Ceana lowered herself in the wicker chair Margaret had abandoned. "He is to marry soon. It would be folly, and unkind to the girl."

"Elizabeth," Sorcha said, as if testing the name on her tongue.

"Aye. Elizabeth. I like her. And so does Cam."

"But he doesn't love her."

"Is that my business?"

"From the way you were kissing him—"

Ceana raised her hand. "I shouldn't have anything to do with him. You know that."

"But you did. That was no experimental peck of a kiss, Ceana. That was . . . that was passion."

"Well, it was short-lived passion, because it is no longer," Ceana said snappishly.

Sorcha stared at her. "You're in love with him."

"You forget, my friend. I am a MacNab woman. We don't fall in love."

"Don't you?"

"No."

"Why is that?"

Ceana shook her head. Some secrets were too painful to be told to anyone, even as sweet a friend as Sorcha. "Family secret."

"Ceana . . . Lord. I know you want Cam. You're miserable. You seem too pale . . . and look at how you're twisting your hands in your lap. Is that how you're feeling on the inside too?"

Ceana leaned forward. "I know you're trying to help. But where could this lead? He will marry soon."

"But if he'd prefer to marry you . . ."

Ceana nearly choked. "Marry me? Choose me, a poor Scottish commoner, over a rich English duke's niece with a dowry that's more than a thousand times as large as the sum of all my possessions? He isn't a madman!"

"He's my friend," Sorcha said quietly. "Cam is a man of passion. Not of numbers."

"Say that to him," Ceana returned. "And then listen to him deny you into the ground."

"He didn't learn." Sorcha's shoulders drooped. "Just before he left, he came to Alan and me. He was going to England to find his wife. His love."

"Did he tell you he sought love?"

"No, but . . . I assumed . . . Oh, Ceana, you must convince him to abandon these thoughts of the English girl. He wants you. I know he does. I saw you with him when I came to Camdonn Castle. His eyes followed you everywhere."

Ceana shrugged. "It is too late."

Even if it weren't, she'd never pursue Cam in such a way. *Never.*

"He'll be miserable married to that girl."

"No. He cares for her."

Sorcha's green eyes widened. "Caring doesn't equal happiness, Ceana. Nor does it equal passion!"

Ceana gave her a wry smile. "I know it doesn't. I'm merely saying that I believe they will be compatible. They've a mutual respect."

"Foolish man. Why did he choose her? Why did he go to England at all, when the right woman for him would have appeared here just a few months later?" Sorcha slapped her hand to her thigh. "I shall never understand that man."

"Understand this, Sorcha." Ceana reached out to take her friend's hand. "I am not the woman for Cam. I never have been, never will be. Even if . . . if something more had happened between us, it could never be. Never. I am a MacNab."

"I don't understand."

"I cannot marry. Ever."

"Why?"

Ceana pursed her lips and looked away.

"You make no sense, Ceana. Neither of you makes any sense at all!"

With that, Sorcha sprang to her feet. But she stopped instantly, her mouth open, a strange look on her face. "Ah . . ."

"What is it?"

Sorcha closed her mouth, licked her lips. "A big gush . . . fluid . . . running down my legs." She took several short, quick breaths.

"It's all right," Ceana said mildly. "Let me see."

Leaning forward, she lifted Sorcha's skirts and breathed out a sigh. "It's your water, Sorcha. It's broken."

"Am . . . am I having the baby now?"

"Not necessarily. You can still carry on for several days."

"Is it dangerous to the—" Sorcha let out a strangled cry and doubled over.

Ceana placed her hand flat on the woman's stomach and felt the tightening bands over her abdomen. She didn't want to worry Sorcha, for of course this could just be a reactionary contraction due to her water breaking.

When it was over, Ceana led Sorcha to her bed and had her sit on its edge. Five minutes later, another contraction came over her, and Ceana laid her down and checked her cervix to find it halfway dilated.

She opened the door and yelled for Margaret, who came hurrying up. Her eyes widened when she saw Sorcha curled on the bed in the throes of another contraction.

"I want . . . I want my sister," Sorcha said, gasping. "I need Moira."

"Go get Alan and send someone to fetch Moira Stewart and the midwife from Glenfinnan," Ceana ordered the gaping woman. "And hurry. The baby's coming."

When the castle quieted, Elizabeth slipped behind the tapestry and escaped down the secret passage. Tonight she moved like a dark wraith flitting through the night, covering the distance between the keep and the stables with alacrity.

Rob had left the stable door open, and she slipped in and bounded up the stairs, excitement making her heart beat quickly and blood flush her cheeks warm.

Standing at a counter before the window, he looked up at her when she tumbled in, breathless, and his smile made her light-headed.

"I'm glad you came."

She returned his smile, pushing the hair out of her face. But as soon as she met his eyes, she looked away, suddenly shy.

"How is your maid?"

The question brought her back down to earth with a crash. "She is healing slowly, but—"

"But?"

She sighed. How to explain how she felt each time she saw Bitsy wince? How to relate the guilt that overcame her when Bitsy hobbled out of her bedchamber?

"She is fine," she said in a quiet voice. "She will be all right."

"Ah." He removed his stained gloves, and Elizabeth saw that he'd been using a dirk to work strips of leather—some task pertaining to his horses.

He walked toward her until he reached the center of the room. "Your servant will be all right, but will you?"

He understood. Every time Uncle Walter hurt Bitsy, he opened a wound in her soul. None of the wounds healed; they only festered and grew.

But Robert MacLean was a soothing balm to those sores. The only person she'd ever known who made her feel so safe, so human. He was her medicine, her drug. He could heal her.

Her throat went dry from anticipation. She'd made a decision earlier tonight. Her plan might lead Rob to hate her forever, and it would certainly put her forthcoming marriage to Cam in jeopardy if he caught her. If her uncle caught her . . . She shivered. He simply must never find out.

She took a huge risk, but the compulsion was impossible to resist. Nothing could stop her. Despite the niggling fear of discovery, she couldn't stop herself.

She was madly besotted with Robert MacLean. The force of her need for him was too powerful to deny. When she was apart from him,

every muscle in her body grew restless and achy for him. Panic threatened to overwhelm her. She couldn't focus. She couldn't think. His
presence calmed her, cleared her mind. He grounded her.

"Rob . . ." she choked. She licked her lips and tried again. "I . . . I
won't suffer. I don't. Not when I am with you. When I am with you, I
feel . . ." Her voice dwindled, and she stared at him hopelessly, watching his face darken. "I heal," she finished in a whisper.

"Elizabeth . . ." The warning was evident in his tone. "Don't."

But she'd toed off her slippers. Her dark wool cloak slipped to the
floor. Her shaking fingers tugged at the strings tying the neckline of
her shift. She dropped her hands, curling them over her legs, pulling
the shift higher, exposing her calves, her knees, her thighs. The triangle of hair between her legs, her stomach, her small breasts. She
tugged her shift over her head and tossed it aside.

She stared at him, knowing every part of her body was flushed and
quivering. "I'm not a virgin," she whispered.

She'd bedded Tom the footman. She'd tumbled him on the river-
bank near Purefoy Abbey. But that was different. That was because
she craved the contact, the human connection, because she was curious, and because there was some inexplicable force that drove her to
self-ruin. That had been a rash, impulsive decision. There had been
none of the emotion, none of the intensity she felt now.

"Elizabeth." His voice sounded strangled. He kept his amber gaze
focused on her face. "Put your clothes back on."

"No."

He stood rooted to the spot. "You are to be married."

"It is you I want."

He glanced at the window. The shutters were closed, but the window looked over the keep, where Cam lay in his bed, most likely
asleep.

"He is my brother." His words rasped with the internal battle he
waged. She understood exactly what he felt, for she'd waged the same
battle earlier tonight.

"I know."

"We cannot betray him."

"I don't want to, but I must. We must. We haven't any choice." She stepped toward him. "I . . . need you."

It was a pleading whisper, an entreaty. Couldn't he see she'd stripped herself bare in so many ways?

"Kiss me," she whispered. She daren't step any closer. "I need you, Robert MacLean," she breathed. *Please, please, please.* She'd never needed anything more wholly, more violently. Every drop of blood in her body craved his intimate touch. "Please."

"I . . . can't." He sounded pained. Miserable. He tore his gaze from her.

The blood that had raged through her veins moments ago solidified into ice. "Please."

"Get dressed. Go back to your bed."

"Rob—"

"Go, Elizabeth."

With every word he uttered, his conviction to turn her away grew more solid. She stood frozen. The ridiculous idea of ordering him to take her to bed—like she'd ordered Tom—crossed her mind, and she gave herself a mental slap in the face. Robert MacLean didn't take orders from her.

Her vision blurred. Frantically, she searched for her shift among the items she'd scattered on the floor. She dropped to her knees, grabbed it, fumbled at it to turn it right side out. Rob knelt beside her, but she tried—impossibly—to ignore him as she jerked at the uncooperative fabric.

"Elizabeth . . ."

"Don't speak to me," she said dully, finally finding the armholes. She yanked it over her head and thrust her arms into the sleeves. "I will leave."

She'd never felt so worthless. She didn't know what to do. Where to go. How could she return to that room in the tower where her uncle had beaten Bitsy? That tower room was a prison, cold and dank, like her heart, like her soul. She thought Rob would set her free, but he was unwilling. He didn't want her.

He laid her cloak over her shoulders, and she grabbed the ties, jerking away from his touch. Blinking hard, she rose and shoved her feet into her shoes.

"Elizabeth—"

But she flew down the narrow stairs. Horses nickered as she fled past the stalls, and cool air collided with her body when she threw open the door to the stable.

Where would she go now?

Cam couldn't sleep. Ceana had occupied his thoughts since he'd gone to bed, and he couldn't shake her free. He was too warm, the air too close. He couldn't think, couldn't breathe.

He rose and pulled on a pair of breeches and a coat; then he slipped outside and down the stairs.

The night was cooler than he'd expected. He hadn't buttoned his coat, and clean, fresh air washed through the thin linen of his shirt and over his skin. It refreshed him, revived him. He strode across the courtyard and passed the stables, hearing the shuffling sounds of the animals inside.

Everything was serene, quiet. Beyond the guardhouse to the north, the loch sparkled in the starlight. This was his home. He loved this place. He couldn't fathom why he'd spent so much time avoiding it when he was young. Perhaps because his father was here, spewing venom on his only son whenever he was near. And, Cam realized, on his own people as well. It was his father's legacy he battled now, as much as his own.

Cam wandered down the path leading toward the guardhouse. A dim light flickered from inside, where the man on guard gazed out over the loch.

A frisson of unease crackled through him. Perhaps he shouldn't feel so comfortable here. People existed who wanted him dead, and he wouldn't be surprised if some of those people inhabited his lands.

Cam stopped in the shadow of an imported tree that had been coaxed to an unnatural height by his mother when he was a boy. She'd loved to putter about the grounds, making certain everything was beautiful and welcoming, and he'd always trailed after her, playing in the grass and dirt. In the years since her death, his father hadn't taken such care with the grounds, and now Camdonn Castle was a forbidding place.

Yet this tree remained, larger than ever and still healthy. He leaned against the trunk, closing his eyes and trying to recall images of his long-lost mother. She was dark haired, like he was, thin and lithe, with a ready smile and a tempestuous demeanor. She'd scolded him endlessly, but she'd loved him, and always showed it with embraces and fond words.

When she knew she was sick, she'd searched for just the right governess for him. When she'd died, not long after finding Mrs. Jones, Cam had clung to the older woman until his father had ordered her away.

A soft crunching noise drew Cam from his thoughts. He opened his eyes to see a dark shadow sprinting across the lawn. The woman held up her skirts as she ran.

The moon emerged from behind a cloud, glinting over blond hair.

Elizabeth! Cam stiffened. What in God's name could she be doing outside this late at night?

She slowed, coming close to the edge of the cliff and walking alongside it, looking for something. She paused between two bushes, and then she crouched down and disappeared over the side.

Cam froze, gripping the tree trunk. *What the hell?* There was a mooring for boats at the base of the cliff, and one could climb down the rocks protruding from the cliff face if one was careful. The climb was far less dangerous in daylight, for the rocks were slippery and surely invisible on even a moonlit night such as this one. How could dainty Elizabeth make her way down safely? Further, how could she know about the rough stepping-stones to begin with?

Cam paused in indecision. She had clearly not wished to be seen, and he didn't want to invade her privacy. Should he go after her? If he did, it was likely to cause both of them some measure of embarrassment.

But hell. He couldn't allow her to slip and fall to her death. He stepped forward from the shelter of the tree, determined to assure her safety, when the sound of footsteps drew him back into the shadows.

Another figure emerged from around the corner of the stables. A shaft of moonlight glowed over the man's features, revealing Robert MacLean. He strode to the cliff's edge and paused, momentarily appearing undecided. Then he dropped to his haunches and slipped after Elizabeth.

Cam's chest tightened. As crazy and unbelievable as it sounded, the truth slapped him in the face. There was only one way to interpret what he'd just seen.

His betrothed and his stable master had planned an assignation.

CHAPTER TWELVE

Rob descended to the beach and turned toward the small impression of earth. Elizabeth stood there, her back pressed against the smooth rock wall, her face hidden in shadow.

"Go away," she said in a hoarse whisper.

For the briefest of seconds, he hesitated. When he spoke, his voice was rough with emotion. "I want you. You know I do."

She shook her head.

"I cannot betray my brother. Cam—"

"What does it matter? He has no idea you're his brother. He certainly doesn't treat you like a brother. You're naught but a servant to him." Her shoulders shook. "Just go away."

The tension in his body was so tight, Rob feared moving. If he moved, he might snap. This woman . . . this *English*woman . . . He'd never seen anything like her. She was utterly fragile. She'd been broken over and over, but somehow she'd picked up the pieces and continued on. He didn't want to be the one to break her yet again.

"I am selfish," she whispered.

He couldn't disagree. "There are reasons why you behave the way you do."

Angrily, she pushed the back of her hand over her eyes. "Didn't I tell you to leave?"

He flexed his fingers. Hell, he was so close to letting himself go. His control was stretched on the rack. One touch, one slight brush, and it would break.

"Aye," he said tightly. But he made no move.

"Go, then."

He stood still.

She raised her chin at him. "What, then, do you expect to do to me?"

That was it. Her words snapped his restraint. She didn't make any mention of what she'd do to him—oh, no. It would be what *he* would do to *her*. She understood.

He no longer gave a damn about Cam or anyone else. There was only this haughty woman, this fragile, spoiled, hurting woman he'd wanted since the first moment he'd seen her.

Elizabeth had been left to her own devices to such an extent that she had disconnected from the world. Even her own punishments hadn't been inflicted on her. Whoever had taken her virginity might have performed the act, but she had dictated every moment of it, and the man hadn't gone beyond skin deep. He hadn't affected her.

She was untouched. It was time to end that. She needed someone to touch her. To take that rigid control out of her hands and teach her to be human again.

"Turn around."

After a moment staring at him, she obeyed, slowly opening her palms against the smooth rock face.

He slipped his arms over her shoulders. She was strung tight, nearly as tight as he'd felt moments ago. Reaching around her, he pulled loose the string holding the neckline of her cloak and then her shift. Her cloak fell to her feet, and he tugged the material of her shift down over her creamy white shoulders. She pressed her forehead against the wall.

A tremor buzzed within him. His seed boiled in his ballocks. His cock tightened until it hurt. Discovery meant certain death for him, but God, how intensely he wanted this forbidden woman.

He needed her. Needed this.

So did she. Perhaps even more than he did.

The desire to give her what she needed was a fierce compulsion within him. She wanted his possession; that much he knew instinctively. Maybe this could help rebuild her. And if she was strong, she could bear the rest. Because God knew, Rob had no idea how to stop the duke, and even the earl, from sucking her lifeblood like leeches.

Or maybe he deluded himself. Maybe he was a selfish bastard who wanted her too badly to pay heed to the consequences. Who had abandoned all reason for the simple purpose of easing his lust.

He didn't know. He couldn't consider what drove him anymore. All he could consider was Elizabeth and the smooth skin of her back.

He lowered his head and brushed his lips over the tops of her shoulders, skimming her shoulder blade. Moving her sleek blond hair to the side, he kissed the back of her neck at her hairline. Then he traveled to the opposite shoulder, dropping his hands to clasp about her waist. When he reached the soft flesh on the outside of her upper arm, he bared his teeth and bit down.

She didn't move, didn't cry out. She sighed, long and low, and he felt the deep shudder resonate through her, passing out and up through her hips.

The nip of pain brought her pleasure. His cock grew harder with the understanding, and the gleam of hope that she could be his match strengthened to a bright, burning light.

"You taste sweet," he murmured, soothing the skin he'd bitten with gentle kisses.

She began to turn toward him, but he raised his hand and pressed her cheek away. "Be still."

She shuddered again, and he sank to his knees. Slowly, he worked his hands upward from her ankles, over her calf, lingering behind her knee, pulling up the hem of her shift as he went. How he'd fantasized about running his hands over this woman's flesh. Now he lived the fantasy, and it was every bit as compelling as he'd imagined it would be.

He rubbed his thumb over the sensitive area behind her knee, then kissed her skin. She tasted like an English rose. Sweet and delicate. He'd never feared her thorns, however. He intended to strip them away one by one.

She breathed harshly now, making no attempt to hide her reaction to his touch.

He splayed his fingers and ran them up the backs of her thighs until he reached the rounded curve of her behind. He closed his eyes. How often had he pictured this arse under his hands? How often had he imagined the pink imprints of his fingers on the plump, pale flesh?

He rose, lifting her shift over her head and tossing it aside. It was a cool night, and save her shoes, she was naked. But her flesh was warm under his seeking touch.

"Yes," she whispered, "yes, yes," as his hands found their way around her body, up the smooth flat of her stomach and around the curves of her breasts. Her breasts fit perfectly in his palms, and her nipples were taut, jewel-hard under his questing fingers. He pinched them simultaneously between his thumb and forefinger, and she released another sigh, this one more ragged than before.

He pressed his cock against the cleft of her arse, knowing she'd feel the hard ridge behind the fabric of his plaid.

"See?" he growled into her ear. "Never say you do not affect me. That I don't want you." He grazed his teeth along her earlobe.

"Please," she whispered.

"Please what?" He swiped his tongue over the shell of her ear. "Tell me what you wish I'd do to you."

"Take me."

Not enough. "How? Where?"

"Take me hard."

He feathered his fingertips over her lips. "Do you want me to take your mouth?"

"I—I . . . yes."

"Your arse?"

She gulped.

He slid his hand between their bodies, tracing the crease of her arse, pausing at the forbidden area and circling it gently as she sucked in air and shudders rippled beneath her skin.

He traveled farther, deeper between her legs, until he felt the slickness of her desire. "Your cunny? Is it here that you want me?" he purred into her ear.

Her only response was a whimper.

Gently, he stroked over the wet tissue and teased her opening. Then, all at once, he thrust two fingers in.

She didn't make a sound, but her whole body jerked violently, and her inner muscles spasmed over his fingers. She'd said she wasn't a virgin, but she was tight, so tight that once again he had to school himself to temperance.

"Tell me about the men you've taken here."

"O-only one." She gasped as he pumped her.

"Tell me."

"He was one of . . . my . . . uncle's footmen." Her body undulated against him.

"Did you seduce him?"

"N-n-no. I . . ."

"Tell me, Elizabeth."

"I ordered him to bed me."

"Couldn't say no to the duke's niece, could he?"

"No . . . but he was frightened that we would be caught. It was . . . over very quickly."

"And afterward?" he said silkily.

"He ran away."

"And did you do it again?"

"No." She sighed, long and low. "He wasn't worth the risk."

"But I am?"

"Yes." Her response was instantaneous. "For you I would risk everything."

He chuckled softly in her ear. "Your footman was a weakling, as most men are when it comes to bonny women. To women of a certain class. But I'm not."

"I know."

He continued to slide his fingers into her, reaching deeper with every stroke. He watched her carefully, felt her beneath him, learned her body as he explored it. As the pads of his buried fingertips stroked against her inside walls, she trembled. That one spot deep within her was something he could exploit, use to his benefit when the time was right. But for now, he made his strokes shallower, using his thumb to explore the area behind her cunny.

"Ah," she whispered from behind clenched teeth.

She liked it there, then. The forbidden territory of her body. He wouldn't take her far tonight, but soon he'd know every inch, every piece of her. But he'd take his time—there was a fine line between pleasure and pain, between punishment and reward. He would skirt between those lines, right to the cusp of her tolerance, but he would be careful never to take her beyond her limit. He would never hurt her, never scare her, because, in the end, what he loved most was what he saw in her now: the expression of sweet, compliant agony on her face. The sighs of contentment. Each time she responded to him, his need to protect her, to care for her, and to bring her pleasure grew.

Elizabeth needed him. No one else was capable of giving her what she needed. And if anyone tried . . .

Mine.

He squelched the rage that built in him at the thought. He tamped down the possessiveness rising like a powerful tide within him, growling, *Mine, mine, mine!*

Forcefully, he turned his attention back to the body writhing under his touch. She was so open, so willing. So trusting.

Why did she trust him? What had he done to earn this woman's trust?

"Turn around."

She turned, and he pressed her back against the rock face. She shuddered at the contact, for the rocks against her heated skin must feel like blocks of ice.

"Open your eyes."

Her lids rose, and she gazed at him, the blue orbs hazy with a combination of lust and trust that sent the blood roaring through his veins.

He let her stand alone, panting, as he studied her. Assessed her. She stared up at him. Completely open.

Her trust staggered him, humbled him. He released a breath through his teeth and gathered her against him. She shuddered in his arms, held him, touched him from head to toe as if she sought to get even closer. To crawl under his skin and stay there.

He pushed his hand between their bodies and yanked up the fabric of his plaid. His cock sprang free, granite hard and hot as a torch. She rubbed her belly across it as if she couldn't get enough of the feel of his burning need against her skin.

He reached under her arse and lifted her. She was so small, light as a feather. Positioning his cock at her entrance, he lowered her onto him. Her eyes widened, and she gasped out a breath as he sank deep into her body. Then he pushed her back up against the rocks again as she wrapped her legs around him and clung to him.

Standing still, he stared down at her as her body clasped his cock, shuddered over him, clenched him in a fiery grip.

"Hold me," he murmured unnecessarily, because she already clutched his shoulders as if her life depended on it.

Still, she held him tighter. He stared at her face as he began to move within her, seeing nothing but passion and need reflecting his own. After two thrusts, he gave a long, low groan. He couldn't control the hot tremors erupting through his body.

He let go. Gave free rein to his lust, to his need. Allowing the rock face to support most of her weight, he held her with one hand. With the other, he touched her. Her soft stomach, her rounded breasts, her tight, small nipples. Her long, creamy neck, where he found her pulse beating wildly. Her parted lips, which sought his fingers and sucked his thumb into the wet cavern of her mouth. Her soft cheek and oval jaw, her arched brows, her silky hair. God, she was beautiful.

She was beautiful, and she was his.

Curling his fingers in her hair, he pulled her head to the side, exposing her throat. He lowered his head, continuing to sink his cock deep within her, thrusting hard and then retreating as he sampled her English-rose skin.

The need had been boiling within him for too long, and when she cried out and bucked in his arms, the rush of his orgasm came at him like a cattle charge. He retained some semblance of sanity, some discipline, for he managed to wait until her tremors began to recede. As soon as her head slumped forward, he yanked out of her, then gathered her against him as wave after wave of bliss rushed through him, pulsed out of him to smear between their bodies.

When the spasms jabbed him with interspersed ripples of pleasure, he gently lowered her legs but kept her body pressed against his, her face buried in his shirt. Reverently, he kissed the top of her head.

After several minutes, she looked up at him, blue eyes glistening.

"I never thought it could be like that."

"Nor did I," he said in all honesty. He brushed a bit of hair away from her mouth, then slid his fingers under her chin to keep her looking up at him. "Why? Tell me . . . why do you trust me?"

"I . . ." She shook her head. "Maybe . . . Well, I think it has to do with the first time we met."

"What of it?"

"You were different from anyone I'd ever seen. You didn't care that I was an English lady. You didn't care that I was the daughter of a duke, the niece of a duke. You saw through me; you saw *me*. No one does that, ever. You were the first."

"What do you think I saw?"

"You saw a haughty, spoiled girl. Someone who thought more highly of herself than she should."

He firmed his fingers beneath her chin. "Aye, I saw all that. But I saw more."

"What more?" She shrugged. "That's who I am. Who I'll always be."

"Even you know that is a lie," he murmured.

Her expression turned soft. Vulnerable. "What else did you see?"

"A bonny woman," he said. "A woman who needs to be touched. Who needs to be loved. Who deserves both."

"No . . ."

"Aye."

Darkening with guilt, her eyes slid away. "You don't know anything about me, Robert MacLean. You don't know the extent of my sins—"

"Whatever happened before you came here doesn't matter," he said. "You were a lass then. Now you are a woman. Now you must take responsibility. Whatever happened before were the actions of a frightened, unloved child."

"I . . ." Sudden tears formed in her eyes, and she tore her chin from his light grip. "No. You don't understand. You cannot."

He sighed and pulled her into his arms despite her feeble attempt at struggling, thinking it was she who didn't understand.

He was falling in love with her.

Hell, he had already fallen.

What had led him here? Cam had held the reins, but he hadn't consciously directed the horse anywhere. He'd just needed to ride alone and without guards, to get as far away from Camdonn Castle as he possibly could.

He'd followed Rob most of the way down the cliff. Then he'd stood there, his body pressed against the rocks, and listened. To all of it. From Rob denying Elizabeth because he couldn't bear to hurt his brother, to Rob taking Elizabeth against the back of the shallow cave.

Robert MacLean and Elizabeth: lovers. Robert MacLean and Cam: brothers.

Brothers. Lovers. Brothers. Lovers. The words flip-flopped in his mind until he couldn't distinguish one from the other. One of the revelations he might have withstood in rigid silence. But when he put them together, his mind couldn't digest it. It was unreal, impossible.

Sweet, young, innocent Lady Elizabeth? He'd never understood her at all. Had he even tried? No, he'd made assumptions and conclusions based solely on her upbringing and her outward behavior. He'd never really tried to dig deeper—he'd assumed there was nothing beyond the shallow English facade. As always when it came to women who were important to him, he'd been a fool. Perhaps this was just punishment for his past sins, his indiscretions and unforgivable behavior with Sorcha.

And Robert MacLean. His stable master, his intended bride's lover, his *brother*?

Holy hell. He couldn't wrap his head around it. It was incomprehensible.

And now the thatched roof and stone walls of Ceana MacNab's cottage had come into view. Cam slowed the horse to a walk and stared at the humble structure. He should turn away. It was dangerous to approach Ceana in his current state. Yet he couldn't bring himself to change course, and his mount plodded inexorably closer.

Thin wisps of smoke curled from the thatch, and all was silent as he approached, the horse's hooves making the only noise as they crunched over the bracken on the cleared path leading to the small structure.

Finally, mere feet from Ceana's cottage, the horse came to a tentative halt. Cam stared at the door. Moonlight slanted across it in silvery invitation.

Why did she burn a fire this late at night? Shouldn't she be abed by now?

He pushed his hand through his hair. Should he go away? Should he tear down the door and fall into her arms? The indecision was agonizing. How could he make any rational decision in the face of what he'd witnessed tonight?

And then a bloodcurdling scream tore through the placid night, and Cam jerked into action. He leaped off the horse and threw open Ceana's door, fists clenched in preparation to kill whoever had hurt her.

What he saw made his hands go limp at his sides and his mouth gape open.

Ceana, who crouched over the curled-up figure on the bed, whipped her head around. "Cam! What are you doing here?"

He looked from her to the woman on the bed. "Sorcha?"

Ceana blew out a breath, and curls flew around her face. "Where are Alan and Moira?"

"I . . . don't know."

"Damn it," Ceana spat. "Come here, then. Sorcha needs you."

"Cam?" Sorcha asked in a weak voice.

Cam swallowed. "Is she . . . Is it . . . Is the babe . . . ?"

"Aye, she is, it is, and the babe is," Ceana said. "So come here and hold her hand!"

"Another one," Sorcha groaned, and the groan deepened and became louder and finally transformed into a keening sound that made Cam's feet itch to run for the hills.

"Good God," he said, petrified. "What's happening to her? Is she . . . ? Is she . . . ?"

"No, she's not dying, for God's sake. She's having a baby," Ceana said tiredly.

"I must go." This damn sure was no place for a man.

"No. You will stay. I need you."

Sorcha's pain seemed to lessen, leaving her sobbing softly. Cam gathered himself and dragged himself to the side of the bed. He looked down at her, and she stared up at him.

"Uh . . ." He glanced at Ceana. "Alan . . ." Cam gulped. "Ah . . ." He looked guiltily away as Ceana flipped the blankets over Sorcha, leaving her round, bare belly exposed.

"Oh, come," Ceana snapped. "It's nothing you haven't seen before."

Before he had an opportunity to argue that point, Sorcha said, "If you don't wish to stay . . ."

He returned his gaze to her, keeping it steady on her face rather than the exposed parts below. "Do you want me to be here?"

"Please . . ." Sorcha grabbed his hand. "It hurts so much, Cam. I'm so afraid . . ."

He closed his eyes, remembering that her mother had died in childbirth.

"Just let me look at you . . ." But she couldn't speak anymore, for pain had gripped her again. She managed it more quietly this time, but her body writhed helplessly on the bed.

He met Ceana's eyes as she looked up from between Sorcha's legs. "She's doing very well," Ceana said. "The babe is a bit early, but everything is progressing nicely."

He looked back down at Sorcha. A sheen of sweat covered her face, and she was paper white. Even her lips were pale. This was *well*?

Pain racked her body once more. Her mouth opened in a silent scream, and she squeezed his hand so tightly, he thought she might break the bones of his fingers.

If this was usual for childbirth, he resolved to never impregnate a woman.

But this woman, a woman he'd once loved and who would always be dear to him, needed him right now. He'd do whatever he could to help her through it.

He bent down and brushed his knuckles over her clammy cheek. "I'm here, Sorcha. You have nothing to fear."

CHAPTER THIRTEEN

Ceana looked up over the slope of Sorcha's belly. Sorcha had labored through a long, exhausting night, but now Ceana's blood thrummed with excitement. She glanced at Cam, who smoothed a wet cloth over Sorcha's brow. Cam had been a great help—she only wished he'd come earlier. Where were Alan and Moira? They should have been here hours ago.

She smiled at the mother-to-be. "The baby's crowning, Sorcha."

"Wha-what does that mean?" Sorcha was pale and listless, for laboring with a child was just that: hard work. And Alan had been coddling her, not allowing her to perform her regular activities and duties. He'd insisted his wife go soft, and that had made it more difficult for her.

She waited patiently as Sorcha endured another contraction. When it settled, she knew she had only a few seconds before the next one struck. They were coming one after another now.

"On this next one, if you feel like pushing, go ahead and do it," Ceana said.

Sorcha barely seemed to hear her, but when the contraction hit, she bore down. The dark crown of hair grew larger but receded with the cessation of the contraction.

"One more, Sorcha," Ceana said in her most encouraging voice.

She wasn't unfamiliar with the duties of a midwife. She'd delivered a few bairns in her time, and she'd studied some of the techniques of birthing at Aberdeen. Yet when she'd arrived at the Glen, she'd kept to general healing and, unless there was an emergency, left the birthing to the midwife and Sorcha's sister, Moira.

Sorcha was bearing down in the midst of another contraction. Ceana focused on the emerging head, and when the contraction tapered, the head disappeared.

"Is he out yet?" Sorcha screeched.

Cam looked at her in alarm, and Ceana grinned at him. "Almost, Sorcha. One more big push with the next one, and the head'll be out. I'm sure of it."

Still smiling, she met Cam's eyes, and something sweet passed between them. They were helping Sorcha through this together.

Sorcha moaned, and Ceana returned her focus to the tiny head. This time, Sorcha succeeded, and the small, damp round face appeared. Gently, Ceana adjusted the head to align with the body. "The head's out," she said on a breath. "One more push, Sorcha. You're doing it!"

With its mother screaming out her lungs, the babe slid out with the next push. Ceana gathered the tiny new human in her arms, quickly wrapping a blanket around the little body and working to clear out its breathing passages.

Cam was speaking in low, excited tones to Sorcha, but Ceana was too focused on the babe to hear his words. Finally, the infant took a shuddering breath and released a reedy wail. Sorcha's voice emerged from the haze.

"What is it, Ceana? Tell me."

"What's that?"

"A lad or a lass?"

Ceana's frown deepened. "Oh . . . I don't know." Carefully, she opened the blanket, then smiled up at the two expectant faces. "A lad, Sorcha. A braw, healthy baby boy."

She cut the cord and then placed the squalling infant into Sorcha's arms. Sorcha stared down at him in awe. "He looks just like Alan."

"But he has your coloring," Cam murmured.

Ceana listened to them murmur over the babe, counting his little fingers and toes and making certain he was perfect. She cleaned up and administered a tincture of shepherd's purse and vervain to Sorcha to promote healing and slow the bleeding. Half an hour later, all was serene in her cottage. She glanced at Cam to find his eyes glowing as he stared down at mother and child, and happiness swelled within her. He'd probably never thought to witness such an event. To most, having a man present at a woman's labor and delivery bordered on blasphemy, but Ceana thought it appropriate. Why not? Men did this to women, so they should be allowed to see what a woman went through to bring a child into the world.

She was far too radical in her philosophies—but then, she always had been. She trod carefully through life, acutely aware that people would believe she was a witch in truth if she allowed her authentic self to show. At least tonight she had good reason for allowing a man into a world reserved for women. With Moira and the midwife nowhere to be found, she'd needed his help. Of course, she could have managed without it, but no one had to know that.

She leaned against the wall and crossed her arms, watching them. Cam glanced up at her. "You look tired."

She shook her head. "Not at all." In fact, the opposite was true. Easy births always infused her with energy. She felt like she could stride outside and take flight, run all the way to Glenfinnan. Or even Inverness.

Cam's smile widened, and a look of understanding flared in his eyes. "Nor am I."

"But you look it too."

"*I* am tired," Sorcha said on a yawn.

Ceana's heart clenched at his tender expression when his gaze moved to Sorcha. "You should be. You worked hard. And look at what you've done."

"Aye, look." Sorcha looked down at her dozing infant. "And I survived it."

"Of course you did."

She gave a shaky laugh. "I wasn't certain I would."

"Here, I'll take him." Cam removed the bundle from Sorcha's arms. There was something very sweet in seeing a man as tall and masculine as Cam handling a tiny newborn babe with such delicacy.

Just then, the door crashed open.

"Sorcha!" Alan rushed to the bedside. "God. Margaret said the baby was coming. I've sent a servant to the village to collect Moira and the midwife."

"Oh, Alan, what took you so long?" Sorcha asked.

He cradled Sorcha's hand in his own. "Margaret hurt her ankle and didn't get to the house till late, and I'd already had half the Glen searching for you. I was on my way home from Glenfinnan when they found me, and by that time it was near midnight. I came as soon as I could, love." He pressed the back of her hand to his forehead and lowered his voice. "Are you well? Are you in pain?"

She smiled up at him. "Not anymore."

"No?" Alan cast a questioning glance at Ceana, and in turn she gestured at the tiny bundle in Cam's arms.

Cam rose and moved to the end of the bed. "Alan. Your son."

"My . . . ?" Alan's blue eyes flitted wildly from Sorcha to Cam. "My son?" he whispered. "There's . . . It's . . . There's already a baby?"

"Aye, Alan. Our son," Sorcha murmured.

"He's sleeping," Cam warned, a protective note in his voice. "Be gentle."

Alan took the lad, a trifle more awkwardly than Cam had, and stared down at the sleeping face of his son, his eyes watering. His mouth moved, but he seemed at a loss for words.

"Isn't he beautiful?" Sorcha said.

"Aye." Alan looked up at his wife. "Beautiful second only to you, my love."

"I know it is tradition to name our first son after your father, but I thought . . . I thought we might call him James."

"Aye," Alan rasped, his eyes shining. "For your brother. James it is."

Cam and Ceana slipped outside to allow the three some time alone. Ceana clasped her hands behind her back. The success of the birth combined with the joy on both her friends' faces made her heart swell with an aching sort of happiness.

Tilting her head up, she looked at the cloudless sky, at the glittering wash of stars overhead.

Cam slipped his arm around her. "I am in awe of your skill. You were wonderful."

She leaned into him, content to have this time with him, content with the companionable way they touched. Agonizing over her attraction to him could come later. Now she meant to revel in the beauty of the night, in the welcome warmth of the man standing beside her. Who'd not balked at a woman in the throes of labor, but had held her hand and soothed her throughout.

That took a special kind of man.

"Thank you," she murmured. "For everything." She looked up at him. "How is your shoulder?"

"Good as new. Almost," he added sheepishly.

She snuggled closer to him. "It's cold out here. How can you be so warm?"

"It's . . ." He shrugged. "It's what happened in there. I've never imagined I'd see anything like that. It's like battle, but with a joyful outcome instead of a deadly one."

She wouldn't remind him that on occasion, the outcome of childbirth was just as deadly as battle could be. She didn't want to think about that now. The truth was, this had been beautiful. Everything about it, except perhaps the sheer surprise of it, had been ideal.

"You're right." She sighed.

He stared up at the sky. "It's late."

"It'll be dawn in a few hours."

"Sorcha can't be moved tonight."

"No," she agreed.

"She has no more need of you, does she?"

"No," Ceana said. "She'll be well. She should be up and about to-morrow, with perhaps a bit of soreness."

"And Moira is on her way here."

"Aye." Though it certainly wasn't necessary for the midwife or Moira to come for medical reasons, she knew they would want to see Sorcha and verify that for themselves.

"You can't sleep here, then. Your cottage will be too crowded."

She shrugged. "I'll survive without sleep for one night. I'll wait to sleep until they have gone tomorrow."

"No." His gaze remained transfixed on the dark, shadowy trees of the forest beyond the clearing.

She raised a brow but said nothing.

"No," he repeated, his voice quiet but deadly serious. "You will come with me."

"That's—"

Before she could say another word, he turned and disappeared into her cottage, leaving Ceana gaping after him. Just as she picked up her skirts to follow him, he emerged. Striding up to her, he grasped her hand, tearing it from the wool of her dress and clasping it in his own.

"Come."

"Wh—"

His expression implacable, he tugged—no, *dragged*—her a few feet to where his horse stood, grasped her waist, and lifted her onto the saddle.

"Cam, what are you—"

He mounted behind her, clamping one strong arm around her waist, effectively pinning her against him. "Taking you away."

"But—"

"Hush."

It wasn't until they were out of sight of her cottage that it occurred to Ceana that she was so bemused, she'd forgotten to argue. She should fight him, should object to the way he assumed he could throw her onto his horse and take her away from her home and her patient.

Then again, she realized with no small measure of panic, she had no desire to fight him.

She wanted to be stolen away, and she wanted Cam to be the one to steal her.

More than an hour later, Ceana sat rigidly, internally waging the battle of her life. They'd passed through the darkened village of Glenfinnan and rounded the tip of the loch almost half an hour ago. Cam hadn't spoken at all, and he sat in still, stony silence, but he kept his arm braced around her, locking her against the warm prison of his chest.

Stay with him. Be with him.

Run, fight, get away!

Be happy again, if only for a brief time . . .

Demand he halt; demand he set you free! Before it is too late!

What demon possessed her? Why couldn't she force herself to open her mouth and command him to return at once to her cottage? She knew that was the right thing to do. The honorable thing.

And yet . . . she couldn't. She didn't.

Cam kept the horse at a trot, and she was thankful the moon was so bright; otherwise this would truly be reckless. As it was, she grasped onto the horse's mane for dear life, though with Cam's solid arm around her middle, she hadn't come near to falling from the animal.

They descended a gentle slope, and through the trees a structure came into view. Just beyond the building, the loch shimmered in the moonlight.

Ceana closed her eyes.

A remote shelter. They'd be alone . . . together.

She was doomed.

Nevertheless, the wild part of her took over, whooping in glee and trampling the sensible part of her into the dust.

The trees parted to reveal a pretty cottage about four times as big as her own home, yet to someone of Cam's status a cozy, intimate place.

Cam stopped the horse and dismounted, then reached up to pluck her from the horse's back. He hooked a hand behind her knees, lifted her into his arms, and, holding her tightly against his hard body, strode to the cottage.

He kicked in the door. It banged against the inside wall, but he paid it no heed. She stared up at him, shocked beyond words. He stared down at her, dark intent in his eyes, and she knew he thought of nothing else but her. At this moment, she was his world.

This was what she'd secretly craved. The wicked part of her wanted him to fight for her. To take her. To make her his, damn the consequences.

He walked through an arched doorway, entering a bedroom dominated by a large curtained bed. He walked to the bed and lowered her to her feet just beside it. Then he paused, his hands gripping her shoulders, and stared at her.

She looked up into his face. Slowly, she raised her hand and grazed his lip with her fingertip. Something flared in his eyes, and he caught her wrist in his hand, pressing her fingers hard against his lips.

He opened his mouth, took a finger inside, and sucked. An erotic spasm shot through her, and she struggled to hold herself still.

"What are we—"

He pulled back from her finger with a small pop and then cupped her cheek, his fingers tight over her skin.

"Shh," he rasped.

The look in his eyes shattered her defenses and then crumbled them until they drifted away like dandelions on the wind.

She closed her eyes. God forgive her.

"I want you," she whispered, against all wisdom, contrary to her better sense. It was the truth. She wanted him like she'd never wanted another man. This enigma of a man whom everyone despised but who cared so deeply for those who depended on him. Who'd sat beside a laboring woman for hours tonight just to offer her comfort.

Ceana didn't just want him. She *ached* for him. The ache had grown in every moment that had passed since their kiss in her cottage. That kiss seemed like a lifetime ago.

She slipped her arms around his waist. He was so hard, so tight. Muscles rippled beneath her hands. And here she'd believed men of his class were always men of leisure, soft as dumplings. How wrong she'd been.

"Ceana."

With that word, his lips crashed onto hers. All at once, the pent-up need she'd been holding so tightly inside exploded. She yanked his shirt from his breeches as he pulled at the crisscrossed ties of her dress. Within moments, their garments flew across the room. Cam kicked off his breeches and stockings, and he was naked. Fumbling with her garter, Ceana glanced up at him, and her breath caught.

She'd known he was firm all over, but never had she imagined how the sight of him would affect her. He was all lean muscle, tight, hard. His cock just as rigid as the rest of him.

"Leave the stockings on," he said quietly. He bent down and scooped her up. She shivered at the contact, the collision of their bodies, sizzling hot, igniting a fire beneath her skin.

He tossed her on the bed. Before she could move an inch, he loomed over her.

"God." He stared down at her, glistening emotion crowding his eyes. "How I've wanted to touch you. To be with you. To love you."

"Me too." She gulped, trying to fill her body with air. Her mind reeled from the vision of him bare, from the hard press of his skin against hers.

"My need for you has grown since the moment I first saw you. It won't stop, Ceana. I can't stop it."

The sensations rocketing through her originated from all the points where his skin touched hers, from her ankle to her breast.

"I want to touch you."

"Aye," she murmured. "I want to touch you too."

They turned until they lay face-to-face. Gripping the back of his head, she drew him close. She kissed his mouth, explored every facet, every curve of his handsome, soft lips. She ran her hands through his short black hair, over the rough skin of his jaw, down his neck. She stroked his muscled shoulders and arms, gentling her touch when she passed over the newly forming scar of his gunshot wound.

He explored her too. Warm, questing hands ran down the undersides of her arms, beneath her ear, across her collarbones.

She pulled away from his lips to crawl down his body. His chest was magnificent. Each dip and curve of his lean muscle made her blood quicken and rush to center between her legs. Squirming a little, she brushed her tongue over his tiny, taut nipple. He jerked and let out a low groan, and she smiled against the smooth skin of his chest.

"I love your hair." His fingers sifted through the curly strands and cupped the back of her head as she traveled down his body. She pressed her cheek against his tight abdomen, kissed the jagged scar on his side, then darted her tongue inside his belly button and reveled in his smoky male taste.

Her lips traveled down the light trail of hair dusting the lower part of his stomach, and her chin bumped his cock. He made a strangled noise in his throat.

His cock was long, hot, and hard. She trailed light kisses up and down the rigid length. Closing her eyes, she sank into the glory of it, wrapping her lips around his girth and taking him deep into her mouth. Curling her fingers around him, she pumped him in time to the thrusts of her mouth, pulling the foreskin over the head as she drew up, then chasing it away with a simultaneous pull of her fingers and push of her lips. Each time she swallowed him deep, he hardened beneath her touch, and the veins covering his cock grew more prominent. The knowledge that his orgasm loomed close made her breath release in sporadic bursts.

Suddenly, he hauled her off of him. In a blink, he'd flipped her onto her back and loomed over her, his cock grazing her belly.

"A little . . . lower," she whispered, squirming in a vain attempt to move his cock into position to enter her.

"No," he said, his intense stare focused on her face. There was something new in the way he looked at her. There was such caring in his expression. There was *love*.

"It's my turn to pleasure you." His body slid down hers until he paused at her chest. Caressing the outside of her breast, he sucked a nipple deep into his mouth. The shock reverberated through her. Gasping, she clenched the bedcovers and arched her body toward him, wanting him to suckle her deeper, harder.

His lips grazed over her skin with tender kisses, and he nudged her thighs apart with his body as he slowly traveled downward. Ceana rose onto shaky forearms and watched his dark head nestle between her legs.

He made love in the same way he faced life: with passion and with care. Such strong, sweet feeling surged deep within her, she could have wept with the force of it.

He pressed his thumb against her clitoris, and she gasped, unable to stop herself from wiggling against his finger. Lowering his head, he slid his thumb downward, gently circling her opening and then sliding into her. She fell back as his tongue swiped over her in long strokes, each pass sending a prickling jolt through her body. His thumb worked her, thrusting into her, then retreating to circle her passage, then gliding inward again.

He worshiped her body with his mouth, stroking her in her most sensitive places, driving her higher and higher until she thought she'd burst apart at the seams.

"Too much!" she moaned, her hips jerking against her will. She couldn't stop the twitching movements, the spasming of her muscles. The pleasure contracted and tightened in her, so acute it was almost painful. "Oh . . ."

He didn't stop. He hummed against her, and when his tongue brushed over her clitoris again, she flew apart. The tight ball of pleasure exploded, and a sweet, piercing sensation barreled through her, causing her body to arch and undulate atop the bed. It spread through her belly, and then her limbs, until the tips of her fingers and toes tingled in release.

As the pleasure slowly faded, leaving residual sparks shooting through her, she stilled, moaning softly. Cam released her, traveling up her body, touching every part of her with his hands and tongue as he moved, stoking the subdued flames until they flared to life once more.

The press of his cock moved up her thigh and then settled in the notch between her legs, and she whimpered again, achingly sensitive from the orgasm.

"Ceana?"

She opened her eyes to see him staring at her, the question evident in his expression.

"Yes," she whispered. "Yes, Cam. I . . . want you. Please. I want you inside me."

He gripped his cock and moved it into position, then, with exquisite slowness, slid in, inch by excruciating inch, pausing between each tiny push to revel in the sensation of their joining.

He watched her, and she knew he was aware of and receptive to every expression of pleasure that crossed her face, making it clear that her pleasure was as important to him as his own.

"Oh," she whispered. Her body squeezed tightly around him, and the place where they joined burned with fiery heat. "Oh."

He pushed deeper one final time, sliding the rest of the way inside her. They were lodged together, connected.

They were one.

He held that position, watching her with those dark, expressive eyes that said so much, that revealed his humanity, his care for her. His love for her.

"Tell me what you feel," he whispered.

That emotion surged inside her again. Staring into his eyes, she slid her arms around him and held him tight, his firm skin sending tendrils of warmth through her to wrap around her heart in a sweet, comforting embrace.

"I feel you, Cam," she whispered. "Only you."

Right now, there was nothing between them. He was her world, and she was his. It was so right, so beautifully perfect. Ceana had never been happier.

He slid out and then in, staring at her. She strained toward him, gripping his solid arms. Suddenly, he drew back, and she whimpered her complaint. She clutched him, struggling to keep him close, to keep his skin touching hers, to urge him back inside her, to achieve that perfect connection once more. "It feels so good, Cam. I don't want you to stop. Please . . ."

He lifted her legs and hooked them over his arms. Leaning forward, he thrust again, his invasion so deep she released a strangled gasp.

Lowering himself over her, his forearm resting beside her head, he gripped her thigh with his other hand. All by itself, his hand on her thigh would drive her to distraction, but the combination of that and his cock thrusting into her, his fingers tangling in her hair, and his lips taking hers in a ferocious kiss made her lose all awareness of anything besides the sensations his touch wrought on her.

She trailed her hand up and down his arm, her fingers taking in the flex of his muscle as he held himself over her. He pushed deep into her, so deep his pelvis brushed over her clitoris, and she cried out.

He strained over her, his body surrounding her, a rigid, powerful cage.

Ceana had never felt protected by a man. But this man covered her, worked her, held her within an armor of steel. And the way he looked at her cast a shield of warmth all around her, defending her from all thoughts of harm and death and misery.

She was safe here with him. She was no longer cold. She wasn't alone. And she was so happy.

The sensations in her body and her heart built until Ceana sobbed out every breath, sure she couldn't take any more. But, somehow, he held her orgasm at bay.

His eyes glittered down at her. His muscles flexed beneath her fingers.

Still, he held back, keeping her from coming, holding her on the brink of madness. She was going to fall apart, fly into a million pieces, shatter. She could not sustain this. Sweet release was within reach, but each time she stretched her hand to grasp it, he yanked her back.

"Oh," she whispered. "No. No."

"Yes," Cam growled.

His thrusts roughened, turned savage, his gentle caresses forgotten. Her body was no longer her own. With each thrust, he wiped away her body's memory of every other man it had taken into it. With each kiss, he cleared away every man she thought she'd loved. With each squeeze of her thigh, he obliterated every man's touch on her skin. With each tug of her hair, he reminded her that it was him, Cam, the Earl of Camdonn, who protected her, who took her, who made her his. He softened her like clay and then refashioned her into something she'd never thought she'd be. Someone who was loved, without question and without fear.

She flew apart. Simply exploded, the sensation so intense she stopped breathing, stopped sobbing. Everything stopped except the white-hot rush of liquid pleasure. He went stiff around her, above her, inside her, and the intense pulse resonating through her body could have been coming from him or from her or from both of them as they reached the apex together, completely still and quiet, flooded with ecstasy.

Finally the pulse eased and reality hovered on the fringes, encroaching on the glow of pleasure. Cam lowered himself beside her, and, keeping his still-pulsing cock wedged inside her, he gathered her close. Warm and whole in the cage of his arms, she pressed her face against the solid wall of his chest.

CHAPTER FOURTEEN

They lay in contented silence for a long while. Just as Ceana was about to drift off, Cam slipped out of bed.

"What are you doing?" she asked drowsily. She blinked and rose up on her elbow, watching him as he pulled on his breeches.

"I'm going to take care of the horse. You sleep. I'll be back soon."

She didn't want to sleep without him. She rose, dropped her shift over her head, and followed him through the door into a cavernous room with a sofa near the hearth and a large table in the center. Moonlight streamed in through open windows on the far wall.

"What is this place?"

"It's one of my hunting cottages."

"Do you come here often?" The cottage was clean and well stocked, as if someone lived here permanently.

"I have someone keep it clean and ready, in the event I decide to come on a whim." He met her eyes. "Like tonight."

"Convenient," she murmured.

"Indeed." He exited through the still-open front door and went to the horse, which was grazing contentedly on a bit of lawn just outside.

She watched as he removed the saddle from the animal, crooning that there would be plenty of oats and a long brush-down when they returned home tomorrow. Bemusement drifted through her as she once again took note of the caring and thoughtfulness he expressed to everyone: from the whore on the mountain to a common healer to a horse. It was impossible to reconcile this man with the image portrayed by the people of the cold, uncaring, and oh-so-*English* Earl of Camdonn.

It made sense why Sorcha and Alan had remained such steadfast supporters of the earl. They knew—as Ceana now did—the true Cam. It was a shame his people had misjudged him so grossly.

He gave the horse a final stroke along its muzzle and led it to the side of the cottage. Since she wasn't wearing her shoes and didn't want to dirty her stockings, Ceana waited for him at the doorway. Less than a minute later, he returned and, seeing her waiting for him, smiled. He held out his hand. "Come back inside and get warm."

She clasped his hand and he pulled her inside and led her back into the bedroom.

"You're shivering. I'll light a fire."

"No, please," she murmured, trying to keep her teeth from chattering. "Just lie beside me."

He nodded, and they slipped under the covers. She clenched her teeth when the cold of his flesh seeped through the linen of her shift.

They clung together, slowly warming each other. When Ceana's eyelids began to grow heavy once more, Cam's arms tightened around her. "What am I going to do, Ceana?"

"You will go to sleep," Ceana murmured. "Then, when daylight comes, you will wake up and go home."

"I . . . saw something tonight." Cam's chest expanded as he took a breath. "Rather . . . I heard something."

The raw tone of his voice pulled her into full wakefulness, and she drew back a little, tilting her head to look up at him in question. "What was it?"

He removed his arm from around her waist and pressed two fingers over the bridge of his nose. "Elizabeth . . ."

Ceana frowned. She didn't want to hear Elizabeth's name now. The word grated along her spine and made the magic of the night sizzle like the hearth after someone threw a bucket of water on it. Acrid guilt rose from her gut, and she tried in vain to swallow it down.

"She . . ." He took a breath. "She is having an affair with Robert MacLean."

Ceana remained quiet, struggling to absorb this information. She'd known about Elizabeth and Rob's attraction, of course, but had thought neither of them so foolish as to act on it.

"Are you sure?"

"I saw them together." Distress creased Cam's forehead. "I followed them to the loch, and I heard them . . . I couldn't interrupt them. I was too . . . bewildered."

Ceana still couldn't speak. What could she say to this? How could she place any blame on Elizabeth and Rob when she had similarly transgressed with Cam not an hour ago?

"It is my fault," Cam continued. "I never took the time to learn more about her, to understand her. She is . . ." His voice dwindled. "I never knew her at all."

"Are you angry?" Ceana gazed at him, trying to assess this reaction. She had been Rob's lover too, but it was over between them, and she certainly hadn't expected Rob to remain chaste for the rest of his life. Yet she hadn't expected Rob to cuckold Cam, either. She'd thought him more honorable than that.

The only thing that could have driven the Rob she knew to such an action was a powerful strength of feeling. Could Rob be in love with Elizabeth? She thought of the way he'd stolen those glances at her across the dinner table. The dark look in his eyes. It had been a pained, nay, *tortured* look, a look of unfulfilled, desperate longing.

Yes, it was possible. Rob might have fallen in love with her.

Nevertheless, Lady Elizabeth was the woman Cam planned to marry. The woman he'd selected to stand beside him for the remainder of their lives. Surely he should be furious—despite the fact that he lay naked beside Ceana at this very moment. Such were the different expectations of women and men.

"No, I am not angry with her, though I should be. I am angry with myself. At how I have botched every aspect of this betrothal." Cam released a self-deprecating laugh. "Look at us both. We aren't yet married and we have already strayed."

"What will you do?" Ceana couldn't imagine him doing anything as foolish as challenging Rob or hurting him. Rob would be safe, but Ceana worried for Elizabeth. If Cam canceled their wedding, if he told her uncle what Elizabeth had done, the poor girl's life would be made miserable.

"I don't know." Cam's throat moved as he swallowed. "There's more."

"Tell me."

"Robert MacLean said . . ." He paused, took a breath, and tried again. "He told her that he is my brother."

This time her response was automatic. "Do you believe him?"

Cam groaned. His eyes glistened. "I don't know."

She flattened her palm against his chest. "What do you feel? In your heart?"

Cam stilled under her hand, and his expression turned inward, searching. "I . . . don't know. I think . . . I think . . . Yes. It could be true. It might explain a few things."

"What could it explain?"

"My mother died when I was very young, and my father . . . I found him, once, with another woman in his bedchamber." Cam turned onto his back and stared up at the ceiling. "I knew my mother was gone, that this woman wasn't her, and I was enraged. I . . . attacked him. Even though he was a widower and he had every right to take a woman into his bed, at that age I didn't understand. I felt he had betrayed my mother. Servants rushed in—they dragged me off of him." He closed his eyes. "The woman . . . She sat up in the bed, gripping the blankets against her nudity, staring at me in shock. I think . . . If I am recalling correctly, I believe she might have had Robert MacLean's coloring."

Ceana released a breath.

"He is six years younger than me. That would make him the right age."

"Oh, Cam."

He squeezed his eyes shut. "When I was a boy, I always wished for a brother. When I met Alan MacDonald in England years later, he became like a brother to me. And now he has a family apart from me. Yet I might have a brother of my own," Cam said. "A true brother."

"Perhaps you do."

"Who is tupping the woman I am to marry." Cam's voice hardened, and Ceana finally recognized the glimmer of anger.

"Aye," she agreed mildly.

He stiffened against her. "I should kill him for this."

"Should you?"

"It is my right. Elizabeth is mine."

"Is she?"

He gaped at her for a brief second, and then his lips snapped shut. He returned his gaze to the ceiling. "Yes. Legally, she will belong to me very soon."

"And yet here you lie in bed with me." Her words emerged in a flat tone, successfully hiding the pain it wrought upon her to say them. *If Elizabeth is yours, what am I to you, Cam?*

But she couldn't voice that question. She must keep this encounter light, not add unfounded significance to it. He'd just come from an enormous revelation about his betrothed and her lover. He had just come from a birth that had left him feeling invincible. Only now had he crashed back down to earth.

It was all as should be expected—no more, no less.

In fact, Ceana was relieved that he still intended to marry Elizabeth. Perhaps his desire to marry the Englishwoman would lessen the pain of Ceana's inevitable separation from him.

Turning to his side, Cam slipped his arm around her waist and tugged her against him. "I'm here with you because I want to be with you."

"Not out of retaliation for Elizabeth's betrayal?"

He stared at her. "Is that what you think? You believe that I'd use you to take vengeance on my betrothed?"

"Aye. It seems the natural conclusion." She gave him a wry smile. "Now that you've learned that she has betrayed you, you feel justified in betraying her."

"No. That had nothing to do with it."

"Well, certainly it is part of your purpose in bringing me here."

"No." He grasped her shoulder and squeezed tightly. "Do you hear me? That had nothing to do with it. I'm here with you tonight because . . . It was this night—all of it. The revelations earlier. Sorcha's birth, and Alan's arrival. The look on his face when he saw his wife and child—" Cam broke off. "It was all of it, Ceana. I wanted to share it with you. I wanted to *be* . . . with you."

"And you *were* with me," she said quietly. Already the blood sped in her veins, and arousal prickled along her spine. She ran her hand along the ropes of lean muscle wrapped around his torso.

His hand slid between her legs. "I came inside you."

"Aye."

"There could be a child."

"No. I have already prevented it."

He nodded, and she smiled at his trust in her knowledge of herbs used to prevent conception. "I cannot say the idea of my child growing in your belly is repulsive to me."

She repressed a shudder. It could never happen. Not again. She couldn't bear it.

"But I shouldn't like to see you suffering the pain Sorcha did."

"All birthing mothers suffer it," Ceana said. "And we . . . *they* . . . bear it."

"I have renewed respect for women."

He'd missed her blunder. She nearly sobbed in relief. "Good," she murmured.

His mouth descended to touch hers, so softly, a question rather than a command, and she opened to him.

His hands cradled her body. His lips sipped at hers like a bee probing a flower for the tiniest drops of nectar. Their lips brushed together in a delicate play of advance and retreat. His tongue slipped into her mouth, gently thrusting in a carnal motion as old as time.

Sighing, she matched his slow pace, tasting him, caressing him. Taking her time.

These could be their last moments together.

Cam moved lower, and his tongue flicked over the sensitive bud of her nipple.

"Mmmm." She reached for his head and plunged her fingers into his silky black hair. She held him in place as he worshiped her breast, sucking the nipple into his mouth, a tug that pulled through her like a rope straight between her legs.

He released her nipple, nuzzled it, and she gasped at the sensation of his rough skin scratching over her breast.

Removing her hand from his side, he pressed her palm to his cock. It was in a state of growing arousal—the stage she loved, not quite rock hard but not flaccid. She curled her fingers and pumped, nearly groaning herself at the sensation of it expanding and hardening in her hand.

"Ah, Ceana." His warm breath fanned over her cheek. He bit down gently on the lobe.

A fierce possessiveness shot through her. He was hers. *Only hers*.

As quickly as they had come, she tamped the bubbling emotions down, locked them up, and buried the key deep in her heart.

Even if he were insane enough to forsake Elizabeth for her once they were married—a fate she didn't wish on Elizabeth—she could never have him. He could never truly be hers.

Never.

With a small sob that emerged sounding like a cross between a groan and a whimper, she pushed at his arm until he fell onto his back. He stared up at her with eyes that glittered like obsidian in the dim light.

She straddled him and adjusted herself over his cock, sliding over its length before she reached beneath her and lifted it into place.

Then, slowly, she descended over him, throwing her head back in pleasure as her channel squeezed all around him. His hands slid over her hips and gripped her arse cheeks.

When he was fully seated inside her, she looked down at him.

"This is where you belong," he said in a growling whisper. "Where I belong."

Cam was a dreamer, she realized as she gazed down at his bonny face. Like most gentlemen, he attempted to make rational, wise decisions based on his status in society, but when his emotions came into play, he lost that ability. He clung tenaciously to feeling and desire.

Somehow, he'd engaged that part of her too. A shudder of panic rippled through her.

He felt her tremble. "Move, Ceana." He lifted her buttocks and lowered her over him. Both of them groaned.

"Again." Once more, he lifted her and lowered her. Not wanting to disturb his healing wound, she anchored her palms on both sides of him.

Grasping her upper thighs, he lifted her, then pulled her down. Together, they built a rhythm, he sliding nearly all the way out and then balls deep. Then she bent down and swiped her tongue over his nipple.

He heaved her off him. She didn't know what his intentions were, but she wanted to feel him in her mouth again. She scooted down his body, licking down the length of his cock, tasting herself mixed in with his earlier release, and then cupped his ballocks and took them into her mouth, laving them as the crisp hairs around the base of his cock tickled her nose.

"Holy hell," Cam muttered, his voice rough with desire, and she blew out a breath of satisfaction. He liked this too.

Gently, for she knew this was the most delicate part of a man's anatomy, she rolled his ballocks in her hands. She took them in her mouth one at a time, suckled them, loved them. Then she swiped her tongue over his cock—it was even harder now—and took it into her mouth in a deep, slick glide.

He made a strangled sound. His hands wrapped in the strands of her hair. Ceana wanted to bring him pleasure, and she loved the feel of him deep in her mouth. She loved how he tugged on her hair, and she loved pushing his cock deep against her throat and then, reaching her limit, pulling back until her lips rimmed his crown. Ceana gripped his thighs and worked her mouth over him, closing her eyes as she felt him grow ever larger against her lips.

Suddenly he pulled away. "On your knees."

He crawled behind her as she went to her knees and leaned forward to rest her weight on her forearms.

"Oh!" She gasped when his fingers spread her arse cheeks and his mouth covered her. He stiffened his tongue, darting it in and out of her channel. She wiggled and tilted her hips, giving him better access.

As his mouth explored her, he tentatively brushed his thumb over her topmost hole. Only one man had touched her there before, and it was the most sensitive spot on her body, perhaps due to the forbidden nature of it.

She pushed against his questing finger, urging him onward. But he pulled back and raised his head.

She flung an arch glance over her shoulder and met his gleaming eyes. The look he gave her was intimate, and it was wicked. Knowing. Telling her he knew exactly what she wanted and promising that he would deliver.

Holding her hips, he jerked her body against him. The cheeks of her arse cradled the rigid length of his cock, and she moved, rubbed over him. Then he released her with one hand. With the other, he guided his cock down her cleft, pausing at that forbidden spot.

Ceana held her breath and tensed in anticipation of the invasion. Still holding her so tightly she couldn't move, couldn't push herself down over him, he teased gently at her opening. Ceana gritted her teeth.

He moved lower, finding the slick, spasming notch of her sex. With a long, smooth stroke, he buried himself within her. He began a rhythm of deep glides, and his thumb returned to the area just above the place where his cock shuttled into her, at first rubbing gently, and then, with a long, inward stroke, sinking deep inside her.

Ceana came instantly, her body jerking from the shock of the double penetration. Tiny crackling flares erupted deep within her, and she shuddered as they swept through her body. He didn't allow her to come down; instead he began a rhythm of deep thrusts with both thumb and cock. The flares thinned, but they didn't stop. Instead they built, coalesced until a ball of flame blazed deep inside her.

Cam thrust harder, deeper, making harsh exhalations with every push into her body. The ball of flame retracted, tightened, became so hot and so dense Ceana thought it might burn her from the inside out.

"Oh!" she gasped. With every thrust, Cam pushed all the air from her body.

His fingers tightened on her hip, and the ball exploded into flames that licked over her skin, beneath it, through her veins. Cam held her tight as she shuddered, and his thrust gentled. He leaned over her, crooning lovingly into her ear.

The fire simmered within her now, and her muscles shook with the effort of holding her body up. Gently, he pulled out of her and laid her on her stomach, tucking one of the round, puffy pillows beneath her hips.

She turned her head to look at him. "I want you inside me again."

"Yes." Already, he'd knelt between her legs and his cock nudged at her entrance. She tilted her pelvis to allow him access.

He slid home, and she released a sigh of pleasure. She was sensitive and hot and raw, but he filled her, took away the feeling of emptiness.

He leaned down over her, his breath whispering in her ear, his chest flush against her back. She loved the press of his warm skin against hers. It felt so right. So perfect. So good.

After her orgasm, she was supple and languid. She felt like a warm, smooth river, encompassing him, caressing him. Within moments, his cock hardened and began to pulse. His muscles tightened, banded around her. And then he thrust hard, once, and his cock contracted deep within her, filling her with his seed.

He slumped down beside her and, as she curled into a ball on her side, he curved his body protectively around her. Delirious with satisfaction, they both sank into a deep sleep.

When Ceana opened her eyes, the first vestiges of a gray dawn leaked lazily in through the shuttered windows. She stretched and yawned, noting the pleasant soreness of her body.

"Mmm."

Cam's hand slipped over her waist and then rose to stroke her breast. "Come home with me today."

"Why?" she murmured.

"I want you with me."

She tried not to go stiff. She chuckled. "Impossible."

"I've decided not to marry Elizabeth."

She flipped over to face him, her eyes wide. "But you must!"

Lord, she should have expected this after all that had happened. But even late last night he'd seemed intent on making Elizabeth his wife. From his words alone, she'd assumed she was safe. What a fool she was.

"You must marry her!"

"Why do you say that? We're not even married yet and she has betrayed me. What kind of wife will a woman like that make?"

She reached forward, cupping her hands over his shoulders, and tried not to attempt to shake some sense into him. "You have betrayed her as well."

"That's different."

She raised a brow. "Is it?"

Impatiently, he pushed a hand through his hair. "Hell, Ceana—"

"You must marry her."

"Why?"

Fear for the young woman—for all of them—rose in her chest. "You mustn't tell her uncle about what happened, Cam. You mustn't tell anyone."

"I have no intention of telling anyone. She is a young, well-bred English lady. If word of her indiscretion spread . . ." He shook his head. "No. I see no reason to damage her reputation."

"That is why you must marry her."

"To save her reputation? That's absurd. It is clear neither of us possesses a strong desire for the other. Why would we commit ourselves to a lifetime of unhappiness with each other just to salvage her reputation?"

"You will ruin her if you cancel the wedding."

"Not necessarily. What if I kept quiet about her indiscretion and instead admitted to my own?"

Ceana's hands slipped off his shoulders. She merely shook her head.

He reached forward and wrapped his hands around her neck, his expression intent, his eyes dark and serious. "What if I told them I no longer wanted Elizabeth? What if I told them I wanted someone else?"

She shook her head again, mute, panic clawing at her stomach.

"What if I told the world I wish to be with Ceana MacNab instead?"

CHAPTER FIFTEEN

Cam rode back to the castle in a fog. After they'd eaten a light breakfast, he'd taken Ceana home, where they'd found no trace of Sorcha or any of the others. A patient awaited Ceana at her door, however, an old man with a rattling cough, and her tension visibly melted away the moment she saw him. She'd jumped off the horse, given Cam a perfunctory adieu, and, with nary a glance back at him, ushered her patient inside.

She'd been silent and snappish the entire way to her cottage. Did it mean she didn't want to be with him? Had he broached the topic inappropriately? He hadn't openly offered her marriage. Was that what she wanted? A deeper promise? A lifetime commitment?

He'd never offered to marry Sorcha MacDonald, and that was how he'd lost her. He'd managed the situation with Sorcha like an ass, and he damn well didn't want to repeat his mistakes now. He cared for Ceana too much. The thought of losing her forever was unfathomable.

But what was the proper way to approach this? The events of last night—all of them—had proven to him that he cared for her beyond measure.

That thought clamped his chest so tight he wondered if he'd ever be able to take a deep breath again.

Nevertheless, as much as his gut commanded him to, he could not rush impulsively into a marriage with Ceana MacNab. He didn't want to offer her something that would affect them so significantly without putting a great deal of thought into the repercussions. He had learned at least a few valuable lessons from the mistakes of his impetuous youth and his rash behavior with Sorcha.

Could Ceana give him the companionship he sought? The mutual affection he craved? Could they overcome the political backlash and the potential enmity of the Duke of Irvington? Was it an exaggeration to say that if he broke off his engagement to Elizabeth, it would ruin her life?

Could he take Ceana into society and among his peers? Could he make her happy?

Would she make him a better wife than Elizabeth?

Not politically. He sighed. Too many ties depended on his association with the Duke of Irvington. If he didn't follow through with his engagement to Elizabeth, the most important and influential people in the world would be sorely disappointed in him. Ultimately, that could negatively affect not only him, but his tenants and all the residents of the Glen.

Perhaps that was why Ceana had fled. She was practical to a fault. She knew who they both were. She knew that in the social order in which they existed, their two worlds didn't—*couldn't*—overlap.

Yet Elizabeth had already betrayed him, and he'd betrayed her. The fact that both of them had already strayed did not bode well for the happiness of their marriage.

Still, he could not simply undo the betrothal and discard Elizabeth. There was too much at stake.

He rode for some time, his mind a garble, before he realized he was leading the horse in the wrong direction. Grimly, he turned back toward Camdonn Castle.

The sun had begun to descend in the misty afternoon sky when he passed through the castle gates and dismounted at the stables, where Robert MacLean approached to take his horse.

Cam gazed at the man who'd taken his betrothed against a cavern wall last night. Why couldn't he conjure up a murderous rage? Was it because the man might be his brother? Was it because Cam didn't possess any proprietary feelings for Elizabeth? Was it because he didn't love her?

None of that should matter. She was still his betrothed. She still belonged to him. Despite that, as much as he tried to muster the requisite hate for Robert MacLean, he couldn't find it in himself.

He handed the reins to Rob in silence and turned toward the keep, but the other man laid a hand on his arm. "A large group of your tenants arrived this morning. Charles Stewart and your manservant are with them."

Cam tried to imagine the boyish Stewart and Duncan MacDougall, his aged valet, attempting to keep a hoard of angry Highlanders content in the confines of his study.

He rubbed his fingers over his temple. Between his feelings for Ceana, his confusion over Rob and Elizabeth, and his desire to make peace with his own people, his ability to manage it all was wearing thin.

He went directly to his study and was instantly bombarded by representatives of the poorest of his tenants, begging for work to exchange for overdue rents. Cam sorted through the Highlanders one at a time, and Charles helped him to match skills to the work most suited to each man.

Bram MacGregor hung back, waiting for everyone else's concerns to be addressed before reporting that Hamish Roberts was sleeping out in the open, and his wife and children had been scattered among families who volunteered to house them a few days at a time.

"Why doesn't Roberts make any attempt to care for his family? Why hasn't he tried to keep them together?" Cam asked.

MacGregor sneered. "What does he possess to care for 'em with? He's been evicted, left with nothing."

Cam eyed MacGregor coolly. "He hasn't petitioned me for work."

"Because ye willna grant it."

"No one knows that for certain until he tries."

The fuming MacGregor strode toward the door, but Cam stopped him. "Why do you champion this man MacGregor? He is a thief, and I have it on good authority that he is a drunkard too."

"He's representative of how poor leadership causes the Highlands to suffer."

"Or perhaps how poor judgment can lead a family to ruin? In any case, I suggest you find worthier men to champion in the future."

MacGregor opened the door.

"Oh, and MacGregor?"

His dark eyes brimming with annoyance, MacGregor turned to face him.

"If you know where Mrs. Roberts is, you might advise her to see my housekeeper. My household is growing, and I require more staff. Perhaps she possesses one of the skills Janet is looking for."

MacGregor stilled, and some of the fire drained from his eyes. After a long pause, he said, "I will send her."

With that, the man disappeared. Standing at Cam's side, Charles whispered, "Well-done, my lord."

Cam released a breath and gazed at his empty room. Perhaps he'd someday learn how to lead these people, after all.

That night at dinner, Elizabeth sat at the table demurely as always, eyes downcast, hands folded. As he watched her, Cam's appetite deserted him. He pushed away his bowl of oxtail soup.

"You don't care for the soup, my lord?" Elizabeth asked as a footman took it away. "I find it very pleasant."

"It is excellent," agreed her uncle.

"I fear I'm not very hungry tonight." Cam cupped his glass in his hands and stared at his wine.

"That's too bad, Camdonn, because it is really quite good." The duke swiped a napkin over his lips. He looked from Elizabeth to Cam, and a slow grin spread across his face. "So. A little less than a fortnight now."

Cam slid a glance at Elizabeth. "Yes."

"I must say, I heartily enjoyed hearing your names when the banns were called at services this past Sunday. It made the event seem all too real." The duke beamed. "I know you will be happy together. A perfect match, indeed."

"Indeed." Cam was grateful his tone sounded somewhat honest. Again, he glanced at Elizabeth. She gazed at her lap, expressionless.

"I daresay the two of you will make beautiful children," the duke proclaimed. "The perfect combination of dark and light. Which shall prevail, I wonder?"

Cam couldn't breathe. He braced his hands on the edge of the table, forcing them not to clench, forcing his itching feet not to stride away. He curved his lips into a grimacing smile. "Hopefully we will know the answer to that question very soon."

"Ah, good," the duke said. "Excellent. Lizzy will make an outstanding mother, and I do believe that the occupation of mothering will subdue her."

Slowly, carefully, Elizabeth took a sip of her wine.

The sounds of her harsh gasps last night, her breathless cries of pleasure, rushed through Cam's mind. Would mothering his children subdue her? Take away that passion he'd witnessed?

He kept his attention on the duke. "Why have you never married, Your Grace? Surely you have the wish to beget an heir?"

"Ah." The duke took a long draft of wine. "Perhaps someday soon, but until now I have been too preoccupied with doing right by my only niece—the sole member of my family remaining after my brother and his wife and son were cruelly taken by smallpox." He cast a loving glance at Elizabeth, which she returned with a smile. "Elizabeth was the only one who survived. She had suffered through tremendous pain and heartbreak. She required so much affectionate care to keep her young spirit from descending into permanent melancholy."

"You have done right by her," Cam said.

"Indeed you have, Uncle. And you have my never-ending gratitude."

Cam stared at her, for the first time discerning a hint of disingenuousness in her words. Perhaps if he hadn't heard her liaison with Rob, he wouldn't have noticed. But every moment he was with her, it was becoming clearer that the core Elizabeth was a very different person from the icon of sweet perfection he'd thought he was to marry.

God, the girl was going to drive him mad.

How could he go through with a marriage to a woman he couldn't trust? She'd reveal her true colors to Robert MacLean, but not him.

Never him.

It struck him that she might leave him, might run away with Rob. He pushed away the initial feeling of relief that thought elicited. As much as he'd like to easily solve the problem of his marriage to Elizabeth, he had no desire to face the embarrassment of that scandal.

In any case, from Elizabeth's point of view, that action wouldn't be sensible, or even reasonable. She'd lose everything. Her life would change for the worse. She was a pampered duke's niece, not a woman who had been raised to weather the rough life of a Highland outcast. Surely she was intelligent enough to know all this.

Nevertheless, Cam realized, after that scene down by the loch, that Elizabeth was more than capable of making rash, illogical decisions.

He set down his wineglass on the ivory linen tablecloth. Maybe he should force her to be candid with him. Perhaps if he told her he knew about her and Rob, she would abandon her facade and finally be candid with him.

It might hurt both of them to be honest with each other. While he could easily reveal his heart, his hopes, his fears, and his thoughts to Ceana, the thought of doing so with Elizabeth gave him a sick, anxious feeling, and he couldn't comprehend why.

Still, he must make the effort.

Soon.

A few hours later, Cam prepared for bed as Duncan puttered around his bedchamber. Cam looked up at the older man. "You knew my father, didn't you, Duncan?"

"Aye, sir. I knew him very well. Worked at the castle as a serving boy when he and I were lads, and we became right good friends until he was sent away to school."

"Do you remember the days after my mother died?"

Duncan's lined face turned grave. He looked up from the pile of clothes he was folding. "Aye. Those were dark days. Dark days indeed."

Cam got right to the point. "Do you remember the women he brought to his bed?"

My bed, Cam thought bleakly, staring at the hulking carved oak bed with its heavy green and black damask bed curtains.

"Er . . ." Duncan straightened, eyeing him with perceptive blue eyes. "Why do ye ask, milord?"

Cam shrugged. "Curiosity, I suppose."

Duncan looked thoughtful. "Well, indeed, there was a string of 'em, sir. Just after Lady Camdonn departed this earth. I always thought it 'is way of mourning . . . of trying to find a replacement for her. But none of them was right, of course. They was all lasses from the Glen."

"Who were they?"

Duncan frowned. "I can't say I remember them all. MacDonald lasses. One or two MacLeans . . ." Duncan's frown deepened. "One of them was married. A pretty one, she was. The husband eventually discovered her betrayal, and there was a big row betwixt the three of 'em, and she and the husband stole away late one night to never return to Camdonn Castle. The earl was furious, so he was—I think he was fonder of that lass than he was of the others. He sent a search party to retrieve them. Alas, they were never found."

"What were their names?"

"Marian and . . . Peter, I think it was." He scrunched his forehead as if he doubted himself. "It was long ago."

"Do you remember the year? The month of their departure?"

Duncan gazed at him shrewdly. "Do you think you know them, milord? Have you met them? Do you remember the incident? Indeed, it caused quite an uproar, but everyone thought you too young—"

"Just answer the questions, Duncan."

"I believe it was 1692, and . . . I cannot remember the month. The trees were bare . . . autumn?"

Cam sat in silence. Robert MacLean was twenty-four, which meant he was born after April in 1693. Could the couple Duncan spoke of be the parents of Robert MacLean? There was only one way to find out. He rose and strode to his wardrobe, taking out a fresh shirt and breeches.

Duncan frowned at him as he pulled on the breeches.

"There's something I must do. Go to bed, Duncan."

After the manservant left him, Cam hurried to the stables. Finding the stable door unlocked, he went in and mounted the stairs to Rob's apartment. Light and warmth emanated from upstairs, so he knew the man was at home.

Hell, Elizabeth might be here. He paused near the bottom of the stairs. "Ho, MacLean? Are you here?"

He heard a scraping noise, and then Rob appeared at the top of the stairs. "Milord? Do you require assistance with one of the horses?"

"No. I . . . wish to speak with you about something."

Rob paused, his expression very still, then said, "Please come up."

Cam climbed the stairs and entered the stable master's quarters. Rob led him to a chair Cam recognized as one of the chairs from Queen Anne's time that his father had kept in his study before Cam had ordered the room refurbished for his own use.

"Would you like some ale? I haven't any whisky."

"Ale is fine."

Cam was quiet while Rob poured the frothy mixture into a cup and handed it to him. He dragged a wicker chair close to Cam and lowered himself into it. "What brings you here, milord?"

Cam cleared his throat. "Have you learned anything about the highwaymen?"

Rob shook his head. "No. I've questioned Bram MacGregor. He claims he knows nothing of the attack, but—"

"Do you think he is the one who tried to kill me?" The thought had already crossed Cam's mind. Several times, in fact, but he couldn't accuse MacGregor of anything when he had no proof beyond the disrespectful way in which the man addressed him.

Rob steepled his fingers in front of his chin. "It is possible. He isn't overly fond of you. Or your politics."

"Neither is anyone else in the Glen," Cam said dryly.

"Aye, well, true enough."

"MacGregor is simply more open about it than the others."

Rob nodded his agreement. "The Jacobites respect him. He distinguished himself at Sherrifmuir."

"Did he? I wasn't aware any of my men were at Sherrifmuir."

"He was," Rob said. "He slipped out and joined the MacDonalds when they made their late march south. He reappeared on your lands shortly after the battle, but the MacDonalds speak often of his bravery."

"I see."

He stared at the younger man sitting across from him. What would Robert MacLean do if Cam confronted him with the truth? Told him he'd witnessed what had occurred between him and Elizabeth last night?

No. He couldn't. He didn't want to face any of that. Hell, he was still unsure what he thought about it. He was still damn uncertain of his own reaction to it. The fact that he didn't feel any rage unsettled him more than anything.

Cam rubbed his forehead. Damn it, he didn't want to be thinking of this now. He *couldn't* think of this now.

He'd come for another purpose. At least he might know how to get to the bottom of this particular mystery. And once armed with the knowledge of the truth, he might have an inkling what to do about Rob and Elizabeth . . . and himself and Ceana.

Cam steeled himself. He breathed in the smells of leather and peat—masculine, earthy scents.

"I've a theory," he said in a low voice.

"About the attacks?"

"No." He took a deep swallow of ale. This was more difficult than he'd expected. "Please . . . bear with me. I've a few questions for you. It'll become clear soon enough where this will lead."

Rob's forehead creased. "All right."

"Where were you born?"

"Glasgow."

"What were the names of your parents?"

Rob's features tightened. "Why?"

Cam grimaced. "Answer the question."

Rob swallowed. "My father was Peter MacLean," he said slowly. "My mother died at my birth. Her name was Marian."

It wasn't proof, Cam reminded himself. He could be Peter's son, not the old earl's.

He stared at Rob, who sat very still in front of him.

"Who sired you?" Cam asked, his voice strained as it emerged from his tight throat. "Was it Peter MacLean, or was it another man?"

Rob's face was immobile as stone, doing a fine job of hiding whatever the hell he was feeling. "I think you might know who sired me," he said quietly.

"I think so too."

For what seemed like an eternity, they stared at each other. The peat fire whispered, sending a flickering blue light over Rob's features, and Cam realized for the first time that they were much like his own. Rob was lighter than him, shorter and wider, but his facial structure— the shape of his bones, nose, forehead, and lips—was similar to his own. Similar to their father's.

Cam rose from the chair abruptly. He prowled around the room, analyzing it. This was his brother's home. He studied the discards of old furniture from Camdonn Castle. He paused at the long workbench against the wall below the rows of tall windows looking toward the keep. He gazed down at the tools as well as the strips of leather and birch that covered it. He glanced at Rob. "What do you do here?"

"Leatherwork," Rob said shortly, watching him from his position rooted to his chair.

Cam nodded. His brother possessed skills he'd never have. Skills supposedly unworthy of an earl's son. He continued to study the place, taking note of the small pantry stocked neatly with supplies, the trunk pushed into a corner, the shelves containing Rob's sparse wardrobe. The bed, another secondhand piece of furniture from Camdonn Castle, with scratched wood posts and devoid of curtains. All in all, a serviceable living area, if not a luxurious one. Cam had subsisted in smaller and more dismal quarters at school in England.

He turned to Rob. "Did my father know?"

"No."

"You came here when he was still alive, didn't you?"

"Aye."

"Why did you not confront him?"

"He was not an approachable man."

Cam released a harsh breath. He understood completely. "Would you have confronted me, had I not approached you first?"

"I . . . cannot say."

Cam thrust his hand through his hair. "Hell," he muttered. "I don't know what to do about this." He stopped in the middle of the room, at the foot of Rob's bed. "Are you certain?"

"Aye. My father made sure I knew, and he never let me forget."

"What do you mean?"

Rob still sat stolidly in the chair, his back stiff. "In words," he replied. "And actions."

Again, Cam understood. In a similar way, his own father had made certain Cam knew he wasn't worthy of being his son.

"We are brothers." His voice was a near whisper.

Rob paused. Then, "Aye."

"You've known . . . for a long time."

"Since I was a lad."

An idea struck him. Like a lightning bolt from heaven . . . or hell.

It was an odd plan, perhaps even somewhat perverse, but an irresistible opportunity to view Rob and Elizabeth together. When he worked in the afternoons, he would bring them to his study on the pretense of spending more time with Elizabeth and teaching Rob about managing the estate. Once they were together, he'd analyze their interactions. Maybe he could learn once and for all whether their passion was an ephemeral thing or whether it went deeper. Maybe then he would be able to decipher the problem of what he must do with them. Whether they'd acted on basic carnal urges or on true feelings for each other. In the end, if Elizabeth truly loved Robert MacLean, Cam could not marry her.

"I want you to come to my study tomorrow after the noonday meal."

"I have duties here," Rob said quietly.

"Delegate them to others." Cam took a deep breath and reined himself in. He was treating Rob like a servant. Nonetheless, he was the elder brother, the earl, the legitimate son. Though he knew he should no longer place Rob in the lowly position he was accustomed to, by rights he still held some sway over the man.

He stepped closer to the chair where Rob still sat. "I should like to get to know you better. Teach you more about the workings of my estate, among other things."

Rob raised a brow, and Cam pressed on. "I should like you to come to my study in the afternoons while I work through castle business with my factor. I want you to watch and learn. If you require another man to help take over your duties here, I will approve whomever you choose. You are illegitimate and by law cannot be the heir to my title and entailed lands, but if you prove worthy—and from my current knowledge of your capabilities and intelligence, I have no doubt that you will . . ." Cam paused. "Well, I should like to raise you higher than a stable master."

CHAPTER SIXTEEN

Rob stood before the hearth, his arms crossing his chest, facing the door where Cam had disappeared almost an hour before.

After twenty-four years, his brother finally knew of their blood bond. And in less than two weeks, the man was going to marry Elizabeth.

What could he do?

Turning to the fire, he closed his eyes. She was better off without him. No matter how much Cam intended to raise him up in the world, Elizabeth was a duke's niece, a duke's daughter. She deserved more than anything he'd ever be.

Yet the thought of Cam touching her, being at her side, being intimate, possessing her not only physically but legally, made his gut churn with nausea.

"She's mine."

Rob's voice rang quietly through the space of his apartment. He spoke the truth. No matter what happened between Elizabeth and Cam or between Rob and Cam, for better or for worse, Elizabeth was his.

There was no turning back.

The question was, could he bear it if everyone else, including the earl himself, believed she belonged to Cam?

Perhaps he could, as long as Elizabeth knew the truth. If they both

understood what they were to each other, he just might be able to endure it.

But could he endure the betrayal? The deception? Cam intended
to pull him into the fold of his home and his family. How could Rob
accept that if at the same time he was taking his brother's intended
into his bed?

In the end, Rob couldn't live a life of betrayal and deception. He
couldn't tear honor into shreds, throw it into the fire, and watch it burn.

He heard a sound downstairs, and then footsteps as they ascended
the stairs. He turned to the doorway. Cam again? Or Elizabeth?

It was Elizabeth, thank God. Dressed in her dark wool cloak covering the simple shift she'd worn before.

She reeled to a halt on the landing, and they stared at each other
for a long moment.

Finally, he said, "I'm glad you came. But you shouldn't have."

"I know."

"It's dangerous."

She nodded. "If my uncle were to find out . . ." Fear clouded her
blue eyes. "But I can't stop myself. I . . . need to be with you. I feel so
safe with you."

He went to her and pulled her against him. She sank into his
embrace.

"You looked like you were waiting for someone," she said, her
voice muffled by his chest. "Did you expect someone else? Another
woman?"

He raised a brow and looked down at the top of her blond head.
"What if I were?"

"I don't know," Elizabeth said thoughtfully. "I think . . . I might be
inclined to kill her."

"Is that so?"

"Yes." She pulled back, and, looking up, she met his eyes. "But I
know I cannot stop you from having a woman here. If you wanted another woman, you'd have her, and there isn't a deuced thing I could
do about it."

"I've no intention of taking another woman, Elizabeth."

"You already have a lover," she whispered. "Ceana MacNab."

"No."

She released a breath of relief, but he bent closer, frowning. "How did you know about Ceana?"

A dark flush spread across her cheeks. "I saw . . ."

He hovered over her, very still. "Where? What did you see?"

"I was coming to see you," she said in a rush. "You and she were at the top of the stairs . . . and I watched."

Elizabeth stared up at him, assessing his reaction to her words. God, the way he looked at her tore her open, exposed her. She couldn't lie to him, couldn't pretend to be anything other than herself—showing her base, coarse, diseased core. She had always been deathly afraid of exposing herself to anyone, but something compelled her to strip herself bare before Rob.

He studied her intently. "How did you feel when you watched me take Ceana?"

"Horrid," she said. It wasn't enough. From the expectant look on his face, she knew he wanted more. She took a deep breath and blurted it all out. "Sad. Jealous. Intrigued. Aroused." She blinked away the sting in her eyes. "I wished it were me."

"Do you wish I'd take you over the hay bale, like I took Ceana?"

"Yes," she whispered. She gazed up at him. "If that is what *you* wish."

With a firm finger, he tilted her chin up. "As long as I have you, I won't desire or pursue anyone else. That is my promise to you."

"I promise the same to you," she said gravely. "As long as we are together, I will give myself to no one but you."

His eyes narrowed. "But you will."

"My body I will give to the man I will marry, and only because I must. But as long as I have you, he will never have my soul."

He released her chin, and his fingers dipped beneath her hair until he cupped the back of her neck.

"I wasn't expecting a woman," he said gruffly. "The earl was here earlier." His fingers tightened, digging into her muscles. It was a pleasant sort of pain, and it shot a spike of arousal through her. "Have you told him about anything that has passed between us?"

She felt her eyes widen. "No!"

"Did you tell him he is my brother?"

Shaking her head vigorously, she said, "I did not."

His hand released its hold on her neck. "He knew."

"How?"

"I don't know."

"What was his reaction to the truth?"

The line between Rob's brows deepened. "He looked at me like he'd never seen me before."

"Perhaps he hadn't," Elizabeth said quietly. "I saw you, though. On the first day I met you." Reaching up, she touched her fingers to his cheek. "I knew that you could be the one to give me what I need so desperately."

"And what is that?" he murmured. "What do you need?"

She couldn't say it. Why would he make her say it? She had the feeling he knew as well as he did. She needed *him*. His power, his control. The firmness of his touch.

His hands curved around her face. He tilted her face up to his, but she closed her eyes, resisting the directness of his stare.

"Open your eyes."

Slowly, she did as she was told.

"Look at me."

She did.

"Tell me. Tell me while you look me in the eye. Tell me what you want—what you need—from me."

She attempted to control her breath, but it was no use. She could scarcely draw in thready wisps of air. "I need you," she said in a reedy voice, "to touch me." She fought against the tears pricking at the backs of her eyes.

He cocked his head as if in question, still staring at her. His hands went tight around her cheeks, and a vulnerable look crossed his face. Still, she didn't break eye contact with him.

"There is . . . a darkness in me, Elizabeth."

"I know." That was part of what she'd seen in him that first day.

"You give yourself to me too freely—" His voice broke and he tried again. "You don't understand."

"No, you're wrong. I *do* understand. You won't hurt me."

He shook his head, and his eyes glistened. "How can you be sure? Why do you risk so much by placing yourself in my hands? Why do you trust me?"

"We fit together, but we work differently. Apart, we are incomplete, broken. Together, we are whole."

He shook his head, vulnerability deepening in his expression. "Do you hear what you're saying? Do you understand it?"

"It's what I feel." She raised her closed fist to her heart. "Deep inside. I know you feel it as well. It frightens you. It frightens me too."

She slipped her arms around his waist and leaned into him, resting her head on his shoulder. The feel of his body against hers made her shudder. Everything about him was hard, inside and out. But she'd just seen the crack in his armor. He feared himself. He feared hurting her.

She didn't, though. "I want to give," she murmured. "And you want to take."

His hands slid up and down her back.

"You want my obedience," she said, her voice shaking, "and I want to obey."

"The mistress wishes to turn the tables on the slave," he murmured.

"You've never been a slave. You never will be."

He pressed his lips to her head. "I want to bring you pleasure. I want to love you—touch you—like no one ever has. I want to see your eyes glaze over in agony. I want you to beg for more."

She tried not to squirm, but his words wended their way through her body and buzzed between her legs, infusing her with a sweet ache.

"Is that what you want?" he asked.

"Yes," she said breathily.

"But when I give you all that, I will also take. I will demand."

She shuddered.

"Will you give yourself to me?" he asked in his quiet, lilting brogue.

Her heart thundered in her ears. "Yes."

"Look at me. Tell me."

Pulling back slightly, she looked up at him. "I offer myself to you, Robert MacLean. I am yours." Her legs wobbled, and if he hadn't held her up, she would have dropped to her knees and bowed her head to his feet, such was the intensity of her desire to be his.

"Get undressed and go to the bed. Lie on your back and wait for me."

Nodding, she pulled away from him and began to remove her shift. He walked behind her toward his workbench, but she focused on her task, quickly stripping her clothes away and crawling onto the bed, then rolling over to her back.

He turned to her, carrying something black in his hand. As he approached, she stared at it. "That's what I saw when I came here last night."

"Aye." Dark and possessive, his eyes grazed her bare body.

"What . . . what is it?"

"It's a gift."

"But we weren't . . . We hadn't . . ."

"I thought of you while I was making it."

He held it up for her perusal. It was a strip of birch about a foot long, painted with black lacquer, with several thin bands of leather equally long strapped to its end. He held the end of the birch stick in one hand and brushed the leather bands over his other hand.

Biting her lower lip, she reached for it, but he held it out of reach. "It is for me to hold. It is for you to enjoy."

"What is it?" she whispered.

"It is a flogger."

Her breath caught, and uncertainty infused her voice. "Will you . . . will you flog me with it?"

She waited with bated breath for his response. Her heartbeat quickened, pounded through her. Not with fear, she realized in some surprise. With excitement.

Rob wouldn't hurt her. Despite his warnings about his own dark desires, he wouldn't push her farther than she could go. She trusted him implicitly. Her skin ached for his touch. The touch of his finely wrought strips of leather.

She stretched her body languidly over the blankets, flirting with him. Inviting him. Basking in the fleeting smile that crossed his lips.

"Maybe," he said noncommittally.

She wanted to order him to flick it over her belly. The leather strands looked so soft, so supple—how would it feel? But if she did so, he would more likely put it away than cede to her demand. So she kept her lips pursed, her gaze focused hungrily on it.

He swiped the leather tails over his palm again. "Do you crave the touch of it on your skin, Elizabeth?"

"Yes." Her voice was a ragged whisper.

His gaze lingered on her breasts. They felt full and sensitive, and her nipples had hardened into tight beads.

That vulnerability washed over his face once more, only to be replaced in a blink by the hardness again. She would give her eyeteeth to know what he was thinking.

"Be still. No matter what I do to you, I want you to lie still. No movement unless I tell you to move. If you move without my direction, we will stop, and you will go back to your bed."

She nodded her agreement.

He lowered himself on the edge of the bed, watching her. For long moments, he didn't touch her, just gazed at her, every inch of her, until all the nerves in her body ached to squirm under the intensity of his scrutiny.

But she had to obey him. She must obey him. She gritted her teeth and held still.

After what seemed like aeons of torture, he raised the flogger. It hovered over her, the tails of leather dangling just above her skin, then descended, lightly stroking over her raised nipples. She released a harsh breath as tingles spread through her.

"So bonny," he murmured, his voice harsh, nearly broken. He focused on the movements of the leather bands as they traveled down her stomach.

She stared at him. She'd never seen anyone so devastatingly powerful, so potently attractive.

The flogger hovered at the triangle of hair above her thighs. He tugged her legs open and the bands stroked the sensitive tissue between. Then he drew back and brought the flogger down in a gentle smack. She cried out, not from pain but from the white-hot sensation that barreled through her.

"Oh," she whimpered. "Lord."

"Look at me, Elizabeth."

He gazed at her, again assessing her reaction. Seemingly satisfied, he moved his attention down her body. The leather strands lightly smacked her again.

This time she kept her lips closed, but she couldn't stop the strangled groan that emerged from her throat.

"Turn over." Yet she didn't have to move, because he did the work for her, lifting her and then flipping her body. He arranged her on her stomach, arms at her sides, thighs pressed together.

"Good." He moved her hair aside and bent over her, his sleeves brushing her back as he thoroughly kissed her neck until she trembled beneath him. "You're doing well. Do you wish to move?"

"Y-y-yes," she murmured, then tried to clarify. "My body wants to move. My mind wants to obey you."

"You may move in a while. For now, be still."

"Yes, Rob," she murmured, amazed by the meekness in her own voice.

She was in heaven. Truly. She wasn't fighting for control; she wasn't pretending to be what everyone expected her to be. She had openly ceded power to a man she trusted. To a man who made her weak-kneed and wet between the legs. To a man who cared for her.

And he did care for her; of that she had no doubt. It wasn't only that momentary break in his armor; it was in his gentleness in the midst of hardness. His desire to give her pleasure by taking the power from her. By being the responsible party.

She was tired of being untouched. She was tired of being responsible. So tired.

He swiped the leather strips over her damp neck and then in long strokes down her back, down the crack of her behind. Again she fought to keep from squirming as her arousal roared through her like waves crashing against a rocky shore.

The strips came down, harder this time, over the upper cheeks of her buttocks. She steeled herself, quelling the natural urge to flinch.

He paused as if assessing her reaction, watching to see if she moved. Her behind flared with heat, and his calloused fingers ran over the area, heightening the burn. She groaned, long and low.

And then the flogger came down again, and again, each blow successively stronger, more powerful, until she whimpered with each strike of the leather.

The harsh reality of her life drifted and faded from her mind. She went liquid. Climbed upon a cloud of bliss and floated, each blow lifting her higher. Each touch of leather was a sensuous gift, a ripple of joy, a white-hot golden glow cocooning her.

And then the blows stopped, to be replaced with something else. Rob's lips, she realized in an agony of pleasure. As if from a distance, she heard a muffled whimpering noise and realized the sound came from her.

He kissed her burning buttocks, soothing every stripe of heat with the soft, gentle caress of his lips. She drifted gently down from the cloud as he lifted her onto her knees.

"You may move now, love," he murmured. "You did well. Your arse is so pink, so bonny."

She closed her eyes in absolute pleasure as his words sank through her contented senses. She'd done well. He was proud of her.

On the day they'd met, she'd threatened to whip him, and the look of anger and disappointment in his eyes had shredded her to pieces. And now, that same man who had looked upon her with such disdain wanted her. Craved her. She'd made him proud.

Her throat thickened as his cock probed her entrance, and, still gentle, he pushed in. She was slick and open, ready for him. Her behind burned, but it was a tingling prickle now, not the hot fire it was moments ago. He gripped her hips, thrusting deep, his fingers fanning out over the sensitive area the leather had scored.

Already, her orgasm gathered and built within her, and she wiggled into him, lodging him deeper still. He didn't linger in gentleness, though. He took her hard, savagely, giving no quarter. She was helpless—blissfully so—under the onslaught.

The orgasm crashed through her, leaving her shaking and weak, but he didn't pause, didn't soften, didn't slow. His thrusts were merciless, deep, hard and fast. He moved one hand from her hips to her shoulder, yanking her tighter, harder against him with each drive into her body. She gripped handfuls of the blankets in her hands and accepted the battering, reveled in it.

Suddenly he gave an agonized groan and pulled out. His hand left her waist, and his knuckles slid over her behind as he stroked himself through his release. Warm strands of his seed landed over the burning slashes on her behind. She pushed herself against him, wanting him to cover her with his seed. Wanting to be marked by him like some primitive animal.

He released himself, and his fingers slid over the warm substance on her lower back, scooping it from her skin. He leaned forward and touched his fingers to her lips. "Take it, Elizabeth. Taste me."

She opened her lips and sucked his fingers into her mouth, savored his salty, masculine essence, swallowed all of it.

Gently, he pulled away from her and lay beside her. She remained on hands and knees, waiting for his instruction.

He reached up and moved strands of hair out of her face so she could see him. "Lie down and look at me."

She scooted onto her side and lay face-to-face with him.

She'd just come down from so much pleasure, but his soft, tender expression sucked the breath from her lungs and made tears prick at her eyes. He made her feel . . . whole. Inside and out. Treasured. Desired. *Loved.*

His hand settled heavily, possessively, on her hip. "You please me greatly."

She bit her lip, suddenly shy. Her cheeks heated. "You . . . please me too."

"Did you like the flogger?"

"Yes," she whispered.

He gave a thoughtful nod. "I am glad."

"You didn't hurt me," she said.

He smiled, and for once, the expression didn't flit away. It lingered, fortifying her feeling of contentment.

His fingers tightened over her hip. "You must go."

The feeling slipped away. Reality slammed back, and pricking tears filled her eyes.

"I don't want to."

"I know. I don't want you to go either. But you must."

She closed her eyes. "I want to stay here. With you. Forever." She whispered the last word.

"You cannot."

"Why?" she demanded.

"Open your eyes, love. Even if you were not within days of marrying someone else . . . Look around you. I don't possess the means to give you the life to which you are accustomed."

"I don't care about that." Truly, she didn't. She hated the life she'd been forced to lead. Once, ages ago, she'd been happy and carefree. But those days were hazy, distant. Since her parents' deaths, since her brother's death, there had been nothing but stifled suffering. She wanted freedom. Fine clothing and silver spoons were lovely, but they offered only a surface pleasure. The kind of pleasure Rob could offer her was far, far deeper.

"I want to care for you, Elizabeth. I want to protect you." His lips flattened, and his features tightened. "But I cannot even offer you that much. I am the stable master at Camdonn Castle. It is not enough."

"Stable master, earl's brother, pauper or prince. I don't care."

"You would. Eventually. You are new to this world. The life of a Highlander is not an easy one, especially in these times."

"As long as I were with you, I wouldn't care."

"You believe that now . . . but in five years, with your back bowed under the weight of your labors? Would you believe it then?"

"Yes," she whispered. "I hate my life. I hate the position I was born into. Despise it. Everything about it."

He simply gazed at her, his features still hard. Implacable.

"I wish I were a carefree Highland lass," she murmured. "Like Ceana MacNab, or even Gràinne. They are so . . . free."

"Neither of those women is carefree."

"Yet they bear their troubles so well. Far better than I. And they are able to be what they want to be, do what they wish to do. Each of those women, despite her place in society, knows who she is."

He scraped a calloused thumb over her cheekbone. "You bear your troubles better than anyone I've ever known."

She just shook her head. "I want to be yours."

"You will be mine. Whenever we are alone together, whenever we are in this room. I won't have it any other way."

"Can you accept that?" she asked. "Part of me rather than the whole?" He seemed like the kind of man who'd demand every bit of a woman, body and soul, and who wouldn't share.

A muscle bulged in his jaw. "I must accept it," he said tightly, but agony sifted into his eyes, lightening them. "I've no other choice."

CHAPTER SEVENTEEN

Cam leaned back in his chair, arms crossed over his chest, looking first at Elizabeth, who sat on the sofa across from him, her head bent over a book, and then to Rob, who sat in Charles's place at the desk beside him.

They made a handsome couple.

Cam flinched at the thought, but he couldn't deny it. Elizabeth's honeyed hair, held up today by a pearl-encrusted filigree comb, complemented Rob's darker brown locks. Rob's hair wasn't pulled into a queue today. It was longer than Cam's, and it brushed his shoulders in loose waves.

When Rob had first walked into the room an hour earlier, the shock on both his and Elizabeth's faces was palpable. Nearly painful. Both had recovered, however, remarkably quickly. Cam had communicated the plan he'd formed in Rob's apartments last night: Elizabeth and Rob would join him here in the afternoons from now on. He desired to spend more time with his betrothed, so Elizabeth was to engage in whatever quiet pursuit she preferred, while Rob was to study Cam's ledgers and plans for his improvements to Camdonn lands.

Unsurprisingly, they both had looked wary. Cam had instructed Rob to close the door, and when the man turned to do his bidding, he said to Elizabeth, "I've learned something that interests me greatly."

"What . . ." She paused, and her pupils dilated, the subtlest evidence of her panic. "What is that?"

"I've discovered my stable master is my half brother."

Elizabeth's azure gaze flickered to Rob and then back to Cam. "Oh."

Cam had taken a seat. "I'm hoping to teach him about the running of my estate."

"I see," Elizabeth had murmured.

They had all settled to their respective tasks, though Cam hadn't accomplished anything in terms of working, and he doubted if they had either. He'd scribbled away, but the words he scrawled were nonsensical. Every sense was attuned to the man and woman sitting on either side of him.

Cam cleared his throat. "Shall I call for some refreshment?"

Elizabeth glanced at Rob as if to defer to him, and the stable master looked up from his ledger. "Aye. Thank you."

Cam rang for a footman and, when the man entered, he gave his instructions and then relaxed back into his chair.

A contented feeling settled in him as he watched them pretend to return to their work.

His reaction to seeing them together was unnatural. Hell, he should have run Rob through that night a week ago. And every night since then, for he knew, he *knew* she'd been going to him.

What was wrong with him? Why couldn't he conjure up the requisite anger?

The truth stared him in the face. It was clear as day, crisp as an autumn breeze.

He liked Elizabeth, but he felt no ownership over her. He didn't love her.

He was in love—desperately, irrevocably, in love—with Ceana MacNab.

"There, now," Ceana murmured to Merry MacDonald, a widow who'd come complaining of stomach pains. Ceana believed it was a temporary affliction and had prescribed a tonic to soothe the gut. "You'll be healed in a few days' time."

"Thank ye, Ceana."

She waved her hand. "It is nothing."

"I've brought a bag of barley, if it'll suit ye."

"You know it will." She took the small sack of grain the woman handed her. The last time she'd been paid in money was at Aberdeen. None of the Highlanders of the Glen possessed much silver, and Ceana didn't covet what little they had. Barley was far more edible than silver.

"I've some vegetables near ready for harvesting, and with your barley, I'll make a fine pot of soup. Come back next week and try it." She'd also check to make sure the woman's stomach pains had passed.

Merry clucked and nodded as Ceana walked her out and watched her hobble away until she turned the bend in the path, bent over from her pain and clutching the tonic to her chest.

The sun had disappeared, and the late-spring gloaming lingered. The air was warm and still, heavy with moisture. Ceana breathed it in. She loved the birth and rebirth of late spring. It soothed her healer's spirit.

She walked to the bucket of water she'd fetched earlier from the burn and bent down, taking a handful of the liquid in her palms and splashing her face. The water was cool and crisp, invigorating. She remained crouched for a moment, then stood, wiping her hands on the wool of her skirts.

Hands descended on her shoulders, and she stiffened, but then the voice whispered through her, melting her muscles like butter. "Ceana."

She turned—she couldn't stop herself—and sank into Cam's arms. Had it been only a week since she'd seen him last? It seemed like a thousand years had passed.

"I missed you." Her voice was a near groan. She stiffened all over again when she heard it emerge. She sounded desperate for him.

"Who was that woman?" he asked. "She's a MacDonald, isn't she?"

"Aye. Merry MacDonald."

"A patient?"

"Aye."

"What is wrong with her?"

"Nothing, I hope. Just some passing discomfort. She should be well in a few days' time." She sensed him looking past her in the direction Merry had gone. "How did you know she's a MacDonald?"

His chest rose beneath her cheek as he sucked in a breath. "Despite her malady, she looked . . . content. Happier than my tenants."

"Alan takes care of his own."

"Are you saying I do not?" he asked quietly.

"You haven't been here, Cam."

"I'm here now. I . . . I'm working on it. It isn't easy. The people are resistant to change. They're resistant to me."

"I've no doubt you'll prevail." Already the common sentiment toward him had improved. In the village yesterday, someone had complimented his strict stance against thievery. Before he'd returned from England, she'd never heard him mentioned without the speaker spitting on the ground afterward.

"Do you think so?" he asked.

"Aye. They will love you."

He gave a cynical chuckle. "Nobody loves me."

I do.

Swallowing those words, she looked up at him. "Why are you here?"

"I . . ." He reached up to trace her brow with his fingertip. "I missed you too."

The blood heated in her veins, and her skin prickled. Oh, this was so dangerous. So very dangerous. Already, she felt as strongly for him as she'd once felt for Brian . . . and Brian was dead because of her, sure as if she'd killed him with her own hand.

She swallowed her panic and took a deep breath. "Will you come inside?"

*   *   *

Rob and Elizabeth lay facing each other, Elizabeth's shoulders tingling pleasantly from the flogger. It was the first time he'd used it since that night a week ago, and equally as arousing.

She'd risked coming to him three times. Latching the inside bolt so no one could come into her bedchamber, she slipped down the secret passageway and sneaked across the courtyard.

The chances of someone discovering her absence from her bed were slim to none. The most dangerous part of the venture was crossing the courtyard. She always came very late, when most of the castle residents slept, and she wore her dark cloak with the hood covering her hair. If someone chanced to see her, they likely wouldn't recognize her.

Though she took every precaution she could, she still worried that Uncle Walter would find out about her nighttime escapes to Rob. Yet she couldn't stop herself from going to him. Even as her mind argued against the folly of taking such a risk, she couldn't prevent her feet from carrying her down those secret old steps or from rushing across the courtyard to the stables.

She needed this. She needed Rob. He'd taken the crumbling pieces of her soul and begun to rebuild them.

Stroking his fingertip over her cheek, Rob smiled. She loved how his smiles came more frequently, more easily now.

"I want you again. Once more before you go."

He slid his hand over her waist and over her thigh, lifting her leg over his hip. Positioning himself at her entrance, he slid into her. She sighed in pleasure as he took her in a slow, gentle glide. She didn't take her eyes from his face, nor did he break his gaze from hers.

They rocked together, smoothly connected in body and spirit. Their connection filled her with contentment, wiped away all the feelings of emptiness that had pervaded her soul since her family died.

His hands roamed her skin, stroking her lips, circling her neck, grazing over her nipples, and raising the fine hairs on her arms. She explored him too, his solid chest, the tight male nipples, the shadow of coarse hair covering his jaw.

Finally, he caught her wrist in his hand, jerking her gaze back to his face.

"Turn over," he rasped, his eyes dark in the dim glow of the fire.

Without releasing their intimate connection, he guided her to turn onto her side, away from him, simultaneously tugging her buttocks to his pelvis, locking her against him. She groaned softly as he glided through her wet, willing flesh. The angle of penetration made him press over the most sensitive places inside her, and sweet, sharp sparks of pleasure resonated through her.

His hands scraped over her the area of skin still sensitive from the flogger, and then cupped over the hot flesh of her shoulders.

"You're so tight," he whispered. "So tight all around me."

"Yes." She closed her eyes, glorying in how her muscles clenched over him. Separate from her control, her body squeezed him, as if to grasp him and keep him there forever.

"Elizabeth," he whispered. "Elizabeth."

She came in a shuddering onslaught of emotion, her body shaking against his. He held her tightly through it, keeping them solidly connected, keeping her safe as she flew out of control.

Before she settled back to earth, he groaned long and low. "I can't . . . I can't stop it."

He pulled out of her, pressing his shaft between their bodies. He drew her back against his hot, hard chest and shuddered his release.

There they remained for several long moments, until their breath evened. Then he released her. "Go now."

She knew he wanted her to go about as much as she wished to leave him—not at all. She sighed, but when his arm lifted from her waist, she heaved herself from the bed and dressed.

At least she'd take the evidence with her. His seed, now partly dried, still covered her body, front and back. It represented his possession, and she gloried in that. She wouldn't wash it from her skin until just before she came to him tomorrow.

He sat up and watched her dress in silence. When she'd pulled the cloak over her shoulders, he reached out his hand, and she went to him.

"Good night."

"Good night, Rob."

Both of them left so much unspoken. There wasn't much time remaining before her marriage. How could she continue to go to him when she was married to Cam?

She couldn't.

Quickly, she obliterated the thought. They'd agreed to take this one day at a time, never to think of the future, but to live solely in the present. That was the only way they could survive.

If she considered a future without Rob, she'd drown in a vat of misery within a matter of seconds. She didn't want to dive into that vat. When those thoughts hovered on the fringes of her consciousness, she pushed them away and focused on something else.

Rob pressed a kiss to her palm. "Go."

Pulling her cloak over her shoulders and her hood over her head, she slipped down the stairs. When she closed the heavy stable door behind her, she turned toward the keep.

A menacing shadow blocked her path.

Elizabeth's heart leaped to her throat. Slowly, she raised her eyes until her gaze clashed with the man's dark, furious face.

"It's about time," Uncle Walter said. "I was wondering how long we'd be here before you gave in to corruption and vice."

Once Ceana had drawn Cam into her cottage, she couldn't keep her hands off him. Within moments, she'd stripped him of his coat, breeches, and shirt. He groped at her *arisaid*, fumbling to unclip the pin holding its edges together, and then he yanked awkwardly at her shift.

Soon they were both naked, and the door to the cottage still stood wide-open. Ceana glanced at it, but then focused her attention on Cam. She didn't care if anyone saw them. It had been days since she'd seen Cam. *Days.*

She kissed him. Down from his jaw to his chest, lower. She paused at his erection, taking its length in her hands, stroking, pressing her lips to it, opening her mouth and taking it, as deep and as far as she could. Oh, how she loved sucking him. It was her favorite thing to feel him harden and pulse beneath her lips. She loved his taste, the way his hands tangled in her hair.

As soon as he touched her, she lost the ability to think. Cam took over her mind, possessed it with a fiery need for him. He drew her close, closer, nudging his velvety cock deeper into her mouth until she felt crisp hairs against her lips.

Ah, he tasted so good. She swallowed him deep, and he groaned in unison with her.

"God in heaven," he said in a strangled voice.

"Mmm." She wrapped her fingers around his steely shaft and began a steady rhythm, pumping with her hand and mouth, guided by the pressure of his fingers on the back of her head.

Under her tongue, he grew harder, larger, until he filled her mouth completely. She wanted all of him. He was close; she could feel it. The vein on the underside of his cock bulged, the lust flowing through it about to explode.

She moaned with every pump, feeling her lips and tongue resonating over the sensitive skin of his cock. He was long, hard, beautiful. So masculine, pumping in and out of her mouth. She devoured him.

"Oh. Hell." His fingers tightened in her hair. He took over, thrusting deep, pushing her hard, but never too much. He gave her as much as she could manage while still gleaning breathtaking pleasure from the experience. And then he tightened, froze, and exploded. In wave after wave, his cock pulsed, and his seed splashed over the back of her tongue. His male, salty essence overwhelmed her senses. Closing her eyes, she swallowed convulsively.

Working carefully, she milked him of every drop. And when she could coax no more from him, she looked up at him from beneath her lashes. His face shone with a sheen of sweat.

"I . . . I have to sit," he murmured. Gently, she pulled away. Staying in her crouched position, she watched as he stumbled until the backs of his knees collided with her bed; then he flopped onto his back and threw his arm over his head. "Good God, Ceana."

She grinned. "Are you quite well? Do you require a healing tonic?"

His only response was a muffled moan.

Rising, she went to join him in bed, burrowing into the crook of his arm. His skin was hot, his body long and hard. She pressed her cool flesh against him, sighing at the perfection of the fit.

They lay together in silence for a long while, both awake, their breathing deep and contented. With her fingertips, Ceana lazily traced small circles over his torso.

"Ceana?"

She shifted to look up at him and saw that he'd moved his arm away from his eyes and stared intently at her.

"Aye?"

"Marry me."

Elizabeth's uncle wrenched her inside and shut the door behind them with a definitive click. She stumbled forward, then regained her balance and spun to face him.

It had begun. That quiver of terror deep within her.

Uncle Walter had punished her several times in the past. But none of her transgressions had ever come near to equaling the one she'd been caught in tonight.

Bitsy . . . Oh, why hadn't she run away when Elizabeth had told her to?

"Well, Lizzy." Her uncle leaned against the door and crossed his arms over his chest. A cold, deadly steel chilled his voice, freezing the nerves at the base of her spine. "Imagine my surprise when, unable to sleep, I took a walk around the grounds and saw you sprinting toward the stables."

She stared at him.

Uncle Walter rubbed his fingers over his sagging jowls. "'Is she

going for a ride at this hour?' I asked myself. So I followed you inside
in order to discern what, exactly, your intentions were."

She couldn't move, couldn't speak.

"I saw your skirts moving as you ascended the stairs. Then I heard
you speaking with that . . . *servant*." His lips turned down in an expression of disgust. "When it became clear that you intended to engage in
carnal relations with that man, I turned on my heel and commenced
to wait."

She stared at him. Why hadn't he stopped her and Rob before
their encounter? As soon as the question crossed her mind, she knew
the answer. Uncle Walter didn't want anyone else to know about her
punishments. Heaven forbid anyone think her different from the pristine English girl he'd raised her to be.

It would be a secret between the three of them. As it always had
been. As everything was.

She clenched her teeth, forcing them not to chatter. Fear froze
her, made her unable to move, to speak. Her mind churned. She must
do something—anything— but she could not.

His face darkened. "Have you nothing to say for yourself?"

She didn't answer.

"You little slut." He shook his head. "Tell me, was this your first?
Or have you been sneaking about for years, tupping your inferiors in
the cellars at Purefoy Abbey right under my nose?"

Again, she didn't respond, and he took a menacing step forward.

"Cat got your tongue?"

Her throat was so thick, she could scarcely breathe. Spots swam in
her vision.

"Well, Lizzy. You're not stupid. Foolish and impulsive, perhaps, but
not stupid. You know as well as I do that anything you say won't help
you now." He sighed. "I pray your husband won't find a sudden need
to return to England to pursue a career in politics. But I have no reason to believe that will be the case. I believe . . . yes, I believe you'll
be quite safely out of my way."

She knew it was why he'd agreed so readily to her betrothal to

Cam—it had given him the opportunity to ship her off to the far end of the kingdom, where there would be a smaller chance of her embarrassing him. *Exposing* him. Now he intended to finish off his lie of a life by finding a woman to take to wife and beget an heir upon without any risk of Elizabeth revealing the truth.

She hated him. She hated what he did to her. In his presence, she was so weak. Her insides had turned to jelly. Her knees wobbled. She despised herself for her weakness.

Why couldn't she fight back? Why couldn't she sprint away like a gazelle and slip behind the tapestry and downstairs, through the kitchens, and across the courtyard, into the safety of Rob's arms?

Uncle Walter's voice was flat, emotionless, but his pale blue eyes boiled with hatred. She knew he hated her. Despite her usefulness to him, he'd always hated her. Because she knew everything about him. She was the only soul in the world who knew how evil he truly was.

His gaze sharpened on her. "You know what you have done is beyond the pale. This punishment must be very severe. As severe as the punishment young William endured for you."

Nausea rose in her throat. William—her little brother. Thirteen years ago, Uncle Walter had killed him as she'd watched.

Tonight, he intended to kill Bitsy.

"No," she whispered, amazed at how calm her voice sounded. "I'll do anything. Please don't hurt Bitsy."

"You must be punished."

"Please, Uncle. Punish me, not her. She didn't do anything. I—I don't care if you hurt me."

"I know." He sighed. "Perhaps that's part of why I've no wish to do it."

"I don't understand." He'd so easily hurt her parents, her brother. Why not her? Why keep her in a state of purgatory for so long? Had he left her in this world for the mere pleasure of watching her suffer? How was it possible that anyone could be so cruel?

"It hurts you much more to watch."

She glanced up at him and found his icy pale eyes studying her.

He tilted his head. "You're all I have left of my brother. So precious. I couldn't hurt all that remains of him, bless his departed soul."

"You're a liar," she whispered. "You wish to punish him through me. I am all that is left of him, so I am all that is left to hurt. And I was a child, an easy target, a simple way to wreak your revenge. You knew he'd wish me to be happy, to be *alive*, and you did whatever you could to stifle that. Why did you hate him, Uncle? What did he do to you to make you so vengeful?"

His lips twitched and then lifted. "What does it matter? We're almost finished with our time together, Lizzy. This, in fact, is likely to be my last opportunity to punish you. So I'm going to make certain I do it well. It shall be a punishment you'll never forget."

She tried once more. "No. Please."

He sighed. "And then I'll have to do something about that man who dared to touch you."

She couldn't move, couldn't talk. Strangling fear gripped her throat.

He raised his hand, and his fingers curled round the door handle and began to turn it.

"Wait!"

His hand stilled. Keeping his grip on the door handle, he turned to face her.

"Tell me one thing, please," she whispered. "Why? Why did you hate my father?"

He shrugged. "It's nothing you could understand." He looked past her, his eyes distant. "He was the first son, the prodigal son, the beloved boy who could do no wrong. He had it all, from the very beginning. I had nothing—not because I deserved nothing, but because I wasn't born first. I deserved it, though. I deserved the dukedom and all the riches that were destined for him. I was smarter than him, a far better leader. What stupidity is it that demands a firstborn son inherit when it is more logical that the superior son should acquire everything?" He shrugged. "I merely corrected a wrong, Lizzy."

"You're mad."

He shook his head, his expression somber. "No. I'm quite lucid and quite aware of my actions and their consequences. Your parents and brother dying when they did was convenient, but to have you die too . . . No, and after such a miraculous recovery from the pox—that would have been far too convenient. How much better to prove to the world what a benevolent, noble man I was, first to take you under my wing and raise you, and then to marry you to a peer. It was a brilliant plan." The lamplight caught in his eyes, making them glitter as he turned toward the door.

"Now wait here, Lizzy, dear. I'll return shortly."

CHAPTER EIGHTEEN

"What?" Ceana asked dumbly.

"Marry me."

She went still. "You know that is impossible."

"Nonsense."

"You're marrying Lady Elizabeth. You can't just walk away from that."

Cam slid an arm over her waist, keeping her pressed against him. "I can, and I will."

"You wouldn't do that to her," Ceana said in a quiet voice. "She'd be ruined. Disgraced."

"I wouldn't throw her to the lions. I have an idea . . ." His voice faded.

"You're a dreamer, Cam." He shrugged lightly, and she sighed. "In any case, talk of Elizabeth is beside the point. You know I cannot marry."

"No, I don't."

Pulling away from him, she rolled onto her back. "Well, it is the truth."

"Why?"

"It's just the way of it. MacNab women don't marry."

"What nonsense."

"No," she said, utterly serious. "It isn't."

Lying beside her, staring up at the ceiling as she was, he thrust a hand into his hair. "Do you expect me to simply accept such an obtuse announcement?"

"Aye."

"Well, I won't, damn it! I've fallen in love with you."

All the breath whooshed out of her body. She stared helplessly up at the beams crisscrossing the thatched ceiling. God forgive her, but she was in love with him too. A MacNab healer besotted with an Earl of Camdonn. They had to be the two most divergent souls to ever have fallen in love.

There were so many reasons for them to stay apart. Their differing social classes. The requirements he'd have of a spouse—a *countess*. And the thought of her as a countess was laughable even to her. His need to maintain stable political ties with England. His betrothal to Elizabeth and his duty to protect her reputation and future.

Cam, her beloved dreamer, thought to overcome all those obstacles and marry her.

God help her if all of it didn't make her love him more. She turned to him and studied the sharp planes of his face. Such a beautiful man. A good man. Why did so few see it in him?

He rolled to his side and those deep, compelling eyes fixed on her face. "I want to be with you, beside you, always."

"No."

He just stared at her.

"I'm a lowly Highland healer. A commoner. Some call me a witch. Elizabeth brings you the political ties you need. She is a lady. She possesses a dowry. I bring nothing but a sharp tongue and misery to all who profess to love me."

"You're wrong." He spoke quietly. "You bring me happiness. I don't give a damn about the English. My own home and my own people are all that matter to me now. I've the feeling that a connection with you will only improve my reputation."

Fear squeezed her chest, tightening it, cloaking her heart and pressing in on her from all sides. She wrapped her arms around her body. "I cannot marry you."

"Why?"

Ceana stared at him. She must tell him before he became so enamored with this idea of marrying her she couldn't change his mind. She must reveal something she'd never revealed to another soul.

"Because . . . if a MacNab woman agrees to marry any man, that man must die."

His lip curled. "Is that why MacNabs don't marry? They're murderesses?"

"No! That's not it." She sucked in a breath. Cam had spent most of his life in England, and it was likely he didn't understand the veracity of Highland beliefs. Not in the same way she did. He'd probably laugh at her, but she had to make him understand.

"A curse was placed on the women of our family a hundred years ago."

His brows crept toward his hairline. "A curse?"

"It's true, Cam. I was the same as you, once. I didn't believe. But it's a true curse. It is real; I swear it. And I cannot risk it again. I can't risk losing—"

He held up his hand. "Shh." His voice was tender and soothing. "Calm down, Ceana. Tell me more about this curse."

She gulped in a breath, trying to calm her racing heart. "My great-great-grandmother was a healer, and when she was a young woman, she failed to cure a witch's lover. When he died, the witch went mad with grief and cursed MacNab women for all time. She pronounced that a MacNab woman shall never marry. If she attempts to mock the curse, the man will die before they are joined."

Cam listened silently, stroking her hair in a gentle motion as she continued. "From the time I was a wee lass, my mother and grandmother tried to make me understand. They attempted to warn me. They told me their stories again and again."

"What stories?" Cam asked.

"My grandmother once agreed to marry a man, but he died of an apoplexy the day before their joining. My father made grand promises to my mother to get her into his bed. When she announced to him that she was with child, he promised to marry her, but then he disappeared. To escape from being shackled to her, he tried to cross the mountains in the dead of winter. They found his body in the spring—he'd frozen to death."

Cam studied her. Understanding had dawned in his expression, giving her some relief, but the most difficult part was yet to come.

"Even with evidence of the authenticity of the curse and the dire warnings of my grandmother and mother, I laughed at them. I rebelled. I"—she blinked hard—"I fell in love."

Ceana turned back to face the ceiling as the memories surged through her in hot, painful waves. "I was at Aberdeen. I went there after my mother died, and I met a man named Brian Ross." Dear God, she hadn't spoken his name aloud in years, and saying it sent a knifing pain through her chest. "Brian was studying medicine at King's College. He was very kind. He encouraged me to tell him about myself, and instead of mocking me or turning me away, like every other learned man I'd known, he was interested in the theories and techniques passed down to me from my grandmother and mother. In return, I was fascinated by his travels and his exploration of medicines from other peoples. He began to encourage my participation—secretly, of course—in his studies. We became friends . . . then lovers."

She couldn't move. She was vaguely aware that she stared at the ceiling of her little cottage in the Glen, but she didn't see it. All she saw was the whirlwind of those happy, intense, erotic days. Brian, her tall, blond Lowlander. Debating medical theories with him. Studying poison antidotes with him. Spending sweaty, naked nights beside him, loving him. Him loving her—or so she'd thought.

"I'd forgotten all about the curse my mother and grandmother tried so hard to warn me about. I was certain Brian and I would be married. He was a gentleman, but he treated me with an abiding respect. He saw me as an intelligent woman. An equal. And then . . ."

She drew in a tenuous breath, trying to keep her voice steady. "I discovered I was with child."

Cam stiffened beside her, but she'd gone too far to stop now. "I was with child before marriage, just as my mother and grandmother had been. I told Brian about the babe, and he promised we'd marry after Michaelmas.

"I did as he asked. I didn't see him for weeks. Michaelmas came and went, and still I waited. Finally, when the babe began to show, I went to his house, only to be turned away by his servant. I didn't know what to do, so I lingered outside, meaning to catch him when he went out. When he finally did emerge he was with another woman. A lady from his own class." Every word sent the dagger twisting deeper into her heart, increasing the pain until she gasped in every breath. "I ran to intercept them. I held out my hand and introduced myself as Brian's intended. The woman stared at me, aghast, and Brian . . . He pushed me aside. He told me to go away. He told the woman he'd never seen me before."

Forcibly, Ceana swallowed down the sob crowding her throat. Her arms had begun to shake. She'd never spoken of this. She'd pushed the memory of it deep inside and tried not to think about those days. She tried not to remember her baby. Her sweet wee baby girl.

"I became obsessed," she whispered. "I investigated his affairs, spoke to people he knew. It wasn't long before I discovered that the woman was his new bride. He'd married her two days after Michaelmas.

"One night I went to his house, and I pounded on the door until I had the attention of everyone inside. I didn't care about the woman— it was best, I thought, if she knew what kind of a man he was. When he appeared from his laboratory to see what the disturbance was, I screamed at him, told him he was a lying worm, that he should rot in hell for leaving me and his child alone. Then I walked away, never intending to see him again."

Ceana rubbed the moisture from her eyes. "But I came back two days later. Because I was so hurt and lost, and I wanted to apologize.

Brian might have deserved it, but his poor, ignorant wife did not. I found . . ." She paused to take a strengthening breath. "As I approached the house, I saw his wife outside speaking to a group of men. I remained out of sight and listened as she told the men I'd killed Brian, that I was a madwoman who'd come to them spewing crazy lies, and I must be his murderer. I slipped away, frightened, and I went to the morgue. I saw him." She shuddered. "I'm sure he was poisoned. I think it likely, knowing Brian, that he used one of his experimental medicines on himself, and it killed him. But by that time, the authorities intended to arrest me for his murder. I ran. I wanted to come here, to the Glen, to hide and be with my grandmother, but on the second day of my journey . . . I lost the child."

She lapsed into silence, and Cam spoke, his voice ragged. "What happened?"

She rubbed her hands up and down her arms, trying to stave off the gooseflesh that had broken out over them. "I began to bleed. I gave birth alone in the wood. She was very early. She never took a breath."

The dam burst, and Ceana let out a low, keening sob. Twin tears trickled down her face. She had hurt—she *still* hurt. She had torn open the wound, and it bled, and she couldn't stop it.

My baby. My poor innocent child.

It was her fault. She had killed Brian, and she had killed her daughter, all because she'd ignored the wisdom of her mother and grandmother. She'd mocked them, mocked the curse.

She couldn't let it happen again. She could not—*would not*—be responsible for another person's demise. Cam's death would be too much for her to bear. She loved him too much.

Slowly, tentatively, Cam's arm slipped over her waist. He meant it as a gesture of comfort, and it did comfort her. She sighed as his gentle heat seeped beneath her skin. If only there were no curse. If only he weren't an earl and she a simple healer. If only he weren't already betrothed. *If only . . .*

She spoke in a low, cracking voice. "I hadn't realized how much I cared for the child, even after what Brian had done. I was too sick at heart to come here, to listen to my grandmother and her 'I told you sos,' so I went to Inverness. I remained there until I received word that she had died."

"How long were you in Inverness?"

"Four years."

"Come here, my love."

Ceana turned to him, squeezing her eyes shut as two more tears trailed down her cheeks. Her voice muffled against his chest, she said, "The curse is real. I cannot agree to marry you. I cannot risk it happening again. If you were to die . . . I couldn't bear it."

"Shhh." Holding her close, he arranged the plaids over her and rubbed smooth hands up and down her back. She'd grown cold as ice, and she shuddered in his arms. Never in a man's presence had she felt so small, so vulnerable.

"You are brave, Ceana," he said quietly. "You are intelligent and honorable. I've never met a woman as strong as you."

Burrowed into his chest and shaking with the force of her sobs, she gave a cynical bark of laughter. She'd never felt weaker than at this moment. Remembering her most difficult, frightening days. Reliving her pain. And knowing she'd been stupid enough to fall in love all over again.

"You were unlucky," Cam said in a low, soft voice. "Your mother and grandmother were unlucky too, devastatingly so. What if I married you right now? Would the curse end?"

"It could never happen."

"Why not?"

"A marriage between us would never come to pass. You . . . you would die first." Again her eyes filled with tears, and she clutched his arm, combating the fear that he'd perish this instant for having the audacity to even consider such a thing.

Cam released a frustrated breath. "No, Ceana. I am healthy as an ox, and I'm not going to die. I want to marry you. I want you to bear my children." His arm tightened around her. "I want to erase that painful time from your memory and fill the remainder of your days with happiness and joy."

Ceana's heart broke. No, it exploded, shattered into thousands of sharp, deadly shards. Slowly, she turned her head to look at him. "You haven't listened to a word I've said."

"I heard every word."

She shook her head. "No. You weren't listening. I told you I can't marry you. I told you why. So why are you doing this?"

"Doing what, Ceana? I love you—"

"Stop it!" She jerked away from him, scrambled off the bed, and snatched her shift from the floor. "Stop all these protestations of love. That's exactly what Brian did."

His voice hardened. "I'm not Brian."

It was hopeless. *God*. She had to do it again. It had nearly torn her apart to deny Rob, but she'd known he didn't really love her. But Cam . . . It would destroy her to hurt him.

But hurt him she must.

"Lies, Cam. You think so now, because you find me pleasant bed sport. But soon you will regret these rash words."

He sat up. His dark eyes remained fixed on her. "I want to spend my life with you, damn it, to hell with the repercussions. I'm not going to change my mind."

He was utterly convinced, and it shook her to her core. She gathered herself, then gave a hollow laugh. "No one will accept a marriage between us. It will destroy you politically. It will earn you the enmity of the Duke of Irvington, the Duke of Argyll, the king . . ."

"They can all go to the devil. I don't care about them. I care about you."

"We've known—both of us—from the beginning that this was an impossible match. We are too different."

"Our differences don't matter anymore," Cam growled. Anger flashed in his eyes. "I know what I want."

She narrowed her gaze at him. "Do you bother to take into account what I want?"

"You want me too. You're being stubborn about this foolish curse business . . ."

"No! I don't want you!"

He ground his teeth. "Ceana . . ."

She pulled on her *arisaid* with jerky movements as she continued. "I have a profession, and it's something I love, something that's part of me to my soul, something that you know nothing of. I heal people. You are not part of that. I have no wish to waste my days away as the wife of a nobleman. I have no desire whatsoever to be your wife."

"Then stay with me. Become my mistress. Later, I will convince you that it can work. I'll prove it to you, Ceana. There is no curse. And as for the rest—I'll find a way, goddammit. Everyone will accept this match—unlikely as it may be. And then you will marry me."

She gave a bitter laugh. "Pretty dream, isn't it?" Yanking at her belt, she leaned over him. "Until you find another woman you wish to bed. Because that's all it was with me, wasn't it? You wanted to tup me. I saw it in your eyes. You wanted me more than you wanted Elizabeth, and you are overcome by the guilt of it, confused by your carnal desire for an old heathen healer over the bonny daughter of an English duke. Well, you've had me, Cam. It should be enough."

Please, God, let that deter him. If she were forced to continue this charade much longer, she was going to fall apart.

He blinked at her. Then he stood up from the bed, his magnificent nude body nearly overwhelming her. Ceana tore her gaze away from it. He reached out, captured her arm. "No. It's not enough. It'll never be enough. From the beginning, I knew it was more. You mean so much to me. For God's sake, believe me. I've fallen in love with you, and nothing can revoke that."

She recoiled as if he'd hit her. And then she laughed. She laughed and laughed, the sound high, eerie, impossible. Finally, wiping her eyes with the backs of her hands, she smiled at him.

"Well, love. To me, it was just as we both knew from the beginning, and I never allowed it to grow deeper. You were a pleasant fuck. Just like Rob MacLean was."

His eyes narrowed, and she knew then that it was over. She had won.

It didn't feel like a win. It felt like a devastating loss. It felt like a piece of her had died.

"That's right," she forced out. "I've bedded Rob just as I've bedded you. And then I tired of him, and I left him. You don't mean anything more to me than he did—don't you see?"

She reached for her jacket and began to work the row of buttons down its front. "So the truth has been revealed. I was trying to hand it to you delicately, to cause you as little pain as possible, but you didn't listen. So now I must reveal the truth, just as I did with Rob a month ago. I'm finished with you. I don't wish to marry you, be your mistress, or even sleep with you again. I've had my fill of you, my lord."

He stared at her. Shock, pain, confusion, distress, disbelief. Anger. All of it raged across his face. His fists clenched and unclenched at his sides, and his jaw worked spasmodically.

She straightened, looked down her nose at him. "You'd best believe me, Lord Camdonn. If you approach me again, I will turn away. I will pretend I didn't see you. If you need healing, turn to your underworked castle surgeon. I am a MacNab woman. You're a fool if you think you could ever take one of us to wife. MacNab women never marry. *Ever*."

With that, she turned and stalked outside, slamming the door behind her. Once she was out of sight of her cottage, she ran into the forest until she was certain nobody would find her. And then she collapsed to her knees, buried her face in her hands, and wept.

Rob surged up from his bed just as Elizabeth flew into his room.

He knew it was her right away. He knew the sound of her heavy breathing, the sound of her sobs. He leaped out of bed, and she flung herself into his arms, trembling like a terrified butterfly.

"Elizabeth? My God, are you all right? What happened?"

"It's . . . it's Uncle Walter," she said, gasping. "He saw . . . me coming to you tonight. Rob . . . he's going to kill Bitsy. And then . . . and then he's going to . . ."

"Are you certain? Where is she?"

"I . . . don't know . . . Please, Rob, we must leave this place. We must go!"

"Shhh," he soothed, trying to calm her even though his own heart was galloping like a racehorse. "Look at me."

She raised her head slowly. Tear-streaked cheeks, red, blotchy skin, bloodshot eyes, liquid seeping from her eyes and nose. God, she was beautiful, even racked by terror. He reached up and, using his sleeve, wiped some of her snot away as if she were an infant. "Keep looking at me," he ordered in a soft, soothing voice. "Tell me what has happened."

"He saw me leave here earlier. He knew . . . he knew we were together. He said he was going to kill Bitsy as my punishment, and then he's coming after you."

He pulled away from her. "I must stop him—"

"No!" Elizabeth clutched at him and yanked him back to her, wrapping his shirt in her fists, her eyes wild. "No, please. Oh, God, Rob, he'll kill you. Please don't. I know what we must do. It is the only solution."

Tears welled over her bottom lids and streamed down her cheeks. He wiped them away with his thumbs. "Your uncle cannot hurt me, Elizabeth."

"You don't know the whole story, Rob. You don't know what he's done. What I've done in cowardice and selfishness."

"Tell me, then," he said quietly.

"There's no time! We must leave this place, for Bitsy's sake! She'll be safe only if we go. Please. *Please*, Rob."

He paused, considering, staring at her, and realized he trusted her implicitly. If she said they must leave, then that was what they must do.

Moments later, with Elizabeth hidden beneath a plaid, they rode past the guards and through the gates of Camdonn Castle. When they turned onto the shadowy path and were out of earshot, Rob slipped his arm around her middle. "Tell me now. How can leaving your maid behind help her?"

"I ran away once before. If I am not there to participate in the deed, he has no reason to hurt her."

"What of when you return?"

She heaved in a breath and whispered, "I cannot return."

He took this in, and they rode for long moments in silence, the only sounds those of the horse's hooves and Elizabeth's intermittent sniffles.

Finally, he asked, "Is that what you did in cowardice and selfishness? Returned home knowing your maid would be punished?"

"No."

"What, then?"

"I was six years old when they died. My mother and father . . . and my brother."

"Aye. They died of smallpox, you said."

"I brought it home from the country house we'd visited for the summer. I recovered, but by the time I was well, they had contracted it. They were very ill."

She hiccupped, and Rob's chest tightened in sympathy. She felt guilty for her parents' and brother's deaths, for she had brought the disease to them, and she had recovered while they hadn't.

"You know you're not responsible for their deaths, don't you? A child cannot help the illnesses she contracts and passes along."

She didn't answer him. Just stared straight ahead. "There's more. One night, late, I woke myself up coughing. I wanted my mother, so I slipped into their room and found them both sleeping. They looked so peaceful, and I didn't wake them, for I'd been told when I was ill that sleep would help me recover. But then I heard someone at the door. I'd been banned from their sickroom, so I hid under the bed, terrified that one of the servants would find me and I'd be punished."

She paused, and he tightened his arm around her middle. "It was your uncle?"

She nodded. "Yes. I don't know what he did." Her chest shuddered in a sob. "I think he . . . smothered them. I heard them struggling, but I was too cowardly. I just wept and listened to him murder my parents. They were too weak from their illness to fight him.

"He stayed there for hours. I hid under the bed, too terrified to move or sleep. And then he began to pace the room. A bit of my nightdress must have been peeking out, and he discovered me there."

Rob swallowed. Goddamn, he would kill the man with his bare hands if he ever saw him again.

"He coaxed me from under the bed, and there, standing beside my dead parents, he scolded me. He said that it was very bad of me to go there, for I wasn't allowed into the sickroom, and he said it was very, very bad of me to hide. He said I must be punished. So . . ." Elizabeth gulped in a breath, and her chest shuddered under his hand. Rob pressed his lips to the back of her head.

"So," Elizabeth continued in a whisper, "he took me to my brother's room. He said since I was well and whole, he couldn't punish me. But . . . but . . . he could punish William, who was very sick. I . . . I didn't understand . . ."

Her body shook, and she bowed her head.

Rob's jaw went tight. "He killed your brother too?"

"He said it was my fault. If I was naughty again, he'd have to punish me again. And he did . . . he beat Bitsy whenever I was bad, and I knew if I did something truly terrible, he'd murder her too."

She dissolved into a shaking ball, and Rob curled his body protectively over hers. Hatred surged through him.

"I should have done something. I should have stopped him. I was weak. A coward."

"No. You were a frightened lass who wanted her parents. You did nothing wrong. There was nothing you could have done to save them."

The Duke of Irvington had destroyed a family. He'd destroyed the woman in Rob's arms. The woman he loved.

She trembled in his embrace, and he knew he must care for her. Take her to safety. Protect her, and heal her. She'd reached her limit, and so had he. Nothing—not his relationship to Cam or his knowledge of her uncle's power in England—could stop Rob from doing what needed to be done. The only thing that mattered now was keeping Elizabeth from the danger her uncle presented, not to her body, but to her soul.

Tenderly, he touched his finger to her chin and turned her face to his. "He'll never hurt you again, love. Never again."

Cam could dredge up no emotion beyond the dull ache in his chest. After offering every signal that she felt the same as he did, Ceana had spurned him. Cruelly.

He couldn't believe she honestly accepted this absurd story of witches and curses her mothers had fed her. But if she didn't believe it, that meant the second part of her story was true. She didn't love him. She'd used him.

Cam's heart was a stone in his chest. The more he thought about it, the more he believed the latter theory. She'd shown him some measure of kindness and compassion—far more than her MacNab reputation warranted—but beyond that, she'd never said, or even implied, that her feelings for him went beyond the carnal.

And what kind of woman would admit to using men? She'd said she'd used Robert MacLean in a similar way, grown tired of him, then discarded him.

Hell, maybe she *was* a witch. Seducing men, crawling into their beds, into their hearts, and then casting them off as easily as the ashes from her hearth.

Her cottage felt lonely, almost eerie, without her presence. He had a strong feeling she wouldn't return until he'd gone away.

Weary and heart-worn, he dressed, went outside, and mounted his horse.

He'd ride for a while, then go home and sleep the day away. When he awoke . . . *Hell.* He needed to have words with Elizabeth. He'd arrange a private meeting with her, and he'd lay down the truth of what he knew and what he felt.

He didn't relish the thought of confronting her. He didn't know how she'd react. But she deserved the truth . . . and so did he.

Fog bathed Gràinne's cottage when Cam stopped in front of it an hour later. He stopped his horse, both man and animal staring at the small structure. One of the guards appeared, but Cam waved him away, and the man disappeared back behind the wall.

He had no desire to wake Gràinne. She was still recovering.

Since Cam was a green youth, she'd been there, always supportive, always soothing—offering him physical and mental comfort. Gazing at her little cottage, he realized he no longer thought of her in a carnal way. When had that stopped? Even during Cam's obsession with Sorcha, he had come to Gràinne for physical release.

Now, while he still thought of her as a friend, he had no desire to bed her. He knew that, even if he waited here until she awoke, he wouldn't bed her today. Or ever again.

What an odd thought. Something had shifted, altered his life beyond recognition. Hell, he didn't know who he was anymore.

He'd changed since he'd returned home. First there was Ceana. When the highwayman shot him, he'd been so certain he was dead. But then he'd awakened to her gray-blue eyes staring down at him, and he'd been reborn. There were the families he'd talked to, those he'd helped, and his plans for the future of his lands. There was Robert MacLean, his brother, and there was Elizabeth. And then there was Ceana. It all circled around to her, didn't it? She had changed him. It had all started when he'd first seen those gray-blue eyes. Now, for the first time in his life, he could see, really *see*, the world around him.

Cam dismounted and led the horse to the nearby watering trough. They made shuffling sounds in the silence, and fog swirled around the horse's legs as it lowered its head and drank. When the animal had taken its fill, he tied it to the post beside Gràinne's cottage.

Just then, Gràinne walked out her front door. Her doe-brown eyes widened, and she fumbled with the bucket she carried in her good arm. "Cam?"

He grimaced. "Did I wake you?"

"No, no, this is my regular waking time. But what are you doing here?"

Unable to answer, he simply shrugged. She pushed a red curl away from her eyes and gestured at the door. "Come in."

"Are you sure? It's early, and you haven't even dressed—"

She snorted. "I wouldn't deny you anything, love; you know that. Especially my house. Come inside. I was just going to put some porridge on, but I'll double the amount. You look like you could use a bite."

"Thank you."

She followed him inside and shut the door behind them. As always, the room was tidy and comfortable. The elegant furniture Cam had supplied grossly mismatched the packed-dirt floor, the lack of a chimney, and the simplicity of the architecture.

He helped himself to one of the chairs at the table and leaned his head in his hand, every muscle in his body weary. It'd been a long night, and he hadn't slept at all.

He smiled up at the woman. His onetime mentor, lover, friend. "Are you well?"

"Aye. Ceana came up day before yesterday. Said I'm nigh good as new."

"I'm glad."

She put the water on over the fire and then took the seat across from him. "What ails you? Looks like you've been trampled in a cattle stampede."

He twisted his lips at her. "Thank you for that."

She shrugged. "'Tis only the truth." When he didn't answer, she cocked her head. "I gather you haven't come to bed me."

The woman was direct, as always.

"No." He cast her an apologetic glance, and she smiled.

"Och, no need to explain. I imagine that between Ceana and the lady you're to marry you've plenty to keep your hands—and cock—more than occupied."

He groaned aloud. Gràinne leaned forward a little. "So, have you bedded the wee lass yet?"

"Elizabeth?"

"Aye."

"No."

"Ah." She settled back in her seat, a smug look on her face. "Then I gather the look of misery on your face wasn't etched by her. Which means, then, that it was bonny Ceana who has affected you thus."

"Observant, as always," he said dryly.

Her expression gentled. Reaching forward, she covered his hand with hers. "What happened, love?"

The whole sordid tale spilled from his lips, unchecked and uncensored. He finished with his departure from Ceana's cottage and his random ride, ending on Gràinne's doorstep.

She sighed. "Oh, Cam. You know you mustn't pursue her."

Cam had risen and commenced pacing the small space of her cottage. He spun round to face her. "What? Why?"

"She will never risk your death; don't you see? If 'twere to happen to her again, she wouldn't survive it. And God knows, it would happen again."

"Of course it wouldn't!"

She raised a red brow at him. "What makes you so sure?"

"Curses? Come, Gràinne. I'll not allow a superstitious fancy to rule—or ruin—my life."

"That's foolish. You'd risk your life, and perhaps hers, to test it?"

"There is no risk!" he bellowed, no doubt waking the occupants of the entire row of cottages.

She recoiled a bit. "Well. You seem confident."

"Of course I am confident. Why must I suffer because the woman I love chose to fall in love with the wrong man years ago? I would never betray her like he did! Never!"

"And what of the poor girl who's promised to you?"

"She's bedding my stable master."

Gràinne's brows rose higher. "Oh?"

"Yes. I caught them . . . the first time. She's been sneaking to his rooms most every night since."

"And how do you feel about this?"

He shrugged. "I don't know Elizabeth. I never did. For some reason I cannot fathom, he seems to understand her. I cannot comprehend it, but then again, how can I explain anything about love? How can I explain how I feel for Ceana?"

Gràinne crossed her arms over her chest. "Why have you come to me, Cam?"

His hands dropped to his sides. He stared at Gràinne. "You've always helped me. I need your help now. Please, you must tell me what to do."

"You don't need me, love."

His hands flew upward in frustration. "Yes, I do! I don't know what's up and what's down. I can't think . . . unless it is about her. Hell, I'm obsessed . . . like with Sorcha, but . . ." He thrust his hands through his hair, cupping the back of his head and holding it. "Different."

"How?"

"I don't know. It's . . . it's . . ." He shook his head helplessly and dropped his hands. "With Sorcha I thought only about myself. After the fact, I realized I hadn't taken her into consideration at all. I didn't give a damn about her reputation, about her happiness, not even about her marriage to Alan. With Ceana . . . I don't want her hurt again. Ever. I want to protect her, to make her happy. Hell . . ."

He paused to catch his breath. Ceana's pain, so evident in her voice and expression as she'd told him her tale, had become a part of him, and it hurt to remember.

"I want her to be content," he said in a low voice. "I want her to feel at ease, satisfied, safe. With me."

Gràinne nodded slowly. "Then what do you need me for?"

"You must tell me what to do."

"Ah, Cam. Stop fooling yourself. You know what you want, and I've the feeling you know how to get it. You already know what you must do."

He stood helplessly in the center of Gràinne's cottage and watched her kneel before the hearth and spoon the porridge into bowls.

She rose and placed the bowls on the table and then motioned him over. "Come, love. Eat with me."

After a moment, he nodded. He'd need his energy. Because, damn it, he was going after Ceana MacNab. And then they were going to marry, whether she agreed to it or not.

CHAPTER NINETEEN

Elizabeth opened her eyes to a muted dawn. Light filtered through the trees and streamed onto the ragged path laid out before them.

Rob's body pressed against her from behind, and, closing her eyes, she melted against him.

"Good morning," he murmured.

"Good morning." She couldn't fathom, really, how she had possibly slept atop a horse, wedged between the front edge of the saddle and Rob, but she did feel better. Somewhat.

The night's events began to encroach on the edges of her consciousness, and she hurriedly thrust them away. She was with Rob, she reminded herself. She was safe. Bitsy was safe.

She straightened a bit and took in her surroundings. The horse descended a gentle slope. The loch gleamed dully through the trees to their left, but she'd never traveled this particular rutted path before.

"Where are we going?"

"Somewhere they won't think to search for us."

She nodded. Judging by the position of the loch to their left, she assumed they must have rounded the end of the water and were now traveling away from the village of Glenfinnan.

They rode for another half hour, climbing the mountainside and gazing at the loch far below, and then descending again to the shore. Finally, they rounded a bend on the bank, and a lone cottage came into view.

"There," Rob said, his breath whispering over her ear.

"What is it?"

"It's one of the earl's hunting cottages. We'll stay here tonight, and tomorrow we'll move on."

"Toward Glasgow?" she asked. That would be the most logical place for them to go, given that Rob had spent most of his life there.

"Aye."

She nodded.

"We'll use the cottage only for shelter today. We must not take anything of his lordship's."

"Of course," she agreed.

They dismounted, and Elizabeth turned her face to the warmth of the sun, twisting and stretching her weary back. Left free to meander, the horse walked to the loch's edge and drank. Around them, spring grasses bloomed in a variety of pastels, but green prevailed. It carpeted the ground and washed over the trees. It was truly an idyllic scene.

An image crossed her mind. Of her and Rob remaining in such a quiet, tranquil place for all their days. Making love, working side by side, raising children.

She closed her eyes. Someday, perhaps. Not today. Not anytime soon. Her uncle would come after them. He might be close. They were still in a great deal of danger.

Rob's arms slipped around her from behind, and she leaned against him. "It is pretty here."

"Aye, it is. It is one of my favorite places on Camdonn land. When I first came here, I imagined . . ."

"What did you imagine?" she prompted when his voice faded.

His chest expanded against her back as he took a deep breath. "I imagined I'd someday tell the earl I was his son and that he'd grant me this land." He gestured to a flat area beyond the cottage. "It is enough for a small farm, and I could build a stable on the flatlands above the bluff."

"You'd have been isolated out here," she murmured. "But self-sufficient, I suppose."

He shrugged. "Isolation suits me."

"I think it would suit me too," she said thoughtfully, "though I haven't experienced much of it."

"Nor have I." His lips feathered across the shell of her ear. "It was crowded where we lived in Glasgow. Only at Camdonn Castle have I been afforded some measure of privacy."

She rested against him, content for this moment before they'd need to start running again.

"Elizabeth?"

She turned to look up at his face.

He gazed down at her, his liquid brown eyes somber. "You're not questioning my choice to bring you here."

"I trust you," she said simply. "I know you'll have brought me to a safe place."

"We're not safe yet . . . though . . ."

Unsure where he was going with this, she simply waited for him to explain.

His hands tightened around her waist. "I want to marry you, Elizabeth. Today. Right now."

Every nerve in her body flared to attention. Her spine straightened; her eyes widened. "What?"

"Marry me."

"But . . . who will marry us? There is no minister here. The banns haven't been read."

"It doesn't matter. All that is required in Scotland is a declaration of marriage by both parties. We needn't have a church wedding, though we can do that later, and if there is no church wedding, the banns need not be read. All that we must do is agree that we're married, and thenceforth we will legally be joined."

She stared at him, astonished. "It cannot be that easy."

"It is. Unless one of us were to deny it verbally, we would be married, with all the benefits and responsibilities such a bond entails."

She absorbed this information in silence. All she'd need to do was say yes, and they'd be husband and wife in the early fog of a spring morning on the green banks of the loch.

His hands closed over her shoulders. "Do you love me?"

She remained silent.

"I love you, Elizabeth. I wish to care for you. I wish to keep you safe, always. The thought of your uncle hurting you, of Cam touching you—" He broke off, swallowed hard. His eyes darkened as he gazed down at her. "I won't force you. If you don't want this, I'll find another way. But . . . I want you to be mine, by right and by law. I want you to belong to me. Not to your uncle, not for another day, another minute. Not to Cam. It is me you need." He glanced at the ground and then back to her face. "And I need you," he added quietly.

"You said we were too different," she said. "You said I could not bear to live the life you lead."

"I won't lie to you. I won't say it will be easy. I'll be a fugitive now. Your uncle will pursue us, and perhaps Cam will too. But I'll take that risk. And I think . . . I think after the choice you made last night for your maid that you will too."

She nodded.

"I cannot offer you what you had, but I know now that's not what you desire. The life I can offer you will be difficult, but I'll be there. By your side. Taking care of you and keeping you safe."

It was more than she'd ever hoped for. Not just a husband, but someone who understood her, who'd know how to protect her. Rob could do both better than anyone in the world.

Reaching up, she cupped his face in her hands. The bristles on his chin scraped her palms . . . palms she supposed would be work-hardened and calloused soon enough.

"Marry me, Rob. Please. I've never wanted anything more."

"Do you understand what you have walked away from?"

"Yes. My life as Lady Elizabeth is over. Lady Elizabeth is dead, and

I'm happy for it. I wish for nothing more than to be reborn as Mrs. Robert MacLean."

His eyes shone, and he bowed his head. "You honor me."

"No. You honor me."

He looked up, meeting her eyes once again. "You are my heart, Elizabeth. My soul. I will protect you and care for you. I will stand by your side, and I will love you until the day I die."

It was a dream. She stared at him. "I . . . I never thought I was deserving of anyone's love."

"You were wrong," he whispered. His hands slid down her arms until his fingers twined with hers. He spoke quietly. "It is as you said. We are two parts of a whole. Whenever I am with you, I am complete. I have never felt this way with anyone else."

She could scarcely breathe. "I have felt the same way, from the beginning. I didn't understand it at first—"

"Nor did I." He lowered himself to one knee, and she dropped to her knees in front of him, keeping her hands clasped with his.

"I take you, Elizabeth Grant. I make you my wife in Inverness shire on the ides of May, 1717. I will never deny you, never betray you. I wish to make you mine and mine alone, and in return I will belong to you, flesh, spirit, and soul. I love you, and I will love you and keep you until the day my life ends."

She tightened her fingers over his. "I take you, Robert MacLean. I make you my husband on this day, the fifteenth of May, 1717. I shall always love you. I want you to be mine, always, as I shall be yours. I shall love, honor, and obey you until I take my last breath."

They knelt in silence, facing each other. Elizabeth stared into her husband's face, and as the moments passed, the sun shone brighter, burning away the dark stains she'd thought permanently resided in her heart, burning away the morning fog. Bright, puffy clouds dotted the jewel-toned sky. A beautiful day for a beautiful new start.

"I love you," she whispered.

Rob rose, tugging her up with him, and he gathered her in his arms, stroking her hair. Emotion resonated through his body as he held her tight, his fingers sifting through the long strands of her hair. "I love you too, Elizabeth," he murmured. "So much it hurts."

"We're married," she said softly. "Truly married." She gazed up into his golden brown eyes. She spoke slowly, testing the words. "You are my husband."

She could repeat the words all day long, for when she did, a primal joy surged through her.

"Aye." He gazed down at her with that unfathomable expression. Yet his hands tightened possessively around her waist.

"It is right that we are married."

"Aye. It is."

"It is how it ought to be."

"Elizabeth . . . if something should go wrong . . ."

Her eyes widened.

"Don't panic," he soothed. "We are safe, for now. But if something happens . . . if we are caught . . ."

"No—"

"I want you to go to Cam."

"No," she whispered.

"He will keep you safe if I cannot."

No, no, no. She didn't want to think of this now. Not while the beauty of what had just happened between them still surged through her.

He pressed his finger to her lips. "Promise me, Elizabeth."

"We're safe. Nothing's going to happen."

"Promise me."

She allowed her heavy lids to sink and pushed out the words. "I promise."

He bent down and kissed her tenderly, his lips stroking softly against her own. Holding him tightly, she kissed him back.

"Let's go inside," Rob murmured. "I wish to make love to my wife."

Ceana trudged through the forest, her footsteps heavy. Full daylight bloomed over the land, promising warmth for the ides of May.

She'd made a decision. One that flayed her already broken heart.

She couldn't remain in the Glen. So close to temptation. So close to disaster. The only solution was to return to Inverness. She knew many people there, and her healer's skills would keep her, as they always had.

Before she left, however, Ceana must set aside time to do one thing. She couldn't go without saying good-bye to Alan and Sorcha.

Sometime later, Ceana followed Sorcha's maid through the entry hall toward the parlor. Though Sorcha and Alan had moved into their new manor house just a few weeks ago, Alan still supervised the finishing touches on the residence. It was beautiful, lavishly cared for, and so modern, with plastered walls and ceilings with fancy molding, wooden floors, and furniture imported from the Continent.

The house was a large rectangular building, a sparkling white gem on a high plateau, with a far-reaching view of the loch. On a clear day, one could see for miles up and down its shores, across to its steeply sloping opposite bank, and up to the tops of the snow-crested mountains.

Sorcha was embroidering when Ceana entered, and the babe slept in a cradle nearby. Ceana bent over him, and Sorcha rose to stand beside her.

Little Jamie had a round, cherubic face, and long, dark lashes that arced over his plump, pink cheeks. His lips were pursed and he sucked gently in his sleep, dreaming about his mama.

"He's truly a love," Sorcha murmured. "Such a sweet, happy lad."

"I'm glad to hear it." Ceana took Sorcha's hand in her own and squeezed. "You and Alan must be so proud."

"We are."

"And how are you, Sorcha?"

"I feel good as new."

Ceana studied her for a moment. Her color was good, and she looked well rested. She supposed that was one of the benefits of being a laird's wife—every woman of the clan was there to help with the babe at night. "Has your milk come in?"

"Aye, and he eats constantly."

"Ah, well, that's as it should be." She tried to smile at her friend, but feared it fell flat. "Where is Alan this morning?"

"He's in Glenfinnan meeting with his tacksmen. They're debating whether to take the cattle to the shieling early this year."

"I'm sorry to have missed him. I would have liked to say good-bye." Sorcha's eyes widened. "But you're not leaving us!"

"I am," Ceana said somberly.

"Oh, no, you cannot!"

"I must."

"Come." Sorcha tugged on her hand and led her to the sofa at the opposite end of the room, giving them distance from the babe so they wouldn't wake him. She nudged Ceana until she sank onto the soft lavender velvet, and then sat beside her, taking her hand again. "Tell me why you think you must leave the Glen. Is this Cam's doing?"

"No!" Ceana hesitated. "No, it's not his doing. But . . . it is because of him I must go."

Sorcha's frown deepened. "Why?"

Ceana took a breath. There was no reason to hide the truth from Sorcha; she didn't doubt that the other woman would learn it eventually. Beyond that, however, Ceana needed someone to talk to, someone to understand. She had held it all in for so long. Too long.

"He wishes to marry me."

Sorcha took a measured breath. "And this is a reason to run away?"

"You know I cannot marry. I am a MacNab."

Sorcha huffed. "Your grandmother despised men, and now you insist you cannot marry one. Why do MacNab women insist upon dissuading the intentions of the male sex?"

"A curse was placed on the women of our family four generations ago. It forbids us to marry."

"What is this curse?"

"If I agree to marry any man, he will die before the wedding takes place."

Sorcha tsked. "A powerful curse indeed."

"Even more so," Ceana said quietly, "when you consider that all three of us—my grandmother, my mother, myself—tried to defy it. We all intended to marry, and we all lost what was most important to us. I know some might accuse me of succumbing to superstitious fancy, but I have lived through it once, Sorcha, and I could not bear to do it again. I couldn't endure seeing Cam die because of me."

She stopped talking to battle the encroaching tears, to calm her pounding heart.

"But if he loves you . . ."

"It doesn't matter," Ceana whispered. "His level of love for me, great or small, will not affect the outcome."

"Surely there must be some way to defy this curse!"

Ceana shook her head. "My grandmother tried. She spent many years trying to break it, from learning secret witch's potions and chants to cloaking herself with the mantle of Christianity. None of it helped. By the time my mother reached womanhood, my grandmother thought she'd conquered it, and my mother was reckless. She suffered terribly."

"Was it your father who caused her suffering?" Sorcha said quietly.

"Aye."

"I'm so sorry."

"So now you see why I must leave." Ceana rose from the sofa. "I cannot stay here. I cannot resist Cam, knowing he is nearby. I will conjure excuses to visit Camdonn Castle, and he will invent ailments to come to my cottage. We will be lovers. Worst of all, he will be married." Tears pricked at the backs of her eyes, and she blinked hard. "I cannot bear to see him married to another, you see. But he must . . . he *must* marry Lady Elizabeth."

Cam dismounted at Ceana's cottage. Leaving his horse, he walked across the dew-covered grass to her door. When there was no answer to his knock, he pushed it open.

Every muscle in his body tightened. She'd been back, but she'd left again, and from the state of her cottage, he deduced two things. The first was that she'd gone in a hurry.

The second was that she was gone for good.

Within a quarter of an hour, he dismounted before Sorcha and Alan's house. Leaving the horse and brushing past the servant who hurried to meet him at the door, he strode inside.

When he threw open the door to the parlor, Sorcha looked up at him, wide-eyed, and he reeled to a halt. She was seated on a sofa opposite him, her bodice open. She held the child at her breast, showing more of her white flesh than was decent.

"Oh, hell," Cam pushed out.

Sorcha's brows peaked.

Cam backed away, intending to search for Alan, but she stopped him. "Good morning, Cam. Care to hand me that plaid?" She gestured with her chin to a blanket thrown over the back of a chair.

He went to the chair, took the blanket, then strode to Sorcha and handed it to her, averting his eyes.

She chuckled, enjoying his discomfiture.

"Let me guess," she said softly, arranging the blanket to cover the exposed parts of her flesh. The child in her arms sighed in contentment and smacked his lips. "You're looking for Ceana."

He instantly forgot his embarrassment. "Was she here?"

"Aye."

He gazed expectantly at Sorcha. "Well?"

"She's gone. I'm sorry. She'll not be coming back."

"Where has she gone?" Cam demanded. "I must find her."

"No, Cam. I'm sorry, but you must not. You must forget all about Ceana MacNab."

Elizabeth opened her eyes. Late-afternoon sun streamed in the window of the hunting cottage, and she stretched her naked body languidly under the covers.

She and Rob had made love twice, and then they'd fallen asleep.

He must have risen a while ago and gone to the other room or outside. As soon as it fell dark, he'd told her, they'd be on their way again. So it was imperative they sleep as long as possible during the day.

Rolling to her side, Elizabeth smiled. He'd made love to her beautifully, sweetly, staring down at her naked body as if in awe that she belonged to him. Touching every part of her as if she were a magnificent, priceless gem. And every touch she'd bestowed on him had left her feeling overwhelmed that someone so perfect for her, someone whom she loved and trusted as much as Rob, should be her husband.

He'd come inside her for the first time, and it had left both of them breathless, not only in body, but in spirit. The fact that she carried his seed inside her solidified the significance of their joining.

The door creaked open, and her smile widened. She turned over to face her husband.

But it wasn't her husband standing at the door. It was Uncle Walter.

He wore no wig, patch, or face paint, and his clothing was askew. The rawness of his appearance sent her heart stuttering in her chest. Even when he was angry with her, he was always careful about how he presented himself.

Instinctively, she curled into a ball and covered her bare flesh with the blankets. Sweat beaded over her body, but the ice-cold terror made gooseflesh break out across her skin. Before she could stop it, a small whimper escaped her.

He just stood in the doorway, the look on his face inscrutable.

Don't freeze, Elizabeth. Not this time. You must not. You must protect your husband.

She surged up in the bed, clutching the blanket to her chest. "Where is Rob?"

Her uncle grimaced. "You mean the servant boy? You know, Lizzy, I'm quite distressed there is no boat at hand, for if there were, he'd be at the bottom of the middle of the lake by now. But, alas, there is no boat. I've other plans for your friend."

Terror barreled through her, more intense than anything she'd ever experienced. Her vision went black. She blinked hard, tightened the balls of her fists, struggled to regain control.

"H-h-how did you find us?"

"I followed you last night, but unfortunately I was alone. Your paramour could prove to be violent and unpredictable, so I determined I would need assistance. I followed you, and, content you would root yourselves here for a few hours at least, I returned to Camdonn Castle to collect my men. I was correct in my assessment of that boy, by the way. He put up quite a fight."

"What did you do to him?"

"He will die, of course. He deserves no less for trifling with an English duke's niece."

The cold wash of terror grew thorns and transformed into rage. "I hate you."

He pressed a hand to his heart. "That is a very unkind thing to say to your uncle, who took you in, raised you, cared for you, gave you all the presents and baubles your heart desired."

"You've done naught but bring me misery."

"Ah, but you bring that upon yourself, my dear." He sighed and straightened, the bulk of his body completely blocking the doorway. "Now get up and get dressed. We haven't much time."

He turned around, facing into the adjacent room, but he didn't walk away. With shaking hands, Elizabeth pulled on her shift and the *arisaid* Rob had brought for her.

Turning to her uncle, she finished buckling the leather belt.

"Where are we going?"

"We're taking a short journey to dispose of your friend, and then, of course, we're returning to Camdonn Castle. You're to marry the earl in four days' time."

Elizabeth brushed past him. Picking up her skirts, she flew out of the cottage. One of her uncle's black-lacquered carriages stood on the lawn, looking more shabby than elegant, its golden crest spattered with dirt and mud. The four horses pranced nervously before it, and the coachman sat up front, his attention focused on controlling the animals. Two men hovered nearby on horseback, weapons glistening at their sides. One held the reins of Rob's horse. Rob was nowhere to be seen.

Ignoring them all, Elizabeth yanked open the carriage door.

"Rob!"

He was slumped on the bench inside, thoroughly trussed at the wrists and ankles. He was unconscious. A man with pinched lips and brows sat across from him, pistol in hand aimed at him as if intending to shoot him the moment he awakened.

Nearly tripping over the steps in her haste to be at Rob's side, she lunged at him. She cupped his face in her hands. His cheeks were clammy, but his breath feathered over her cheek when she bent down to feel it. She clamped back a sob of relief. As long as Rob lived, there was still hope. If he died . . .

No.

She flung a glance over her shoulder. Sure enough, her uncle stood just beyond the carriage door, surveying the scene dispassionately.

"What have you done to him?"

Uncle Walter shrugged. "He's suffered a bit of a bump to the head, that's all."

She sucked in a breath, unsure whether to believe him. She tried to adjust Rob into a more comfortable position, paying no attention as her uncle climbed into the carriage and sat beside the other man.

The carriage lurched into movement as she spoke softly to Rob, heedless of the men watching her. She didn't care about anything but saving her husband. She wished desperately that he'd wake up. She prayed for it. Her hands slipped over the ropes that bound his wrists, but the barrel of a gun nudged her fingers away.

"No, milady. You mustn't touch his bonds."

She kept speaking to him, murmuring, whispering words of encouragement, and finally, she said, "I love you."

"I've heard quite enough," Uncle Walter snapped. "Not a word more from you, Lizzy."

She looked up at him through blurring eyes. "Why not? What will you do to me if I speak? Kill someone? Kill me? Rob?"

"I will make you regret it," was his ready answer, and she did not doubt him. She kept her words to herself, but they ran rampant in her thoughts. If Rob could hear them, he'd know he needed to wake, and soon. He'd know how much she loved him.

He didn't wake. The carriage plodded slowly, resolutely, across the uneven terrain. Elizabeth was certain she could have walked faster. The road to the hunting cottage wasn't a road—it was a rough path, and a narrow one at that, riddled with rocks and holes. It was amazing that her uncle had brought a carriage there at all. Then again, the carriage was a convenient prison in which to hold them captive.

They bounced along for hours. The air inside the small space grew thick and warm, and sweat crept in rivulets between Elizabeth's breasts and down her hairline. Rob's eyes fluttered and opened once, but then he dropped into what seemed like an even deeper sleep.

She was hungry, she was thirsty, but none of that mattered. She stared across at Uncle Walter, a potent mixture of hatred and fear tangling within her. Why had she been such a coward? There had to have been a way to stop him long ago. She'd been too stupid, too childish . . . and now, once again, if her uncle had any say in the matter, the only person she had loved since her parents and brothers would die too.

Rob was hurt. If Uncle Walter had his way, he would die.

This time, she had to stop him.

CHAPTER TWENTY

Rob remained dead asleep, and Elizabeth sat in stony silence, her mind churning with her options for escape while the two men across from her exchanged small talk. Such was Uncle Walter's confidence in his scheme that he hadn't tied her or bound her at all—surely that could work to her advantage. Yet if she moved, Uncle Walter had directed the henchman to kill Rob.

After they'd traveled for the better part of the afternoon, the carriage drew to a rumbling halt. "Move aside, I say," the coachman shouted, his voice muffled by the wall of the carriage. "Allow us to pass."

A small commotion sounded outside, but her uncle remained serene. "No doubt a herd of sheep has blocked the way."

Finally, the coach jerked into slow movement again, and Elizabeth saw from the window on Rob's side that a cart, its contents covered by plaids, had pulled onto the grass to allow them to pass. A blond-haired youth drove the cart. Another person, a woman whose head was covered by a tartan shawl, had alighted from the bench and faced the forest. She didn't turn to look at them as they drove past.

Elizabeth sank into her seat. She'd thought of calling out for help, but what good would it do? Even if the strangers were inclined to help them, chances were that her uncle's man would shoot Rob before they reached the carriage door.

They traveled on. The shadows lengthened, darkening the interior of the carriage. Rob occasionally stirred, sometimes groaned, but still he did not wake.

Elizabeth sat very still, continuously schooling herself to be calm. Else she'd lash out, try to kill Uncle Walter, and end up dead. Or, much more likely, Rob would end up dead.

She stared out the window, studying their surroundings. They'd ascended a steep slope and had ventured inland, high above the loch. The trees grew thick and tall here—pines, junipers, rowans, and other species she could not name, in thick patches on either side of the path, casting the way in shadow. This deep in the forest, the fading sunlight penetrated the thick leaves and dappled the ground in spots like a faun's.

Rob's eyes fluttered, and she stroked the line of his jaw, willing him awake.

Across from her, Uncle Walter plunged his hand into his coat and pulled something out. On the fringes of her vision, she saw him pinching a clay vial between two fingers. He turned it over in his hands, studying it with a musing expression on his face.

"Belladonna. The deadly nightshade."

Shivers cascaded down Elizabeth's spine.

"I acquired it when last I was in London, where I saw it put to work on a criminal. It is a most expedient poison, and best of all, if anyone finds the body afterward, there is no external wound to point to murder. No one need know that the person's death was not a natural one."

So that was why they were heading into the forest. Uncle Walter planned to poison Rob and dispose of him before returning to Camdonn Castle.

"No."

He raised his gray brows.

"I won't let you do this."

He sighed. "Oh, Lizzy. I fear you cannot stop me."

She must stop him, but how? She glanced surreptitiously at the man sitting beside her uncle. As the hours had passed, he had grown lax. He had assumed a relaxed position, the pistol held loosely on his lap. If she was quick enough, she could grab the pistol, thrust Rob out of the carriage, and leap out after him. She'd never shot at anyone, but she'd seen a gun being fired before. All she'd need to do was squeeze the trigger. She'd have one shot to battle off her uncle and the man beside him, the coachman, and the two on horseback. Even if Rob awakened, he could do nothing to help with his wrists and ankles tied.

One desperate woman against five men. The chances were so slim as to be negligible. Yet what choice did she have?

The carriage slowed to a crawl as it had done repetitively over the past hours, making a tight turn. Outside, mud and grass encroached onto the path, and the carriage wheels sank into the soft earth, slowing them even further.

It was now or never.

She bunched her muscles, and as the carriage began its turn, she launched herself forward, grabbing the gun from the man. Instantly coming alert, he lunged for her. They wrestled, and Elizabeth's finger pressed the trigger. There was an explosion of glass as the bullet went through the window. Uncle Walter cried out.

It seemed like everyone was fumbling, crawling on top of her, grabbing at the weapon. But the gun had been shot, and she carried no ammunition, so it was useless to her now. She dropped it onto the carriage floor, climbed over Rob and opened the door latch, thrust the door open, and managed to push Rob until he toppled out with her on top of him.

The action of the fall woke him, and instinctively he curled his body into a ball, his shoulder absorbing his impact with the muddy ground. Elizabeth fell partially atop him, partially into a mud puddle. As soon as she fell, she yanked the dirk from his stocking, scrambled to her feet, and spun to the carriage. The true villain was inside—all these men merely followed his orders. If she could bend him to her will, the rest would follow.

From inside the carriage, her uncle shouted. Rob groaned lightly, but she kept her eyes on the vehicle as it ground to a halt not five feet from where they'd fallen.

First the man jumped out and then her uncle. A piece of glass had sliced his cheek, leaving a trail of blood to drip from his chin. A whinny sounded behind her as one of the riders stopped his horse, and she heard the sucking noise as boots sank into the spongy earth.

She kept her gaze, and the dirk, trained on her uncle.

"Go away," she said steadily, her voice hard. "Leave us alone."

"Elizabeth . . ." Rob's voice was a rasping whisper of warning from the ground at her side. She didn't dare look at him. She sensed movement as he struggled to rise.

Her uncle held up a conciliatory hand. "Come now, my dear . . ."

She tightened her grip on the handle of the dirk.

Uncle Walter's eyes flicked to the side, betraying the stealthy movement of the man behind her. At the same time, his shadow fell over her. She spun around just as the man lunged at her, slamming them both to the ground. She landed hard on her side, knocking the wind from her lungs. As soon as she could move her arm, she swung it around, stabbing the man in the back, the force of the action jolting her all the way to her shoulders. Hot blood poured from his back, painting her tartan print *arisaid* in a thick spray of red before he rolled away.

Someone leaned over her. Dimly, Elizabeth realized it was Rob. She met his eyes for a fraction of a second, and the sadness reflected in his expression washed through her.

They were surrounded. They had no weapons. They'd lost.

The man from the carriage hauled Elizabeth to her feet while another held a pistol trained on Rob.

"Hold her still," her uncle commanded harshly.

But she wrenched away and lunged for Rob. Just as soon as she reached him again, she was yanked back and dragged through the mud.

"Here!" someone shouted, and a loop of rope sailed through the air and landed at her feet. She managed to kick it away, but it was no use. A second man came to help the villain holding her, and together they tied her ankles and wrists.

Dragging her beyond the copse of trees and bushes at the path's edge, they gagged her and secured her to the trunk of a pine, and, leaving her unable to move, they returned to Rob.

He put up a brave fight, but he was injured and bound, ineffective against the three brawny men who dragged him near where Elizabeth was tied. Her uncle followed with his fists on his hips, a look of righteous victory on his face.

"Belladonna, Lizzy," he said, when the noise of struggle had ceased. Once again, he withdrew the vial. He glanced at the largest of his men. "Hold his mouth open."

"No!" she sobbed through the gag. "No!" She struggled against her bonds until she was certain her arms would snap in two. It was no use. Even if she did break her arms, she wouldn't free herself.

Two of the men held Rob still while the other forced his mouth to open. Uncle Walter uncorked the vial and glanced up at Elizabeth, his expression forlorn. "Yet again, Lizzy, you drive me to extreme lengths to protect you."

"No!" she shouted, her voice muffled and indecipherable. "No, no, no!"

Uncle Walter tipped the vial, and a thick, black liquid oozed into Rob's mouth. He coughed and sputtered, but firm hands clamped his mouth and nose shut, forcing him to swallow the poison.

Watching Rob's throat work, Elizabeth went limp. The fight drained out of her.

Uncle Walter had just killed her husband.

She sagged against her bonds and dropped her head in defeat, willing her life to rewind to the day she'd brought misery and death upon every person she loved—the day she brought home the smallpox.

Ceana had asked Sorcha to help her find someone to transport the bulk of her medicines and possessions, and her friend had readily agreed, instantly engaging the services of one of the MacDonald men.

With hugs and kisses, and a special kiss bestowed upon little Jamie, Ceana had taken her leave of the MacDonalds. She'd walked home and, with a heavy heart, packed her belongings. Bowie MacDonald, Alan's young cousin, had arrived with two horses and a cart just as she finished packing. They'd loaded the cart, and by the time they finished the task, it was just after noon.

Bowie was a garrulous companion, friendly and open. In a way, he reminded Ceana of his cousin Alan. It was in the open expression in his blue eyes, she supposed. Just one encounter with either man would be enough for anyone to grant them their trust.

Nevertheless, Ceana ached all over with grief. She'd lost something precious to her, and even though she should feel content that she'd left Cam healthy and whole, shaking off her misery wasn't as easy as she'd hoped it would be.

Since the Duke of Irvington's carriage had passed them at the beginning of the wood, however, Ceana had remained silent. Deep in her thoughts, she'd spurned all of Bowie's attempts at friendly conversation, and eventually he too fell into a contemplative silence.

Where was the duke going? Who'd been with him? Was Cam inside the carriage? Were they looking for her? But Cam would be on horseback rather than in the enclosed compartment of a carriage, wouldn't he?

Did this have something to do with Cam and Elizabeth's marriage? Now that Ceana had left him, had Cam seen reason and decided to go through with his marriage to Elizabeth? If so, though, what was the duke's carriage doing this far from Camdonn Castle? His niece was set to marry Cam in four days.

Shadows lengthened, and both Ceana and Bowie stiffened when they heard a hollow boom.

"Gunshot," Ceana whispered.

"Aye," Bowie said. "Sounded like it."

They continued on, their senses on high alert. They had ridden halfway to Inverlochy, and soon it would be time to stop for the night. Ceana had planned to spend the night on the western bank of Loch

Eil, at the home of her grandmother's friend Anne Tynan, and it would probably be near to full dark by the time they arrived.

As the waning light trickled through the trees, Bowie directed the animals up a steep incline. Ahead, riders on chestnut and black horses appeared at the top of the hill. Seconds later, the familiar sleek black-lacquered carriage, now covered with dust and grime from a full day's worth of muddy travel, crested the rise. The duke's party was returning from wherever it had gone. Odd, since there were no houses or other visiting destinations within miles. Doubly odd, given the gunshot they'd heard earlier.

Surrounded by shadowy green, the carriage rumbled slowly, carefully, down the path leading toward Ceana and Bowie. Her heart began to thrum in her chest. Anything to do with Cam, even remotely, was apt to fire her blood. Add to that the mystery of the duke's presence out here, along with the gunshot, and Ceana's every nerve was on edge.

"Looks like they expect I ought to be the one to pull off again," Bowie grumbled.

"I don't doubt it." Ceana sighed. Last time they'd moved to the side of the road to allow the duke's party by, the cart's wheels had sunk into the deep mud, and it had taken them a good half hour to push it out. She pointed at a small clearing at the edge of the wood. "Looks like a safe enough spot over that way. Might as well stop and wait for them to pass."

Bowie agreed, and within a few moments they had halted the animals and waited patiently for the duke's party to go by. Ceana pulled the plaid low over her brow. This time, Bowie frowned at her. "You don't want them to know you?"

"No. It's the Duke of Irvington, and I've no wish to exchange words with him."

"Ah." Bowie nodded in understanding. He spat over the side of the bench. "I dislike the earl myself. He is not one of us."

"It isn't the earl I dislike," Ceana explained patiently. "The Earl of Camdonn is a good man. It is the English duke I'd rather avoid. And you shouldn't be so stupid," she added in an acerbic tone, "as to despise a man solely based on his political bent."

"Aye, well. You weren't here when the earl wronged Alan."

"No, but I heard about it."

Bowie scowled at her. "And you still maintain he is a good man?"

"I'd trust him with my life," Ceana said softly. "And your laird would too."

Bowie sighed. "Everyone loves Alan, 'tis true, but all agree he is too soft."

"Perhaps you just haven't tried to know the earl as Alan has." *And I have.*

"Aye, and I've no intention to know him."

"Well, you'd best remember one thing, Bowie MacDonald."

"What might that be?"

"The man has paid for his sins. Alan's honor has been redeemed. How honorable is it to hold on to a grudge? Without forgiveness, men would have driven humanity to extinction long ago."

The rumble of the carriage wheels and the clomp of hoofbeats grew louder as the party rounded the bend up ahead. Ceana pulled the plaid tight around her, but she watched them from the corner of her eye.

A man on horseback went by first. As he passed, Ceana's heart lurched. There was a dark, wet stain on the rider's buckskin coat.

Ceana was a healer. She knew what freshly bloodstained fabric looked like.

The carriage rumbled by next, and Ceana strained her ears, for it almost sounded—aye, it did—like a woman sobbed inside.

She remained silent until they'd passed, and Bowie worked to start up the animals and get them back onto the road. When they were once again plodding forward, Ceana spoke in a low voice. "Mark the wheel ruts."

She pointed at a small rise of mud ahead; the mark of the carriage wheels made clearly delineated grooves over it. The duke's carriage was the first conveyance of that sort to pass since the last rain.

Bowie frowned at her. "Why?"

"I want to know where they stopped and turned back."

They traveled on. Darkness began to overtake the dusk, and they were within a mile of Anne Tynan's house when Ceana sucked in a breath. "Stop."

He did as she asked, for he'd seen what she had. The carriage had come to a rapid stop here, and the grass on the side of the road was crushed, as if the conveyance had pulled to the side, then turned around to return home.

"Over there," Bowie said in a low voice, gesturing with his chin to the bushes beyond the grassy area.

"Aye." Some of the branches were broken, as if men had stomped through them without regard.

Ceana jumped from the bench, and Bowie followed. She turned a slow circle, studying the area.

Bowie whistled out a breath. "Come look at this, Ceana."

She went to where he stood looking down at the ground, an expression of disgust on his face. "Blood, isn't it?"

"Aye." Kneeling down, she lifted a red-stained leaf and sniffed at it to make sure. Fresh blood, and it looked like whoever had been bleeding had been dragged a short distance before he had either stopped bleeding or someone had picked him up to carry him away.

Lifting her skirts, she hurried over the trampled terrain. It wasn't difficult to follow their path. She paused in a small clearing, where they must have stopped for a time near a thin-trunked pine, for multiple boot heels had churned the earth here.

"There." She pointed to a trail of trampled grass leading toward a large copse of trees. From this clearing, the party had plunged even deeper into the forest. Ceana retraced their steps, pushing through the shrubbery, heedless of the branches scratching at her hands and tearing her *arisaid*.

The brush grew thicker and the trampling more obvious. Then, all of a sudden, the disruption to the environment simply stopped. Ceana reeled to a halt, with Bowie just behind her.

She turned in a slow circle, eyes narrowed. A dense screen of bushes and trees surrounded them, innocuously fluttering in the evening breeze. All she could hear were Bowie's harsh exhalations.

"Something's not right," she murmured. "Why would they come so deep in the forest, just to turn around and return?" Since they'd left the clearing, she'd seen no signs of blood or struggle.

A flash of red caught her eye, deep in the brush. She squinted at it, then pushed through the bushes.

It was a man, half buried in forest debris and mud. She knelt beside him, her knees cracking branches, and pushed leaves from his face.

"Rob!"

He looked dead. God in heaven, he was so pale. But his skin was pliant, and, pressing her fingers to his neck, she detected a faint pulse.

"Rob MacLean?" Bowie whispered.

"Aye."

She transformed into her healer persona seamlessly—she could virtually feel the impassivity of her trade flooding through her, and she welcomed it with open arms. If she held on to her humanity at this moment, there would be too many questions, too much emotion. But there was no time for any of that now. She had to save Rob.

She checked his pulse again. Thready and rapid. She checked his eyes—dilated.

Poison. It had to be. Rob was too healthy for this to be anything else.

His lips and mouth were completely dry, and when she pulled open his shirt, she saw that his skin was also dry, and a red rash covered his chest.

Belladonna.

She turned to Bowie. "I must go back to the cart for my medicines."

Bowie nodded.

"Try to rouse him while I'm gone. He might seem deranged, but he'll be too sick to hurt you."

"Aye, Ceana," Bowie said gravely. As with all the residents of the Glen, his trust in her capability was absolute.

She sprinted back to the cart, even more heedless to the damage to her skin and clothes wrought by twigs and branches. Time was of the essence in cases of poisoning. Belladonna was utterly lethal. If she got to him too late—and dear God, she knew just from looking at him that she was close to that point—he was no better than dead.

She reached the cart and climbed into it, tossing aside the plaids that covered her belongings. She threw clothes and small items of furniture over the side. Her medicines were toward the front of the cart, and she stumbled her way to them. The first items she needed, emetic wine, coffee, and plain water, were common enough, and easily found.

Piling the items on the bench, she focused on her packed medicines, sifting through them in rising frustration and fear. She'd used the jaborandi that she'd acquired from one of the ships that had come from the Americas only as an experimental medication, but she and Brian had theorized that jaborandi might be effective against nightshade poisons.

She released a sob when she caught sight of the tiny glass container containing the jaborandi tincture. Dropping the other items into her sleeve pockets, she grabbed the vial, leaped out of the cart, and ran back through the brush. By now they'd created quite a clearing, and she reached Bowie and Rob in moments.

Bowie looked up at her. Fear shone in his blue eyes. "He's awake, but . . . And he's shaking badly."

Ceana sank to her knees beside him. "Rob? Rob, do you hear me?"

"Elizabeth?" he asked, his voice slurred.

"No, Rob, it's Ceana."

"Elizabeth?"

She ground her teeth. Confusion was a common symptom of belladonna poisoning. "You must sit up," she said sternly. "I'm going to give you something to drink, and you must drink it all."

"Thirsty," he agreed. His muscles weakened from the poison, he couldn't lift himself, so Bowie helped him to a seated position.

Kneeling at his side, Ceana held the emetic to Rob's lips. "You must drink all of it. It will help you, I promise."

"Ceana?" A muscle worked in his jaw, and he squinted at her. "I can't see you."

"Aye, it's all right. It'll go away once we get some medicine into you. Drink."

He opened his mouth, and Ceana tilted the jar. He gulped it all down, and she met Bowie's eyes. "Hold him to the side," she said quietly.

Bowie did as he was told, and within moments Rob was retching violently onto a pile of twigs. Bowie and Ceana held him until he'd expelled all of the emetic wine and the remaining contents of his stomach, of which there was very little.

This didn't bode well. It meant he'd been given the belladonna on an empty stomach, and his body had probably already absorbed much of the poison.

Bowie continued to hold him as he retched, and Ceana drew back to mix the jaborandi tincture into the coffee.

Rob leaned back, shaking even harder. "I see Elizabeth," he murmured. "Elizabeth?"

"Spectral illusion, Rob. It's one of the effects of the poison. Elizabeth is not here."

He continued to rave about Elizabeth and the duke and Cam, half of his mutterings unintelligible.

"Now, Rob," Ceana said, holding up the cup, "this medicine you must keep down. It's coffee with some other medicines added, and it should not taste as horrible as the last. You *must* keep it down, Rob— do you understand?"

"Will it cure the headache?" he slurred. "My head's about to burst."

"Aye, it'll clear your headache in time." Either it would cure his headache or he would die, she thought grimly. Either way, he'd no longer feel the pain.

He took the cup from her. He shook so badly she feared he would spill all her precious exotic tincture, so she held her hands over his, keeping them steady. "Good, then. Drink it."

Dutifully, he brought the cup to his lips and took a drink.

And retched, bringing every drop of the fluid up.

"Damn it, Rob," she ground out. "You must keep it down. You must! It is your only chance, do you understand? Don't be such a man. Be strong, like a woman. Swallow it, and don't allow it to come up or you will die, do you hear me?"

He blinked in confusion, then muttered, "Witch." He pushed her hands away from the cup, and under his own power, he drank it down in one gulp. Then he leaned forward, face flushed, panting heavily. He squeezed his eyes shut. "Holy hell. I'm going to vomit."

"No. You are *not*. You will *not*."

He groaned. "Uh, I am, Ceana. I am . . ."

"No." She took a deep breath, leaned forward, and spoke into his ear. "Elizabeth needs you, Rob. If you die, she will suffer under her uncle's hand. I know she will. Is that what you wish?"

Rob swallowed hard. Bowie exchanged an alarmed glance with Ceana, and she didn't know whether it was because of what he'd just learned about the earl's betrothed or if he was worried Rob wouldn't be able to hold the medicine down.

Rob did hold it down, however. He began to tremble harder, and then his eyes rolled back in his head, and he slumped. Bowie caught him halfway to the ground and lowered him gently upon the dirt.

The young man stared down at him. "Is he going to die?"

"I don't know, Bowie."

"What do we do now?"

"Now we wait."

CHAPTER TWENTY-ONE

"I should like to confer with Lady Elizabeth," Cam said flatly. For two days, Elizabeth had sequestered herself in her bedchamber pleading illness, and Cam hadn't pestered her. He hadn't had the strength.

He'd drowned himself in work, avoided thoughts of Elizabeth, tried—and failed—to push the loss of Ceana from his mind.

But his time was running short. He was to be married in two days, yet he still hadn't determined what he was going to do about his betrothal to Lady Elizabeth Grant. He needed to make a decision— *today*, damn it—about his upcoming nuptials.

The compulsion to go after Ceana, to find her and force her to succumb to his will, was still powerful—in fact, it had driven everything else in his life to a screeching halt as he struggled to combat it—but he wouldn't be a fool this time. He would not repeat his mistake by dragging her away and risking her hatred.

He also knew, from speaking with Sorcha, that Ceana wouldn't allow him to find her. It was over between them. Finished. He'd lost her forever.

With that fact tearing at his heart, his marriage loomed ever closer, and a decision needed to be made. He'd put this dreaded conversation off long enough.

Duncan was across the room, folding one of Cam's shirts. "Aye, milord. She's been unwell, however . . ."

"Ask her to come to me," Cam said shortly. "If she's not able, I'll see her in her bedchamber."

"Yes, milord." With that, Duncan bowed and withdrew.

Elizabeth stared at Cam's study door, blinking hard in a futile attempt to push away the grief clawing through her.

Two nightmare days had passed. Unaware of the events occurring around her, she'd lain curled up into a ball in her bed, overcome by black, dark grief. It covered her like a shroud pierced by hundreds of tacks that sliced beneath her skin, releasing all the poison that had accumulated since Uncle Walter had killed her parents and her brother.

Again, she was responsible for the death of someone she loved. Again, she'd failed.

She'd lost Rob. She'd caused him to suffer. She couldn't rid her mind of the look of pain on his face after he'd ingested the deadly nightshade. He was already dead, and he knew it. She knew it.

She'd drift off into a hard sleep, and nightmares plagued her. Watching him die. Watching him endure the effects of the poison as she stood by, helpless, tied to that damned tree. Unable to move. Unable to do anything but watch the man she loved succumb to death.

This morning, Duncan had come into her room and said the earl had demanded to see her. He'd mentioned that Bitsy was gone, that she'd disappeared three nights ago, and that he'd send a maid to help her dress.

When he left, Elizabeth forced herself off the bed and dragged herself over to the drawer where she kept the diamonds she'd offered to her maid.

They were gone. Bitsy had finally come to her senses. She'd taken Elizabeth's diamonds and fled, hopefully to Gràinne and the other women on the mountain.

The maid arrived and helped her dress, and now she was at Cam's door. Somehow standing, though the grief made her as heavy as granite, made motion so difficult, she had to grit her teeth with every straining step forward. With power she didn't know she possessed, she raised her hand to knock on Cam's door.

Marry Cam.

Those were the last words Rob had mouthed to her as they'd dragged him away.

She would do it. If she succeeded at nothing else, she would fulfill Rob's dying wish and marry his brother. In this, she would not fail.

She was a master at deception, at pretending she was something she was not. At pretending she loved her doting uncle. At pretending she was happy, even when grief darkened her soul and made her heavy as stone.

She didn't know when—whether it was day or night, whether it was this morning or when they'd first returned to Camdonn Castle— Uncle Walter had come to her. He'd threatened that if she revealed anything of what had happened, he'd abandon his idea of marrying her to a Scotsman. He'd use the belladonna on Cam and then take her home.

She didn't doubt him. Uncle Walter always came through on his threats. He *would* kill the Earl of Camdonn.

Uncle Walter knew, he *knew*, that she had given up. If it was just Elizabeth he threatened, she would have bared her chest to his sword. But he threatened Cam now, and he knew she'd do whatever she could to save him from her uncle's poison.

So she would somehow find a way to hide her grief. Pretend that nothing had happened, that she knew nothing of Rob's disappearance, and that she was ready—and eager—to marry the Earl of Camdonn.

She needed to endure only two more days of pretending, and then she'd be free. Uncle Walter would go back to England, and Cam would be safe.

She'd do this for Cam. And because Rob had asked it of her.

From inside, Cam called, "Yes?"

She took a moment to harden herself. Breathing deeply, she closed her eyes and pictured the numbness she knew so well coating her— mind, body, and spirit. Then she lifted her head, cleared her throat, and spoke in a clear voice.

"It is me, Elizabeth. You called, my lord?"

"Come in, please."

She smoothed her buttercream satin skirts, so different from the rough wool of the *arisaid* Rob had given her on the morning of their marriage, and entered Cam's domain.

"Good afternoon, Elizabeth."

Clenching her fists so her hands wouldn't shake, she curtsied. She twisted her lips into a semblance of a smile. "Good afternoon, my lord."

When she raised her head, his eyes widened. She knew how awful she looked. Her eyes were bloodshot and puffy, and her face was lined with grief.

She breathed deeply, imagining the air entering her body and strengthening her. Today her act of self-possession was more difficult than it had ever been before.

Cam spoke gently. "There are a few things we must discuss."

Pressing her lips together, she nodded.

"Please sit down." He gestured to one of the silk-covered chairs, and she walked over to it and lowered herself onto it, smoothing her skirts to keep her hands busy.

Panic.

She couldn't do this. She didn't want to do this. Why not fall at his feet and explain everything? Beg, plead? Cam had always been kind and understanding. He'd help her.

No. No, she couldn't. This wasn't about her or her grief. This was about Cam, his safety. She must keep him safe. She must pretend. Just for two more days. Just until Uncle Walter was gone.

She swallowed her fear and, battling the never-ending crush of grief in her chest, raised her eyes to his.

He took the chair across from her after pushing it a few feet closer.

Their knees nearly touching, he leaned forward. "Are you still unwell? What plagues you?"

For a long moment, her lower lip quivered. Then she gathered herself yet again, battling off the threatening tears. She straightened. "Just a . . . woman's complaint, my lord. I am feeling much better this afternoon."

"Please call me Cam."

She nodded.

"There is something very serious I wish to speak with you about, Elizabeth." He paused, then said, "It is about Robert MacLean."

The world spun around her, and she clutched the carved chair arms, battling to maintain her equilibrium. She sat very still so she wouldn't betray herself. Yet her grief threatened to erupt with every second that passed.

Cam leaned back in his chair, steepling his fingers under his chin and watching her. "Elizabeth, it is time to stop pretending. You've engaged in carnal relations with my half brother. More than once."

Panic overtook her. She couldn't stop it, couldn't prevent it from flaring in her eyes and over her skin. He *knew*. He knew at least part of the story. Her mind struggled to regroup, to assess, to calculate the changes she must make to her plan.

Save him. Save Cam from Uncle Walter's belladonna. Nothing else matters anymore.

She must lie to Cam about Rob—there was no other choice. It was too late for Rob, for happiness, for love, but it wasn't too late for Cam. He was a good man. She must see her uncle gone from Scotland without him hurt.

She blinked, then blinked harder. Again she composed herself.

"I don't know what you're talking about," she whispered.

"Stop," he said gently. "I saw the two of you, out by the loch. You've left your room at night several times since to meet with him."

She sat very still, and the solution came to her in a rush. With relief, she released the stopper she'd stuck behind her eyes and allowed the tears to brim and then spill over.

"Will you turn me away?" She still clutched the chair arms, the carved ridges digging into her fingertips. "Please don't turn me away."

He leaned forward. "Listen to me. If you love Robert MacLean, you cannot marry me. I've no wish to be second in your estimation."

"No!" She shook her head emphatically. "That . . . that could never happen."

She sobbed wholeheartedly now, and Cam leaned back, a stunned expression on his face.

"Rob has gone," she lied through her honest tears. "He hates me, hates what he's done to you. It was my fault, every bit of it. He said he couldn't stay, knowing how he betrayed you. So he left. He's gone. He left me, and he left you. Forever. He'll never return. Please, my lord. Please . . ."

She slid off the chair and sank to her knees before him, lowering her face to her hands and sobbing.

"Rob has gone?" Abruptly, he rose and walked away from her. Clutching her skirts in her fists, tears streaming down her cheeks, Elizabeth watched him as he went to the window overlooking the stables, parted the curtains, and looked out. "Why haven't I been informed of this?"

"I don't know," she pushed out over a sob. "He . . . he left the night before last."

He turned from the window, frowning at her from across the room. "I don't love you," he said quietly. "I know nothing about you. You pretend to be someone you are not. How can I marry someone like that?"

"Never again." She twisted her skirts in her clenched hands. "I was so stupid. I shall never lie to you again." After they were married and Uncle Walter was gone, that was. She had to maintain the lies until then. When Cam was safe again, she'd be honest. She'd tell him everything.

"You still wish to marry me?"

"Yes!"

"Why?"

"I . . . I need this life. I want it. I want *you*."

"Why?" he asked again.

Rob wanted her to live. He wanted her to prevail over Uncle Walter. He wanted her to marry Cam and ensure both their safety. She knew all of it was true. He wouldn't want her to succumb to helpless terror, nor would he want her to stop caring.

"I will be cast off by my uncle, discarded by society. I will be shunned by the entire world." Her sobs had receded, and she stared up at him as he came to sit across from her once again. "I know you are a good man," she whispered. "A kind man. Please do not throw me to that fate. *Please*."

Cam narrowed his eyes. "I doubt your uncle would allow your reputation to suffer. We will end the engagement congenially. Perhaps we could say the Highlands did not appeal to you—"

"No!" She gazed up at him through blurring eyes. "Please. I love Scotland, I truly do. I want to learn Gaelic. I want to be a Highlander in truth . . ."

"Those are girlish notions. They have naught to do with what a life with me would be."

"But it's true; I swear it. Please believe me. I don't want to go back to England. Ever." She swiped at the stray tear carving a trail down her cheek. "I'm sorry about Robert MacLean. I was foolish, stupid. I never meant to betray you. I'm so very sorry."

Cam didn't appear persuaded.

"There is so much at risk," she said. "I'm not ignorant of the political importance of our match, and neither are you. You need this union. Perhaps more than I do."

His dark eyes narrowed. "Do you love me, Elizabeth?"

She paused, then bowed her head. "What does it matter? Ours wasn't a love match; it was a political pairing." She looked up at him and tentatively laid her hand on his knee. "We could be happy together, my lord. I will be the best wife I can possibly be to you. I promise you on the lives of all I hold dear that I will never betray you."

He blinked. His eyes turned glassy as she stared up at him, her hands clasped in supplication.

"I must marry," he whispered. "I must marry and produce an heir. It is my duty."

She gazed at him, unable to interrupt his thoughts for fear he'd turn away.

"What does it matter who it is?" he said thoughtfully. "I've made promises to your uncle. To Argyll and the king. Despite our transgressions, despite our mutual lack of love."

She clasped her hands before her as if in prayer. "I will make you a good, dutiful wife. I swear it on my life. On my parents' graves, God rest their souls." *On Rob's grave* . . . She choked with the resurgence of her tears and froze on her position on her knees, paralyzed with grief.

Cam reached down, took her hand, and helped her to her feet with an unhappy sigh. "Very well. We will go through with the marriage, as planned."

The next morning, Cam sat in his study. He intended to give the pretense of working on the accounts stacked upon his desk, but hell if he could work. Between the losses of Ceana and his brother, and the promise he'd made to Elizabeth, he couldn't focus on a damned thing.

He was still stunned by Elizabeth's reaction to his knowledge of her affair with Rob. Instead of unearthing a girl happy to call off the marriage to a man she didn't love, he'd discovered a woman begging him to wed her. Yet she admitted she didn't love him.

And Rob? What the hell had happened? Why had he left without so much as a word? Cam had assumed Rob's feelings for Elizabeth went beyond the desire for a quick tup or two. And now he'd abandoned her out of guilt for what they had done?

Cam didn't know Rob well, but Rob never struck him as the kind of man who'd allow guilt to overcome him. He seemed far too proud to slink off into the night, too frightened to face the consequences of what he'd done.

In the end, whether they were a conjured performance or not, Elizabeth's arguments had swayed Cam. It was his personal, political, and social duty to marry. He had made promises to her, to her uncle, and to others—promises he could not renege on the day before their marriage.

Elizabeth was not the woman for him. But then again, who was? None whom he could have. He was clearly doomed to failure in matters of the heart. He'd learned time and again that matters of the heart and matters of honor could not overlap.

Sorcha and Ceana were right: He must marry Lady Elizabeth.

Alan and Sorcha were busy with their new lives, their new house, and their son, and had no time for him. Rob was gone. Ceana was gone, damn it. Tomorrow he would marry a woman he didn't love and who didn't love him.

He supposed he should make sure the preparations for his wedding were going smoothly. He left his study and went in search of Janet MacAdam, the housekeeper, who had assumed responsibility for the festivities.

The tension in Cam's shoulders built as he strode downstairs to the kitchens. Halfway down the final flight, he came face-to-face with Bram MacGregor. The man glared up at him.

"I was just coming to look for you. Milord."

Cam raised a brow. Despite the man's surly demeanor, surely the *milord* appellation was a step in the right direction.

"I haven't the time to meet with you today, MacGregor. Can you return next week?"

Bram shook his head. "'Tis of no importance. Just wished to . . . well, I wished to thank ye."

"For what?"

"For the help ye offered the Roberts family." His lips curved. "They're fattening up, looking more hale than I've seen 'em in a long while."

"Well. Your concern for the Robertses is exemplary."

Bram shrugged. "Aye, well, they are my clansmen."

"Good. I was glad I could help. Any news of Hamish?"

"The bastard has gone."

Cam sighed. "Well, we all know he's a thief and a sot on top of it, so it's probably for the best."

"Aye," Bram agreed. "I daresay you're right, milord."

Cam was mildly surprised by Bram's change of heart, but perhaps Berta Roberts's new position in his kitchens had served to convince the man that Cam intended to work for the benefit of his tenants rather than their demise.

Cam moved down one stair. "Now, if you'll excuse me, MacGregor, I'm on my way to the kitchens to speak with my housekeeper."

"Oh, aye? Might I accompany you there, sir?"

"Yes, you may."

They walked a few steps in silence; then Cam cast a sidelong glance at the brawny man. "Robert MacLean told me you're a tracker."

Bram's chest puffed up. "Aye, sir, that be true enough. I've a nose like a hound."

Cam paused, considering, then took the risk. "Did you hear that my party was set upon by highwaymen last month as we went through the mountain pass?"

"Aye, I'd heard."

"Do you know who was responsible for the attack?"

"Nay." Bram's voice was hard, flat, and final. Cam believed him.

Cam slid him another look. "Well, then. Perhaps you might look into it for me."

Bram hesitated. "They weren't thieves, were they, milord?"

"No. They were after me alone."

"Jacobites."

"Yes. Your kind."

Bram's lips twisted. "Nay. My kind doesn't rely on pernicious, murderous ambushes in the woods. My kind possesses more honor than that."

"I am glad to hear it."

Bram sighed softly. "There be better ways to achieve victory."

"Yes, there are," Cam agreed.

"Killing our earl isna the answer."

"No, it is not," Cam said. "You should know—my current heir would take pains to destroy my land and its people."

"Och, then ye must marry and produce an heir as quickly as possible."

"Yes. I must."

Bram took a breath and clenched his fists at his sides. "I'll find those highwaymen, milord."

They walked the remaining way to the kitchens in silence.

CHAPTER TWENTY-TWO

Ceana woke before dawn. She'd awakened often to check on her patient, so her sleep had been restless for the past two nights. Rob remained in a coma through the day yesterday, but, though insensible, he had begun to wake for brief periods at dusk. The waking periods lengthened throughout the night, and the dilation of his eyes had reduced. He remained weak and shaky, and still didn't have the strength to lift himself to a seated position on Anne Tynan's bed.

The widow herself slept on a pallet in the other room, separated from them by only a thin screen, and Bowie had chosen to sleep under the stars along with the cart and horses.

Ceana stood and stretched, then went to check on her patient. She lowered herself to the edge of the bed, watching his chest rise and fall with easy, steady breaths.

He would survive. Closing her eyes, she thanked God.

"Ceana?"

She opened her eyes and smiled down at him. "Saints, Rob, you scared me for a while there."

"Where . . . am I?"

"We're in the cottage of the widow Tynan." He looked confused, and she pressed a hand to his cheek, finding it clammy, but the fever that had flared last night was gone, and the jaborandi had done its work to counteract the drying effect of the belladonna. "How do you feel?"

"Terrible."

"Can you manage a bit of a mild tea?"

He looked doubtful. "Maybe."

She fetched the cup of green tea she'd prepared for him last night. "You've used up all my most expensive medicines," she said lightly after she'd helped him take a sip.

He frowned at her. "What happened?"

"You were poisoned. By the Duke of Irvington, I suspect." She said the man's title with a shiver. He'd probably discovered Rob's liaison with Elizabeth and thought it worthy of murder.

Rob's eyes widened. "Where is my wife?"

"Your wife? Rob, love, you're not mar—"

"Elizabeth!" he exclaimed, lurching up on his own power. "Where is Elizabeth?"

"Lady Elizabeth?"

"Aye, Ceana, my wife . . . Oh, God. Oh, hell."

He shuddered, and sweat glistened across his upper lip. Ceana grabbed his shoulder. "Rob, you must lie down."

"Where is Elizabeth?"

"I don't know," she said firmly. He'd gone insensible again. She thought he'd passed that stage. "Now lie down before you make yourself faint."

Stiffly, he lay back in the bed and remained quiet until the violent shudders died down. When his body had calmed, the feral light began to drain from his eyes. He licked his dry, chapped lips.

"Tea?" Ceana asked.

"Aye," he croaked out.

She propped his head and held the cup to his lips. He took a deep draft and settled back into the blankets.

"We're married."

Ceana stared at him in confusion. "Who's married?"

"Elizabeth and I. We married . . . before the duke found us."

"What?" she said breathlessly. "Are you . . . *What?* Why?"

"She was in danger, so I took her from Camdonn Castle. I tried to save her . . . I failed." He grabbed her hand and squeezed it tight. "Please, you must believe me."

"I . . . Of course I believe you." Either he'd succumbed to madness or he spoke the truth. Insanity was easier to believe, and yet there was no lunacy in the manner in which he spoke.

"What day is it?" he asked quietly.

"Thursday."

They stared at each other. For they both knew the truth: Thursday the nineteenth of May was the day the Earl of Camdonn intended to marry Lady Elizabeth.

It was about five o'clock in the morning. In the best conditions, Camdonn Castle was a six-hour drive away. Cam and Elizabeth's marriage was set for ten o'clock this morning in the chapel, to be followed by a feast in the castle courtyard.

"Elizabeth will not marry Cam if she's already married to you," she said soothingly.

"She will if she thinks me dead. She'll believe she has no other choice." His throat moved as he swallowed. "She knows that's what I want her to do. Just before they took me away, I told her to marry him."

And Cam would marry her. Not only because it was his duty to follow through with the betrothal, but because Ceana had left him. Ceana's own actions had stripped him of any other choice.

Ceana stared down at Rob. He was strong. He would continue to grow stronger by the hour. He would survive, even if she pushed him to his limits today. She took his hand and squeezed it.

"Rouse yourself, Rob. We've a wedding to stop."

"The Lord sanctify and bless you. The Lord pour the riches of His grace upon you, that you may please Him and live together in holy love to your lives' end."

Elizabeth blinked at the man. As if through a thick pudding, she slowly turned to Cam as the reverend finished his blessing.

Cam stared down at her, and the confusion she felt simmered in his expression.

They were married. They were husband and wife now, until death separated them.

Oh, Lord, what had they done? How would either of them survive this?

They must. They both must.

Cam's hands cupped her shoulders, and a brief, forced smile crossed his face. He bent down and kissed her gently, chastely, on the lips.

"Wait!"

A woman's voice, shrill and loud, sounded from behind them, from the door of the chapel. Both Elizabeth and Cam spun round.

Ceana.

She was breathing hard, and her skirts were muddy. From the corner of her eye, Elizabeth saw her uncle rise from the pew just beside her. Clothing rustled as the other attendees—nearly every occupant of Camdonn Castle was packed into the tiny chapel—turned to stare at Ceana.

"Ceana?" Cam said. "What are you doing here?"

Ceana ignored the crowd. Her eyes latched onto Cam. "You cannot marry her."

He stared at the woman for a long moment, and then closed his hand over Elizabeth's. "It is too late. We are already married."

She shook her head wildly, curls flying. "No. You can't marry her, Cam. She is not free to wed."

Uncle Walter snarled. The crowd began to murmur. Ceana held up her hands.

"You cannot marry Lady Elizabeth," she announced, "because Lady Elizabeth is already married."

Cam blinked hard as Rob appeared at Ceana's side. He looked awful, pale and haggard, and it didn't appear he could walk save for the help of Bowie MacDonald, who supported most of his weight.

Beside Cam, Elizabeth gasped. Her hand fluttered in his own.

"Elizabeth is my wife," Rob grated out, his voice sounding as haggard as he appeared.

Gasps echoed through the small chapel.

"This is an outrage!" Irvington blustered. "How dare you come in here and make these accusations? You . . . you swine!"

Ceana narrowed her eyes at the duke. "Robert MacLean claims he is Lady Elizabeth's husband. If she agrees that they are married, there has been a declaration of marriage *de presenti*, and their marriage is legal and binding."

Elizabeth squirmed, but Cam held her hand tightly, keeping her beside him. Rob stood at the door, his dark eyes focused on Elizabeth. God, Cam realized, he'd been right: Rob did love her. Whatever had happened, he had not left her intentionally.

His attention moved to the bristling Duke of Irvington. Irvington was furious—his face was lobster red and his lips were twisted into a snarl.

"You lie," the duke growled. "You are a commoner, a servant. You would not dare to touch my niece!"

Irvington knew, Cam realized. He knew all about Elizabeth and Rob's liaison, and, somehow, he'd tried to stop Rob.

Rob looked like . . . *Oh, hell.* Cam blinked hard. He looked like a corpse—pale and peeling. Ceana propped up one of his shoulders while Bowie stabilized the other. Had the Duke of Irvington tried to murder him?

Cam glanced again at the duke. Rage built within him, but he contained it and returned his focus to Rob.

"Is it true, Rob? Are you and Lady Elizabeth married?"

Rob's attention moved from Elizabeth to him. For a long moment, the brothers held each other's gazes. Then Rob nodded. "Aye, my lord. She belongs to me."

Cam breathed out. God help him, it was a sigh of relief.

The reverend's gentle voice sounded behind Elizabeth. "Are you already married to this man, child?"

"Yes," Elizabeth said as she sobbed quietly. "Yes. Robert MacLean is my husband. We are married."

Cam's gaze shifted to Ceana.

This was as it should be. Elizabeth was Rob's and Ceana was his. He would not allow her to escape from him this time. He wouldn't allow her to be separated from him. Ever again.

The murmurings rose to a crescendo as the dark figure of the Duke of Irvington burst forward from the front pew. He wrenched Elizabeth's hand from Cam's, and she screamed as he dragged her backward along the front row. Cam leaped to tear her away from her uncle's grasp, but reeled to a stop when he saw the barrel of a pistol pressed against her temple.

It all became sickeningly clear. Cam's friend, the Duke of Irvington, had tried to kill Rob. He now held a gun to his beloved niece's head.

Cam quickly tamped down his surprise. His brother needed him now. Elizabeth needed him now.

Dressed in his ceremonial plaid, Cam carried no gun, only his dirk tucked into his hose. That would do little good against the madman whose finger already rested on the trigger.

"Get back!" the duke snarled. "No one is to touch my Lizzy. Not some Scots bastard, not anyone! Everyone stay away!"

Wedding guests shrank back from the duke. Elizabeth stared at Cam, her sky-blue eyes round as saucers. Cam raised his hands in a conciliatory gesture.

"Irvington. She's your niece. You wouldn't hurt her."

The duke's lip curled. "Better to see her dead than married to a Highland pauper."

"Nonsense," Cam said.

Irvington turned to Rob, baring his teeth. "You were as good as dead when we left you."

He still looked it, Cam thought bleakly. "Let her go, Your Grace," he soothed.

"Never!" Irvington dragged her toward the side door of the chapel.

Cam calculated rapidly even as his mind rejected this impossible turn of events. The duke couldn't get far—his carriage wasn't ready for travel. Where the hell did he intend to take her?

One of Irvington's men kicked open the door, and he dragged Elizabeth over the threshold, his arm clamped around her waist and his gun digging into the side of her head. She didn't resist him. She looked truly petrified.

Cam's fingers inched toward his dirk. From his position at the door, Irvington couldn't see Cam's weapon—his legs were hidden behind the pews. Still, the duke kept his focus solely on Cam, as if Cam were his only adversary. Perhaps he was. Rob was too sick to fight for Elizabeth, and beyond that, who would take a stand for the Sassenach wench?

Cam grasped the hilt of the dagger, wrapping his fingers around it and sliding it from its sheath. From the corner of his eye, he saw a flurry at the front door of the chapel.

Cam didn't take his gaze from the duke. Their stares remained locked, a whimpering Elizabeth between them.

And then Irvington broke their connection. He swiveled his head, distracted by the movement at the door. Cam latched onto the opportunity. He raised his dirk, aimed, and, praying to God he still retained the skill he'd practiced endlessly with Alan as a youth, he flung it at the duke's upraised hand—the hand holding the gun to Elizabeth's head.

The dagger did not hit the duke's hand. It clanged against the barrel of the pistol, yanking it out of Irvington's grasp. But not before he pulled the trigger.

The boom of the gunshot resonated straight into Cam's soul. With an agonized cry, he lunged for the duke and Elizabeth.

Elizabeth was on the ground. Blood was everywhere—coating her face and her dress. But—thank God—she wept. She was moving.

Cam dragged Irvington to the ground in a full-body tackle. He rolled beneath him, the duke's full weight slamming him to the earth, but then he gained the upper hand, sank his boot heel into the soft mud, and propelled himself on top, all the while slamming his fists into the older man's chest.

Irvington had hurt his own niece, whom before now he'd loved and cosseted as if she were the most important, precious gem. What kind of a deranged man—

"He murdered them! He killed my parents! He killed my brother! He tried . . . tried to kill Rob!"

The shrill accusations came as if from a distance. Cam was too busy staving off the duke's attack to register them for several moments. Then they sank in.

Elizabeth had screamed the words. The Duke of Irvington had murdered his own family. He'd tried to murder Cam's only family.

With renewed fury, Cam slammed his fist into the older man's face. But somehow Irvington managed to slip out from beneath him. "Roger!" he screamed. "Help me!"

Suddenly another pistol materialized in the Duke of Irvington's hand. He wrenched the weapon around, aiming it at Cam's chest.

Cam knew he was going to die. In the next fraction of a second, he was going to be shot through the heart.

He heard the bang of the gun. He felt the impact shudder through him.

But there was no pain.

He opened his eyes. There was blood, more blood, so much, staining everything crimson. But not his own. The Duke of Irvington's eyes stared up at him, glassy. There was a hole in the side of his head, and gore oozed from it. His arm lay at his side, finger still curled around the trigger of the gun his man Roger had thrown to him.

Cam surveyed himself, slowly coming to the realization that he hadn't been shot, that it wasn't the end. The Duke of Irvington lay dead beneath him.

He glanced up. People surrounded them, some of them shouting, their voices muffled by the din in his mind. Rob knelt not two feet away. Slowly, Rob lowered the pistol with shaking hands, swaying a little, looking more green than pale. His voice pierced Cam's shock. "Sorry. Took so long. Didn't trust my shot from a distance."

"Elizabeth?" Cam turned, searching for the girl amid the crowd of people surrounding them. He'd seen the duke shoot her. He'd seen the blood.

"The shot grazed her arm as the gun fell," Rob said. "The wound isn't fatal."

Cam's eyelids sank, weighted by steel. "Thank God."

Suddenly, an arm slipped over his shoulders, and Cam opened his eyes. Rob had staggered away, probably to see to his wife.

"Here, let me help you. Can you get up? Where does it hurt?"

He looked up into Ceana's heart-shaped face, framed by that wild, irresistible mop of curls.

He allowed her to help him off the dead Englishman. He stood on unstable legs and, with a strange detachment, watched the flurry of people rushing about. Then he pushed through the crowd surrounding Elizabeth and went to her side.

Rob knelt beside her, holding her in his arms. Blood smeared between them and stained the ivory silk of her wedding dress, but she'd found the strength to wrap her arms around Rob, so Cam felt reassured the injury wasn't dire. He touched her shoulder. "Elizabeth?"

She turned to him, sniffing. Her eyes were bloodshot. "My lord."

"Will you be all right?"

"Yes," she whispered. Tears slipped in twin streams down her face. "Thank you."

He smiled at her, brushed a tear from her cheek, then nodded at Rob. "Take care of your woman, brother."

"Aye. I will."

Tenderly, Rob brushed Elizabeth's tousled hair out of her face and cradled her in his arms, though he looked near to death himself.

It would be folly to try to separate them. Cam had no wish to do so. They both might have to be carried to bed later, but let them sit in the mud and comfort each other. There was no harm in it. Hell, they were husband and wife.

Cam rose. His legs felt stronger now, more in control. He saw to the arrests of Roger and the remainder of the Duke of Irvington's men, and had the body removed. When the tumult died down, he scanned the crowd. Where was Ceana?

There she was, her head bent as she gave a servant orders for medicines and a bandage for Elizabeth.

The castle surgeon stood at her side, scowling. "You will irritate the wound if you clean it in such a manner."

Ceana looked at the man, raised a brow, then turned away as if she found him unworthy of a response. Cam nearly smiled.

She was a true MacNab.

But Cam didn't believe in curses. And he wasn't going to allow her to believe in them, either.

He intended to break the MacNab family curse. *Now.*

Ceana ground her teeth when fingers closed around her elbow. That damned surgeon again, thinking he could put his filthy hands on her . . .

She turned, hand raised, prepared to shove him away, but instead of the surgeon, Cam hovered over her. That intense expression hardened his face. The one that sent heated shivers bouncing through her core and scared the wits out of her.

"What—"

"You're coming with me," he growled. "Now."

"Cam," she huffed. "Really. I haven't the time. I must dress Elizabeth's wound, and Rob—"

"Leave them alone," he commanded. "They're happy where they are."

He tugged—no, *dragged*—her inside the chapel. She sighed heavily. "What do you want?"

He remained implacable, stubbornly pulling her along until they stood at the altar. She glanced around. Only a few people remained in the chapel after the earlier uproar. One of them was the reverend. He was turned away from them, his bald head bowed as he tended to the candles.

Cam cleared his throat. "We're ready."

"Ready for what?"

"Hush," he reprimanded.

She cast her gaze to the heavens, frustrated. "Good Lord."

Cam raised a brow at her. The minister turned to her, eyes wide, and she huffed out a breath. "Forgive me, sir."

The man inclined his head at Cam. "Are you certain, my lord?"

"Absolutely. It is what I've wanted, what I've known to be right since the day I returned to the Highlands."

The man began to intone in Latin, blessing them both.

A heavy feeling descended in Ceana's stomach.

Oh, hell. Oh, no.

"No," she murmured. "This is impossible. The banns haven't been read!"

The minister paused, then smiled benevolently. "Oh, aye, indeed they have. I've read them these three Sundays past."

"That's impossible!"

"But it is true."

She glanced at Cam, who gave her a serene look, and she turned back to the minister. "You read them for the earl and Lady Elizabeth Grant. I'm Ceana MacNab. You didn't read them for me."

"Oh, but I did." His eyes twinkled. "Indeed I did."

"I've been present at every one of those Sunday services, Ceana," a voice called out from behind her. Ceana turned to see Janet Mac-Adam's round face beaming from within the gathering crowd. "I am certain it was your name Reverend Anderson called."

"Oh, aye, it certainly was," said a man beside her. "'Ceana MacNab,' he said, loud and clear."

Agreement rang out from all corners of the chapel, and every single head in the suddenly crowded space nodded in smiling agreement.

"Aye, it was Ceana MacNab's name."

"Indeed it was."

"I don't believe our earl ever considered marrying anyone else."

They were all joining together in support of her marriage to Cam. The reverend nodded in grave agreement, and even Ceana was almost convinced.

They were Highlanders. All of them. They stood behind what they thought was best—what they thought was best for their leader, the Earl of Camdonn. Their *laird*. And even though Lady Elizabeth's name was the true name that had been called out at the services for the past three weeks, nobody would ever admit it. They'd insist, to their dying breaths, that the reverend had called Ceana's name and no one else's.

Ceana's heart began to beat rapidly, fluttering in her chest like a hummingbird's wings. Her eyes stung, and she began to tremble.

Cam was serious. The reverend was serious. The people surrounding them were serious. They all wanted her to marry Cam today . . . *now*.

"Cam—"

"Hush."

He held her arm in an iron grip. *Oh, God.* She could run if she wanted to. She could wrench away from him and run until she couldn't move another step.

The reverend began again, resuming the service where she'd interrupted him.

God help her, she wanted this. So badly. She'd dreamed of hearing these words spoken to her. She'd never thought she would.

She slid her gaze to Cam. He stood beside her, his face cast in stone, staring hard at the clergyman.

"Repeat after me, my lord," Reverend Anderson said, his gaze fastened on Cam.

She watched in fascination as Cam dutifully repeated all the words the reverend recited. Tears pricked at her eyes. Would the devil smite him on the spot? Would he run away? Would he change his mind? Would someone run in and shoot him in retribution?

She looked wildly about, but though more people had entered the chapel, they were all men and women she knew from Camdonn Castle, and all wore benign, encouraging expressions. She blinked back at them in owlish disbelief.

"Now, Miss MacNab, it is your turn," the clergyman said.

Janet MacAdam gestured toward the altar, mouthing, *Go ahead, lass.*

Ceana swung her head around to face the reverend. He gave her a gentle smile. Cam's hand tightened on her elbow, and she glanced at him.

"Please," he whispered. "I love you."

She burst into tears.

Instantly, people surrounded her, handing her handkerchiefs, murmuring their support. All the while, Cam caressed her. He rubbed his hand on her sleeve, gently touched her cheek, her nose, her lips.

"Look at me, my love."

She raised her teary eyes to his, and the world around them disappeared.

"I love you," he said again. "Break the curse with me. We can do this, Ceana, right here, right now. I'm not going away. I'm not going to die. I don't want any other woman—since the first moment I saw you, there has been no one else for me. Be my countess, Ceana. Be mine."

"I'm so afraid." She couldn't stop shaking.

"We're almost there." He didn't beg, didn't plead or grovel. He knew what he wanted, and he was going after it. His face remained hard, determined. "We're moments away. I'm here with you. I'm not going anywhere. Ever."

"I love you," she whispered. Fresh streams of tears cascaded down her cheeks. Her hands shook in his. "No matter what happens . . . never forget it. I love you, Cam."

"Are you ready, miss?" It was the reverend. His voice came from far away.

She looked into Cam's dark eyes. So much love shone there. It sank through her pores and spread deep inside her, lending her strength.

"Aye," she murmured.

She repeated the lines, hardly knowing what she said. There was beauty to every word, though, simply because she shared each one with Cam. He mouthed them along with her, squeezing her hands tightly, keeping them safe within his own.

Moments later, the reverend uttered the final blessing. "The Lord sanctify and bless you. The Lord pour the riches of His grace upon you, that ye may please Him and live together in holy love to your lives' end."

Applause erupted in the small space, almost deafening in its intensity. And then they were surrounded by people. Men slapped Cam's back, offering congratulations, while women dabbed at Ceana's tears with their handkerchiefs and kissed her cheeks.

The men grinned at them, and the women bowed and blessed them both. Over it all, she met Cam's eyes, and they smiled at each other, the love they shared at this moment made more powerful by his people's support.

Bram MacGregor, the man she'd cured of ague, approached the earl and gave him a short bow. A wide grin split his cheeks, and he took Cam's hand to give it a hearty shake. "Congratulations, milord."

Ceana released a breath, and with it, all her fear of Cam's never winning his tenants' affection evaporated. His people finally, wholeheartedly, approved of their lord.

And she was married to him. The curse was broken.

"I have good news," Bram continued. "As you requested yesterday afternoon, I took some men with me to follow the trail of the highwaymen who attacked you."

"I hadn't expected you back so soon," Cam said.

"We found the men, sir, including one who made mention of the whore from the mountain, Gràinne. Said he remembered her from Inverness."

Ceana saw Cam's features tighten and she squeezed his hand.

"I questioned the woman, and she confirmed it was the man who attacked her."

Cam nodded.

"They were Jacobites from Inverness, milord, all of them. On a quest of folly to rid the Highlands of its loyalist lords. We've thrown 'em all into the dungeon."

"Excellent, Bram. Well-done."

"One more thing, milord. There was an English servant woman on the mountain. Gràinne wished me to deliver a message to ye on her behalf."

Cam frowned in confusion. "An English servant with Gràinne? Why?"

"She didn't say, milord. She said to inform ye that Bitsy was well, and that as soon as the duke left for England, she'd return forthwith to Camdonn Castle to serve her lady once more." Bram shrugged. "She said, 'I'll return with the diamonds.' Whatever that means."

Still frowning, Cam nodded. "I'll tell Elizabeth."

Bram turned to go, but Cam placed a hand on his shoulder, stopping him. "I thank you, MacGregor. From the bottom of my heart."

Turning beet red, Bram made his obeisance and left. Grinning, Ceana took Cam's arm. "You've won them over," she whispered.

"Have I?"

"Aye, all by yourself." Without her help, without the help of Alan MacDonald. Cam's own generous nature had accomplished the feat.

Again she was torn away from Cam by someone's grip on her hand. She looked up into Elizabeth's smiling face. "Oh, Elizabeth, your arm." She'd forgotten all about her intention to bandage it.

"It's perfectly all right," Elizabeth said quietly. "I just wanted to congratulate you. I'm so glad Cam dragged you to the altar. I—I didn't know . . . I didn't understand that his heart was promised elsewhere."

Ceana smiled. "As was yours."

Elizabeth inclined her head. "Indeed . . . my lady."

She frowned at Elizabeth, who grinned back at her, and then they both glanced at Cam. He stood shoulder-to-shoulder with Rob, and Ceana was gratified to see some color had bloomed over the younger man's cheeks. Ceana paused, her gaze narrowing as she studied the two men side by side, and then she gasped. "You *are* brothers!"

Cam nodded and reached out to take her hand. "Yes, love." He glanced at Rob, clasped his shoulder, and then smiled at Elizabeth. "A rather inauspicious start to our newly formed family, I suppose. But we will make it work."

Elizabeth sighed. "We had planned to go to Glasgow, but—"

"Of course not," Cam said. "You'll stay here."

"At Camdonn Castle?"

"If that is what you wish." He gave her a soft smile. "Until your house is built."

"House?"

"You're a duke's daughter." Cam met Rob's steady gaze. "You're an earl's brother. You'll require a home of your own. Consider it my wedding present to you."

Elizabeth glanced at Rob. "As a matter of fact, we already had a place in mind."

Cam frowned. "Did you?"

"You've a little hunting cottage across the loch—"

Cam waved his hand dismissively. "That place is too small for the two of you."

"No," Elizabeth murmured. "No, it is perfect."

Cam paused, then took her hand in his own and squeezed it. "Then it is yours."

Ceana took Cam's and Rob's hands in her own. They formed a solid square at the altar of Camdonn Castle's chapel. A unit. A family. One that had come within a hairsbreadth of never existing. But, Ceana knew, the four of them were strong together. They'd make an indestructible team.

Happiness so great she nearly burst with it flooded through her soul. She squeezed her husband's hand, and he leaned toward her, kissing her softly on the cheek.

"Do you believe in curses now, Ceana?" he whispered in her ear.

"Aye," she said solemnly. "But I believe you've broken mine."

"We broke it together."

"But what of everything else, Cam?" she asked in a quiet voice. "Your responsibilities—"

"My responsibility is to you first and foremost. Then to the rest of my family." He glanced at Elizabeth and Rob, who had stepped away and were speaking in low tones to the reverend. "And to my tenants." Looking around at the clustered people's smiling faces, he grinned. "I'd say I'm managing my responsibilities rather well."

"What about the Duke of Argyll? The king—"

"They knew nothing of Irvington's treachery."

"Still"—she motioned to herself, from her wild hair to her simple garments to her stained and frayed shoes—"they expected more for you than this."

"God, no." Slipping his arm around her waist, Cam drew her close and pressed his lips to her hair. "They expected less."

Ceana's lingering doubts and resistance fled. Closing her eyes, she leaned against him, and for a long moment she basked in the bliss flooding through her. Nothing had ever felt so right.

But how could it be? She was married to the man she loved. To an earl. The curse had been broken. Her husband was alive and well.

"Are you certain this isn't a dream?"

"Come with me."

She opened her eyes and allowed Cam to usher her out of the front door of the chapel. The sun cast a spring glow over the keep, making it shine silver. Beyond it, tiny sparks, like stars fallen from the night sky, shimmered on the crests of the loch's little waves. "This," Cam said, "is yours now. It is ours. It is real." He gestured at the crowd behind them, smiling at them. "These are our tenants." He turned to her. "You are mine, and I am yours."

She turned slowly, taking in her surroundings, expecting it all to go dim and fade away. But it didn't. The sun continued to shine. The people continued to smile. The loch continued to glimmer.

Cam still stood beside her.

The curse was broken. Never again would she fear losing her love.

"See?" he murmured.

"You were right." She turned to him, happy tears pricking at her eyes, and he gathered her into his arms. "It's not a dream," she whispered against his shoulder. "It is heaven."

Dawn Halliday has earned degrees in computer science and education and held various jobs, from bookselling to teaching inner-city children acting, but she's never stopped writing. When she doesn't have her head buried in a book, you can find her playing video games or posing as a baseball mom in California, where she lives with her husband and three children. You can learn more about Dawn on her Web site at www.dawnhalliday.com.

Read on for a sneak peek of another passionate tale in
Dawn Halliday's Highland romance series,

Highland Obsession

Available now from Signet Eclipse.

Scottish Highlands
October 1715

Cam dismounted and tethered his horse to the spindly trunk of a juniper. Though a full moon had brightened the night sky earlier, clouds had gathered and now a soft mist fell. The horses' heavy breathing steamed the air and their intermittent snorts contrasted with the whisper of water on the bushes and grass.

Ignoring the needles scraping his arms, Cam glanced back at Mac-Lean, who remained mounted, waiting for Cam's instruction. The man and his horse formed an inky shadow in the increasing gloom.

The ground sank under Cam's feet and leaves rustled as he moved to take measure of the small valley below. He scanned the stables and few dark outbuildings hardly visible through the rain, but his gaze came to an abrupt stop when it collided with the largest dwelling in the enclave— Alan MacDonald's two-room cottage near the banks of the loch.

Sorcha and Alan were inside. Alone at last on the first night of their marriage.

Hours ago, from behind an old cairn, Cam had watched the villagers dance around a bonfire as the lively tune of their fiddles and pipes echoed through Glenfinnan. Cold to the marrow of his bones, he'd stared past the stones down at them, at *her*. Sorcha smiling shyly as Alan led her in a reel, her skirts swishing around her calves. She looked as a young bride should: beautiful, happy. Innocent.

But she wasn't innocent.

Her father had tried—and failed—to keep a tight rein on her. Now it was Alan MacDonald's job. Cam knew Alan would do it better.

Smoke puffed in small clouds from the chimney and light spilled· out from the cottage windows onto the water, making it glitter as it splashed gently against the pebbled shore.

Again Cam glanced at MacLean, who sat patiently upon his horse, reins held loosely in his meaty hands. "Wait here. Come only if I call for you."

MacLean nodded. Cam didn't allow his gaze to linger on the big man—he didn't want to see any sign of disapproval, though logic told him MacLean followed him blindly with no interest in separating right from wrong. If Cam saw disapproval in MacLean's expression, he'd be conjuring it from a blank slate.

Swiping the back of his hand over his stinging eyes, Cam stared at the cottage. He had no choice but to go down there. He had to see it through to the end. Maybe then his obsession with her would end.

"Stay out of sight," he murmured to MacLean.

"Aye, milord." MacLean's rough voice came from behind him, but Cam hardly heard. He was already striding down the wet slope toward the cottage.

Sorcha. Her name rose in his mind, peaked and receded like a delicate wave. How had it happened this way? And why, for God's sake, did it even matter? He'd thought Sorcha was a toy, an entertaining plaything. A dalliance. Nothing more. How wrong he was.

More than a month ago, her father had left Cam's service and moved his family to Glenfinnan. The day before she'd gone, she met him in his bedchamber. After they made love, she'd clung to him, and her eyes had glistened with tears as they'd murmured their farewells.

Cam assumed he'd forget about her. He predicted he'd easily find another skirt to amuse him. Instead, he'd thought about her daily. He ached to see her, to hold her again. To touch her silken skin. To see her generous smile, then kiss her into submission.

When he learned of her upcoming marriage to Alan MacDonald, something had snapped in his consciousness. Thoughts of her began to occupy his every waking moment. He'd tried to stop. He'd schooled himself to restraint and resolutely kept out of her affairs.

Today was her wedding day. And, God help him, today he hadn't been able to stay away.

He reached the edge of Alan's cottage and placed his palm flat on one of the cold, wet stones. Slowly, he walked around the back to the closest window, dragging his fingers across the jagged surfaces of the stones as he went. Now completely hidden from MacLean's sight, Cam peered inside.

There was Sorcha, closer to the window than he'd expected, facing away from him. She stood still, her dark hair a satin waterfall cascading down her back. Beyond her, the large, cluttered space contained a rough-hewn dressing table, several chairs and chests, a long bench, and a bed built into the wall. A peat fire flickered in the fireplace at the room's far end. Rustic, but comfortable. Nevertheless, far below Alan's means.

Cam sensed movement deeper within and ducked away, his pulse surging to a frantic cadence.

Breathing heavily, he leaned back against the wall. Out of all the men in the world, why did it have to be his closest friend who'd taken her to wife?

Cam turned his face up to the rain and savored the feel of the stones digging deep into the flesh of his shoulders. What in the devil was he doing, slinking about like a common low-bred thief? Longing for something he could never have? He hated himself for it.

Yet he couldn't stop.

He turned and looked in the window once again. Alan sat on the edge of the bed now. He'd removed his plaid, and his white linen shirt covered him to midthigh. He spoke softly, much in the same way Cam had seen him calm a jittery horse.

Sorcha took a step away from the window. Cam couldn't see her expression, only the dark fall of her hair shimmering in the light of the tallow candles as she moved. She wore a thin linen nightdress that shifted provocatively with the sway of her hips.

Alan was ignorant of Cam and Sorcha's previous carnal acquaintance. If he knew, he never would have married her. Cam was familiar enough with his friend's personality to know this as absolute fact. It was clear Sorcha hadn't revealed anything of her experience during the short period of their engagement.

Ultimately, Cam couldn't blame her for hiding the truth. Her father had placed her in this position, and she would die before dishonoring him. Furthermore, her blasted Highland morals wouldn't allow her to embarrass or anger Alan, her laird and future husband.

And now they were married. Joined together . . . as one . . . until death. Cam winced. *Bloody hell.*

Would she continue to play the part of the timid virgin tonight? Would she cry out as she had when Cam took her maidenhead? After she had made that small, frightened noise, he had frozen in place, hating to have caused her pain. But she'd clutched him tight and whispered to him, saying it was all right and encouraging him to continue. Soon she had arched up to meet him, making a little sound of pleasure with each thrust.

Cam would never forget that night. When he had broken through the shield of her virginity, her reaction had been honest. With Alan, it would be a deception. Cam tried to take some comfort in that, and failed.

Sorcha sat on the edge of the bed beside Alan, turning so Cam could see her profile. Her eyes were downcast. A lock of hair fell across her face, and she reached up to brush it away with trembling fingers.

So she did choose to play the pious fraud. Cam grimaced, clutched the windowsill, and watched.

Sorcha couldn't stop shaking. It wasn't that Alan MacDonald didn't appeal to her—in fact, the opposite was true. He was handsome in a rugged, fierce way, yet there was a kindness about him that inspired trust. Only a month had passed since his return to Scotland after a nearly twenty-year absence, yet the MacDonalds of the Glen already respected their laird as if he'd never left at all.

She was not as quick to trust as her kinsmen. She didn't know this man at all. Alan had spent so many years on English soil, he was little more than a stranger to her.

She possessed only one memory of him before he and his mother had gone. They'd visited Camdonn Castle to see her parents. Sorcha had been just a small child and he'd paid her no attention, but she'd clung to her mother as he'd cast narrow, furious glances at everyone, his lips turned down in a scowl. Later, she'd been told the poor lad was angry because he didn't want to leave Scotland. Nobody blamed him.

He'd finally returned to acknowledge his birthright—his lands on the southern side of Loch Shiel, bordered by the Earl of Camdonn's property on one side and the village of Glenfinnan on the other.

Within a week of his arrival in the Highlands, Alan had met with her father and negotiated their betrothal. Her father was delighted, but Sorcha had never been so afraid. And Sorcha was not the kind of woman who frightened easily.

"Come, Sorcha. Lie beside me."

Trying to calm her roiling tension, she turned to him and lowered herself to her side of the bed, her body rigid.

Alan scooted down beside her. Facing her, he stroked her hair behind her ear. She shuddered at the intimate contact. Only one other man had touched her like this before, but that was such a different man. Dark where Alan was light. Whipcord lean while Alan's body rippled with muscle. Everyone was suspicious of the Earl of Camdonn and approached him with anything from guarded wariness to outright hostility, while Alan had earned the clan's trust in a matter of days.

"Such beautiful hair you have, Sorcha," Alan murmured. "Soft and silky, and black as a raven's."

Would he still think so in ten years when it started to go gray, like her mother's had? Mama had died giving birth to Sorcha's brother . . . would Sorcha die in childbed too?

The years stretched before her, brimming with the unknown and now under the control of the man lying beside her. She forced a smile and pushed out a response to his compliment. "Thank you. That is very kind of you to say."

"I'll go slowly," he said. "I know you are frightened."

Sorcha blew out a breath and nodded, but she couldn't meet his eyes. Yes, she was frightened, but not for the reason he imagined. She had experienced sexual congress in many different forms, in many different places and positions, and she had taken great pleasure from it.

She didn't fear this man's inevitable invasion of her body. No, she feared the future. Living with a stranger day in and day out. Would they grow to love or despise each other? Would he be kind to her or cruel? Years down the line there might be a brood of children for her to care for. What would her life be like then? Would Alan take mistresses? Most of the men she knew did. Even her father, though he was always discreet, kept a woman on the mountain.

She would never take another lover. She didn't know what her life with Alan would be. Nor did she know whether he'd rule her body as Cam had, though she supposed she'd learn soon enough. In the end, it didn't matter whether Alan satisfied her. She was married now, and she would honor that to the death. She would never bring shame upon herself or her husband.

She feared for her future. For her life. Surely it was not so odd to do so. Would she die a year hence, in this very cottage, in childbirth? Or would she survive it to birth a dozen babies? Would Alan ever return to England? Would he take her with him?

She knew nothing, and it frightened her.

His fingers, warm against her skin, paused at her temples. "Sorcha, we are hardly acquainted with each other, and I was thinking it would be best to wait awhile before I got you with child."

Sorcha's breath caught, and she spoke without thinking. "What?"

His palm cupped her cheek. "Are you anxious to have children, lass?"

"No." She drew in a breath and shook her head, stumbling over her words. "What I mean to say is that I should very much like to bear your sons, of course, but . . ." Her voice dwindled. She felt so awkward, so green and uncertain in her own skin.

He shook his head, reading her easily. "Don't tell me what you think I want to hear. Be honest with me. Speak the truth."

"My mother died in childbirth when I was ten years old," she blurted. She clamped her lips shut. How to explain that she'd held on to her younger sister as her mother suffered horrifically? That she'd always feared a similar fate?

"Aye, I'd heard that, and I'm sorry for it." Alan's hand moved to her shoulder and stroked down her arm. Tiny hairs rose in a line on her skin, following the path of his fingers. "It is natural you'd fear it after losing your mother in such a way."

"But don't you want a son?"

"I do, eventually." Alan's fingers laced through hers, coaxing her clenched hand to open. His soothing touch was beginning to calm her. "I would like sons *and* daughters. But we have the rest of our lives for that, don't we?"

Sorcha swallowed hard. "Aye, we do."

He spoke gently. "How much do you know of how children are made, lass?"

She blinked at him. She knew he thought her a virgin, but surely he didn't mistake her for a complete innocent. Perhaps he'd languished in sprawling English mansions for too long and forgotten that the people of the Highlands lived in close quarters. She formed her words carefully. "I know everything, I think. Before my mother died, we lived in a one-room cottage. I am the eldest of four children."

He sighed—it sounded like a sigh of relief. "I don't want to hurt you. Or surprise you."

After her experiences with the earl, not much Alan could do to her body would surprise her. "Thank you," she said in true appreciation for his kindness.

This was so different from her first time with Cam. That joining had been rushed and surreptitious, on the floor of an unlocked closet, where anyone could walk in at any moment. Cam had slowed only after he had first thrust impatiently into her, and she had whimpered at the sudden, sharp pain. Stricken with guilt, he had apologized over and over for hurting her as he'd rained kisses upon her face and neck.

This time the circumstances were different. Premeditated, slow, calm. She and Alan were husband and wife, taking their time, in the private comfort of their own home. Alan moved at a leisurely pace, as if he had the rest of his life to make love to her. She supposed he did, after all.

"I will spend outside of you, for now. But you must realize that's not as fulfilling for a man. And it's certainly not guaranteed, though it will reduce the chances of my seed taking root within you."

To keep from saying "thank you" like a fool again, she merely nodded. Cam had spent on her belly and in her mouth most of the time, though in his fervent haste he did come against her womb more than once. She was lucky he hadn't gotten her with child.

More than lucky. She knew her dalliance with the earl could have cost her everything. Yet at the time, even that knowledge hadn't stopped her. She had lived her days desperate to see him again, to feel his hands on her body, to succumb to the sensation of him inside her.

She'd known her actions were impulsive and foolish. Perhaps that had been part of the pleasure in it—the innate excitement in furtive trysts and secret rendezvous.

When her father had taken her from Camdonn Castle to live in Glenfinnan, she'd secretly mourned losing Cam, but their separation was for the best. She'd never been enough of a fool to think there was a future for them—she was a factor's daughter and he an earl, for heaven's sake.

Alan grinned suddenly, jolting her attention back to the here and now. This man was her future, not the Earl of Camdonn. She'd best remember that.

"It seems odd that one of our first conversations should be of such a personal nature. But I want to be candid with you, Sorcha. I believe honesty to be the basis of a strong marriage."

She smiled back at him, and this time it was real. "As do I."

And then her own hypocrisy struck her. She truly believed honesty was important to a marriage. Yet she lay here, deceiving her husband on their first night together, playing the part of the virgin wife. What a liar she was.

Dawn Halliday also writes as
Jennifer Haymore!

ON SALE NOW

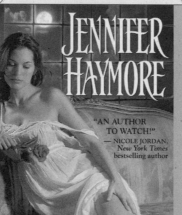

A TOUCH OF SCANDAL

Garrett, the Duke of Carlton, has one enemy in this world:
William Fisk—a man who nearly destroyed him. Nothing can distract
him from exacting revenge until he meets the mysterious Kate, a woman
who stirs a passion in him unlike any he's ever known. But Garrett
makes a shocking discovery: Kate is Fisk's sister. Can he trust the
blood relative of the man who tried to ruin his life—and can Kate
ever love the man determined to kill her brother?

"Jennifer Haymore is an author to watch!"

—Nicole Jordan, *New York Times* bestselling author

ISBN: 978-0-446-54027-8